Rave reviews for Brynn Kelly's *Edge of Truth*

"*Edge of Truth* has it all—danger, desire, and heart-pounding action. Brynn Kelly captures you on page one and doesn't let go!"
—Laura Griffin, *New York Times* bestselling author

"Brynn Kelly will capture your heart and leave you breathless in this passionate, harrowing novel of romantic suspense. A must-read!"
—Brenda Novak, *New York Times* bestselling author

"Dark and deep—a twisting romantic suspense that will grab you and never let go."
—Cynthia Eden, *New York Times* bestselling author

"*Edge of Truth* is a breathtaking romantic thriller. The characters are so real they leap off the page, the love story is hot and the action never lets up. I couldn't put it down."
—Karen Robards, *New York Times* bestselling author

"Kelly is rapidly demonstrating that she is highly skilled at developing intricate stories that are packed with intrigue and jeopardy, while also rich with human emotion. This book is a nonstop thrill ride.... Kelly is proving to be a gift to the romantic suspense genre!"
—*RT Book Reviews*, Top Pick!

Rave reviews for Brynn Kelly's
Deception Island

A *Booklist* Top 10 Romance Debut of 2016!

"Intense and exciting...romantic suspense at its best!"
—Carla Neggers, *New York Times* bestselling author

"Smoldering chemistry, cunning twists and a whole lot of heart. Brynn Kelly delivers everything I love in a romance."
—Heather Graham, *New York Times* bestselling author

"Kidnappings and pirates and romance—oh my! *Deception Island* is a keeper."
—Cindy Gerard, *New York Times* bestselling author

"[T]he perfect book...one you'll never forget."
—Sharon Sala, *New York Times* bestselling author

"Brynn Kelly pens a raw, dark, emotional novel of danger and intrigue that will keep readers turning the pages."
—Kat Martin, *New York Times* bestselling author

"*Deception Island* is nothing short of brilliant. I love this book and am salivating for more!"
—Award-winning author Lena Diaz

"A taut romantic thriller readers won't want to put down."
—*Library Journal*, starred review

BRYNN KELLY

EDGE OF TRUTH

HQN™

HQN™

ISBN-13: 978-1-335-05092-2

Edge of Truth

Copyright © 2017 by Bronwyn Sell

The publisher acknowledges the copyright holder of the additional work as follows:

Forbidden River

Copyright © 2017 by Bronwyn Sell

Recycling programs for this product may not exist in your area.

www.HQNBooks.com

Printed in U.S.A.

Don't miss a single book in The Legionnaires series
from Brynn Kelly and HQN Books

CONTENTS

EDGE OF TRUTH

CHAPTER ONE

TESS CLUTCHED THE bare mattress and gulped a lung-ful of stale air, her heart jackhammering against her ribs. A nightmare? No—men were shouting, outside. She widened her eyes, then squinted. Open, closed, open, closed, it made no difference. Black was black was black.

She sat up with a lurch and shuffled back against the damp stone wall to at least get a fix on which way was up. Not a sliver of gray slid between the floorboards above. Had to be night. She'd been asleep? For how long? She laid her palm over her face and blinked, the lashes tickling her skin. Definitely open. This wasn't the kind of nightmare you got to wake from. As further proof, her big toes throbbed in unison where Hamid's men had ripped out the nails.

A door squealed, and something solid was dragged across the floor overhead. From their nest in the cor-ner of her cell, the mice scratched and squeaked—even they knew something was up. She shakily exhaled. Six days she'd been here, and each night had been heavy with silence until the distant song of a muezzin's call to prayer. What was different about tonight?

A flashlight beam flickered through the cracks. More voices—instructions, perhaps. A series of clinks, a heavy scrape—they were opening the bunker hatch. Was she to be freed? She swallowed. Or executed?

Fresh air puffed over her face as the hatch lifted. She drew up her knees and hugged them. The flashlight beam tracked around the cell, pausing on a food tray the mice had finished up, and a scattering of empty plastic water bottles. The light flicked to her, scorching her eyes and drilling pain into her brain. She shut them tight and sealed her palms over top. Even then her vision pulsed bloodred.

If they were planning to make another video, or if Hamid was coming to ask again if she was ready for death, the next sound would be the rasp and bump of the rope ladder being lowered. But this early? This felt more like the hour of...

Enough overthinking. She breathed deeply through her mouth—she'd stopped inhaling through her nose days ago, so she couldn't smell herself rotting.

People had survived years like this. She had to keep believing that the kidnap of a high-profile American TV journalist would prompt a large-scale search, even in East Africa. She had to keep visualizing a company of marines scouring the arid terrain. Or would they be out to get her, too?

Overthinking.

The rasp didn't come. More scuffles and scrapes. She forced her eyes open. Shadows circled the dirt floor. Above the hatch, figures moved and a man grunted, as if with great effort. Something blocked the square hole, returning the cell to darkness. It wasn't the hatch cover, so what was—?

The thing dropped. She shrank back as it thudded down a few feet away. A strobe of light flashed on a large curled shape before the hatch thunked shut. Metal scraped on metal—the bolts sliding home. She shivered. Voices and footsteps retreated, a door squealed shut, a key clicked in a lock, leaving the darkness absolute. She let her crown drop back on the cold stone. Not execution, not yet. Maybe they were storing something down here. But at this time of night?

As her shuddering breath subsided and the mice settled, she made out another sound. Air rasping, in and out, in and out. Holy crap. The thing was alive.

"Hello?" Her voice caught. She cleared her throat. "Hello?"

No answer.

She crawled off the mattress and felt her way along the packed dirt. Her right hand hit something warm, covered with smooth fabric. It flinched. Human, at least.

"It's okay," she said.

She splayed her fingers. Under the fabric the skin was firm but yielding. A stomach? A groan rose up—a man's voice. Her left hand touched something hard. Bones—a row of them. He shuddered and arched away. His spine? Which meant her other hand was currently exploring a particularly solid butt. She released her grip.

He muttered something unintelligible. French?

"Are you hurt?" In the cloying silence, the walls whispered back.

A grunt. She'd have to find out for herself. Maybe they'd sedated him with the same drug they'd used on her after they'd dragged her from the Land Rover. She glided her hands over his curved back. No sign of injury—nothing but hard ridges of muscle, under a thick cotton jacket. At his shoulders, her finger caught in a loop. An epaulet. Military? An enemy soldier to

Hamid and the al-Thawra network was likely to be an ally to her—and there'd be more where he came from.

Unless his team was dead, as hers might well be. Her cameraman had taken a volley of bullets within seconds of the ambush. Every time she closed her eyes she saw his face—the flicker of disbelief and realization before he slumped, lifeless. Just a young Zimbabwean news junkie who thought working with her would propel him into the big time, and all it got him was... She sucked in air through clenched teeth.

Her translator better still be alive. Last she'd seen him, al-Thawra thugs were dragging him feetfirst along a stony road. He was just an honest, reliable local dad who'd needed the money. Had she been explicit enough about the risk of working for her, about the need for secrecy? He'd been so eager for the job. If she'd got him killed, too...

No. Cling to hope. She'd been the target, not him.

She dipped two fingers under the soldier's collar and scooped. No dog tag. Thick, corded neck, suede buzz cut. His crown was hot and...sticky. Ugh. She snapped her hand away. Had to be blood. He moaned. A bit of light would be handy—she'd rather not stick her fingers in his brain.

"You've got a wound up here. I'm going to check it. Hold still."

Like he was capable of anything else. She closed her useless eyes and brushed her fingertips over the spot. An inch-long gash gaped over a lump the size of half a tennis ball. Ouch.

"It's not too bad," she said. Like she had any idea. "I have a first-aid kit."

He needed sutures, but alcohol wipes and adhesive

strips would have to do. God help him if it got infected down here. He muttered again. She caught a guttural *R*. Definitely French, maybe from Djibouti—no other army this side of the Congo would speak French. Or L'armée de Terre? But why would a French soldier be out here?

"Is anything else hurting?" Silence. "I'm just going to check."

She leaned over him, her knees touching his back. Her hair slipped loose. She looped and twisted it into a knot. One benefit of hair that hadn't seen shampoo in a week—it was greasy enough to tie without a band.

She ran her fingers over his shoulder and a rolled sleeve, down to his right hand. Jesus, the guy had muscles. As she slid her fingertips into his palm, his hand closed. Just a reflex, but she gave in to it, letting the flicker of comfort shoot right up to her chest.

"Merci, madame."

The deep words came from so low in his throat she could have imagined them—she'd been imagining a lot of crazy things lately. Maybe not a reflex, then? She squeezed back.

"De rien," she said, her choked *R* giving away her rusty tourist French. God, was he ever welcome, whoever he was. She shouldn't be thankful some other luckless schmuck had wound up here.

Reluctantly, she eased her hand from his. He'd be more comfortable on the mattress but first she should make sure moving him wouldn't worsen any injuries. She patted his stomach, then stroked up. At his chest, hard pecs tightened. Nothing wrong with those reflexes.

His neck and jaw were rough with stubble—almost a beard—rising up to a sharp, smooth cheekbone and speed bumps of tiny wrinkles beside his right eye. His forehead was unlined, though a little rough and peeling. The skin between his eyes was bunched into two crevasses. Was this how blind people built a picture of someone? The bones were in the right places, though the nose felt wonky. He didn't recoil when she skated her fingertips along it, and there was no open wound. An old break, perhaps.

"Can you roll onto your back?"

He sighed, and seemed to understand, shifting and resettling and—she guessed from the sound of rubbing fabric—straightening his legs. He was moving freely enough. She checked his other arm. A gravelly graze on his elbow but otherwise okay. The fingers of that hand didn't curl around hers. Which was fine.

She skipped the business part of his trousers—nothing much she could do about *that* if it wasn't working, and she already knew there wasn't a thing wrong with his butt. His legs felt fine. Very fine—powerful thighs slid into long, strong calves. His trousers—combat pants, presumably, given the number of pockets—were tucked into socks. His boots were intact. Best leave them on—in this filth, his feet were better off contained.

"Back in a sec," she murmured.

She felt her way to the mattress and found her backpack, which had been ransacked for everything but her first-aid kit and a few toiletries. No phone, no laptop, no documents, no notes—little more than Band-Aids, sunscreen and lip gloss. *I need you to stay pretty for my videos*, Hamid had said, shoving the backpack into Tess's stomach.

Hamid had stood there, a few feet from where Tess now sat, flicking through her notebook. *You've been trying to find my base. Congratulations, my friend. You succeeded. If I'd known you were so keen to drop in, I would have invited you much sooner.*

How did you find me? Tess had demanded.

The same way I usually find people. The same way I found your whistle-blower, the traitor Latif. Hamid held up Tess's phone. *With the help of America's very useful National Security Agency. My job is a bit like yours, you know. It's all about the contacts.*

That's impossible. I was careful. She hadn't been online in a fortnight. She'd been using burner phones, contacting no one she knew. *We were all careful.*

Not all, Hamid said. *Not all. Your translator texted his wife several times.*

Tess's face went cold, all over again. She removed the first-aid kit from her backpack. She could do nothing for her crew now but she could help this soldier. Returning to him, she coaxed his head onto her lap, cradling his shoulders with her thighs while keeping her bandaged feet clear.

What had this guy done to incur al-Thawra's wrath? Or was Hamid trying to draw France into their phony conflict?

"I'm going to clean the cut on your head. It might sting a little."

At his solid weight, a memory flashed up of her final weekend with Kurt, when he'd taken leave and met her in Cairo. Ugh. Turned out even a Medal of Honor didn't make a man honorable—even if half of America swooned over him. No more military heroes for her.

Next time she'd go for a dependable small-town accountant whose chief attribute was loyalty. Someone who could be relied on to come home after work—

alive, and not smelling of another woman. Charm and
bravado spelled trouble. She frowned. That was if she
got a chance at a next time and didn't end up in two
pieces like the last unfortunate American kidnapped
by Hamid.

She ripped open an alcohol wipe and ran it over her
hands. Working on feel and guesswork, she smoothed
the next few wipes over the lump, wringing out the alcohol so it dripped on the wound. He hissed, his shoulders tensing against her.

That'd have to do—she was low on wipes, and she
might need to change the dressing in a day or two, if
they both lasted that long. She squeezed her eyes shut,
trying to send the message to her other senses that they
were on their own, as she held the wound closed with
one hand and pressed on the suture strips with the other.
Several times the strips tangled and she had to start
over. She finished by winding a bandage around his
head. Better than nothing.

Would twice the people be looking for al-Thawra and
their hostages now? Soldiers were full of no-man-left-
behind macho crap. At least they'd be a whole lot more
enthusiastic about looking for one of their own than for
a pain-in-the-ass reporter. More than a few American
politicians and military brass would be greatly relieved
to pay their respects at Tess's funeral.

"Done," she whispered. Now, how the hell would
she move him? His head felt heavier, suddenly. *"Monsieur?"*

He groaned. "Oh."

"What's wrong?"

"Oh." She heard him swallow, with effort. "Water."

"Of course. Hang on." Duh—he was saying *"eau,"*

not "oh." No kidding he'd be thirsty. The air out here was so dry it felt like you'd swallowed a cup of salt. She eased his head off her lap and crawled to the mattress, waving her arm as if she were divining the water. She knocked over a bottle and caught it before it rolled away.

"Here," she said, scrambling back. "Can you sit up?"

No answer. Unconscious, again. Crap, how was she going to do this? She heaved him upright, cradling his back against her chest. She sensed his head slumping, and caught him as he tipped sideways. Her foot grazed his thigh, searing pain up her leg. She adjusted under his weight, her arm muscles burning as she guided his head back onto her shoulder. Man, he had to weigh two hundred pounds. *Help me out here, buddy.*

Grunting with effort, she closed her arms around his torso and twisted the cap off the bottle. It couldn't be a good idea to pour liquid down his throat. She splashed a little water into her palm and lifted it to where she guessed his mouth was. She got his prickly chin, instead. She tried again, a little higher. When her palm touched his dry lips, she eased the water into his mouth. He moaned and straightened a little, relieving the pressure on her muscles. On her next attempt he darted out his tongue and licked her palm, shooting fissures of awareness up her arm.

Well, if he was strong enough to do that... She brought the neck of the bottle to his lips and raised it. Water trickled down her arm but his throat made swallowing sounds. She flinched as something warm and rough closed over her fingers—his hand, guiding the bottle to a better angle. She couldn't bring herself to extract her hand. Maybe he was a hallucination—her isolation and fear playing on her subconscious—but whatever he was, whoever he was, calm spread through her for the first time since her translator had slowed for that damn roadblock near Hargeisa. Hell, she'd take any relief she could get.

He released her hand. "Beaut," he gasped.

Beaut? Was that French? Something about the accent was familiar—something that didn't fit this picture. When he'd said "water" in English, he hadn't used the French *R*. He'd trailed off with no *R* at all.

"Can't…see. Eyes…"

Definitely not a French accent. Was he English? But why the French words earlier? A multilingual local? Or maybe his accent was just messed up after too many years away from home, like hers.

"Nothing wrong with your eyes. It's pitch-black down here—I can't see anything, either."

His back collapsed against her chest and she fought to catch him. Conked out again? She laid him down and extracted herself. She found the graze on his elbow and dabbed and dressed it. It couldn't be healthy to leave him on the dirt—at night the cold seeped up through it. The mattress was filthy and scratchy but it provided a couple of inches of insulation and comfort.

Well, if she couldn't take him to the mattress… She felt her way across the cell and shoved the squab up against him. Screwing up her face, she rolled him onto it. He shuffled and settled, with a sigh that might have been gratitude. After checking he was lying clear of his wound and breathing okay, she let her shoulders slump. God, it felt good to not be alone. The chances of him being a psycho killer had to be low, right? This compound already contained more than its fair share.

So where would *she* spend the night? No way was

she taking the floor, not when there'd be a little space right in front of him she could *just* fit into. If he was sedated he was likely to sleep soundly, and she probably wouldn't sleep at all—she'd dozed off only a few times in the long days and nights she'd been locked up. By the time he returned to his senses in a few hours she'd have disentangled herself. In his current state, he was no threat to her—or anyone else, unfortunately.

After gulping some water, she crept to the top of the mattress and slipped down into his outstretched arms as if sliding into a sleeping bag. One heavy forearm weighed down her waist. She wriggled until his other biceps pillowed her head. Was this a little creepy of her? He'd understand, surely.

Arrested by a thought, she trailed her fingers down his rough, corded left arm and over his knuckles. No ring. Not that that proved anything—plenty of married military guys didn't wear them, much less abide by them—but at least she might not be taking advantage of another woman's semiconscious husband. Just a regular semiconscious guy. She curled her legs around his bent ones. He mumbled and pulled her closer, burying his face in her hair and sliding a hand down her outer thigh. Uh-oh—he wasn't about to have some drug-addled wet dream, was he?

She held her breath but in seconds he relaxed—with her firmly in his grip. And, hell, that felt good. She dared to press her nose to his arm and inhale. Gravelly. Tangy. Real. His sweat probably smelled a damn sight fresher than hers.

Still no dusty beam of gray spilled through the cracks overhead—she couldn't even see the boards. Dawn had to be hours away. She yawned. If these were the last

hours of her life, at least they'd be comfortable ones—
even if the relief was stolen from an unwitting stranger.

Don't you dare die on me, soldier.

FLYNN LEAPED TO his feet, blinking to clear the fuzz from
his brain. What the fuck? A dim bunker. No door, no
window. Underground? A woman, pushing herself up
from a mattress—not naked, at least. Christ, his head
thumped like a drum solo. He brought his hand up to
it. Bandaged. Not a hangover, then.

"What the fuck?" They were the only words he
could get his mouth around. He cleared his throat. It
felt stuffed with acacia thorns.

The woman straightened to full height, which wasn't
much, palms upright as if calming a snorting bull. Her
face registered somewhere deep in his mind—young,
hot, in a pointy-jaw tough-girl way. Even in near darkness her eyes shone blue. Was he delirious?

"You're okay," she said.

"This doesn't look like okay." Except for her. She
was a damn sight more than okay.

She shrugged. "Relatively."

"What is this?" He swept an arm around, blinking
moisture into his eyes. *This*, meaning: What the hell was
this place, what the hell was he doing here and who the
hell was she? He patted his pockets. Empty. No holster, no
pistol, no knife, no tac vest, no utility belt. No helmet—
had he been wearing one?

"You're Australian?"

"You're American." He swore as his brain caught up.
"You're that missing journalist."

So this was what deep shit looked like. He shut his
eyes tight and pinched the top of his nose. The dressing

pulled at his scalp. *Think.* His unit got ambushed, right? The last memory his brain could locate was of running through a village—goats scattering ahead of them, Angelito shouting commands, the *thuck-thuck-thuck* of enemy fire. They dropped back behind a concrete hut. Levanne went down, in the open. Flynn dashed out to help him. Then, a crunch—hot pain in his skull, bullets zipping around, fabric smothering his face. No, no helmet—just his useless beret. He'd been chucked onto a truck bed or something, fighting to breathe, retching on a chemical smell.

He gagged at the thought. He'd been captured—by al-Thawra, seeing as he was with the reporter. What was her name—Newell, right? Tess Newell. A big deal in the States—her kidnapping had been all over CNN. She didn't look it now, with blond hair pulled back and dirt smearing her face. Pain twisted behind his eyes. He winced, which made it worse. What'd happened to Angelito and the others? So much for their routine patrol.

"I have painkillers." She limped past him and unzipped a bag. "Only over-the-counter stuff, but it might take the edge off. Here."

He took the offered trays and popped out four, for starters. She zipped away her first-aid kit and passed him a fresh water bottle from a plastic-wrapped stash in the corner. He slugged back the pills.

"You fixed me up," he said, pointing to his head. As she nodded, a memory filtered in. More like a feeling— of relief, of knowing he was looked after, of surrendering the fight to stay awake, to stay alive. Hell, how far had he lowered his guard?

"You know where this place is?" he said. "What this place is?"

"A compound of some sort, somewhere remote."

He swallowed another mouthful of water. "Narrows it down." *Remote* described 95 percent of the Horn of Africa—assuming they were still in Africa. They could have crossed over to the Middle East. Hell, they could be in the Bahamas. "You were sedated when they brought you here?"

"Yes… So you're Australian?"

"French," he corrected, automatically.

"You don't sound French."

"Eees zees betterrrr, *mademoiselle*?" *Dickhead.* Nine years of faking a French accent whenever he spoke English to strangers, and he chooses a hotshot journalist to slip up to? "I was taught English by an Australian. It comes out in the accent sometimes." Not a lie. He'd learned English from a whole town of Australians—the shit heap where he'd grown up.

"Wow, that's a strong influence. So you're—what?—French Army?"

He patted the *Tricolore* on his left arm. She squinted, her gaze drifting up to the legion patch. With luck she wouldn't know what it meant.

"'Légion Étrangère,'" she read awkwardly. "You're Foreign Legion."

Bloody hell.

"But aren't their soldiers foreign—hence the name?"

"Not all," he said quickly. Several Frenchmen in his company had masqueraded as Canadians or Belgians to get a new identity, but he wasn't about to tell a journalist that. "Anyway, I'm a lieutenant—officers are drawn from regular army." Usually. They'd made an exception for him and Angelito. He went to shove his fingers through his hair, but hit the bandage and stopped, clenching his teeth. "Too many questions, lady. What is this—*60 Minutes*?"

She started. "Sorry—habit." Her tone softened. "I've had a while longer to get my head around this."

And there was that feeling again. It was her voice—quiet and husky. That voice had filtered through the haze last night like some angel's prayer. At his fuzziest he'd wondered how a reprobate like him had made the cut for heaven. Lucky he hadn't been able to see her—he'd have immediately sold his soul to the nearest deity, even if her clothes looked like they'd been washed in mud. The stench of mouse piss should have been a giveaway that this was nowhere close to heaven.

He checked his watch. Nearly 0800. Late. Angelito would be going apeshit—if he was alive. He'd better bloody be alive. *Tu n'abandonnes jamais ni tes morts, ni tes blessés.* You never abandon your dead, your wounded. Angelito would have risked everything to save Flynn—they all would have.

She tilted her head. "Have we met? There's something about you…"

No. Anything but that. "Believe me, I'd remember. I just have one of those faces, that's all…" *Deflect, soldier.* "Have they hurt you?" No obvious injuries, but he couldn't see jack in this hole.

"Nothing too bad. Hamid wants me looking pretty for the execution."

"Son of a bitch—Hamid Nabil Hassan is here, in person?" Shit was getting worse. The man at the top of every terrorist watch list, here. "Is this al-Thawra's headquarters? What country are we even in?" *Think.* His brain clunked over. "Intel has you being held in Somalia."

"I wouldn't trust it. But that's possible."

Something clattered—a key in a lock—and a door squealed. Footsteps thumped above. Metal clunked. She grabbed his wrist with a cold hand and pulled him clear of a square hatch cut into the boards overhead, a few inches above his six-three height. Lucky he hadn't smacked his head on the roof when he'd leaped off the bed. Bed. Hell. Somehow he'd wound up curled up in bed with *the* Tess Newell—spooning *the* Tess Newell.

Above them men spoke—and a woman. He caught a breathy *"eshi"*—*okay*, in Amharic. So maybe this was Ethiopia? "It's Hamid," Tess hissed.

Flynn pulled her behind his back. She was half the size she looked on TV—he could hide two of her.

The hatch shifted, releasing square-cut blades of light. Someone grunted, and it lifted. They were in a dugout under a concrete-block building, by the look of it. An M16 barrel poked into the hole. "Do not move, soldier," said a thickly accented voice. A rope ladder dropped down.

As the rifle eyed Flynn, two men in camo gear jumped through the hole, landing with knees bent and barrels aimed. One looked Middle Eastern, maybe Ethiopian. The other was darker skinned and taller—Somali? They fanned out as a figure descended the ladder, his shape masked by a robe. Tess sucked in a breath and stepped out from behind Flynn, drawing away one of the rifle barrels. Her face was set in the don't-feed-me-bullshit expression he knew from TV. A mask, probably, but bravery usually was. If you weren't scared shitless in a situation like this, you were a fool.

The robed man touched the floor, spun and pushed back his hood. *Her* hood. Holy shit. A column of dusty light revealed a woman—witch-thin and only a few inches shorter than Flynn. She was backlit, so he couldn't get a fix on her face. Nothing in the intel had suggested a woman was high up in al-Thawra.

"Bonjour, soldat," she said, stepping forward. *"J'espère que tu as bien dormi?"* She arched thin eyebrows toward Tess. She wasn't a native French speaker but he couldn't pick the accent. She was maybe fifty, tanned, a pale blue scarf tied around her hair. In France you'd call her *une femme d'un certain âge*. In Australia a MILF. Not what he'd expected.

"With the drugs you lot gave me, I didn't have a choice but to sleep well." He answered in English, for Tess's benefit, with his adopted singsong Corsican accent. Tess would wonder what'd happened to his Australian twang, but she'd become threat number two. Until he figured out how much the terrorists knew about him, he was safer playing to expectation. "Who are you?"

The woman raked her gaze up his body as if checking out livestock. As she reached his face, her kohl-rimmed brown eyes lit with a challenge. "I am the one you know as Hamid Nabil Hassan. The most wanted man in the world."

CHAPTER TWO

FLYNN GROUND HIS heels into the dirt. This was the *man* America had been hunting since the Los Angeles terror attacks? "You don't look like a Hamid."

She laughed, the sound dull and harsh in the thick air. "You don't think a woman can be a powerful adversary?"

Oh, he knew all about how dangerous women were. "You're American?" Bloody hell, their intelligence really…wasn't. "You're supposed to be Somali. And a man."

Her eyes narrowed slightly. "In the twenty-first century we no longer need to be defined by lines on a map or the accident of our birth. I am a person of the world, as you are. I am defined by the things I can control, not those I can't. Gender, age, lineage, provenance—these are outdated concepts."

"You forgot to mention religion," said Tess, sounding like she was clenching her teeth.

"Oh no," the woman—*Hamid*—said, her heavy eyes drifting to the bearded soldier next to her. "Religion can still be very useful."

She and Tess looked like they were about to shoot lasers out of their eyes at each other.

"Why am I here?" Flynn said.

Hamid didn't take her eyes off Tess. "Because my

captive here was lonely and I like to play matchmaker. She's pretty, don't you think? You are well suited."

"My government will not pay a ransom for a lowly soldier."

Hamid tilted her head, assessing him again. "I would pay a good deal of money for a man like you. But, yes, I'm counting on that."

He fisted his hands against his thighs. "Then why?" Like he didn't know what was about to happen.

"I requested a pretty French soldier and my men did not disappoint."

She stepped forward, lifting her hand to the square patch sewn on the chest of his jacket and tracing her fingertips over its twin stripes. "And an officer. Even better." She glanced at Tess. "The French lieutenant's woman—it has a certain allure, right?" She hooked a finger under the thin red foulard looped around his shoulder and tugged it. "And what does this mean? This scarf?"

"It means it's dusty out there." He resisted the urge to swallow. If she didn't know he was legion, she'd figure it out when she saw his patch. Once she knew how expendable he was to France he'd be worth less. And it wasn't like Australia would give a damn.

Her fingers grazed his cheek. One movement and he could have his hands around the throat of the psycho who'd ordered the deaths of thousands of civilians.

"Yes. My men chose well. The world will be twice as incensed by the brutal execution of two beautiful people as they would by the deaths of regular people. Unfair, yes? You will look handsome indeed on television, next to your new friend. I think we will kill you first and make her watch. Maybe she will cry for you—people love that kind of thing." She flipped her hand and slid the backs of her fingers down to his jaw, lowering her voice. "Did you make the first move last night, or did she? And was it as good as I was imagining?"

"*You* are Hamid?"

"It depends who's asking, and what story fits your worldview." She spoke just above a whisper. "To the Western world, yes, I am that shadow from their worst nightmares, the one who could invade their comfortable lives and blow them up any second." She clicked her fingers, right next to his ear, the snap echoing off the walls. "Your supermarket, your cinema, your school. I can be anywhere, take any form. A former soldier driven mad by war. A frustrated immigrant whose dream of a new life never came true." She rested her palm on his chest, her breath smelling of coffee and toothpaste. "If you are poor and powerless and from this side of the world, I am a rallying call, a raison d'être in an otherwise disenfranchised life. No, not a raison d'être. A reason for *dying*." She smiled.

He made a point of eyeballing her. "You expect me to believe that a mob of jihadists would take orders from an American woman?"

She trailed her hand across to his shoulder, sliding a sideways look at the goon next to her. "You mean these people?" Her lashes were so thick with mascara he was surprised she could keep her eyes open. "Oh, *they* think I am Hamid's jihadi bride, and if they play nice little jihadists I will introduce them to the oracle. I make them call me Mrs. Hamid. You see? Different things to different people. I am whatever you want me to be." She stroked one side of his neck. "And what would you like me to be, Lieutenant?"

He swallowed, drawing her focus to his throat. She laughed. "I make you nervous. Don't worry. I make everyone nervous."

Flynn's gaze flicked to the nearest weapon. If he tried to strangle "Hamid" he'd be dead before her heart stopped and she'd be revivable. Breaking her neck would be quicker and more permanent. He unclenched and clenched his fists. Taking out a mass murderer would be a fitting end to his life—and better to die with his secrets safe than have his face broadcast in one of al-Thawra's snuff videos.

"But why are you telling me all this?" He made his words come out slow and halting, like he was settling into a long speech. "Aren't you worried that—?"

He sprang to her midsentence, spun her and caught her in a headlock with his left arm. Shouts bounced around. One chance. As his right hand gripped her jaw and yanked sideways, pain slammed into his skull. The room twisted. His crown exploded with heat.

A force grabbed him by the shoulders and hauled him backward, as Hamid scrambled away—gasping but alive, fuck it. The silhouette of a sidearm rose above him. The pricks had pistol-whipped his wound. He bit down on his cheeks, internalizing the pain pinballing through his head.

A female soldier leaped down in front of him, a reinforcement from above. Flynn pulled at his captor—captors, now, one pinning each shoulder. They bore down as he dragged them across the dirt toward Hamid. He tossed forward to flip them but the reinforcement launched a boot to his gut. His breath yelped out.

"Don't touch his face," spit Hamid as she repositioned her scarf and hood. "The rest of him is yours."

The woman pulled out a cable tie and sprang round back of Flynn as the other goons pinned him. It clicked as it tightened around his wrists. Warm liquid dribbled down his forehead and into his eye. Blood. He blinked to clear it but a filmy smear remained, coloring the room red.

Damn sedative must have slowed him. No point fighting now. Better to concede and hope they didn't take it out on the journalist. Light flashed in his face. A phone camera. Taking his picture for their press release? His vision swam in blues and reds.

At least with a dirty face, a bandaged head, an eye socket running with blood and a scruffy half beard he'd be unrecognizable from the teenager Australia remembered. A soldier shoved him to the floor face-first. Something smashed into his lower back. A knee? He inhaled through the pain. In his peripheral vision, the woman stepped back and leveled her rifle. One chance and he'd screwed it up.

"We'll take a more attractive photo once we get you cleaned up," said Hamid, her voice ironed smooth. "Maybe I'll shave you myself. And now, my other pretty one, you must write a note for me."

With his cheek rammed into the dirt, Flynn watched Hamid tower over Tess. Tess lifted her gaze, defiant, her fists clutching her cargoes. Hamid snapped a command—in Amharic?—and something small pelted through the hole. A soldier passed it to Hamid. Baby wipes.

"Clean your hands first," hissed Hamid, handing them to Tess. "You're filthy and I don't want the paper smudged."

"A note?" said Tess, with a hint of challenge.

"To your producer. You will write exactly what I tell

you." Hamid's robe swished as she lifted something from it. "Use this."

"My notebook." Tess said it like an accusation.

"Date it a week ago, exactly. Write, 'Quan. There's nothing in the story linking al-Thawra with Denniston Corporation. Hyland's clean.'"

Tess scoffed, a tick from the back of her throat. "Let me guess. Quan will receive this after my death?"

"Write it or I'll remove your hand and write it for you. And no tricks—I know your handwriting."

Shaking her head, Tess pulled a pen out of the notebook's spiral top and began writing.

"Good," said Hamid, peering over her shoulder. "Now add, 'I can't trust using a phone, so I'm posting you this.'"

The pen rolled over the pad.

"Sign it with 'Ciao' and two small *X*s. And now a *T*, with a full stop."

Tess looked up, her forehead creased. "You've been reading my emails."

"Do it."

Biting her bottom lip, Tess returned to the note. When she was finished, Hamid snatched it, smiled and stomped on Tess's right foot. Tess yelped. The pen skidded onto the dirt by Flynn's nose. Hamid ground in her heel a couple of seconds before releasing. Tess crumpled to her knees, air scraping into her lungs. Jesus. Flynn bucked against his guards but all it got him was a smack on the head.

Hamid stepped back, sniffing. "Oh, and thanks to the information on your laptop, I've discovered the identity of your other whistle-blower. She will soon meet the same fate as the first. Nice and tidy."

A cry squeaked out of Tess.

"It's over."

"Never," Tess breathed, raising her chin. "If I found out the truth about al-Thawra, someone else will, too. They'll take you down, along with Denniston and Senator Hyland."

Wait—Senator Hyland? *He* was in on this? Shit, Flynn was even more dead.

"No. You have kindly revealed a crack in this organization and I am fixing it. I am going through your so-called evidence piece by piece to ensure there will be no more lapses."

Tess pushed to her feet with a slight grunt. "You can't win this."

"I already have and your death will seal it. In a matter of days, the US and its allies will announce war on Somalia. Very soon, the senator will be president."

"With you behind the scenes doing his dirty work." If Tess was scared, she hid it well. *Wrap it up, sunshine. This ain't comfortable.*

"You say that as if you think it is *he* who is in charge of *me*," Hamid said, brushing a streak of dirt from her robe.

"He's got you believing you hold the power here? You know that sucking people in and spitting them out is what he does best? You're his pawn, as much as these people."

"Oh, I am looking forward to the hour I get to spit *you* out."

A swishing noise. Hamid was climbing the ladder. The pressure on Flynn's lower back released. More scrambling marked one soldier's departure, followed by another. The one remaining guy rubbed Flynn's face in the dirt and let go.

Flynn inhaled dust, pain stabbing his chest. A cracked rib? The hatch clonked shut, sucking up the beam of light.

"I have nail scissors," Tess said weakly, nodding to his bound hands. "You took me by surprise with that move on Hamid. I should have done something, tried to grab a gun, or..."

"You couldn't have done anything. And for future reference, don't try. I can look out for myself. You should, too."

In a minute she'd snipped off the ties. He rolled onto his back with a groan and pressed his fingers into his ribs.

"It was worth a shot," she said. "Broken?"

"Don't think so." *Hope not.* He hoisted himself onto his elbows, suppressing a wince, and wiped his eye clear with his jacket sleeve. "Your foot..."

Tess swept her leg around in front of her. Even in the gray light a scarlet bloodstain stood out, spreading over the toe of her sock, following the path of a darker stain like fresh lava over old. The sock was stuffed with something—a bandage?

"They ripped out your toenails." The pricks. As torture went, it was old-fashioned but painful as hell, by all accounts. At least nails grew back—given the chance. "What did they torture you for?"

"A dossier of the evidence I have on them—they wanted to know whether there were copies and where they were."

"Did you tell them?"

"Everything." Her answer was strangely short.

"There's some shit going down here, isn't there?"

"Oh yeah."

He caught her other leg and trailed his hand down to the foot. More blood, but dry. She pulled both feet away.

"Hamid's a psychopath, in case you hadn't worked that out," she said.

"Hamid's a woman."

"You noticed. I'd better take a look at your head—I might have to close the wound again."

"And an American. What's with that?"

She pushed to her feet and unrolled his bandage. "Yep. Born and raised in Chicago. Ex-marines, ex-CIA. Her real name is Sara Hawthorn."

"Sara. The most wanted man in the world is a hot Chicago cougar called Sara."

"Hey, if *she's* your type, you have problems."

"A woman heading a jihad?"

"Al-Thawra is no jihadist group, despite what their thugs believe."

"Really? They kind of give it away with all the 'death to the infidels' shit."

"That's what Hamid—Sara—wants people in the West to believe," she said, her voice cut with bitterness. "Hell, it's what we're quick to believe, isn't it? That we're under attack from whacked-out extremists from the other side of the world? It's harder to understand if the cracks are in your own country."

"Now you're sounding like her."

Featherlight fingers drew through his scalp. He bit down on his cheeks.

"This doesn't look too bad—the strips have held." She knelt in front of him, her knees and legs splayed awkwardly. To protect her toes? With a finger under his chin, she raised his head so his eyes were level with her chest. What could he do but explore the hint of cleavage diving into her T-shirt? Sure, he could shut his eyes, but he was no monk, and hey, this could be his last happy moment.

He inhaled. Earthy and musky. He shouldn't find that sexy, but…damn. He'd never been into women who reeked of perfume—or worse, tasted of it.

Crap, she was talking. *Mind out of the cleavage, mate.*

"…goons are mostly Muslim, answering the call to jihad, but they're being fooled as much as anyone. It's all a cover." She bent slightly to get something from her bag, bringing her cleavage within millimeters of his nose.

Focus. "A cover for what?"

She snipped something—surgical tape?—and pressed it on his wound, shooting sparks through his skull. He forced himself to imagine what was under that T-shirt, seeing as he didn't have a real anesthetic…

Man, he was screwed up.

Like he didn't already know that.

"Long story." She wound the bandage on, sat on the mattress and removed a wipe from the packet Hamid had left. She ran it across her forehead, leaving a pale streak.

"So you said. We have time."

She scrubbed her cheeks like she wanted to erase them. "God, I hope you're right."

She studied the wipe, now the same dusty gray as the floor. How long had she been here—a week? In solitary, under threat of death, with a couple of rounds of interrogation and torture. Enough to send a commando berko but she seemed calm. Tougher than she looked, maybe. Or just good at hiding the damage.

Dirt—technically mud, now—was swirled over her face, mixed with scoured pink streaks. He itched to lean over and finish the job, so he could stare at something beautiful for a minute. He hadn't seen much of that in a long time.

Not that he was about to hit on Tess Newell. Hell, no. Journalists cared about headlines, not people, no matter how much they pretended otherwise. He wouldn't fall into that trap again, just in case these weren't his last days.

"Hold still." She leaned forward and smoothed a clean wipe over his forehead and around his eye. "So," she said, sitting back and hugging her knees. "Interesting times to be a soldier. Where have you served?"

Changing the subject? "Classified."

She sighed. "And here's me thinking it might be nice to have someone to talk to."

You want polite conversation, you got the wrong cell mate. He dragged his sorry arse along the floor and sat on the mattress cross-legged, a hair short of touching her. So the warm, pliant body he'd woken up pressed against was hers. He'd thought it was a soldier from his commando unit. Pity he hadn't figured out the truth before he'd panicked and leaped up—or maybe just as well.

Ah, crap, her guilt trip was working—she looked genuinely bummed by his brush-off. He could give the woman some company without going into details. "You don't last long in this business without seeing a bit of action. I've served in a lot of places. Too many. One dusty, pointless conflict after another."

"What had you expected?"

He shrugged, shamelessly watching as she drew out another wipe and attacked a cheek. At least talking gave him an excuse to stare. "I didn't get into it to be noble, if that's what you mean." Even at twenty, when he'd signed up, he hadn't been naive enough to think it was all exercises and hard drinking—though that would've suited him fine. But he hadn't counted on seeing so much death and misery in so many places. Like he hadn't lived through enough of that growing up. He scratched his elbow and found a Band-Aid on it. Did she do that last night, too?

She closed her eyes and ran the wipe over them. It felt weirdly intimate, watching a woman clean her face—the kind of thing you only usually saw if you were screwing her. And this was not a woman he'd be screwing.

"Why did you get into it?" she said.

Deflect attention, a-sap. "You said al-Thawra's a cover—for what?"

"You tell me. Who benefits from those conflicts you've been sucked into?"

"No one," he spit out. Pain stabbed his torso, where that bitch had kicked him.

"Really?"

"No one I've seen," he gasped, clutching his side.

"Maybe I should take a look at your ches— I mean check your *ribs*."

He held up a palm. If he could survive broken ribs without medical help as a kid, he could survive them now. Anyway, if his ribs were cracked, a Band-Aid and nail scissors wouldn't do shit. And the last thing he needed was those pretty fingers skating all over his chest. "Just bruised."

A pause. "But someone benefits, right?"

"From war? Yeah, journalists."

"You think?"

He shuffled back to rest against the cool stone wall, buying himself a few inches of space. "Gives you a job, doesn't it?"

"I could say the same about you."

"I'm guessing your job pays better than mine."

"But there are easier and safer ways for both of us to make a living, right?" She stretched her legs out, angling them awkwardly to avoid his. "If the US and its allies invade Somalia tomorrow, to crush the supposed threat from al-Thawra, who benefits?"

"*Supposed* threat? That's a whacked comment coming from a woman sitting on jihadist death row—or whatever kind of death row you think this is. Who benefits? How about the people who don't get blown up in the next terrorist attack?"

"Oh, come on—you don't believe the PR about war making us safer?"

"Ah, crap, really? I'm stuck in a hole in I-don't-know-the-hell-where, about to have my head sliced off, having some philosophical debate with…" With a woman who was getting more attractive—and formidable—by the second. He swallowed. "With some lefto greenie… tinfoil-hat-wearing conspiracy-theory crusader."

"Power and money, right?" She bulldozed on, but with a hint of a smile. "That's what it's about—what it's always about."

"Not from where I'm looking. You missed survival and the fact that some of us actually like defending innocent people." God, now *he* sounded like he was on *60 Minutes*, or whatever self-righteous program she worked for.

"Yeah, but you're looking at the foot soldiers, right? And the victims—the poor people just trying to keep their goats and children alive. Who benefits from a war in Somalia?"

"Ah. That would be no one."

"No one in Somalia, sure. But how about in America? In the UK, in France, *in Australia*, in every other country al-Thawra's trying to provoke?"

"Sunshine, my brain's too fuzzy to decode your conspiracy theory. And I'm guessing you've had no one to lecture for an entire week, so how about you lay it all out for me?" At least she wasn't interrogating him about his yo-yoing Australian-French accent.

She smiled again, the pale light catching her eyes. He could get used to looking at a face like that. Pity he wouldn't get a chance. "What about the good old-fashioned war profiteers? In the Civil War they were the carpetbaggers. In World War II, the industrialists. Now they're the contractors and suppliers."

"Bloody hell, I'm gonna need more painkillers—you're saying al-Thawra's a military contractor?"

"Not directly, but I have—I *had*—a paper trail proving that al-Thawra is controlled by the biggest military contractor and supplier in the world—Denniston Corp."

"Seriously?" Half the legion's supplies were stamped with that logo. "Okay, that could be interesting, if it's true."

"Oh, it's true. It was the story I was chasing before I was captured. Denniston's about to go bankrupt, and when they do, a whole lot of dirt will wash up. Not just

the ties to al-Thawra, but money laundering, terrorist links, political corruption... Kickbacks have been
bouncing around the world for years, and a lot of people
have got very rich and very powerful—senators, mem-
bers of Congress, business leaders, at least one prime
minister. Jail terms all round."

"Wasn't Denniston the company set up by—"

"Senator Hyland, yes. When he left the marines,
that's where he made his money. Officially he's sold
out of it, but unofficially he still calls the shots—in
Denniston *and* al-Thawra."

"Isn't he the guy running for—"

"President. Yep. If Denniston goes bust, he loses
everything—including his liberty. The one thing that'll
save them is a lucrative multigovernment contract, and
soon."

Whoa. It was like having his own live news service.
"And they'll get this contract if there's another war?"

"Bingo. Things aren't profitable right now, with
troops withdrawing from Iraq and Afghanistan, and
the US and its allies wary about getting mired in another conflict. So Denniston and Hyland and his buddy
Sara invented al-Thawra and Hamid, and she master-
minded the LA attacks—using foot soldiers who genuinely thought they were martyring themselves in a
jihad—and made it look like Somalia was sheltering
the terrorists. This invasion would not only get Hyland
out of the crap—it'd make him look good."

"The presidential candidate was behind an attack on
his own country? Bullshit."

"You think al-Thawra kidnapped me just because
of my profile?"

"Hey, I was kidnapped and I don't know about any of this."

"I'd just verified enough evidence to run with the story and, bam." She gestured at the room.

Okay, the fact she was in an al-Thawra dungeon might back up her story. "Does anyone else know?"

"My producer knew I was chasing the story, and my crew, but I had to keep it contained—many people would do anything to prevent this getting out, or find a way to discredit it." She chewed the corner of a fingernail. "I don't know what happened to my translator—we were separated when al-Thawra sprang. The cameraman was killed."

"The translator—Somali guy?"

"Do you know what happened to him?"

The woman was in her last days—did she need the details?

She swore, and rubbed her eyes with the fingers of one hand. "Oh God. Really?"

"I didn't say anything."

"I could see it in your face. Dead?"

Very. "Afraid so."

She tipped her head back and stared at the ceiling, her shiny eyes reflecting the light. His gut twisted—he knew the pain and guilt of losing buddies. Hell, he might have just lost all the friends he had.

"So all this stuff about them kidnapping you because you offended Islam…?"

"As you so eloquently put it? 'Bullshit.'" She lowered her head and stared at a stain on the mattress. "Hamid will play the publicity for all it's worth, then kill me, live—so to speak. She'll want to generate more anger in the States, so Hyland can stir up the political will to get over the line in Somalia." She lifted her gaze. Strength had returned to her eyes, cut in with new anger. "She's also eager to pull France into her game. Your execu— your *capture* could tip them."

Subtle she wasn't. "Hamid will assume you've told me all this, that I know her secret."

She winced.

"Guess I was dead anyway," he said.

"Didn't want to say it."

A clink and a squeal—the door upstairs. Footsteps crossed the floor above. Dirt drifted down between the boards, lit by slits of weak light. One soldier, by the sound of it.

"I'm just pissed I'm going to die before I get this story out," she added.

A grin tugged at his mouth. Smart, gutsy *and* hot. If he could have chosen one person to share his last days, it might well have been someone like her. As the room lightened she was looking paler and more fragile—but there was fire in her, for sure. He twitched with competing urges—to fold her into him and hide her from all this, and to tease that flame out of her in a far less honorable way. He stayed rigidly still.

Above, one bolt shot across, then another. She gripped the mattress, knuckles blanching.

"Tess, look..." he whispered, ignoring the burn in his ribs as he leaned closer. He stopped short of making it *Tess Newell*, as he'd heard hundreds of times on TV. *Tess* seemed incomplete. "Them kidnapping me buys you more time. Sounds like they plan to kill us together, and if your theory is true—"

"It *is* true."

"—they'll want to drum up anger about me in France first, right? That's got to give us a few days."

"You're a real comfort," she said flatly, but her knuckles returned to a normal color.

"I'll find us a way out of this."

She smiled, sadly—acknowledging his attempt at solace even if she didn't believe it. Well, damn, he'd just have to prove her wrong.

The hatch yawned open. He tensed. Or he could be wrong about the whole time thing. One burst of fire down that hole...

A rope lowered, from the hands of a woman in gray camo gear and a hijab. Flynn shuffled in front of Tess but she exhaled, pushed to her feet and hobbled past him.

"What's going on?" he said.

"Trust me, we want to cooperate with this." She grabbed a yellow bucket from the corner of the room and hooked it up.

"That what I think it is?"

"Hey, at least they change it twice a day. Otherwise I guess the smell would float up."

"Real hospitable."

The bucket rose and disappeared. Something fell. Before he could warn Tess, it clonked her on the head. Another bucket. Clean, at least.

"You okay?"

"Peachy," she said, rubbing her head. She ducked as a brown plastic packet thunked onto the dirt, then another. She threw one to Flynn.

"An MRE?" he said.

The hatch dropped and was bolted.

"The finest field rations Denniston produces. They

earn a dollar in profit from every meal, and they supply dozens of forces around the world—sometimes both sides in a conflict. And that's only one of their contracts. They might not be making the bombs but they're sure making the money—or they were. Most countries have a stockpile of these things now, so they're not renewing their contracts."

He ripped open the plastic, went straight for a brownie and bit in. Scam or not, he was as hungry as a wolf. She sat on the mattress and hugged her knees again, pulling her socks away from her toes. He got the idea she'd spent a lot of the week sitting like that. It'd sure suck to be alone down here. Hell, it sucked anyway, but it sucked a little less with her next to him.

"You not eating?" he mumbled.

"Later. Hard to drum up an appetite for something with a shelf life of three years."

"Takes that long to go through your system."

"I don't want to know about your system."

There was that unexpected smile again. He'd have to watch that smile—better yet, not watch it. He studied the packet, speaking through a mouthful of brownie. "This one expired two years ago." He shoved the last of it in his mouth.

"So now you're speaking with a French accent."

"Am I?" he said, trying to sound offhand as he fished out a packet of crackers. "I don't speak English much, so I'm all over the place." That was true enough. French had become his official first language when he'd signed his life to the legion nearly a decade ago. The less of his old identity that remained, the better.

He felt her gaze as he crunched, the sound bouncing off the walls like shrapnel. He glugged from his water bottle.

"What are you hiding?" she said.

He choked, and the water splattered his jacket. "What?"

"I once did a story on the legion. It's not a career path for well-adjusted kids from good families. They say everyone's hiding or running—or both. So what's your story?"

"No story. I wanted adventure."

"Come on—we could be dead by dawn."

"Not if I can help it."

"I'm not taking notes. You could at least be civil—this could be the last conversation of your life. Between you and me, what are you hiding?"

Between him and her and her audience of millions? "Maybe I'm just an idealist."

She raised her eyebrows. "Uh-huh."

"What you said, about escaping—maybe it's true of some of the foreigners. But for French officers it can be a quicker trip through the ranks, if you're prepared to put up with a platoon of lunatics." Again, not exactly a lie.

"And are they—lunatics?"

"Non," he said. *Watch yourself.* "Most just need a job. Others want to earn a European passport. Sure, some are running, but they're not serial killers." He gulped. The words had slipped out. Dumbass. "They're more likely to be escaping bitter ex-wives."

"Ah. And do you have one of those?"

"No, thank God."

"Where are you from?"

"I told you—France," he said, too quickly.

"You already said that. I meant, where in France?"

Damn. "Corsica, where my regiment is based."

"Corsica, huh? That's the…parachute regiment."

Mate, she sure paid attention. *Proceed with caution, soldier. "Oui, le 2E Régiment étranger de parachutistes."*

"The elite force—paratroopers, commandos."

He shrugged. "My parachute training is about as useful down here as your notebook."

"Do you spend much time at the French base at Djibouti—Monclar?"

"When I'm in town."

"Maybe that's why you look familiar—maybe I saw you there, when I was researching my legion piece. I watched a few training sessions."

Yeah, that wasn't why. "That's it, then." *Let it go, lady.* He scanned the ceiling. Enough chitchat. "Is that the routine here—bucket goes up, food comes down?"

"Twice a day—morning and evening."

He stood, and ran his hand over the wooden planks that marked the ceiling, ignoring the sting in his ribs and his throbbing head. At one point the gap was wide enough for a few fingers. He scanned the ceiling, then the hatch, then the room.

"Looking for something?" she said.

"Hooks, nails, staples, bolts. Anything that could attach to the wood up here."

"It's all rocks and dirt. You have an idea?"

"I'll tell you if it works. What's above us?"

"Some storage bunker, I think."

"Empty?"

"Mostly."

"Number of guards?"

"They come and go, usually in pairs. They might beef up patrols now—I don't think I was much of a threat."

You are to me, sunshine. "When they bring the evening rations and do the bucket thing, does one person do it, like then?"

Her gaze shot to a corner of the room, thinking. "Yeah."

"Is it light or dark outside?"

"Dark—right after sunset, I think. They don't seem to have electricity in this building—this is as floodlit as it gets."

That presented possibilities. Maybe if he could create some leverage... "Give me a look at your bag."

She chucked it over. "You planning to bust us out with tweezers and diarrhea pills?"

"Beats waiting for the execution."

CHAPTER THREE

TESS WATCHED THE soldier palpate gaps in the ceiling. His brain better be as honed as his body, because she sure wasn't seeing a way out.

Damn straight he was a pretty boy—or would have been, once. Caramel-colored hair blended with his tan, and his grim expression made his cheekbones look sculpted, his defined lips determined and his jaw even squarer. His narrowed eyes were pale—blue or maybe green. And still his face nagged at her memory, like meeting a guy you hadn't seen since junior high and searching his features for the boy you remembered.

But the stubble, the crooked nose, the lines dug out between his eyes, the sun-worn skin… He was rough and a little frayed, too. And there'd been nothing delicate about the solid body pressed against hers last night. Just the thought… *Whoa.*

Hell, she didn't even know the name of the guy who'd lulled her into her first proper, blessed sleep in nearly a week. Evidently it'd once been stenciled on his chest pocket but only a few faded strokes remained. An *F*? Or an *E*?

"What's your name, soldier?"

A pause. "Flynn."

"That doesn't sound very French."

He tugged at a board, acting like he hadn't heard. It

shifted, and dirt showered him. He was hiding something, for sure. Debts? Petty crimes? Recruits to the legion could change their names—was it the same for native officers, if he even was French? His French accent sounded kosher but she'd have sworn his Australian accent was authentic, too. *Beaut*, he'd said last night. Did anyone but Australians say that? Wouldn't his native language be more likely to slip out in a drugged daze? And he'd said *bloody hell*—the French didn't say that. Any minute, the neurons would connect, telling her where she knew him from. Something told her it wasn't her visit to the French base—it went further into the past, to somewhere unexpected, somewhere dark. Damn, that was annoying. When she'd taken her first good look at his face, a frisson of danger had crawled up her spine—her subconscious issuing a warning? Why?

"Flynn who?"

"Does it matter?" His gaze was locked on the ceiling.

Well, hey, if he was a mystery, he was a welcome one. She froze. Unless he'd been planted down here to extract information. Crap. Al-Thawra had a rainbow of nationalities. Was he pretending to be a French soldier to earn her trust? That could explain the erratic accent and her usually reliable instinct pricking up.

Maybe Hamid was still trying to figure out if Tess had a copy of her dossier—using a carrot this time, rather than a pair of pliers? Tess chewed her lip. She'd know from the emails, as carefully worded as they were, that Tess hadn't had a chance to get the evidence to Quan in Addis Ababa, and she hadn't risked storing it online. Thank God caution had stopped her short of mentioning the backup of the dossier to Flynn—if that was his name. Could he be here to stage a bust-out so she'd lead him to it?

No. She was going loco. Too much time alone, locked in her head. If he got her above ground, at least she'd have options. In the meantime, it wouldn't hurt to do what she did best—prod him for information, push him a little, see if he slipped up. A wee game. Hey, she didn't have anything else to do.

"Do you have a big family in Corsica?" she said.

He stiffened. "No."

She waited, but he offered nothing more. Could be a good sign. In her vast experience with liars, they usually spoke too much, not too little.

"Did you grow up there?"

"Does it matter?"

"Just making conversation."

"How about we focus on the task at hand? You'll have the rest of your long life to make meaningless small talk."

"Humor me. I've had no one to talk to for six days— and days last a mighty long time down here."

"Fine. You want to talk, let's talk about you. Where are you from?" He didn't even pretend a genuine interest. Though if his French accent was faked, too, why did his words roll over her skin like velvet?

"The States," she said, with a sly smile.

"Well, yeah. I meant…" He met her eye, then looked away. She detected a faint curse—called out on his own caginess. He crouched beside a wall and began examining it. "You know what I meant."

Ah, what the heck. It was all on the internet. "I'm based in New York when I'm in the States, which isn't often."

"Where are you mostly?"

"I live in Addis Ababa, not that I'm there often, either. I cover Ethiopia, Kenya, Somalia, Djibouti, Sudan, South Sudan… So I'm mostly on the road."

He was silent a few seconds, regarding her with raised eyebrows. "Wow, you didn't land the cushy job. Did you piss off your bosses?"

She laughed. "I begged to be posted here."

"What are you running away from?"

"Nothing. I like it here."

He returned focus to the wall. "Where did you grow up?"

"Fort Bragg, mostly, though we moved around."

"The army base?"

"That's the one. My mom and brothers are still headquartered there." She swallowed. And her mom had just become an al-Thawra target, too. *Your other whistleblower will soon meet the same fate as the first. Nice and tidy.* Was Hamid bluffing? Tess could only hope Lieutenant Colonel Newell was one step ahead of Hamid—it was her job to know what people were thinking before they thought it, to outmaneuver them before they took a step. Which had sucked when Tess was a teenager, but now…

"You're an army brat." He ran his hands down the padded straps of her bag, frowning. "That ain't gonna work," he muttered.

"What isn't?"

He fished around in the bag, emerging with a small rolled bandage. "Fort Bragg. That's in the South, *oui*?"

"North Carolina, yeah."

"You don't sound Southern."

"My accent comes and goes, a little like yours."

"We did a joint exercise off Hawaii with some guys from there," he said, his voice tight, evidently ignoring her dig. "Stevens, Porter, Luiz... Know them?"

Common enough surnames and it was a big base. Lucky guess?

"Mauricio Luiz?" she said.

He unwrapped the bandage and snapped it taut. It ripped. He swore. "Sounds right."

"Blond guy?"

He looked at her sideways. "With a name like that? Nah, Colombian or something. Short guy, burn scar across his neck, tattoo of a...snake, or something. Arrogant piece of shit."

"Oh yeah, that's him." So Flynn probably wasn't faking the military thing. "He's a good buddy of one of my brothers. God knows why. Last I saw him, he'd bleached his hair."

"That'd be right."

"Have you trained elsewhere in the States? Maybe that's where I've seen—"

He held up his hand, listening, as a car engine surged and fell away. "We're near a road?"

"Yeah. Not a lot of traffic but it seems to be a public road. I've heard children's voices, buses, donkeys..."

He scanned the room for the twentieth time. "So what stopped you signing up, like your brothers?"

Wow, he was as seasoned at changing the subject as a politician. "Hard to be a lefto, greenie conspiracy theorist and shoot people."

"You forgot the tinfoil hat." His lips pulled up into a lopsided grin. It made him look boyish. Cute, even. Green—his eyes were green.

She pulled focus. Like it mattered. "I was more interested in keeping the higher ranks honest than doing their bidding. I saw the crap my mom and brothers had to put up with." She left her Bronze Star–winning father out of it—he'd been the type to serve up the crap, while cheating on her mother on every tour. "Mom was only too happy to send me to college to keep me out of uniform."

"Bet she didn't imagine you'd be the one winding up here."

"Guess not." Or the child who'd bring killers to her door. What was her mom doing now? No one in the family would sit back and wait for the authorities to act, despite their respect for the chain of command, but she'd know Tess's abduction had put her at risk. It was only after she'd put Tess in touch with Latif six months ago, while he was still working as an IT security analyst at Denniston, that the conspiracy had started to become clear. And now Latif was dead—"collateral damage" in a drone strike against al-Thawra, as if that could be believed—despite Tess's promise to protect him, and the evidence he'd left behind was her only hope. Too many deaths already.

Flynn pushed a finger through the gap he'd widened in the floorboards, then retracted it, his forehead wrinkling. Was he planning to yank the whole floor down?

"What do they do—your family?" he said.

Warning bells jangled—was he fishing for information? Something to hold over her? But, hey, her family was no secret—*Rolling Stone* had profiled the entire clan last year on the third anniversary of her "American hero" father's death.

"My brothers are Special Forces—all three of them. Mom's in Intel."

"Is that why you're obsessed with this Somalia story—you're afraid your family will be deployed there?"

"I don't like to see any soldier go to war without a very good reason."

He ran a hand over the boards. "Neither do I. Hell, *I* could end up deployed there... So this dossier—can you do your story without it?"

A chill tiptoed up her spine. "My bosses would never run it without hard evidence—it's too damning, too dangerous."

"So you need to get it back."

"I don't imagine that's an option."

She picked up her MRE. Maybe force-feeding her stomach would stop it churning. This guy might be radiating mixed messages but at least he brought hope.

"How long have you been in the legion?" she said. If he was hiding something, she'd catch him out. If in doubt, ask the same question ten different ways until they got flustered. The Human Lie Detector, Quan called her.

Half a minute passed. He poked and prodded and shifted the floorboards. "Nine years," he said.

She waited. Nothing. Sheesh, the guy didn't offer much.

"How old were you when you signed up?"

Another pause. "Twenty."

She pretended to focus on opening a packet of gray mush that claimed to be oatmeal. That made him three years younger than her. With his cynicism and frown lines she'd have picked older. "I thought you'd transferred from the regular army?" She forced an offhand tone. She sensed him stilling, imagined him looking down at her and frowning as he assessed the question.

"Yeah, that's where I signed up, L'armée de Terre. That's what I meant. I transferred to the legion after graduating the academy."

"And where did you do your officer training?"

"Sunshine, we could be here for weeks. You wanna wear me out the first day?"

"I'm just interested—and I'm trying to figure out where I've seen you before."

"I told you—one of those faces."

No, that wasn't it. Maybe a less direct approach... "I've never been to Corsica. Is it much different from mainland France?"

Pause. "It's peaceful. People don't ask questions."

She smiled, the movement unfamiliar on her lips. He was probably right, at least within the legion, where "Don't ask, don't tell" took on a far wider meaning. The legionnaires she'd met all had Flynn's cagey look, the sideways glances, the spare details, as if the ghosts of their pasts were about to jump them and haul them back.

Something shot across the floor. She gasped, clutching her chest. "Damn mouse."

"There's a nest in the corner. You want me to get rid of them?"

She screwed up her face. "I don't know. We've been together awhile now. I was present at the birth."

"Don't tell me you've named them."

"Minnie and Mickey and... Huey, Dewey and Louie."

"Pretty sure those last ones are ducks. How about I send them to a happier place and I'll be your friend instead?"

"Let them be. They're trapped here, too."

What just came out of her mouth? She was fighting for the rights of mice now? There it was—proof she'd gone crazy.

"Just what I need to be stuck with—a *vegan*, lefto, greenie conspiracy-theory crusader. Trust me, not all life deserves to be preserved."

"I'd rather not have a pile of bodies rotting in the corner—the smell is bad enough already. Unless you're sizing them up for lunch?"

"Couldn't eat another thing. Don't worry, princess. I won't kill them if you don't want me to. I'll repatriate them." He raised his chin to indicate the newly widened slats above his head.

"They won't fit through there."

"The fuckers can get in anywhere. They go flat as paper. You wanna help? Tip the mattress on its side to block their escape that direction."

As she hoisted it up, he ripped open a packet of peanut cookies, crumbled one and threw the remains into a corner.

"You're assuming they'll recognize that as food." She found herself whispering, like the mice could understand English.

He crouched, motionless, the shape of his butt outlined by his faded trousers. How good had that felt under her hand last night? Round, but firm and muscular. She nibbled her lip. Small pleasures were about all she could hope for.

She spent far too many of the next ten minutes admiring his rear view. Finally, the mother mouse scampered to the crumbs. The babies weren't old enough to venture from the nest or Tess might not have come over all Cinderella.

"Okay, very slowly, bring that mattress closer." Flynn inched in until he was between the mother and the nest, as Tess slid the rectangle of foam along the floor, flush against the wall, closing in. Each time the mother looked up, twitching, they froze. Time ticked by. His thighs had to be killing him, quads of granite or not.

Tess stumbled. The mouse took off. In a blur of desert camos, Flynn flung forward and shot out an arm. "Got it."

Dang, he had the reflexes of a cobra.

"Grab the babies, one by one, and ease them through that gap up there."

"I can't reach that high." *Thank God.* She wasn't squeamish, but wild mice weren't on her preferred list of things to handle. Flynn's butt, on the other hand, was currently sitting in the top ten. Top five. Top—

Stop it.

He swore, his fingers clamped around the mouse's tail as it clawed air and gyrated. "Then you'll have to hold her while I move them."

She widened her eyes. "Hey, I'm tolerating them— just—but I don't want cuddles."

"If I release her first, she'll come back down to the nest." He met her gaze. "I didn't take you for a wimp."

Damn, exactly the kind of crap her brothers dished up. "Hand her over." *Oh man, really?*

He edged behind Tess, his breath teasing the top of her hair as he encircled her with his arms. "Her instincts are going mental, so you'll have to hold tight. Clamp down on the tail, either side of my fingers."

Yuck, yuck, yuck. But she followed his instructions.

He hovered a palm underneath their hands as he let go. "Got her?"

"Got her."

"Spin her gently so she can't arch back and bite you." He backed away. "Can't believe I'm busting my arse to liberate mice."

"Think of it as earning karma. But hurry up."

He knelt by the nest. "It's okay," he crooned in a falsetto, "you dirty little fuckers. Just call me Uncle Scroo—"

He froze and plucked something from the nest. Not a mouse. String? He passed it under a shaft of gray light, and it glinted.

"What is it?"

"A wire. You said there was no electricity in this building."

"Not as far as I can tell."

"Seen any electrical cords? Wiring?"

"Nothing."

He scraped at the dirt where the stone wall met the floor, just shy of the nest.

"What are you looking for?"

"Tell you when I find it."

Minnie pawed the air like she was on a mouse wheel. "Ah, could you look quickly? She's about to turn herself inside out."

He crawled along one wall, digging into the dirt at its foot, then shoved aside the mattress and crept along the next wall, doing the same. Halfway along he stopped and dug faster, like a dog after a bone. Maybe that head injury was affecting his brain.

"You beauty," he muttered.

"A secret tunnel?"

"Not quite, but looks like that karma might have come round pretty quick."

He tugged something. She jumped as a long shape scooted along the floor. More mice? Crap—a snake? Minnie's claws scraped her wrist. "Yeouch." She arched her hand.

Flynn was holding something—the end of a piece of rope, embedded in the dirt. She squinted. Not rope—an electrical cord, tapering off to a frayed end. He gazed up at the ceiling, frowning.

"Excellent," Tess said. "Now we can fire up my hair straightener and singe our way out of here."

"You have a hair straightener?"

"Does it look like I have a hair straightener?"

He shrugged. "Pity. Could be a useful weapon."

"Would you mind hurrying things up with those mice?"

"Just a sec." He clawed at the dirt farther along and ripped up another cord.

"Do you think it's live?"

"I doubt it—the mouse managed to chew right through without getting electrocuted." Holding each cord by its white cover, he touched the frayed ends together. "Yep, dead."

"Flynn…? This mouse is about to explode."

He stood and ran his hand over a floorboard, biting the inside of one cheek.

"Flynn!"

"Yeah, yeah. On it."

He sauntered to the nest, evidently distracted by mysterious calculations running through his brain. Kneeling, he shoveled half a dozen balls of gray onto one palm and enclosed them with the other. He stood and eased the creatures through a crack one by one, eyes crinkled in concentration. Oh boy, a tough guy being gentle—it got her right *there*. And that was her problem. *No more tough guys, you hear?* Dependable, loyal accountants.

"Now for Minnie." He came up so close beside Tess the warmth of his body reached out and caressed her. She stood straighter. This was not supposed to be an intimate experience. He maneuvered his hands around hers. "Separate your fingers a little. Got her. Let go."

"Gladly."

He gripped the mouse's body and lifted it to the gap. It sniffed, found purchase with its scrabbling claws and blessedly disappeared. Tess shook her wrist.

Flynn looked at his palms, grimacing. "Got any more wipes?" Suddenly he shut his eyes tight, like someone had stabbed his voodoo doll.

"Flynn?"

"Too much…action for this soldier." When he opened his eyes they looked like they were retreating into his skull. Nothing fake about his head injury. A fraction more force and the wound could have been fatal.

She kicked the mattress flat, caught his arm and guided him down. "More painkillers?"

"I'll hold out… Need to keep sharp." He sounded anything but. God, what if his wound did prove lethal? He could have internal bleeding, swelling…

She grabbed the wipes. "Give me your hands," she said, kneeling in front of him. She scrubbed at one, then the other—muscular, tanned, callused hands that flinched at her strokes. She fought the temptation to bring one up to her face, to feel the roughness against her cheek. Yep, desperate *and* pathetic. And eager for him not to die, whoever he was.

He yawned. She echoed, her eyelids feeling as heavy as his looked.

"We should…sleep," he said. "Store our energy. Must have been well after midnight when I… I'll take the floor."

"Don't be silly. We're adults. We can share. You don't want to pick up an infection, and this place is far from sterile."

His lidded gaze ran the length of her body, her skin goose-pimpling in its wake. *Earth to Tess.* He was probably just figuring out how they'd both fit on the mattress. Did he remember anything of the previous night? Her face warmed.

"I…need to use the facilities." He jerked his head toward the bucket.

"Sure," she said. She swiveled away and concentrated on popping a couple of painkillers. Trying to ignore the noises from the other half of the room, she brushed dirt and stones off the mattress, lay straight and rigid on one side of it and closed her eyes. Her muscles pulsed as they eased up. The toe Hamid had stomped on throbbed double time, at least eclipsing the pain from the other.

Sometime last night she'd awoken on her back, Flynn's forearm heavy on her belly, his hand curled around the side of her waist, his stubbly cheek against her shoulder. It would have been so easy to turn into him so their bodies were flush together and hunker down into a place of refuge. When she was single, that was what she missed most—the physical contact. Yes, she missed sex, but it was plain old touch she ached for—a strong, rough man's body cocooning hers. That was when she felt safest, when she felt loved, when it felt like nothing could sneak in to destroy her happiness. It wasn't even necessarily about being *in* love. Had she ever been in love with Kurt? Or just in love with the idea of him, the fantasy that it might actually work out, despite her misgivings?

Behind her, the mattress shifted as Flynn lowered onto it. His body grazed her spine, then settled, his warmth radiating into her. He had to be half an inch away, at most. She risked a peek. His body mirrored hers, facing the opposite wall, spooning air. She nestled down and ordered her eyes to close. She could still steal comfort from the pinpricks of electricity heating her back. It seemed impossible that a body so warm, so *alive* could be so…not, in a matter of days. Hours, perhaps. Hamid said she'd kidnapped him to be a double act with Tess. Another life on her conscience.

Even with him there, sleep didn't come. Ten, twenty minutes later she remained rigidly awake, her thoughts pushing into ever darker places. She sighed.

"This is stupid," he said huskily. She sensed him rolling over. He propped himself up on an elbow. "We're lying here like corpses."

"Did you just say 'corpses'?"

"Okay, not the best word choice. Point is that I can't sleep like this and neither can you. Come here."

Without waiting for a reply, he slipped his hands around her waist and pulled her in until his chest skimmed her back. Shock waves of awareness buzzed into her stomach. She caught her breath. That shouldn't feel so good.

"Relax," he said, skating a hand down her arm. "I'm

not hitting on you. Priority one is to get some rest, and this way we can both be comfortable. I'm just glad I didn't get chucked in here with a guy."

Mercifully, he kept his hips away from her butt—*that* kind of contact would not be conducive to sleep. She forced herself to inhale deeply. On the exhalation, she let her body settle into his. Something nudged her hair—his nose? Oh man, lips?

"Better, huh?" he whispered. Yep, his lips. Better, yes. And so much worse.

"Yeah," she said, high-pitched and wooden. "That's fine." *Idiot.*

Just take the respite. Last night was a godsend, but this was a gift straight from him—offered, not stolen. And despite her instinct blinking neon warnings, she genuinely liked this prickly, brazen guy—maybe a little too much.

Outside, something banged. She tensed. He squeezed her forearm and they waited in silence. Nothing.

"Don't worry, sunshine. We'll be out of here as soon as that hatch opens tonight. Meantime, I've got your back."

Right now, she'd let herself believe it.

FLYNN WAITED UNTIL near darkness to thread the first length of electrical cord through the gap in the floorboards for the first of his handholds. He'd coated it with mud but the white would still glow through, catching any light that passed. Still, the guards seemed confident about the security of their prison—boots crossed over the boards just once every hour.

Apart from the odd shout or footfall outside, the only sounds for the past thirty minutes had been him scrambling around and Tess's steady breath. Her curled shape on the mattress was melting into black, with just her hair still picking up the light. He'd let her rest as long as possible. With injured feet, she'd have a hard enough time keeping up.

Hell, how long since he'd had an encounter like that with a woman? Gentle and innocent—except for the dirty thoughts running through his head. For nearly ten years his few relationships had been short-term and only about sex. In one fling, with a Canadian tourist, he'd pretended he didn't speak English to avoid conversation. Yep, he was that much of a lowlife. Stick around and they'd start asking questions.

The last time he'd stuck with a woman—with a journalist—too long, she'd torn his life apart. The bitch had pretended to be into him just long enough to paste his face and whereabouts all over the media, leaving him no choice but to leave Australia. Oh yeah, he'd learned his lesson, about journalists *and* women.

He twisted the cord and tried to angle it to fall over the gap on the other side of the board, so he could pull it through and secure it. Bugger, this would take more time and effort than he'd budgeted. He was fast running out of light, and his head wound pulsed every time he looked up. He made himself breathe—in, out, in, out. At least the pain in his ribs had eased.

After ten minutes he took a break and a handful of painkillers. On his next attempt, success. The cord flipped into the right spot and he used Tess's tweezers to grip the loose wires and urge them to a point he could grab them. He pulled both ends tight and tied them, then swung on the cord, tentatively lifting his feet off the floor. It held. Sweet.

With the scissors, he sawed off another length of cord at the point it disappeared between the rocks. It was shorter—just enough for a second handhold. Threading it through would be even more of a bitch than the first.

Tess shifted. Mate, the light had fallen fast. This was taking too long. If the soldier returned before he was ready, his plan was screwed. He tucked the cord under his arm and crouched over Tess, his fingers finding her neck, then navigating to the safer territory of her shoulder. He gently shook it.

"Tess, wake up."

She groaned and sat. He kept his hand on her. Maybe because he didn't want her getting disorientated. Maybe because the smooth curve of her shoulder felt good. With his other hand he searched for the open bottle of water.

"It's dark," she said.

"Ready to bust out? Here, have a drink." He let his hand fall to the middle of her back while she gulped. "Can you get your boots on?"

"Maybe, if I strip down the bandages on my toes. It'll be…tight."

"Leave them off for now. Put them in your backpack— it's leaning on the mattress. I've packed it. You might have to take out one of the water bottles—I've stuffed in as many as can fit." She'd run faster in socks, if she could run at all. He'd have to steal a vehicle.

"What's your plan?"

"Get us above ground."

"And then?"

"Wing it."

Her silence told him everything about her faith in that.

"Sunshine, winging it is what I do best."

Anything was better than sitting down here, rotting. He got back to work on his handholds, giving her his watch so she could direct its light up. Even the faint blue glow cast shadows.

"Someone's coming."

Damn, she was right. Footsteps neared, thudding on dusty ground. "A few more seconds." The frayed end of the second cord was poking up through the boards, but he still needed to catch it, yank it back down and tie it. "Kill the light. I'll do it blind." He hadn't had time to check everything, let alone practice his maneuver. Could he wait? And then what—risk escaping in daylight? They might not be alive by tomorrow night.

He let his head drop forward, taking the pressure off his wound, and left his fingers to do the work, snapping the tweezers blindly into the gap. A scrape and a click—the key in the lock.

"Put the backpack on," he whispered. He'd intended to carry it, but plans were evolving too fast.

A door squeaked open. The tweezers snagged something. Shafts of light fell through the cracks. He pulled the end of the cord and caught it in his fingers. Footsteps passed overhead—one person, too heavy to be the woman. Flynn held his breath. One flick of the flashlight in his direction and the cords would gleam like strip lights.

He drew the cord down. Screw it, no time to prepare, test the angles, experiment with his run up. The diagram in his head would have to do. As the bolts shot across, he tied the ends and tested his weight, wincing as the cords rolled, shuddering, along the floorboards. He lowered to the floor, released the handholds and backed into the wall, wiping his sweaty palms on his combat pants. Chalk would be good, like at high school gym. He settled for dirt. No shortage of that.

The hatch squealed as it was levered off, the flashlight beam dancing out from the soldier's hands. The handholds glowed. *Now.* Flynn sprang out, launched himself off the floor and into the loops, and swung his feet up. The guy squawked. Flynn's boot collected something as his feet flew out of the hole. The rest of his body didn't make it. The flashlight cracked into a wall and flickered off.

He hooked his boots on the edge of the hatch, his torso swinging down wildly. Bugger. Not enough momentum. High school gym was too long ago. The guy shouted something. Flynn crunched up, flailing with his right hand, his ribs burning, his skull complaining about being upside down. Pressure dug into his back— Tess, pushing him from underneath. He got a fingerhold on the side of the hatch, then a hand. The guy shouted again. *Merde*, how long until reinforcements arrived?

Pain slammed into his shins. Something pushed on his soles. The guy was trying to tip him back in. Funneling his strength into his right arm, Flynn hoisted himself, with a grunt. One foot slipped but his upper body was out. He rolled clear of the hole and sprang upright.

Footfalls rapped from outside, flashlight beams jiggling through the open doorway. His opponent's eyes lit with fear. Flynn smashed a fist in his solar plexus, dropping him. The guy scraped for breath but kicked out, catching Flynn in the nuts. Flynn swore, unbalanced, slipped sideways. Something skidded out beside him and dropped into the hatch. The MREs the guy had been carrying.

As Flynn picked himself up, another soldier reached

the doorway, running, an M16 aimed. A flashlight beam skidded over the wall, revealing an alcove. Flynn dived. Bullets ripped up the room; warm liquid sprayed his face. *Putain*.

Suddenly, the gunman flailed, reared up and smacked into the floor at Flynn's feet, his rifle flying up. What the—?

No fucking way—the guy had tripped on the looped cords sticking up through the floorboards. The first soldier lay still on the floor, his skull flipped open like a lid. More shouts outside. Five or six men, a couple of women. Some closing in, some farther away.

Flynn dropped on the gunman, smashing an elbow into the back of his neck. "Look out below," he called, lifting the guy in a spear tackle and launching him headfirst into the hole. He landed with an unhealthy crack. Hell, Flynn should have taken his rifle. Not thinking quickly enough.

He pressed into the alcove, reining in his heaving breath, as another guy approached the door. A splintering crack ricocheted from the other side of the room. Shit. A second external door had been forced open. Two goons spilled in, silhouetted in a floodlight, rifles glinting dully. Enemy left and right. Nowhere to retreat. He needed a plan B.

CHAPTER FOUR

"Flynn!"

Something skidded across the floor and smacked into Flynn's boot. He crouched, felt for it, flinched. Hot metal—the M16 barrel. Tess had chucked it out of the hole. Legend.

Gunfire tore into concrete an inch above his head. He slotted the rifle into his arms and let loose a burst. One enemy went down. Two. Three. As the echoes faded, stillness settled. Someone gurgled. Shooting unidentified targets wasn't Flynn's style, but neither was dying for a principle. Dusty beams from two fallen flashlights crisscrossed the floor. Voices pinged around outside, closing fast. They had thirty seconds, tops.

In the light spilling in from outside, he made out the ladder, attached to bolts in the wall. He flung it into the hole, his gaze—and rifle barrel—flicking between the doorways.

"Tess," he hissed. "Climb, quick."

The rope jerked and swung. She yelped. "He's got me. My ankle."

Flynn peered down, barrel first. "Let her go," he warned. He released a volley over the guy's head. Tess sprang up a little as he wisely took the chance Flynn had offered. Flynn grabbed her forearm and hauled her out. "Stay behind me."

He unhooked the rope ladder and tossed it into the hole, then leaned against the concrete beside the gaping second doorway and scoped out the exterior. No movement, no sound. He felt behind him for Tess but his hand hit air. She was leaning over a dead enemy.

"Tess!"

She tugged at something, then ran to him in a loping stride, shouldering an M16 like she knew how.

"What now?" she said breathlessly.

"First, we get out of the light." Adrenaline surged through his veins and lit up his nerves. *This* was more like it. "And then I'm going to fucking kiss you."

TESS STUCK BEHIND Flynn as they sprinted to a patch of darkness, ignoring the bolts of fire in her toes. Pain was just her nerves yelling to her brain that there was a problem. She knew there was a problem—her nail beds were pulpy masses of blood and goo—so her nerves could shut the hell up.

Her brain threw together a jumpy picture of her surroundings. It wasn't the concrete-walled compound she'd imagined, more a sprawl of huts ringed by a ten-foot chain-link fence. Ahead, beyond an open gate, was a dirt road, otherwise there was a whole lot of dark nothing. A desert? Crap. Urgent voices carried from the far side of the bunker—half a dozen goons getting closer. Far off to the right was a sprinkling of lights—a village? A pair of headlights bumped toward them along the road. She couldn't hear the engine over her own panting.

Light spilled from a hut next to the gate. A gatehouse. It looked deserted—the guards must have rushed to the bunker. A lucky break but they'd have to be quick. She sped up—and was yanked back.

"What are you doing?" she whispered.

Flynn's hand encircled her biceps. "It's exactly where they think we'll go."

"That's because it makes the most sense." She tried to tear free but he held tight. "We could flag down the car."

"Again, that's what they'd expect us to do."

She clenched her teeth. "Again, that's because it makes sense."

"Got a better idea. Trust me." His eyes glittered. Green, definitely.

Stop it.

Trust him? Right now instinct urged her to, but instinct had got her into bad places where men were concerned. Still, there didn't seem to be anything wrong with *his* survival instincts. If he got them to safety, she'd return the favor and ditch him. She didn't need another death on her tab.

"Fine," she said.

She followed him behind a small wooden shack near the fence. A hole-in-the-ground toilet, by the smell of it. She pressed her back into its rear wall, and he did the same. Sheltered from view, for now.

The car neared, its headlights lighting them up. Flynn leveled his rifle.

"You're not going to shoot it?"

"Nope," he whispered, tracing its progress with the barrel. When it was a foot or two past the gate he opened fire. She smacked her palms over her ears, craning her neck. What the hell? Dust rose along the path of the bullets, lit red by the taillights. He'd missed. Was that good or bad? The car revved, tires squealing. Footsteps and shouts sounded from the compound, closer now. A woman barked orders. Hamid.

The car bumped and skidded, engine straining. Poor guy driving it had to be terrified.

"What the hell was th—?"

"Wait," he whispered, hardly louder than if he'd mouthed it. Something soft touched her ear—his lips. His hand pressed on her thigh. Just a warning to keep it together, that he had this under control—like hell— but she allowed herself to close her eyes for a second, to breathe. Whatever his plan, she had no choice but to go along with it. This kind of situation had to be his day at the office.

Sheesh, he'd promised to kiss her back there. A throwaway comment, obviously, but it'd heated her up all the same, just as his lips and hand were doing now. Man, she was messed up. How soon could PTSD set in? Was that also the reason for her paranoia about him? Well, paranoia was part of her job, but she was finding whole new levels.

Great, so now she was paranoid about being paranoid.

A vehicle door opened and slammed. And another. One, two, three more. An engine growled to life. Wheels skidded. Another engine started and whined into a cre-scendo as it accelerated, tires crunching along the rocky road. The fleeing car reached panic pitch.

So that was Flynn's plan—make Hamid and her goons think Tess and Flynn had flagged down the car. God—imagine if they had? If it had been her choice... As the cars left and their noise faded, Hamid's voice rang out. A one-sided conversation—on a phone? She could be speaking English, but Tess couldn't make out the words over the pulse pummeling her eardrums. Behind them, a guy shouted. Another answered.

The compound was otherwise quiet. Flynn had taken out four or five goons. Maybe five more had left in the cars. How many were left? They all had to be focused on that car, having assumed Flynn's gunfire had come from one of their guys in pursuit. And the driver had, naturally, hoofed it, making the car the target Flynn wanted it to be. Two birds, one stone. Smart—and ruthless.

Flynn appeared to be tracking something, out of her vision. Hamid's voice receded—she was walking to the gate? His hand left Tess's thigh and he silently lined up a shot. She settled her breath like it was her finger on the trigger. A man's shout. Footfalls across the compound, toward Hamid. Flynn pressed back into the building, lowering the rifle, and gave a quick shake of the head. No shot. He gestured that Tess should lead them along the fence line, behind the buildings. Back into the compound? No kidding he was winging it. But, hey, if it confounded her, it'd confound Hamid.

She peered around her side of the shack, away from the gate. No one. She scampered into the open, her breath catching, and slipped into the darkness behind the next building. A few feet separated its concrete wall from the fence. How long until Hamid's goons caught up with the car and figured out the truth?

Rocks pricked her feet through her socks. At least her tread was silent, though the car rally out front would mask a wildebeest stampede. Flynn walked so quietly she had to check he was following. Was that something military guys practiced—tiptoeing drills?

The fence didn't let up. They came to a corner, near

a long, low concrete building with barred windows and several doors opening to a veranda. Dark and quiet.

"We'll have to go over the fence," Flynn whispered.

"I don't think I can. My toes—I wouldn't be able to get a grip."

He frowned, first at her feet, then at the fence. He could leave her behind, of course, but self-preservation stopped her suggesting it. If he was a selfish guy, it would occur to him. If not, he'd refuse.

"Wait here," he said.

"Where are you—?"

He'd gone. Her breath hitched. Maybe he *was* the selfish type. He tried the first door in the building and pushed it open, leading with his rifle. He disappeared inside. After a silent, tense half a minute, he reappeared and did the same with the next door, and the next. He jogged back, something glinting in his hand—a pocketknife.

He knelt at the fence and slashed, the clinking and tearing echoing through the rear of the compound. She cringed.

"Give me the bag and your weapon."

He slid them under the fence and lifted the makeshift flap. She shimmied through, the back of her head brushing his arm, followed by her shoulders, back and butt. She reached back to do the same for him but he retreated a few paces, charged, flew at the fence, clung on about halfway up, cleared the top in some flippy maneuver and landed at her feet, knees bent. Nimble and quiet as a kitten.

"What now?" she said, trying not to sound impressed. Exactly the kind of stunt her brothers liked to pull. He could just as quickly have shimmied under.

"No idea," he said, throwing the backpack on. "But it's been pretty fucking ninja so far."

"Show-off." Still, her lips curled up. Hey, she adored her brothers, though she'd never let on to them.

Gunfire popped. She gulped. Had they got some innocent driver killed? Flynn stilled, head cocked, gaze locked on hers. The car race had stopped—the engines were idling. He pushed the fence back in place and kicked some scattered rubbish around the break.

"If I'd gone under I would've had to make the hole twice as big. With luck they won't notice till morning, at least. They'll have to waste resources searching the compound."

Somewhere a dog howled, answered by several others. Or were they hyenas? Did hyenas howl? Tess looked left, into blackness, and right, also into blackness.

"Seriously, though," she said, "do you have a plan?"

FLYNN SHOULDERED BOTH RIFLES. "You're not easily impressed, are you, sunshine?"

He inhaled deeply. Adrenaline was good for jumping out of pits and scaling fences, but not for strategic thinking. Case in point: his comment about kissing her. Not that the urge had passed—the woman was lighting up dark parts of his brain. The sooner he got her to safety and returned to his unit, the better.

"First, we get out of the open," he said. "Then we find transport or comms—preferably, both."

"This is kind of all 'the open.'"

"See that?" He pointed out a large shape a few hundred meters away, a hulk of charcoal against the dark. "Could be a hut or a vehicle. We shelter there and make a plan."

Engines revved in the distance, getting louder. "They're returning." He ripped the bandage off his head and stuffed it in a pocket—it'd glow like a flare. "Follow in my footsteps but keep a couple of meters behind— there could be old land mines around. Can you run?"

"I can try."

He set off in a jog, listening for her footfalls to judge his speed. Rocks jarred his feet even through his thick boots. Socks wouldn't last her long but at least the ground was too hard to hold footprints. Her stride faltered, like she didn't know which foot to favor. He slowed, though it near killed him.

To their left, a beam of light flashed and skidded across the ground. Damn. Probably just a large flashlight but it meant they had eyes on the ground already.

"Go faster," she hissed. "I can keep up."

He obliged. Hamid's soldiers would split up— searching the compound, the road, the wasteland, then fanning farther out… Would she call in reinforcements? He and Tess would need to be long gone by daybreak or they'd stand out in this dead-flat terrain like hippos in a bathtub. Hamid would guess they were headed for the distant village lights, but what choice did they have—hijack a camel?

As they neared their target, he slowed. Something jutted out at forty-five degrees, aimed their way. A large gun, looming out of an abandoned tank. He skidded around to the far side of it, perched on one of its exposed, trackless wheels and swung the backpack around.

"You planning to start this thing up and roll us out of here?" Tess huffed as she caught up.

"I wish." He pulled the pocketknife from his combat pants. "It's a Russian T55."

"Meaning?"

"Meaning it's been sitting here rusting for thirty years or more. It'll be from the Ethiopia-Somalia war, abandoned where it was put out of action—or broke down, more likely. Which means we're probably near the border of the two. Dunno which side, but maybe on the road to Hargeisa."

"I was taken from Somalia—near Hargeisa—so that would make sense."

"And me from Djibouti, along the Somali border. Not in such easy striking distance, but they could have used a chopper."

They'd gone to some lengths to find a French soldier. Was Tess right about Hamid wanting to suck France in? He found his watch in the backpack and strapped it on. They must have screwed up by capturing a legionnaire. The whole point of the legion was to give France an expendable force—he was cannon fodder no one cared about. No one except his *frères d'armes*. His unit would fight to the death for him. He cricked his neck. He needed to make contact, a-sap.

"What were you doing in Djibouti when you were captured?" she said.

"I'm not at liberty to talk to the media."

"I'm not writing this down."

He pulled her boots from the backpack. "Quit asking questions. You might not like the answers."

Silence.

"No big story," he conceded. No point firing up her curiosity. "Just on terrorist watch, like always. Guess we hit the jackpot."

"They're not—"

"Sunshine, if it looks like a terrorist, smells like a

terrorist and shoots like a terrorist, I'm calling it a terrorist. Do you remember anything between being kidnapped and landing in the dungeon?"

"Vague flashes of being on the back of a truck. You?"

"Not a bloody thing." He stabbed the toe of one of her boots and dug the blade into the leather.

"Hey! That's the only footwear I have."

"I'm giving them air-conditioning. We might be on foot awhile. We can duct-tape them later." He sawed the toe off one side. "Or you can buy more with your superstar salary. Try this."

She slipped it on, wincing as she worked her foot in. "Do you really think there are land mines here?"

He started on the second boot. "Abandoned land is often abandoned for a reason out here. But these thorn bushes and acacias have been cut back recently—for cooking fires or goat pens—so we're probably safe." A shout sailed out from the compound. "Relatively. You gotta watch the scrubby areas that are untouched."

"Are we heading for those lights—the village, or whatever it is?"

"We don't want to be in the open come morning. Here." He passed her the boot.

"That's where they'll expect us to go," she said, her voice tight, anticipating pain.

"That's because it makes the most sense."

She forced a thin-lipped smile and yanked up the laces. A shaft of light landed beside the tank, casting a shadow of the gun. He gripped her leg in warning—needlessly, it turned out, seeing as she was tense as concrete. Voices drifted over, conversational rather than urgent. Hopefully Hamid assumed he and Tess had headed out the gate, and had sent only a couple of schmucks around back to cover their bases. The light lingered on the tank's turret, then moved on in a steady sweep. He realized he was still holding her, right around the thigh. He let go.

"Don't suppose you know how to use one of those?" He nodded to the weapons beside them.

"I did some skeet shooting growing up, and I've shot an AR-15 in a firing range, but only on…"

He picked up a rifle and ejected the clip. Nearly full. He checked the next one. Full. "Only on…?"

She finished tying her laces and stood, testing a few steps. "Only on dates."

"You messing with me? What kind of guy are you dating?"

"The wrong kind. And sometimes I go to the firing range with my mom and brothers. Thanksgiving, Christmas, birthdays—we've always been a little… competitive. I've never used one of those, though. Is it an M16?"

"Yep." He gave her the 101 of readying and firing. Dating the wrong guy, huh? And that information had zero relevance. She was a celebrity; he was a recluse and planned to stay that way. Not a combination that'd work. Well, any relationship involving him wouldn't work.

He shortened the sling to fit her frame and fitted it over her shoulder. "For you, this is a last resort. Your clip's nearly full, so you have enough for four bursts. Don't use it needlessly—and don't use it on me."

"Depends on the circumstances," she said, with not nearly enough of a teasing tone.

"Don't forget who busted you out." And who'd had his arms around her much of the day. He'd lain awake for the last half hour of their nap while he'd mentally run through his plan, trying not to think about how soft her skin felt and how neatly she fit into him. Sicko. "You good to go?"

"You're speaking Australian again."

Bugger. When had he switched? "Told you my English is all over the place."

He peered around the hull. Might as well stick with Australian now—the less his brain had to compute, the better. He'd be rid of her soon enough, and then he could ease back the paranoia lever.

The searchlight had moved off. Headlights trailed along the road, toward the village. Out in nowhere land, maybe three klicks away, a warm light flickered. Campfire. Probably nomadic herders—little chance of a phone there. With no moon, stars lit the sky like holes in a sieve. He scanned the horizon.

"The village is to the west. Hopefully the road continues the other side so we won't have to pass the compound on the way out of town." West was more likely to mean civilization—Addis Ababa, or maybe they could scoot back up to Djibouti. North likely meant Somalia, east a whole lot of nothing.

"How do you know the village is west of us, if you don't know where we are?" She tugged the laces of her second boot.

Man, she was the suspicious type. He pointed above their heads. "I checked the map."

"You can navigate by the stars?"

"You got a compass?"

Satisfied with her boots, she tipped her head back. "Prove it."

He grunted. What a pain in the arse. He didn't need to prove anything, but if it made her ease up on the interrogation… "North Star." He pointed. "We're about ten degrees north of the equator so you look about ten degrees above the horizon. The rest is easy. Bit of trust here?"

"Show-off."

"You asked. Time we moved. But first we need to dirty up your T-shirt."

"I've been wearing it for a week—it's not dirty enough?"

"I can still see some white—it'll show up like a reflector if that light catches it. Here." He picked up a handful of soil, grabbed her wrist and dropped it in her palm. "Spit on this and rub it into the front. I'll do the back. We'll turn it into desert cammies."

He picked up another handful and moved behind her. He could almost cover her back in a single hand span. She was all shoulder blades, spine and ribs—she'd gone easy on the MREs. Lucky he was into curves. *Just you remember that, soldier.*

"You like this stuff, don't you?"

"What stuff?" Having his hands all over a beautiful woman? Too right. He liked *her*, that was the problem. She lit him up and she wound him up. A dangerous combination.

"Playing soldiers."

"I am a soldier. It's no game."

"Isn't it? Isn't that why you joined up—you wanted to make the computer games a reality? Dive inside that Xbox?"

"You're fishing for information." And way off the mark. He'd been one year off an engineering degree when that journalist bitch outed him. With the walls closing in, he'd fled to Paris. Before that he'd been more into "Tetris" than "Call of Duty." "Is that why your brothers joined up? And your boyfriend?"

"I don't have a boyfriend," she snapped.

"Whoa." Mission Change of Subject accomplished. He spun her. "Your face is glowing." He smoothed the dirt in his hands over her cheeks, nose and forehead before running his fingers around her neck and into the exposed V of her chest. She took a sharp breath. A few inches lower and—

Shut it down. "Better," he said.

She clicked her tongue. "And I just cleaned my face."

"Waste of time out here, if you're playing soldiers or not." He ripped a strip of reflective metallic fabric off the bag and pocketed it, and rolled the rest in the dirt. "Same rules apply—keep your distance and step where I step. Sound's gonna travel, so we go steady and careful. I do this…" He brought his palm level with the ground and lowered it, quickly. "We drop flat. If their lights pick us up, we run like lightning." His gaze slid to her feet. "If you can. And try not to step on anything shiny."

"What should I do if something goes click?"

He grimaced. "It won't."

"How can you be so sure?"

"It'll just go bang."

"O-kay. Nice reassurance."

"You want reassurance, hire a life coach. We'll stick to tracks wherever possible—human, goat, donkey, camel… And, hey, if this area is mined, Hamid's soldiers might not come after us."

"I guess there's that."

"Ready?"

"After you, Lieutenant."

CHAPTER FIVE

TESS'S INSTINCTS PING-PONGED with red alerts. She focused on following Flynn's boots, trying to ignore the pressure in her toes and the hyperawareness of every noise. Not that there was much sound, bar her panting and the distant drone of vehicles.

Maybe a mile away, maybe five, three sets of headlights crept parallel to them, casing the road. Flynn's head was skewed in that direction, his hands cradling his rifle. He'd better be looking out for shiny things, too—she'd met too many people in this part of the world with missing limbs.

Her chest tightened at the thought of putting her fate in the hands of a stranger, even one who made her stomach do flippy things. *Especially* one who made her stomach do flippy things. Rule number one in Africa: beware of the strangers who approached you, who tried to befriend you, to offer directions or some other "help." They were the ones with an agenda—invariably involving relieving you of money. If you needed help, you sought out the ordinary people keeping to themselves, plying honest trades. Which category did Flynn fall into? Maybe falling drugged from the sky wasn't the same as sidling up to her at a bus station, but he was hiding something. He wasn't bothering with the French accent anymore. He had to be Australian.

A stone flicked off his boot and rocketed onto her exposed left sock, shooting fire up to her shin. She stumbled to a halt, scooching in a breath.

Flynn spun. "You okay?" She bent double, her eyes watering. He crouched and rested a hand on her shoulder. "Your toes?"

"Stone," she gasped. Wow, she was such a princess. It was only a freaking toe. Who knew it could hurt so much? Flynn had a gaping head wound.

"You want me to carry you?"

"Hell, no." She managed an expansive breath. The pain would settle—she just had to wait it out. "I'm good. Keep going."

"If you need a break, I'm serious about carrying you. You probably weigh less than the backpack."

She straightened. He kept his hand on her shoulder. He could be right. She hadn't been eating well since she started chasing this story. The stress diet. Maybe she should quit journalism, write a diet book, make millions.

In the distance a pair of headlights flared—too far off for the beam to reach her and Flynn, but resolutely aimed their way.

"Flynn, the car's turning."

"I see it."

"What do we do?"

"We hope. They get too close, we hit the deck, make like rocks and hope some more. It's a massive patch of land and a dark night, so if their lights don't get a direct hit we might be okay. Even then we might get lucky if our camouflage works. You sure you're good to move?"

"Yes. Go."

He released her. She swayed. She hadn't realized

how much she was letting him prop her up—in all sorts of ways.

It had to be healthy that she recognized she was in danger of falling for him—out of some sense of fear or gratitude, perhaps, some outdated feminine impulse to secure protection. And if she was aware of it, she could damn well make a conscious decision to resist it.

She settled back into his stride, faster now, the rifle bouncing against her back. Maybe that was why her instinct was going mental, like the mouse mom's. Not because there was something familiar in his face, but because her brain was intent on protecting her from another Kurt-esque debacle. Clever brain. She should let it take charge more often.

The closest headlights grew bigger and brighter. Another light swept from the side of the vehicle—someone hanging out the passenger seat with a flashlight. The village lights weren't getting any closer. Flynn was near sprinting, Tess stumbling along behind as if he were dragging her on a tow rope. Her breath was getting shallower, her toes jarring with the shock of each step. *Tough it out.* A good run wouldn't kill her. Plenty else around here would.

Flynn glanced back.

"I'm fi—" she began.

But he wasn't looking at her—he was looking over her shoulder, frowning. She followed his gaze. Another set of headlights was barreling straight for them. Oh God.

"Could we hide in those trees?" she gasped.

"What trees?"

"At your two o'clock."

"I don't see them."

She pointed, though his back was to her again. "You can't see that?" True, they weren't much—a tangle of spindly branches—but they were clearly outlined, black against gray. The more she looked, the more trees she made out. Could you summon a mirage at night?

"Wait. Now I do." He changed direction, angling toward them. "We don't have a choice."

It was all she could do to keep breathing. The trees didn't seem to be getting bigger. The headlights behind her were.

"Down," he whispered, hitting the deck as the flashlight swept their way.

She didn't land quickly enough. The beam lit her up. Crap. It passed on without hitching. *Keep going, keep going.* It stopped and lurched back, burning straight into her retinas. Flynn sprang up, grabbing her hand. Her vision swam with black and red and purple. They hurtled toward the trees, her shaky legs threatening to give out.

"They still want us alive, right?" she shouted.

"I hope so. If anything, they'll take me out and haul you back."

"I'm not going back." She upped her pace. Gunfire cracked around them.

"Just warning shots," he yelled.

"How do you know?"

"We're not dead."

Her eyes adjusted. Both sets of headlights were trained on them, bouncing light and shadows on their path. The engines screamed. Flynn pulled her to the left—skirting the bleached skeleton of an animal. At least, she hoped it was an animal. Half a minute later, she heard it crunch and snap under a wheel. They passed the first tree, then the second. Another hundred feet and the goons would have to follow on foot.

The terrain changed. They plunged downhill, her knees wobbling as the ground steepened. Flynn's hand tightened. Spindly trees panned out around them. It was a gully. Crap.

The headlights flared on something red, to her right—a warning sign, with a skull and crossbones.

"Flynn, it's a minefield."

"Good."

"Good?"

"That's what I hoped." He released her hand and skidded down a bank. "Stay behind me. Some of them spray sideways."

Oh Jesus. Behind, a vehicle skidded to a stop. More gunshots, too close. She braced. No pain—nothing new, at least. She was still on her feet, her body still taking orders from her brain. The second engine roared closer.

"Out there we have a hundred percent chance of death," Flynn shouted. "In here, maybe less."

They careered downward, slaloming between trees, ducking under branches. It was hard to figure out where Flynn even was, let alone follow his path or watch for mines. Her mind was about to blow, with all the warnings it was pelting at her. Gunfire smacked into dirt by her feet. She yelped. Shouldn't warning shots go upward?

The second vehicle slowed. As the engine silenced, another motor filled the gap, farther off but pushing fast. Possibly more than one. Among the clatter of gunfire she caught shouts edged with panic. Hell, *they* were worried?

A beam of light swept past them. Something glinted on the ground ahead of Flynn.

"Stop! Flynn!"

He kept charging. Her scalp went cold. She lunged for his waist and dragged him to a shuddering halt, her toes bouncing on the stones.

"What are you—?"

"Don't move." She drew upright, practically climbing his body, and clung to his left arm. "Something shiny."

"Where?" His biceps was rigid.

"An inch in front of your foot."

"I can't see anything."

"Like a bunch of nails sticking up."

"You're kidding me. That's a bounding mine." He shook his head. "I still can't see it. You must have superhuman sight."

"Guess I got used to the dark."

To their left, the light snagged on trees.

"Maybe I should go first," she said. God, that was the last thing she wanted.

"No."

"I can see better than you."

He caught her waist and lifted her sideways, moving them behind a tree trunk that was half his width. "I don't want the responsibility," he whispered into her ear. "You stay behind me, you're safe."

"Until you get blown up and then I'm on my own anyway, if I'm even alive."

"Most of these things will be buried. Just then, we got lucky."

Gunfire burst out. She shook him off. "And we might get lucky again if we can see. Come on."

She took a step. He pinned her arms to her sides, his chest grazing her back. "I go first."

"I'm quite capable of taking responsibility for my own death."

"I can see that. I'm still going first."

Wow, he sure had a hero complex. "Oh, I get it," she said, changing tack.

"Get what?"

"It puts me in their line of fire. If I get shot, you get away."

"What? No!"

He loosened his grip. Taking advantage of his indignation, she set out, her heart thumping hard enough to break a rib. Best-case scenario, she got lucky. Second-best, she died quickly. Her mind flashed up an image of a boy shepherd she'd met after his leg had been blown off midthigh. She'd forced herself to watch as a doctor had removed his filthy dressing, and then she'd swallowed vomit. The black, pulpy mass had writhed with maggots.

Sometimes knowledge wasn't power.

Crap—Flynn wasn't behind her. She glanced back, slowing. He was crouched over the mine. What was he doing—defusing it? He grabbed something from his pocket and laid it beside the spikes. The reflective strip he'd ripped off her bag. A warning to others? He would stop to be considerate, now?

He started running, waving her on. The land began to rise again up the other side of the gully. She stuck to where the trees were thickest. More gunfire. Not potshots—they were spraying the wood. Branches swooshed and cracked like a windstorm. She hurtled across the stony ground, bent double, scanning for shiny things. Or dull things. Anything that didn't look right. Could the goons see her, or were they shooting blind? A burst clapped out behind her—Flynn had caught up and was returning fire.

A dark hulk loomed. She stopped, an inch from smashing her nose into it. A boulder. She swiveled, thrusting out her hands. Flynn was running sideways, looking back over his shoulder. "Fl—"

He rammed into her chest, slamming her spine into the rock. Pain spiraled through her torso. His rifle smacked her elbow, deadening her arm.

"*Merde.* You okay?" He bounced off and caught her, his hands pressing up and down her back.

Breath rasped back into her lungs. "Peachy," she squeaked. It felt like she'd been hit by a rhino. A bullet cracked above them, showering her with rock chips. He pulled her into a crouch, leaning over her as the stone rain settled.

"Come on," he said, grabbing her hand.

Blindly, she stumbled after him, rounding the boulder. He yanked her down on the other side and scooted in beside her. Cover. Thank God. Her feet pulsed. Ahead, the land flattened out again—the top of the gully easing out into a plateau.

She let her head fall backward onto the rock and took a shuddering breath. Gunfire tore through the trees, their echoes alone loud enough to burst an eardrum. Dozens of bullets, maybe hundreds. A lot of fingers on a lot of triggers.

"Still warning shots?" she said.

"Their orders have changed. My guess? They're cutting their losses. They've realized they can't risk you getting away."

"So they're shooting to kill."

"It's a good thing. It means they think we have a chance of getting out of here, which means we must have a chance—we just need to find it. This can't be a dead end."

"Wow, you're quite the optimist."

"Nah. An optimist sits back and waits for good shit to come to them. I don't expect anything good to come to me—you gotta go out and make that shit happen. If you get lucky, you get lucky. No such thing as karma—you die or you don't, whether you deserve it or not."

"So right now, are we lucky or unlucky?"

"Depends what happens next." He unzipped the bag and passed her a water bottle. "But don't go all philosophical on me. My head hurts too much for thinking. Let's just try not to die today."

"Hey, it was you doing the philosophizing."

"Hardly. I can't even pronounce that word."

She drank greedily, the water loosening her stuck throat. To her left, a bullet whacked into the dirt. Something pelted her temple. She gasped, fumbling the bottle, but it flipped out of her grip. She'd been shot in the head?

"Tess?"

She patted her face. No broken skin—just a burning sensation. Her T-shirt was soaked. "A stone, I think. Must have ricocheted up." She grabbed for the bottle but it rolled away, into the line of fire. She lurched forward. A force hauled her back—Flynn's hand, gripping her waistband. She flew for a second and plopped down, jamming his fingers into her butt crack. Graceful.

"Leave it," he said, tugging his hand free.

"They'll see it."

"They're more likely to see you—I don't think they have your superhero vision."

He grabbed a fallen branch and coaxed the bottle within reach. As good as empty.

"They could keep this up all night, all week," she said. "Starve us out—if there's anything left to starve by the time they run out of ammunition."

"I'm counting on Hamid not having the patience for that. If what you say is true—"

"It is tr—"

"Then there's too much at stake. The longer this goes on, the more anxious she'll get, the more likely she'll make a bad call. You said she reports to someone higher-up?"

"She runs al-Thawra, but al-Thawra reports to Denniston and the senator."

"Then that's where the bad call will come from. Bad decisions always come from bosses who aren't on the ground, aren't reading the conditions." He punctuated his words with the bottle. "They want a black-and-white outcome, no matter the cost and screw the circumstances."

She raised her eyebrows. "Personal experience?"

He scoffed like she'd asked an intimate question. "Human nature. They'll be telling Hamid to find you before this gets out of control. Minefields aren't put in dead ends. They're designed to stop the enemy getting somewhere—they're laid in shortcuts, thoroughfares." He shook the last drops of water onto his tongue. "Which means this patch of scrub leads somewhere useful and they know it. It's not just some oasis."

"No kidding it's not. Maybe it leads up into those hills?"

"Hills?"

"There." She pointed. "Silhouetted against the stars."

He squinted. "Yep, that's where they'll expect us to go."

He flipped onto his belly and scooted to the far end of the rock. "Man, I could kill for NVGs." He shouldered his rifle, let off a burst and ducked back under cover.

"What are you doing that for?" He couldn't take on a couple of dozen soldiers.

The return gunfire surged. "Confirming we're still alive."

"If they think we're dead they might stop shooting."

"Hamid won't believe we're dead until she spits on our bodies. I want to make her nervous, impatient. Staying put and strafing this scrub to keep us pinned—or, better, kill us—is her best strategy. I don't want her choosing the best strategy."

He slid into his firing position and let off another round. She shoved her fingers in her ears, though they were already ringing like church bells. As he rolled back, she could smell his adrenaline—sharp and tangy and spiced with scorched metal.

"Aren't you worried about giving away our position?"

"Not the way these shots are echoing. And there's enough scrub to mask the muzzle flash. I'll give it a rest now, anyway. Hear that?" His teeth gleamed. She could no longer figure out where one surge of fire ended and the next began. "The sweet sound of panic. We're relatively safe here, and sooner or later they'll figure that out. Meantime, I have a plan."

"Which is…?"

He looked above their heads. Checking the stars? "I'll tell you, if it works."

"Flynn..."

"Hey, the last one worked, didn't it? Kind of?" He flattened against the rock and pointed along the ridge in the direction of the village, as near as she could tell. "You see any more rocks we could shelter behind?"

"Yeah, maybe a hundred feet away. Man, they are not letting up."

He dragged the backpack toward him, unzipped it and pulled out the open MRE.

"You're eating?" she said. "Now?"

"Gotta keep up the energy. Here." He slapped a bar of something onto her lap.

"You have it. My stomach is flipping around so much the food might bounce right out."

"Eat the bloody thing. You don't look like you're carrying a lot of reserves and I'm not having you flaking out on me."

In the darkness, her glare was wasted. She fought through a sickly sweet granola bar, a nibble at a time. Oh, for a fresh, crisp apple. At the thought, saliva poured into her mouth. Flynn laid into something that smelled like curry. At a time like this. As they ate, the gunfire became sporadic then eased off, leaving them cloaked in silence. She stashed the bar's wrapper in her pocket, wincing at the crackle.

Flynn scooted to his vantage point and beckoned her over. They lay on their bellies, shoulders touching.

"What's that superhero vision telling you?" His murmured words vibrated right through her.

She blinked, hard. "Nothing," she whispered. "Wait,

something's moving. A person. More than one—maybe half a dozen, entering the gully." Crap.

"Spread out or in single file?"

"Spread out."

"Good."

"Was that your plan?"

"They're doing what the bastards who buried these mines hoped. The mines are laid out under the theory that soldiers spread out. You go in alone, or single file, odds are you'll get out alive. A whole unit spreads out, chances are one will set off a mine that catches his buddies with shrapnel, so it lowers everyone's odds. It's a numbers game, like the chance you'll be the one picked by the shark at the beach." He fell silent. "Maybe a little more likely than that."

"You'd think they'd know that, living here."

"They'll be following orders—bad ones, and they'll know that and resent it. You can't do a grid search in single file. I bet they're praying to Allah." He caught her eye. "Or God, or Buddha, or their mothers."

"They've stopped shooting, at least."

"*Merde.* They might be flanking us."

Her neck prickled. She rolled onto her back, peering into the trees on the plateau while he watched the other direction.

"You cover our backs," he said, creeping behind her. "Don't fire unless you have to, but don't hesitate, either. I'm going to create some chaos. On my say-so, we pull back to that other rock."

She flipped the catch to full-auto as he'd shown her. God, she hoped he was wrong about them being flanked. She adjusted her grip and forced her breath to settle. It was just like on the range, shooting at targets.

Except targets didn't shoot back. She widened her eyes as if they were satellite dishes. The bigger the disc, the more it picked up, right? Movement wasn't always immediately obvious—like before, seeing the soldiers among the trees, sometimes you had to sift through layers of darkness to catch it.

Gunfire burst out next to her. She jumped, her pulse rocketing. Flynn again. A shifting noise as he changed position. He fired again. A boom split the air, rocking the ground. Oh man. That was no gunshot.

A throaty scream echoed up the gully. Light flashed, right up to the plateau, illuminating the unmistakable figures of two men, dressed in camouflage, walking straight toward her, rifles panning left and right.

Her throat dried. She flattened, holding in her stomach—as if that would make all the difference. The explosion from the gully flared, like something was burning. One of the men looked directly at Flynn and raised his weapon. Shit. *Shit.* Should she fire?

The light flickered and cut out. Darkness swarmed back in. She blinked, blinded. Of course she should fire. But where had they gone? Around her, gunfire cracked, thwacking along the earth, pelting the rock. Incoming, not outgoing. Oh God, had her hesitation got Flynn killed? Where the hell were the men?

CHAPTER SIX

SCREW IT. TESS had an automatic rifle—no need to pin-point the bull's-eye. She squeezed the trigger, fighting the kickback as she peppered the trees. The recoil shook her skull, strobing her vision. Her hearing muffled. Far away a man was talking. She couldn't release her finger—the trees were becoming men, one by one, then a dozen at a time, closing in from all sides.

Something gripped her forearm. "Stop."

She let go of the rifle with a start. The voice—it had been Flynn's. Her hands reverberated—hell, her whole body shook. The hordes of enemy morphed back into trees. Crap. Had there been *any* real soldiers?

"You got them," Flynn said, his voice soaring down from the stratosphere, his hand tight on her arm. From the gully the screams continued—or was that in her ears? Gunfire rattled, like a million balloons bursting in her head, the shouts of a dozen men laid on top. "We need to move."

He swept the backpack on and pulled her up. She'd shot the two goons? Were they dead? She grabbed her rifle and stumbled after Flynn, clutching his hand like a lifeline. So much for keeping her distance. Hell, they were deep in this together; they might as well get blown up together.

The screaming rose in pitch, and broke into a shout. *"La. La! Laaaaa!"*

No, in Arabic? A single shot rang out above the rest. The screaming stopped. Flynn's hand tightened. A faint buzzing circled, like a toy helicopter. She clicked her jaw but her ears wouldn't equalize. She couldn't hear her feet hitting the ground, though she could feel them, all right.

Something moved through the trees. She yanked Flynn's hand. Too late. A guy ran toward them, raising his rifle. Flynn released her, spun, lifted his weapon. Kaboom. Everything exploded into light—the ground, the air, the trees. A force rammed her back and shoved her down, slamming her nose and mouth into the earth. She couldn't breathe—she was buried under something huge and heavy. A boulder? A tree?

Someone had hit a land mine. Her? Flynn? Hail pelted the dirt—not ice but shrapnel, sticks, stones. The hulk on top of her shifted and groaned. Oh God— Flynn? His breath rasped like his throat was crammed with gravel. Then he went still and silent. *No, no, no.* She was panting so hard she couldn't tell if his chest was moving against her back. She forced her face to the side, scraping her cheek on stones.

A flame flickered, lighting up a swirling fog of dust, flaring just long enough for her to identify the shape in front of her face. An arm. *Only* an arm. Too skinny to be Flynn's. Oh crap—hers? She clenched both hands, scraping her fingernails through the dirt. All fingers accounted for. Her feet were evidently still attached— nothing phantom about the pain shooting from her toes to her thighs.

She gagged on the smell of dirt, smoke and she didn't

want to think what else. Footsteps approached. Flynn remained dead still. She swallowed a mist of hot dust. Beyond the bloody arm she made out two figures, slinking closer. Quiet, urgent voices carried. One of them kicked something, with a fleshy thud. Any second, they'd spot her and Flynn. Her rifle poked into her ribs but she couldn't budge, let alone grab it.

The voices trailed off. The goons didn't seem to be coming closer. They were…retreating? No way. Flynn was in head-to-toe desert camo gear, no doubt coated with dust and ebris—maybe they looked like a rock? *We might get lucky if our camouflage works.*

Dark silence dropped like a blanket. A gulp stuck in her throat. Too scared to whisper, she forced herself to stop panting, ignoring the need in her lungs. Was Flynn's chest rising? Was he breathing? *Be okay, be okay.*

A guttural curse scraped out of him. She relaxed into the ground. A swearword had never sounded so beautiful. He lifted off her with a groan, like it was a huge effort. She lay still a second, the sudden absence of his weight giving her the sensation she was levitating.

"Too close," he moaned. "You okay?"

"You die or you don't," she rasped, rolling onto her back. He leaned over her, a shadow against the stars. She patted down his chest, his ribs. Intact. "I thought you'd…" She swallowed.

"I'll live. You good to walk?"

She lurched to a sitting position. "I think so. You sure caused chaos."

He pushed up into a crouch, grabbed her upper arms and lifted them both to their feet. "It wasn't all me, sunshine," he whispered. "That was some crazy shooting of yours. Not bad for a—"

"I hope you're not going to say, 'Not bad for a woman.'"

He groaned, dropping contact. "Not bad for a woman *who couldn't bring herself to kill a mouse a few hours ago*. Jeez, Germaine."

She wiped her dusty hands on her dusty trousers. "Honestly? I have no idea what just happened. What was going on down below?" She nodded to the gully. "Before we moved, before those guys…" *Before I became a killer*. "Someone else stepped on a mine?"

"I exploded the one you found."

"How…? Wait—the reflective strip. You shot it."

He winced. "It was meant to be a diversion. They were closer than I'd thought."

"The screaming—it stopped. Abruptly."

In the shadows, something crunched. A walkie-talkie crackled with static. Flynn pulled her behind a tree, his arm tight around her waist. Her rifle bumped a branch. She caught it. Beyond the spindly foliage the outline of a man passed, his movements jerky, too fixated on scanning the ground to spot her and Flynn. Chaos was right. These guys were spooked. Hell, so was she.

Another guy appeared—no, a woman—farther away, creeping in the same direction. Flynn tightened his grip, his fingers digging into her hips, his muscles tensed against her, all the way across his arm and shoulder and down his thigh. Last night—was it only last night?— she'd run her hands down those long, powerful legs. *Yes, focus on that, not the goons with guns passing a few feet away*. Then, Flynn had been a very fit body. Now he was every other kind of sexy, too—smart, brave, witty, protective. An all-round menace.

Words buzzed from the walkie-talkie. Nothing

discernible. The woman looked directly at their tree, frowning. Trying to make out the message, or trying to identify the suspiciously thick shape? Tess held her breath. *She's staring into space.* She hissed something to her friend and they skulked off.

Tess stood rigid. The soldiers melted into the darkness, their silhouettes no longer distinguishable from the trees. As silence returned, her scalp tingled. She stretched and fisted her fingers to stop the trembling. It didn't work.

"We're clear," Flynn said, releasing her. "Let's move, fast and quiet."

At the next boulder he pulled out a fresh water bottle and offered it. She bent double, resting her hands on her thighs. She could barely inhale, let alone drink.

"Can you hyperventilate a little quieter?" he whispered. He laid a hand on the middle of her back. She suppressed the instinct to flinch. "Like I say, it's a numbers game. We're the needles, this is the haystack. We'll stay here a minute, let them sweep on ahead. Enough enemy have been through that they'll mark off this sector as checked."

She took a deep, settling breath, resisting the urge to let it out in a hiss as she would to calm her nerves before a live report from the field. Straightening, she took the water. As she gulped, he slid her rifle off her back.

"If luck's on our side, they'll assume we're pressing on toward that hill," he said, ejecting the clip. "You have one more burst left."

"Thought you didn't believe in luck."

"I didn't say that. I said we create our own luck—and we have." He checked his own clip.

Luck. There was a relative term. Was she unlucky to

be stuck in a minefield, stalked by an army of goons, or lucky to be out of the dungeon with a kick-ass soldier on her side? *Probably* on her side.

Definitely on her side. Sheesh.

And the fact she was growing more attracted to him by the minute—would that prove lucky or unlucky?

Huh. Luck? Plain stupidity, more like. About time she cured her weakness for alpha military crap.

After today. Today, alpha military crap was keeping her alive, in body and hope. Next week, when all this was a memory of the did-that-really-happen kind, she'd make a psychiatric appointment. A lobotomy should take care of it.

He silently took the water bottle and slipped it into the pack, and handed back her rifle. "We keep going west, toward the village. You okay to lead? If you can concentrate on the ground, I can look out for enemy."

"Oui, Lieutenant."

She stared downward until her eyes adjusted enough to make out—or perhaps imagine—individual stones among the shades of black, then crept out from behind the rock. It felt like a boa constrictor was wrapping around her chest. Flynn grabbed her arm and pulled her into him. *Oh God, what now?*

"Not on the ridge," he growled. "We stay under it. No silhouettes."

She scooted downhill. They made steady progress, skirting suspect shapes on the ground—too round, too square, too regular, too pointy. She was probably seeing things, but at least it gave her something to focus on. Every foot they traveled eased the tightness in her stomach. Maybe this would be a lucky day.

Don't say that.

Thank God for Flynn dropping into that hole—he might not believe in luck, but for her that'd been a blessing from above. Even if she'd managed to get out by herself, she'd have been caught in minutes. Her mind didn't work nearly as quickly as his—but then, this kind of thing was his job. In her work she didn't *do* anything—she dug into other people's experiences and put them into words and pictures. All talk, no action.

Was that why she liked military guys? They were all action, from boots to buzz cut. Flynn must have some interesting stories—starting with his own history. Drawing that out would be a challenge, for sure.

After twenty minutes, the terrain began to level and they passed another triangular sign, facing away from them. She pinched her eyes shut for a second. Out of the minefield. Thank God. Flynn nodded as she pointed at the sign, but his focus was fixed ahead. Down a slight slope, light filtered through the thinning trees. Male voices trickled up. She squinted as Flynn inched ahead, the weak beam drilling into her brain, right behind her eyes. Two lights—headlights? Yes, a hefty vehicle parked at an angle. One of al-Thawra's white Ford Ranger trucks. Crap.

Flynn made the get-down signal and dropped noiselessly. She crunched into a stack of dry leaves, silently cursing. He crawled over.

"They have NVGs—night vision goggles. Only one of them has them on his eyes right now. They're probably part of a perimeter block."

As her sight adjusted, she made out one of the guys' faces, partially obscured by a cap but uplit by a mobile phone screen under his nose. Her jaw tightened. No mistaking the scar twisting his lip or his outsize military jacket. It probably still had her blood on it. The other guy looked familiar, too.

"Definitely Hamid's guys," she whispered. "So what now?"

He looked over his shoulder. "We can't risk gun-fire. Our advantage is that Hamid doesn't know where we are and I'd rather not give it up. And we're low on ammo." He fell silent, frowning. *Take all the time you need.* She sure didn't have any ideas.

"There are two of them," he said eventually. "We'll have more chance if I can split them up."

He shrugged the pack off his back. In the silence, the zip roared like a fighter jet. Neither goon moved.

Flynn slipped a bottle out, unscrewed the lid and started shoveling dirt and small stones inside. It was the bottle she'd emptied down her top. When it was full, he tested its weight, scanned the terrain and crawled backward—into the minefield. He motioned for her to follow.

Goddammit. She followed him behind a prickly bush, her shoulders tensing. When would this night be over? How long since they'd busted out—thirty min-utes? Several hours?

"There are more headlights to the north and the south," he whispered. "Stationary, like these ones."

"We're surrounded." The words caught in her throat.

"We only have to get past these two guys. Wait here and cover me—but only shoot if you're about to die. If this doesn't work, you can…" He glanced left and right, as if expecting to spot a TARDIS. "It'll work."

"What are you going to do?"

Silence.

"Right—you'll tell me if it works. Wouldn't want

to blow your karma." She raised a palm. "Not that you believe in it."

"I'll signal for you to come out when it's safe." He gripped the neck of the bottle and experimented with flicking movements.

"Be careful—the guy with the phone…" She inhaled. "He's a psycho. Well, they're all psychos, but that guy…"

"What did he do to you?"

She trailed her gaze to her feet, which pulsed in pain on cue.

His jaw went rigid. "I'll treat him with extra care. Stay put."

Flynn left the backpack and retreated into the minefield. She screwed up her face. Watching him creep through it was somehow more stressful than going in herself. He reached a clearing and hefted the bottle. It arced high into the air and landed with a cracking thud in bushes a couple of hundred feet away, on the edge of the scrub. Ah. Another diversion.

The psycho looked up from his phone. He waved the other guy away in the direction of the noise and leaned into the cab through the open passenger door. A radio crackled, silenced as he spoke into it, and crackled again. At what point would he call in reinforcements? Surely they'd first check that it wasn't an animal?

So Flynn planned to pounce on the goon who was checking out the noise, then draw in Psycho and grab him, too? But wouldn't Psycho call for support rather than go in alone? She chewed her lip. And wouldn't the first goon see Flynn coming anyway, through his goggles?

Overthinking. Any plan was better than none. *Trust*

him. Focus on covering him, not second-guessing him.
She eased her rifle into position.

Minutes passed. Not even a twig snapped. Her heart
felt like it was leaving bruises on her rib cage. The second guy had disappeared from her sight line. Psycho
leaned back on the hood of the truck between the headlights and pulled on his goggles. Surely he'd see two
figures, not one? From there he could open fire—she
wouldn't put it past him to take out his own guy, just
to get Flynn. He yelled. His friend replied from out of
sight. *Oh God, Flynn. Stay alive.*

She caught a flicker of movement behind the bed of
the truck. Crap, a third man—bigger than the others.
Flynn wouldn't have factored him in. She fixed him in
the scope, finger light on the trigger. *Don't shoot unless you have to—but don't hesitate, either.*

He disappeared from view behind the truck. Still
no movement at the tree line. The beam of the farthest
headlight flickered as a dark shape shot past. The new
guy. She swung the barrel, searching for him. Psycho
jerked backward. A column of light pinned two grap-
pling figures, one wearing desert camos. Whoa. She
eased her finger off the trigger. The new guy was Flynn.

He had Psycho in a headlock, his other hand clamped
on his wrist, trying to wrestle away a handgun. Psycho
shouted. They lurched out of the light and disappeared
behind the truck. Scuffling, a meaty crack, a thud. Oh
God. Dust puffed across the headlight beams.

The other goon ran out of the scrub, rifle leveled,
shouting into a comms device on his shoulder. Hell,
even if Flynn were winning, this guy would take him
out. And then reinforcements would come...

She couldn't just watch. Screw Flynn's orders.

She jumped up and yelped, as if she'd hurt herself. The guy turned. She let out another screech and flattened onto the dirt, panting, directing her shaky fingers onto the trigger.

The goon's face snapped up, scanning the bushes. Behind him, a figure staggered out from behind the truck, wearing NVGs and an oversize military jacket, tugging down his cap. Psycho. She swallowed a squeak. That crack she'd heard… Psycho wouldn't have walked away if Flynn were alive. Tears stung. Shit, shit, shit. He was dead, and she was screwed.

No. She still had a chance, if she took out both goons before they started shooting.

One burst.

Don't hesitate.

CHAPTER SEVEN

TESS BLINKED AWAY moisture and lined up her shot. If Flynn had died, she'd damn well ensure it wasn't for nothing. When her story went to air, his sacrifice would help save hundreds of thousands of lives. *That* would mean something to him, even if he'd deny it.

Oh God, she really didn't want him to be dead. The second guy glanced at Psycho and returned focus to the scrub, shouting and pointing—right at her. Her nape crawled. If this worked, she could steal the truck. And go where? It was Flynn who was good at winging it. The only things she could improvise were words, and she didn't always nail the first take.

Hanging back in the shadows, Psycho looked more intimidating than ever. He strode up to the second guy, who was raising his rifle her way.

One burst, right to left—the gunman first, then Psycho. No second takes. She nestled her finger on the trigger and tensed, bracing for the kickback. *Now.*

A flash of movement, and both men dropped. What the hell? Psycho had tackled the other guy and they were wrestling. Psycho raised his handgun and crunched the butt into his friend's forehead. The impact rippled through him, and he crumpled, still. Psycho ripped away the rifle and tossed it. He flipped the guy over and forced his arms behind his back. What now? Should she still shoot?

Psycho's cap slipped off, revealing a tawny buzz cut. Wait—Flynn? Her face went clammy. It was Flynn. She'd been seconds away from… Whoa.

She flipped the catch to safety, grabbed the rifle and the bag, and hurtled through the scrub. Land mines be damned, Flynn was alive. Hoo-ah.

As she neared, he was trussing the unconscious guy's hands with zip ties. Where had he found those—on Psycho?

"What happened to the other guy?" she said.

"It got ugly."

"Not for you, I hope." He looked okay. Well, he looked—

Now is not the time to think about how he looks.

"Nothing serious."

In an evidently well-practiced routine, he bound the guy's feet and searched him, then carried him to the trees.

"Hopefully, they won't find him until morning," he said as he returned. He took off Psycho's jacket, fished around in the pocket and produced a keyring. "Bingo."

"We're stealing the truck? Great." Her feet ached at the promise of respite. From the cab, a phone ringtone sang out.

"No, we're not."

"What? Why?"

"Because there'd be a chase and we'd lose. We've been through this before—we have to do what they don't expect."

"We could drive with no lights, be long gone before they realized."

"They're already coming."

"What?"

He nodded along the tree line. In the distance, a pair of headlights was zigzagging—a vehicle, turning. A low hum reached her ears, in stereo sound. She glanced over her shoulder. "There's another one, coming from behind."

"Here," he said, handing her the goggles. "Find me the biggest rock you can carry, and quick."

She pulled them on. No point asking about his plan. He disappeared around the far side of the truck. The driver's door squealed open.

A rock. A big rock. The goggles made everything green and screwy. She couldn't tell a stick from a snake. She shoved them up to her forehead and blinked. The truck started up and maneuvered around. Was Flynn planning to drive it away, draw attention elsewhere while she escaped on foot? The headlights closed in— three pairs, now.

The truck idled. She swallowed past the lump in her throat. Whatever his plan, she'd feel better if they stuck together.

"How are you doing with that rock?" Flynn called.

She focused back on the ground. Stones, stones, stones…rock. She heaved it up and staggered back toward the truck, swaying.

Flynn had turned the truck so it faced the wasteland. He was shoving something big and solid into the driver's seat, lit by the internal light. Psycho's body? Flynn picked up the trussed guy's rifle and jammed it through the steering wheel, then pulled the wheel. It didn't budge.

He ran up. "Give me the rock, quick."

Gratefully, she rolled it into his arms. Another minute and the nearest reinforcement would be upon them. She raised her rifle at it, as Flynn climbed in the passenger side. A thump, a clack. What was he *doing*? The truck whined as it started moving, then accelerated quickly. Oh God, he *was* leaving. Something fell from the passenger door—Flynn. He hit the ground, balled up, rolled to his feet, then sprinted to catch up with the straining vehicle. What the...? Legs pumping into a blur, he reached out and shoved the flapping passenger door. It slammed. The internal light revealed Psycho's silhouette, his head slumped. It timed off.

"Get down!" Flynn yelled over the roars of several engines.

This time she obeyed instantly. As the truck gained speed, a set of headlights swept the ground two feet from her nose. Crap. The approaching truck spun out, tires scraping against stones, and accelerated. Chasing Psycho. The other two pairs of headlights veered away and joined the pursuit. Genius.

After a minute Flynn leaped up, his head snapping around like he was looking for something. "Can you run?"

"Yeah." What option was there? She could internalize a bit of pain. Flynn had bought them another chance. Now it was *she* who had the urge to kiss *him*.

He pounced on something—the handgun—and jogged to her. "Give me the backpack and your weapon. You'll travel light. We'll hug the tree line for a bit, then hit open ground across to the village. They'll have to waste time figuring out what's happened and regrouping. We have to capitalize."

As the headlights receded, the village lights became

obvious again. It was farther than she'd hoped but distances were deceptive out here. She surrendered her gear. In the field she insisted on carrying her share of the equipment, but she wasn't stupid—Flynn would be drilled in running while hauling weight, and that backpack would feel mighty heavy after a few miles. They were in this together. He deftly arranged everything on his athletic frame.

Together. Wow. When had *that* happened? She'd been planning to ditch him as soon as she breathed fresh air, for his sake. And she still would. Just a while longer...

"You set the pace," he said. "We need to go fast but it must be sustainable. I doubt there are land mines— this ground's well traveled."

She had plenty of motivation to run but her legs stayed put. She swallowed.

"You okay? Tess?"

She started. "Yeah. Just... Wow..." She couldn't even form words. That never happened.

"I get it. You're so impressed you're speechless."

"No. *No.* I'm just having trouble..." Her mind blanked. What was going on?

He caught her shoulder with one hand and lifted her chin with the other, stooping to stare into her eyes. "It's shock. Don't stop to think. You don't need to process this now. You just need to run—let your legs take the lead. Get your body moving and your brain will settle. *Oui?*"

Gunfire echoed across the wasteland.

"Oui."

The decoy truck still had a decent lead, as far as she could tell. She slipped away and started running, pushing through her fear. The movement felt unfamiliar, unbalanced—like she was the one carrying the load. She ignored the pinch in her toes every time her foot struck earth. She could do this. One foot in front of the other, for as long as it took. How long could a dead guy drive a truck, out here? Until the gas ran out? Until he tipped into the Gulf of Aden?

They covered the ground quicker than she'd thought possible. Flynn was right—once they set out, the haze in her brain cleared. The village lights began to wink out as night grew heavier.

In the distance something whistled. A boom shook the ground and a ball of fire puffed skyward, lighting up half a dozen Rangers. Behind her, Flynn swore. "RPG. They must be launching from the back of a truck. Jesus, that's ballsy."

He sounded impressed. She was too breathless to respond. She wasn't surprised—al-Thawra were as well resourced as the Marine Corps. Hell, they had the *same* resources. Another whistle, another explosion, with a deadened thud she guessed was the grenade hitting dirt, not metal, not yet. If they intended to scare the driver into stopping, they were out of luck.

The engine noise faded, leaving her ragged panting the only sound between explosions. Her pulse drummed in her ears. She imagined one of her brothers was on her tail, hassling her, like they had as teenagers on the running track. She'd never liked to lose—still didn't. Trouble was, no one else in her family did, either—her parents included. No one had let her win because she was the girl, or the runt. And she sure wasn't complaining about that now.

"Okay, Tess, let's head across open ground. Be ready to drop on my order."

His *order*? What was she—his recruit?

Well, heck, even if she had the breath to complain, he'd kept them alive this far. She changed direction. Hard to believe she'd suspected he was a plant. But still the thought nagged her that she was missing something about this situation, about him. Something she could pinpoint if she only had time to process it, to run his face through her memory banks like the feds might do with the DMV database.

An explosion boomed out, followed by another, louder and higher pitched. Flames balled up, maybe a few miles away.

"They got lucky," he said darkly.

"Should we...speed...up?"

"Don't overdo it. I'll carry you if I have to but I'd rather not. They can't get near the wreckage until it cools, and by the look of those flames, it'll take them a while to figure out what they're looking at—one body, not two, and the wrong body at that. Could take hours without firefighting equipment. Meantime, they'll assume we're safely inside. Their impatience just bought us time."

"Good," she managed. Crap, she'd thought she was reasonably fit, but he could talk in full sentences like he was lounging on a sofa, beer in hand.

They ran in silence—she by necessity. It took her a while to realize her T-shirt was no longer soaked with water, but sweat. When the village lights started zipping around like fireflies, she knew she was done for. She staggered to a stop and planted her hands on her knees. Even then she swayed.

"You need a break," he said, pulling up beside her. "We should have stopped for water. I forgot that you're a—"

"Woman?" she gasped, barely able to summon the indignation.

"*Civilian.* Sheesh."

She heard a zip, and then a bottle of water was in her hands. As she glugged, the world dived. She grabbed at Flynn, catching his elbow. He slipped an arm around her waist.

"Rest. We have a little time." He guided her a few steps to a natural shallow basin in the dirt. "Lie flat. We'll take five."

"Won't they see us?"

"We call it a ranger grave. We're in the middle of a massive patch of desert in pitch darkness, and if we keep under the level of the land we're pretty much invisible. They'll be playing catch-up awhile, and their search area is much larger now—they haven't a shit show of locating us."

She sank to the ground, her body only too glad to take up the offer of rest. Even lying flat, she felt the earth sway. She smacked her hands onto the dirt either side of her, for ballast.

"Tess, you're doing great, but in future you pull up before you reach this point."

"Mmm-hmm." How long a future did he think they had?

He set down his luggage and wriggled in beside her, nudging her hand away. It wasn't a large dip, and it tapered in—their elbows jockeyed for space, and they were flush together from the hip down. The heat of his body wasn't helping hers recover—quite the opposite—

but she didn't pull away. Sucking comfort from him, again. He wasn't even panting.

"All right, I concede," she said, when she was able to speak. "That *was* pretty ninja."

"Child's play. Wait till I really bust out the moves. You'll be so impressed." He held up the pistol and slid something off the top. "Mate, this thing's filthy."

What a surreal night. As she stared up at the sky, layer upon layer of stars revealed themselves until the Milky Way looked less like a thousand pinpricks and more like a smear of, well, milk, across a slab of obsidian.

Unbroken by mountains, trees or buildings, the sky curved in a perfect dome. It wasn't hard to imagine the whole bizarre evening had unfolded within some snow dome—desert dome. This was the moment of stillness after the flakes settled. As a child, she'd loved watching that peace descend in her miniature world.

She rubbed her face with both hands. "What time is it?"

"No idea." He unzipped the bag, pulled out the wipes and began cleaning the dismantled gun. "I don't want to risk lighting up my watch."

Far in the distance, some trucks idled, others cruised. She shivered. If she'd been making the calls, the goons would have their quarry.

"Cold?"

"No." Hell, no. Her skin was cooling fast but Flynn's warmth radiated into her. She ached to snuggle closer.

No. That was the last thing she needed.

"Where do you think your…platoon…is?" she said.

He clicked the gun back together and ran a wipe over his hands.

"My unit. Somalia maybe, going by the intel on you—if they're alive. How about your family?"

"My family?"

"Your brothers are Special Forces, your mother is Intel. That's the kind of people who figure stuff out, make stuff happen. If you were my sister, I'd be going AWOL and parachuting out of that sky tout de suite."

"They wouldn't know where to start looking. And last I knew, two of my brothers were on black ops in Afghanistan." Now she was out, could she get a message to them without it being traced? How? Not the internet, or a phone—too readily monitored. She couldn't risk pinpointing her location or giving Hamid coordinates on her mom. "Not sure how easily they can extract themselves."

"For you? They can extract themselves."

"If there's a way, they'll do it." What she wouldn't give to have them jumping out on her right now. They could holler their hoo-ah crap as loud as they liked. "Their lives would be dull if I wasn't around for them to mock."

"Why don't we call them?" He pulled something from his pocket. "Got a number?"

"A phone?" She sat up and grabbed for it, her breath shallowing out. "You stole that psycho's phone? You idiot."

"Shh. Keep down." He held it out of reach, flipped on top of her and pushed her back down, checking their surroundings. Holy cow. She hadn't seen *that* coming— which she guessed was the idea. An ambush. "Sound travels in a place like this."

She pummeled his shoulder. "We have to destroy it." With one hand, he grabbed one of her wrists, then the other, and held them over her head. Her legs were pinned under his. "They can trace the signal, dumbass—right to us."

"There's a number I can call."

"Not from that you can't."

"Trust me, sunshine, the legion is good at keeping secrets." His mouth was inches from hers.

"I'm sure they are. It's the people monitoring the phone signals I'm worried about. If Hamid thinks we're dead, I want to keep her thinking that. A call to the French military from out here? Why don't you just send up a flare?"

"Wow. I was joking about you being a conspiracy theorist."

"In my defense, I did get kidnapped while chasing the biggest conspiracy theory of my career, so you can cut me some slack. And right now you're trapped in my conspiracy theory, like you've infiltrated my bad dream, so you'd better start believing it."

"Are you a vegan, too?"

"What?"

"Just want to know what I'm stuck with here."

"Give me a steak and I'll show you carnivore."

He chuckled, the movement reverberating through her body. "Don't talk to me about steak. I've had nothing more exotic than goat meat for a month." His mouth flatlined. "Tess, seriously, I have to contact my unit."

"You do that and you lead our enemies right here."

"If you're worried about a phone call, I can send my CO a coded message over the internet. We have agreed procedures for this."

"And is what you're doing here agreed procedure?"

The smile returned to his eyes. "No, this is me taking advantage. *Au combat, tu agis sans passion.*"

French? Seriously? Why was that doing things to her? "Meaning?"

"In combat we act without—"

"—passion. Some kind of rule?"

"Le code d'honneur du légionnaire."

"Would you *stop* speaking French?"

He laughed. "Shh. The legionnaire's code of honor."

She wriggled. Bad idea. He just pressed harder. "I don't think this is the *passion* they mean."

"I don't think this is the *combat* they mean, either."

If she thought about it, she could probably identify each of his many muscles in contact with her—and some other parts. This was *not* like wrestling with her brothers. "Let me go." She was totally half-hearted about that.

"If you promise not to destroy the phone."

"Flynn, you don't know what resources these guys have." Her voice had gone husky and breathless, dammit. "Even if it's switched off, they can track us to within a square mile. You call someone, post something, and they'll be onto it in seconds. It's too dangerous. We have to put it out of action."

"I can be discreet."

"So can a stealth missile. You're not taking that risk while you're on m—*with* me."

"Oui, mon Capitaine."

She rolled her eyes—the only body part she could move. "So you're agreeing?"

"No, I'm still taking advantage."

"Phone, Flynn. Now. We don't have time to discuss this."

"No. I'm using it. I have to contact my unit. I have to know if they're okay. I have to get us out of here."

"We need to find another way out. You heard Hamid. She has the resources of the NSA. She can track a phone call, track internet usage—and believe me, she does. You haven't seen what she's capable of, what her reach is." She closed her eyes—which only brought up her cameraman's dying face. She snapped them open. "No more risks."

"All risk is relative. In these circumstances a phone call is a risk I'm willing to take."

"Well, I'm not, and the longer it's even on us, the more of a risk it is. They could already have tracking up on all their phones."

"And all it would tell them is that the phone's in the vicinity. Like, in that burning truck."

"Until you use it. Then they'll work out it's not burning—and neither are we. You're so big on not doing what they expect—this is what they'll be expecting, what they'll be waiting for, *watching* for. *Please.*"

"The phone is the best chance we have, unless you can give me a better idea. And so far, sunshine, all the good ideas have been mine." He didn't move, though his breath had quickened. Oh, she could think of a dozen better ideas. She suppressed a smile. Oh yeah, she knew *just* how to distract him from using the phone—in a way she never could have with her brothers. But did she have the guts to go through with it?

Yes. Fair means or foul, she wasn't going back to that dungeon. She wasn't taking chances. She would finish this on her terms.

"Ah, crap, I don't know," she said, letting frustration jar her tone. She flicked her eyes to his mouth. Two could play at ambush. "I can't think straight."

"Oh yeah? Why's that?"

She paused, lifting focus to his eyes, unblinking. "Because you're so fucking sexy." Somehow she sounded offhand and matter-of-fact and slightly annoyed. A heroic effort, under the circumstances.

His mouth fell open. His eyes widened. Jackpot. Her turn to take advantage. She arched, flattening her breasts against his chest, her neck straining. With her arms still pinned, her lips couldn't quite reach his. Damn.

"You promised me a kiss," she whispered.

"A rash comment in the heat of the moment." His face was so close she could feel electricity snapping between them.

"I think I'm still feeling that heat."

She tilted her hips. He groaned. It was enough. His mouth captured hers.

CHAPTER EIGHT

Tess sank to the ground and let her mouth fall open, welcoming the slide of Flynn's tongue. Good grief, this was happening. With her hands occupied, sensation channeled into her mouth as he tasted and explored. Ruse or not, heat zapped around her body.

She moaned, and not by design. In the heavy silence the only other sound was their desperate breaths. His hips pushed into her sweet spot. Hell's bells. Another minute of that and she'd explode, right here in a desert, fully dressed, with an army of bad guys hunting them. Not a bad way to go out, but she could think of better—all involving Flynn wearing significantly fewer clothes.

At last he released her wrists and trailed a hand down her raised left arm. She flinched as he reached her underarm, arched as he glided down her side, gasped as he cupped her butt and ground against her. Desire bolted up her thighs. She closed the fingers of one hand around the back of his neck, urging him to deepen the kiss. The world began to spin.

Something thudded—the phone dropping from his hand, the sound she'd been waiting for. The sound she'd almost forgotten she was waiting for. He grabbed her other butt cheek. Oh man. *Concentrate.* With her free hand, she patted the stony dirt. Where was it?

He moaned her name into her mouth. Guilt pinged

in her belly—he was *really* getting into this. Hell, *she* was really getting into this—her brain was struggling to outpace her body.

She crossed her ankles behind his back and shuffled downward, making out she was getting into a more stimulating position. Well, heck, she *was* getting into a more stimulating position. Talk about multitasking.

Still no phone. She swapped arms, splaying the fingers of her right hand over the undulating muscles of his back, and searching the ground with her left. A rock jabbed her spine. She blocked out the pinch. The pleasure was ten times more intense than the pain, anyway. Or maybe both were working together in a hot-cold spiral that was carrying her away from reality. Either way, she was in danger of losing it.

Yes, you go ahead and overthink. Anything to stay present. Her hand closed around something smooth and rectangular. Yes.

Flynn released her mouth. "Fuck, you can kiss."

It's you doing the work, sweetheart.

He dived onto her neck, his silky lips and tongue playing good cop, bad cop with his scratchy stubble. Her breath shuddered. No need for acting. She drove her right hand down his broad back, enjoying the journey—the dip of his lower spine, the curve of his butt. Her turn to explore. She gripped his muscular ass, cursing the fabric in the way.

He was grinding into her red zone, lifting her to a plateau from which there was no retreat. Wow. She let her head fall back, giving him more space to tease her neck, keeping him occupied while she stashed the phone. Where? Thigh pocket? She maneuvered her fingers across to the snap but couldn't pry it open. Meanwhile, *damn.*

He released one of her butt cheeks. *Don't grab my hand.* He lifted his hips just high enough to slip a hand between their bodies, flipped the button on her fly, lowered the zip and slipped his fingers into her panties. She gasped. Yeah, holding hands wasn't what he had in mind.

"Flynn." She didn't know if it was a plea or warning.

Evidently figuring it for a plea, he pushed down the thin cotton and slid his fingertips over her. He made a choked sound. Hang on, no—that was her. Yielding to instinct, she pushed up while he stroked and circled and pressed right where she wanted him. *Oh. My. God.* Heat coursed through her. This was going to happen, right here, any second. He found her mouth, stroking her tongue with his while his fingers sent her soaring— slipping inside her, sliding up to circle her clit. Rinse and repeat.

Job at hand, Newell. She crossed her legs tighter around his back to bring her pocket closer—which also jammed in his fingers. His movements became smaller, deeper, more focused, more...oh. *Oh.*

A squeak escaped her. She was about to splinter, if she liked it or not. Well, crap, she liked it, all right. She reached her right hand over and popped open the pocket. Pleasure coiled under his fingers, pulsing in concentric circles, enveloping her entire body. She rose higher and higher. She shoved the phone into the pocket and fumbled with the snap. Got it. *Bam!* She hit the peak, panting, and clasped his neck with both hands, kissing the bejesus out of him while light and warmth exploded down her legs and through her belly.

As her climax pulsed and ebbed, he rolled onto his back, taking her with him so she sprawled gracelessly on top. She slumped onto him, her breath loud as thunder, his hands framing her hips. As hard as his body was, he was far more comfortable than a bed of stones.

What the hell just happened? It was supposed to be a kiss, a momentary distraction. Oh man—had she totally used him? Should she return the favor? Her stomach tightened at the thought of seeing him lose control in the sexiest possible way.

He kissed her hair, chuckling, his chest vibrating under her cheek. "Bloody hell. That wasn't what I'd planned."

"Me, either." At least, it wasn't supposed to go *that* far. "What had you planned?"

"A rest stop."

She propped her forearms on his chest. "I'm feeling very rested." *And slightly guilty. Okay, very guilty.*

"And me not at all." In the distance, an engine revved. "We should move."

"We should."

She stayed motionless, as did he, their gazes locked. She cradled his face and lowered her lips for another taste, taking advantage while she still could, before he discovered what she'd been up to. He responded, sweeter this time, more leisurely. Wow, the endorphins were doing their trick—she felt like she could take on the world.

But first she needed to take on this soldier.

"That was…mind-blowing," she said, releasing him and sucking in a breath. "And now I need to pee."

He dropped his head to the ground, groaning. "And

there's the passion killer. Make it quick—I don't want any tracers lighting up that sexy arse of yours."

His BACK TO Tess, Flynn zipped the water bottle into the pack. Mind-blowing indeed—and he hadn't even been on the receiving end.

How fucking cool was that? Stupid, yes, but at some point between lying on top of her and glorying in her shuddering against him, he'd figured it was just the respite she needed. And he was only too happy to give it to her. Only. Too. Happy.

Several kilometers away, two sets of headlights bored into the black. One lit a plume of smoke twisting up from the wreckage. The flames had subsided. Had they checked for bodies? They'd be confident no one had survived, but their bosses would demand proof of death. In the minefield, flashlights flickered—still searching, or returning to base? Either way, time to get out of this shooting range.

Something cracked behind him. He frowned, trying to identify the sound. "Everything okay, Tess?" he hissed.

"Yeah, good. I tripped, but I'm fine. Don't look," she squawked, as he went to turn.

"You're choosing *now* to become a prude?" Another crack, morphing into a smashing sound. The back of his neck prickled. "You trip again?"

"Uh—yeah."

Screw privacy. He spun. She was holding the rifle like a shovel, focus fixed on the ground. A snake? She drove the butt down. A snap, a crunch. Not wildlife. He narrowed his eyes. What was—?

Shit. The phone, flat as an impounded car.

"The hell are you doing?" He strode up and grabbed the weapon.

She held firm. "Destroying their tracking device. I'm not finished yet."

"Pretty sure the phone's finish—" The truth smacked him like a mallet. "So that…" He released the rifle and gestured wildly at the ranger grave. "That was all a big ruse to get the *phone* from me?"

She didn't reply, intent on vaporizing the damn thing.

He blinked dust from his eyes. "*Putain.* You could have just asked for it. You didn't have to…"

"I did ask. You said no." *Smash.*

"And this is what you do when you don't get your way?"

The noise was carrying. He grabbed one of her hands, and chased and caught the other. "Okay, it's done. It's well-done. Jesus, we could have talked about it."

"We did." Was it his imagination or had her chin just got pointier? "Look, I'm sorry, okay? I just—"

"Sorry for which part, exactly? Because I could have sworn a minute ago you were the polar opposite of sorry."

She stared up at him, rubbing her lips together. "For the record…that just then, that was…amazing. I didn't expect it to…go that far."

So it *had* been a trick. "Unbelievable." She squirmed—guilt, or was she still feeling aftershocks? Hell, he sure was.

"And, um, thank you, I guess."

"Thank you," he repeated flatly. He'd occasionally had a conversation with a woman after sex, but…*thank you*? Like he'd passed the salt?

She threw off his grip, sifted through the wreckage and snapped the SIM card. What kind of fool was he, thinking something real was happening between them—media It Girl, and regular lowlife? He could still taste her skin, sweet and earthy.

"Tess, one phone call could have got us out of here before they'd woken up to it."

"More likely it would've condemned us and whoever came to our rescue." With her hands, she swept stones and dirt over the electronic remains. "I've devoted a year of my life to this story. I nearly died for it—I could die yet. One phone call could destroy it."

"One phone call could destroy your *story*? How about destroying your life—our lives? What's more important?"

"The two are inseparable right now." She stood, brushing her hands on her trousers. "Look, I'm incredibly grateful to you—for getting me out of that dungeon, for keeping me alive when I could have been dead five times over, for…that…"

A sweep of the arm. Shorthand for him getting her off, like it was already ancient history. And he thought *he* was self-serving.

"Now I have a chance to tell this story," she continued, "and, yes, that's bigger than both of us, certainly bigger than your pride."

"That's what you think this is about—my pride?"

Okay, so maybe it was a little, but there was more going on. While he was lying on top of her, exploring her, listening to her smothered cries, it felt like they were connected by more than just his fingers and her—

Imbécile. As if any woman would want to be with him—the fake him or the real him. As if he'd want that woman to be a famous journalist. Even if by some miracle she didn't expose him in the media, some pal of hers would recognize him and beat her to it. There was no mutual future for them beyond today, if they survived that long.

"Yes, your pride," she said, straightening like someone was zipping up her spine. "You're offended because I have bigger things to think about than a quick roll in the dirt—albeit a very...enjoyable one."

Enjoyable. Like a three-star movie. "Oh, come off it. I'm a big boy."

"You certainly are."

She was grinning. And fuck it if that didn't make him feel even more stupid. What was he, some teenager getting naked with a girl for the first time? *Suck it up, idiot.*

Her smile eased. "Fine. You want to know exactly why I don't want to use a phone?"

"Afraid it'll give you cancer?"

"I had a source, a guy within Denniston who gathered the evidence I needed for my story..."

"This is the whistle-blower Hamid was talking about?"

"Yeah." Her voice wavered. "His name was Latif."

"Was? He's dead?"

"Collateral damage in a US drone strike on al-Thawra in Somalia, officially."

"And let me guess—you don't buy it?"

"It was a little convenient. My sources tell me al-Thawra was nowhere near the strike site. He'd been in hiding in Ethiopia with his fiancée—he'd promised me he'd stay there—but one day he left without telling anyone. He was on his way to Mogadishu—he'd booked a flight to Nairobi using his cousin's ID, had bedded down for the night in a guesthouse and…" She clicked her tongue. "You want to guess how they tracked him down?"

"How?"

"His fiancée rang him on his mobile phone, terrified. They'd been using burner phones—and only in emergencies, from random locations away from their hometown, never using names or other identifiers—so she thought it was a risk worth taking. But Hamid had his number—she boasted about all this when she captured me. It turned out he was still in contact with someone at Denniston, still trying to pin down more evidence, and she found out and put a trace on the phone. She was just waiting for him to use it again so she could pinpoint his location and…boom."

"And you think that the US…?" He shook his head. "No way."

"You heard Hamid gloating about his death, back in the bunker."

"Yeah. She said it was 'neat and tidy' or something." He strained to remember. "How do you know it was a US strike? How do you know it wasn't al-Thawra?"

"The president took the credit for it, probably without knowing the truth. Claimed to have taken out a key al-Thawra target at a nearby house, but the guesthouse took the main force of the hit. All searchable on Google."

"And I totally would do a search except that—oh, wait—I don't have a phone. Why didn't you tell me all this before…?" He waved his arm, seeing as it had become their agreed code for what had happened.

"I have to be very careful about who I talk to and what I say, for your safety as much as mine. I hoped you would just trust me, but…" She sighed. "You think this is all some big conspiracy theory, some joke, but people have died for it. You and I would have been next—might still be next."

He didn't feel much like joking now. "And that other whistle-blower—the one Hamid mentioned? Some woman."

"Yes, she's in danger, too."

He rubbed his face. Bloody hell. This was far bigger than him being pissed that a woman had used him. Damn, where was his mind even at? Most men he knew would be stoked to be used like that. *He'd* been stoked.

He straightened. Tess had a goal that counted for something, unlike most of the crap he did day to day. If he could get her to safety and she could stop a war, maybe his messed-up half life would have been for something. A lot of maybes, but…what if she pulled it off?

Hang on, she'd said herself—without the evidence, she was screwed.

"So Hamid has the only copy of your dossier?"

Tess blinked at the change of subject. "Ye-es, like I told you."

"And without it you can't do your story, you can't stop this phony war and Hamid will keep coming after you."

"Yeah." She spoke in slow motion, like she was trying to figure out where he was going with this. *Me, too, sunshine. Me, too.*

"How do you know she hasn't destroyed it already?"

"You heard what she said—she was still sifting through it."

A rhythmic thump drifted from the minefield. Crap,

a helicopter. Its navigation lights hovered over the tree line. No searchlight, which meant a thermal imaging camera. She was right about them being well funded. She was turning out to be right about a lot of things.

"Break's over, sunshine. *Flip Flap la girafe* on our tail."

She followed his gaze to the chopper. "Did you call that a flapping gira—"

"Gets lost in translation."

"Maybe they know it wasn't us in the truck."

In the other direction, the flames had died to a red glow. "Or they've figured out they've only got one body. Either way, we have to go."

This time he ran in front, setting a quicker pace. They'd spent five minutes too long in the open. He should have carried her rather than let her rest—then all that bullshit wouldn't have happened and he'd have a phone. Though now he didn't know if he wanted one.

Still, on fresher legs they churned up the ground, spurred by the chopper buzzing the edges of the scrub. If the enemy hadn't found the guy Flynn had trussed, they would soon. So much for not being found until daylight. Damn thermal.

Flynn's eyes began to pick up shapes better. More and more stars became visible until the sky looked more white than black. A perfect night for old-school navigation. Angelito had taught him to read the sky, back when Flynn was a recruit and he was an NCO. His jaw tightened. He'd warned his *capitaine* he was tempting fate by agreeing to a last mission before his discharge, but the bosses had left him no choice. *Bâtards.* Flynn would rather not write a condolence letter to Angelito's kid and girlfriend. Still hard to believe he was quitting the legion for a woman. It was a running joke in the unit that they'd all slog it out in the field until they were forced to retire to the legion's Provençal vineyard, joining the other washed-up vets cursed to spend their dying years bickering and making bad wine and drinking too much of it. If an emotionally stunted bastard like Angelito could find a woman, there was hope for anyone. Except Flynn, of course.

As he and Tess neared the lights, several rounded objects took shape, like tatty igloos, then a few dozen of them, then maybe a hundred. Tents. What did the locals call them—*tukuls*? Lights flickered from small fires and beamed from lanterns and flashlights. A truck stood in a floodlit area to the north, with a few people unloading sacks and drums.

Flynn crouched behind a thorn bush and signaled Tess to follow. A dozen green-and-pink plastic bags drooped from its prickly branches.

Tess touched one. "The African flower," she murmured.

That put them in *chat* territory, where men spent their afternoons chewing the narcotic leaf, then tossed the bag to blow like tumbleweed for a thousand years, or however long it took those things to decompose.

"Look at the tarpaulins," she whispered. The huts were tacked together with twigs, wood, plastic, cardboard, fabric—and tarps stamped with the UN logo. "A refugee camp?"

"Looks like."

They fell silent as two thin men strolled around the back of the huts, talking and gesturing with languid movements. They passed within ten meters. One wore a checked Yasser Arafat–style scarf. A woman followed, her long dress swinging with her swaying stride, her head covered. The scent of charcoal-fired stoves and parched dirt hung in the air.

"Somali," he whispered. "That has to put us in Ethiopia—nearly all the camps for Somalis are there." He stood.

She tugged him down. "They'll see you."

"It's a UN camp. There'll be a manager. We'll find help, get a message out."

"This close to al-Thawra's operations? No. Hamid has eyes everywhere. We show our faces and we'll be back in that dungeon before sunrise."

"You don't believe in making life easy, do you?"

"Isn't that what Hamid will expect us to do—show up here?"

He exhaled. "So we sneak in and find a phone or radio without being seen."

"Too easily monitored. If we use a phone—and I'm saying if—it has to be far from here and impossible to connect to me. To us."

"Okay, you've shot down my suggestions. What's yours?"

"That truck—it's from Global Food. They won't plan to stay long. I don't think they'd travel through the night—too much of a risk—but perhaps at first light…"

"We stow away."

Her eyes sought his. She shrugged. "Maybe?"

"A lot of those trucks come through Djibouti, from the port," he said, thinking aloud. "It could be heading back that way. Though right now anywhere's better than here." He checked his watch. "Dawn's a long time off."

"Got a better idea?"

"Nothing you won't smell a conspiracy in. But it

could work. There's a risk al-Thawra would stop the truck and search it, but I can't imagine they'd have more than three or four guys at one checkpoint." He checked the chopper position. "The odds would be better."

Meanwhile, more bloody waiting. He rebalanced his weight across his quads. Worst thing about the military— you wasted 99 percent of your life waiting for shit to happen, and the other 1 percent a squeeze of a trigger finger from death.

Where were Angelito and the others—dead, captured, bugged out to France? He had to assume he was on his own. He glanced at Tess, who was retying her hair. Not on his own. Jesus, did he really just have his fingers down her pants? Surreal. And truly fucking erotic. Would they get a chance to finish what they'd started?

No. Last thing he needed. First thing he wanted, sure, but he wasn't thick, despite appearances. *I have a chance to tell my story, and that's bigger than both of us.* This was it, then, his chance to save the world, or at least a chunk of people in one corner of it. Wasn't that why he joined the legion, if he was honest with himself—which he tried bloody hard not to be? To escape Australia, yes, but also in the naive hope he could do some good to balance out the evil he'd failed to stop in his youth. He wasn't stupid enough to believe that one ordinary person, or even two, could pull off something this big, but suddenly he wanted to do something more than save his own arse.

No. No, no, fucking no. He'd got this far in life without a conscience—why mess things up now? Get the woman to safety, evacuate. Mission accomplished.

"We need to find cover," he said. "Something thermal imaging can't penetrate."

"Thermal imaging?"

"See how that chopper's doing slow circles this way? It's searching for something but there's no spotlight. They have to have thermal. Two people crouched behind a bush will look mighty suspicious."

"What can't it see through?"

"Glass, foam, concrete, rock, aluminium…"

Shouts filtered over the tents. Automatic fire peppered out—a warning burst fired skyward, by the sound of it.

She flinched. "Hamid's soldiers—in the camp."

"So maybe they figured out it wasn't us they blew up."

"We'll need cover from more than just the sky. The Global Food truck? We could hide in the back."

"They'll search it."

"Underneath?"

"Not a defendable position. They find us there, we're screwed."

"But—"

He shushed her. "Listen."

Shouts rang out from several directions. "They'll have split up to search." He'd have to take on only two or three at once, if it came to a confrontation. They had two minutes to get out of chopper range.

A pale-skinned blond man jogged into the floodlit arc around the truck. "Solomon!" he shouted.

A guy in a blue Global Food cap strode up, followed by a taller man. Others gathered, mostly Somali. Flynn caught snatches of the blond's speech, in English with a heavy Afrikaans accent.

"They're being advised to leave," said Tess. "Take their chances on the roads."

"I heard."

"They'll close up the back and go." She went to stand. He pulled her down by her wrist, eyeing the chopper still searching the wasteland. "Flynn, there's no one watching the truck. This could be our only chance."

"Wait." Shouts echoed around the camp—demands, protests, panic.

She tugged at his grip. "They're distracted—we can climb in without being seen. Another minute and we'll miss our chance."

"Wait, goddammit."

"To be captured? No thanks."

He swore. "Give me some credit. That truck will be one of the first places Hamid's crew will search. If it's an obvious hiding place to us, it'll be obvious to them. When they've cleared it, *then* we go."

Her gaze rose above his head. "And the helicopter?"

Crap, it had angled toward them. He stood, lifting her to her feet.

"If we're not hiding, it'll pass right over us."

"What, so we blend in? I'm going to need a better tan."

"The chopper won't see your skin color. Everyone's the same temp on the inside."

"It's not the chopper I'm worried about."

A shout rose above the rest. Fifty meters away, at the entrance to a ragged horseshoe of tukuls, a group of Somali men were debating and gesturing. Women were retreating into tents, bustling children ahead of them.

A cry burst out, in English. The group of men focused on something out of Flynn's sight line.

"Stop. You are not permitted to be here." The South African, also out of sight, his voice higher than before.

"Follow me," Flynn whispered to Tess.

Keeping in shadow, he walked to a dark tukul on the edge of the horseshoe and pulled a couple of burka-like lengths of fabric off a washing line. Stealing from refugees. Low. He tossed one to Tess and they threw them over their heads. The rotors thumped louder.

He casually circumnavigated the tent, swiped a portable stove from the ground and chose a dark spot at the rear of the horseshoe with an eye line to the truck. He sat, hunching under the burka, making out he was lighting the stove. Tess got the idea and crouched opposite, her head bent toward him. The guys would give him hell for hiding behind a woman's skirts but pride be damned. The guys weren't here.

"Your rifle's showing," he whispered.

She tucked it under her shroud. He pulled his pistol from his pocket, keeping it out of sight. It'd better not come to a shoot-out, with this many civilians around.

"Cerise isn't your color," she said.

"Sir—what?"

The chopper drew overhead. She cleared her throat. "Pink. Washes you out."

"Noted."

With all attention on the approaching commotion, no one glanced their way. The men at the truck were moving faster, rolling barrels and hauling sacks. His instinct to wait better be right.

Somewhere, a walkie-talkie stuttered, followed by terse voices and footsteps pounding dust. Flynn tensed, bending in so close to Tess that his forehead prickled.

The men at the top of the horseshoe were getting

more agitated by the second. Under the wash of the floodlight, the cheeks of the nearest guy bulged—the guy in the Arafat scarf they'd seen earlier. An older man shouted at him, thin arms prodding the air, green spittle dribbling into his springy henna-orange beard.

Chat. They'd be wired, like they'd sunk their tenth-straight espresso.

Near the truck, two figures in gray cammies strode into view, M16s strung across their arms. *Here we go.* The shorter Global Food worker stood his ground, big arms crossed—the one the South African had called Solomon. The men who'd been loading the truck had wisely vanished.

"What do you want?" Solomon said, sounding more impatient than scared.

One of the soldiers swept to the side of the truck, his focus aligned with his rifle. The other stopped. "French man. American woman," he said. "Where are?"

"Nobody here like that."

"We look."

Solomon shrugged and stood aside. Wise enough to wait and see how it played out. The chopper hovered away. Flynn inhaled deeply.

The other soldier checked under the truck with a flashlight, then disappeared around to the rear. His boots clanged four times—climbing the loading ramp? Then four times more, the sound descending in pitch. He reappeared, speaking into a comms unit. Marking the truck as cleared? So far, so good. As a reply crackled out, he headed to the horseshoe. The next sector to search. Flynn dipped his head, letting the burka hood his face.

Heavy boots approached. Tess pretended to fiddle

with something on the stove, keeping her hands hidden. The first soldier strode past, not even slowing. Flynn wiped sweat from his palm. He detected movement in the shadows between two tents. Three scruffy round-faced boys were staring right at him. He lifted his finger to his mouth, hoping shush was a universal signal. One took off into the darkness like a spooked rabbit.

The Somalis tracked the soldier's movements, jittery. The Arafat guy spit on the dirt, his gaze zapping around. Flynn could almost feel his adrenaline—he looked young, maybe a teenager, but he wouldn't be here unless he'd seen violence, felt fear. He'd be shit-scared, amped up and high. *Be cool, dude. This isn't your battle.*

Behind Flynn, the soldiers had split up to search the tukuls. "American woman! French man!" Something big smacked against a tarp; a woman cried out; a child wailed. The chopper drummed, its position masked by the floodlight. Flynn could smell the volatility, like fizzing dynamite.

"Nice and slowly, let's walk to the truck," he said. Priority one was to get Tess to safety. But he wasn't going with her, not yet. He couldn't, screw it. A plan was evolving in his messed-up head, one that required a return to Hamid's compound—preferably without a woman to slow him down or get herself killed. Then she could do her story, as long as she kept him out of it, his conscience would be clear—*clearer*—and he could forget about her.

A whisper floated in from the shadows. *"Farangi."*

Crap. The local word for white person. The two boys had been joined by a dozen or more kids, lurking in the dark, watching.

"Your hair is showing," hissed Flynn, slowly standing, raising his finger to his lips.

"And you're a white man in a burka," Tess whispered back. "I think that's our cover blown."

A squeal. *"Farangi, farangi."* More kids, running their way.

Flynn pulled Tess behind the horseshoe, out of view of the Somali men. The enemy were still inside tents, shouting.

In seconds, the dozen kids exploded into a shrieking entourage of thirty, surrounding Flynn and Tess. Pretty much planting a GPS tracker on them.

Tess let out a muted yelp. Beside her, a girl was holding a handful of blond hair. She screeched and dropped it like it was diseased. Another kid went for Tess's head.

"That's enough," he said, stepping forward, his arm across Tess. "Get out of here."

The kids just giggled. The chopper roared closer.

"Ma'a as-salaamah," said Tess, sternly. Arabic for goodbye. She'd be taking a punt—these kids would speak Somali, but some might know both. The nearest kids froze, looking up at her, blinking. She began shooing them, then stilled. The chopper had swept overhead, nav lights blinking, the wind from its blades flapping the half-discarded burkas into the air and peppering stones into the children's faces.

You pricks open fire on these kids and I'm hunting you down.

CHAPTER NINE

FLYNN GRABBED THE fluttering cloth and wrapped it around his head. Beside him, Tess did the same.

"Stay still," he warned, his pulse rat-a-tatting like an AK.

"They must have seen us," she said hoarsely.

"Too many people this close together—that's gonna look like one big smudge of light. Hopefully they'll see a group of kids and move on."

Shading their eyes against the wind and stones, the kids stared straight up, frozen in wonder like the chopper was a UFO. One kid jumped up and down, shouting. Another screamed and bolted, followed by a couple of others.

The roar ebbed. The helo was moving off. A boy shouted, jabbing a finger in the air, and the horde took off after it, yelling. Flynn caught Tess's gaze. If the enemy had been using a searchlight instead of thermal, it'd be all over.

"Holy crap," she said.

"Truck, now."

The Global Food guys had cleared a getaway path. The taller guy cast a wary but unseeing glance in Flynn's direction. No doubt they'd heard the fracas but the floodlights would have blinded them to it. The guy pulled himself into the cab of the truck. The group of Somali men had disappeared.

"You wanna change your mind and ask for a lift?" Flynn whispered. "I don't think they're on Hamid's side."

"No. The fewer people we involve—*I* involve—the better, for their sake as much as ours. And if the truck is stopped, their guilty consciences might give them away. This way we give them plausible deniability."

Damn. She had a point—again. The truck engine shuddered into life. The ramp clattered and moved. The hydraulics were lifting it. In a minute it would fold to vertical, becoming the truck's rear door.

"Come on," he said.

They ran past half a dozen tukuls, sticking to the dark outer edge of the horseshoe. As they rounded the last one, Solomon strode to the back of the truck, watching the ramp lift. Flynn skidded to a halt, shooting out an arm to catch Tess.

Flynn pulled her back until the tukul's curve hid them. Somewhere in the camp the kids shrieked—still following the chopper's path, like some deranged Pied Piper procession.

"Maybe we *will* have to—"

He held up his palm. "Hang on, Solomon," he shouted above the engine noise, in what he hoped was a deep Afrikaans accent. "I need a signature. Come here a minute, yah?"

"Hendrick?"

"Over here, Solomon."

Footsteps approached. Flynn grabbed Tess's hand and looped back around the tukul. Solomon would do a circuit of the tent to find the voice—all they had to do was keep on the opposite curve. As the truck came back in sight, the ramp whined. It was almost shut.

"Hendrick?" Solomon called, from across the tukul.

In the cab, the interior light silhouetted the driver's bent head. He was marking something off a clipboard.

"Now," Flynn whispered. They dumped the burkas and scampered across the lit ground to the rear of the truck. The children's shrill chorus rose to the pitch of a school at lunchtime, backed by the thumping of the chopper. Closing in. He linked his fingers, palms up, forming a step. "I'll boost you in. Quick."

She took a run up and planted her boot. He hoisted with too much force, forgetting she wasn't a hundred-kilo commando. She slipped and caught the edge of the folding ramp with one hand. It shuddered, and stalled at forty-five degrees—the safety mechanism clicking in. *Merde.*

She managed to swing her second hand up, then hung from the top, feet scrambling. He caught her legs and heaved. She flew up and over and thudded down inside, rifle clattering on the metal floor. Damn. With luck, her landing had been covered by the engine noise, the chopper and the kids.

I thought you didn't believe in luck.

Making our own here, sunshine.

Solomon was still out of sight, giving what sounded like one last frustrated call for Hendrick. The ramp clicked and whirred but stayed on its angle. The driver had to be trying to restart it from the cab.

Tess's pale face appeared over the ramp's edge. "You okay to get up?"

Confession time. "I'm not coming."

"What?"

"I'm going back to the compound."

Her forehead screwed up. "What the hell for?"

"Your dossier. What does it look like—what am I looking for? Is it a paper thing, your laptop…?"

She shook her head as if waking herself up. "What?"

He shot a look at the tukul. "You need it, to do your story, right?"

"Yes, but—"

"And if you don't do your story, there's nothing to stop this war, right?"

"Yeah, but—"

"And Hamid will keep coming after you?"

"Flynn, this is—"

"So I'm going back."

She frowned. What was that on her face—fear? The hollering cavalry of kids hit a crescendo. The helicopter was seconds away.

"I'll be careful, Tess." The driver's door squealed open. "I have to go. When you get to Djibouti, go to the French base, ask for Rafe Angelito, or anyone in his GCP team. You can trust him, better than anyone. I'll meet you there."

A thump—the driver jumping from the cab. He shouted, presumably to Solomon, his words swallowed by the kids.

"Flynn! Get in."

"I don't want this to be all for nothing." Like the lady said, there was something bigger at stake than his crappy life. "Tell me."

"Screw it," she said, more to herself than him. "There's another copy. Get your ass in here." Footsteps closed in. The helicopter thrummed—almost overhead. "Flynn!"

A copy? What the hell? Whatever—no time to think. He eyed up a foothold, took a step back and launched off it, landing in a crouch on the truck floor and praying the driver hadn't noticed the vehicle shudder. His veins throbbed, top to toe.

He slung an arm around Tess's waist and drew her behind an empty pallet. As they sank against it, strips of rough wood dug into his back. He fought to get a hold of his breath as the driver checked the ramp, muttering. Overhead, the chopper morphed into a steady whine. Half a minute later the kids stampeded around the truck, screaming.

He was shit sure she hadn't mentioned a copy of her dossier. That fear on her face when he said he was going back to the compound—it wasn't fear for him; it was fear about letting him in. So she trusted him with her secrets as much as he trusted her. Perfect.

The hydraulics whined and shuddered. He grimaced. What if they'd broken the ramp? With a metallic scrape, it began moving—back down. Against his chest, Tess's spine tensed. If the men hauled them out, the helicopter would see the whole thing, clear as daylight. What then? He couldn't shoot his way free, with two aid workers and a tribe of kids in the firing line. Would the chopper let rip on the whole crowd? Too many what-ifs.

The floodlight cast a gray glow into the truck. He shrank below the height of the pallet, though his outline would still be visible through the slats.

"Lie down," he whispered, easing onto his side and taking Tess with him. He pushed his rifle around to his back, slid one arm under her neck and folded his legs around hers. Spooning, again. She curled her arm around his forearm and seemed to turn liquid, yielding and melting until they fit like an oyster in a shell, like she wanted to dissolve right into him. Maybe they'd drop a grenade on the truck and this could be his happy last moment.

The ramp squealed and thumped. Hitting the ground. The helicopter roared steadily—hovering right above.

The kids screeched. He could have made a hundred other decisions—come clean to Solomon or Hendrick, taken out Hamid's soldiers one by one, used a bloody phone. Hindsight only came after a screwup. Tess's hair feathered his lips, releasing a waft of talc—the smell of innocence, of childhood. Huh. What did he know about that? Any innocence he had was wiped away by the creeping realization of who his father was—*what* he was—after years of denial. *I'm imagining it. If I don't say anything, it's not real. After this one he'll stop.*

Yep, drop the bomb now, because his life wasn't getting any better. And probably a damn sight worse.

The truck jolted. Tess's fingers dug into his arm. The floor vibrated, clunking and rattling everything inside. A blunt shadow rose on the aluminium wall in front of them, lengthened and dissolved into gloom. He disentangled himself and peered through the lowest slats. The door was closing. He slumped back down. Yee-ha.

The chopper and the shrieking faded. A door slammed, followed half a minute later by another. Solomon and the driver were in.

The engine hummed and the truck drifted backward and turned. From the cab, separated by the wall and a blessedly dusty glass peephole, came a faint greenish glow from the dash and a murmur of conversation. If Solomon and his buddy were swapping notes about their crazy night, they didn't know the half of it.

Flynn's head thumped so hard he imagined the noise echoing around the truck. Always the way—the second you got to safety, the pain set in. Sometimes it was better to keep on running.

The truck clunked into gear and coasted forward.

Hallelujah. It picked up speed, the driver evidently as keen to scarper as his stowaways.

"Wow, this might actually work," she whispered.

"Don't talk too soon."

"What, you worried about killing the karma?"

She wriggled away and shuffled to sit against the external wall. He grabbed her boot and yanked. She squeaked.

"Shit, sorry," he hissed. He'd forgotten about her toes. "Get away from the side, in case the chopper returns."

She arched like the wall had burned her. "You said it can't see through metal."

"You'll be warming the metal. It'll see the heat signature. We stay low, stay in the middle till we get some distance."

With several pallets closing them in, there wasn't much room unless they spooned again, which he didn't want to do. Well, he wanted to, all right, but...*no*. After some awkward maneuvers they settled in seated side by side against the pallet, their knees folded up. Darkness closed in until he could barely make out the shape of her. They must have cleared the camp. Long minutes passed, as the truck rattled along a rough road. His head pounded like a piston. He patted it. No fresh blood, as far as he could tell.

"So," he ventured. "You have a copy of your dossier."

"Ye-es."

"You didn't think to mention this earlier?"

"I didn't think it was your concern."

"Neither did I. You *got* me concerned—you make a convincing case." He retied a bootlace. "You didn't trust me, did you?"

"I did trust you, obviously. You're here, aren't you? If I didn't trust you, I would have let you go after the dossier. And I definitely wouldn't have let you...you know."

Oh, he knew. "Right, because that was all about you trusting me—nothing to do with the phone."

Their arms touched as she took a deep breath. Her hair skimmed his cheek. It had fallen out of its knot again. "Look, the default option—the safe option—is to tell nobody what I'm doing and go it alone. That way you're in less danger."

"And less likely to mess up your plans?"

"That, too."

He scoffed. She was being honest, at least.

"Oh, Lieutenant, don't come over all naive and hurt, because I know you're neither." A bump jolted her into the air. He grabbed her arm, instinctively, then abruptly dropped it. He needed to stop finding excuses to touch her.

"You know, *monsieur*," she continued, "you're not the most trusting of people yourself, so I know you get it—your life is your business, my plans are mine."

"Well, turns out I'm already deep in this shit. And, unless you wanted to become a martyr in that dungeon, the only plans I've messed up so far are Hamid's."

"I guess."

"You *guess*. Seriously, what do I have to do to impress you?"

The truck slowed. "Oh, and you don't have any secrets? There's nothing you're keeping from me?"

"Don't change the sub—"

Shouts batted around outside. Urgent, threatening. Light flickered through the peephole. The truck rolled to a stop. A roadblock? Flynn rose to a crouch, readying his pistol, steadying his breath. He had a half-full clip in the pistol, a few bursts left in their rifles. This would be over quickly.

CHAPTER TEN

THE DRIVER MUTTERED something to Solomon. Flynn cocked his head but couldn't catch it. He spoke again, louder, his words directed outside: "Your people already searched the truck, back at the camp. Whatever you're looking for, it's not here."

"Wait here." A new voice, sounding like it was leaning in through the driver's window. A muffled conversation carried on outside. A walkie-talkie sputtered. Confirming the driver's story?

"Lie flat, behind the pallet," Flynn whispered. "I'll take care of this."

"I'm not hiding. Two weapons are better than one."

"One death is better than two."

"I'm not going back there, Flynn."

"Too bloody right you're not. Sit tight, sunshine. I don't want you caught in any cross fire."

"I'm going to help, whether you like it or not."

"I don't like—"

"Flynn, I can—"

"Shut up a minute. Fine, you can be backup. Lie down, sniper-style. I'll take care of whoever opens the back, then jump out and circle round. You can catch out anyone who comes looking, after I'm out." Jaw tightening, he waited for the clunk to indicate the hydraulics were engaging. "But identify your target and shoot only if you're in immediate danger. You have one burst, remember?"

The truck surged. He grabbed the pallet; Tess reeled. *Merde*, she was going to slam into the side. He released the wood and caught her waist. She clutched his shoulder and righted. He ground in his heels, his quads keeping balance for both of them. *No sharp turns, driver.* Solomon spoke, his words lost as the truck accelerated. Angry, not anxious. They were through.

Flynn sank to the floor, guiding Tess down beside him. His eyes must be adapting—he could make out her features under the greenish glow. She looked fragile and angular, her cheekbones shadowing the hollows underneath. Later today he was force-feeding her a decent meal—before she wasn't his problem anymore.

"So, the spare dossier," he said. "You're going after it?"

"Flynn, it's not your—"

"Of course you are." He should offer to help. No, he should get the hell away. He wasn't some crusading hero—getting her this far was more than enough. "Want some help?"

What the hell, Flynn?

"Thank you for the *sincere* offer," she said, her voice prickly. He'd spoken through gritted teeth, so it was deserved. "But I can look after myself. Besides," she added, softening her tone, "you're too much of a distraction."

"A distraction. Right. I've been called a lot of things, but…" Mate. Why even bother? He should return to his life, shitty as it was, and clear her out of his rattled head. He was imagining a connection that wasn't there.

"So that's what it was about back in the ranger grave—a distraction?"

"I don't know. Was it?"

"You seemed pretty distracted." He tried to keep his tone casual. Why was he so wound up—adrenaline comedown?

"I was, for the record—very." Her voice went deep and husky, making his stomach tighten.

If he captured her chin and eased it around, he could taste her mouth again. He'd take it slowly, this time, explore her over hours.

No. She was trying to change the subject from his grudging offer to help—playing him, manipulating him, *distracting* him. Yep, she was a master.

Hell, if she didn't want his help, he'd take the exit she was ushering him to. Why risk his life and privacy so a reporter could get a story? She'd steamroll anyone to get her name in lights, just like Katie—now Katherine Miller-Harrison, every freaking syllable emphasized on her TV appearances like it was an achievement. Just like Katie, Tess would get her story and he'd get exposed as the reprobate he was. Scum didn't like sunshine.

"We can move to the sides of the truck now," he said, tiredness pulling at his eyes. "You should sleep—it could be a long trip."

"Why don't you? You're the one with the head wound."

"Suit yourself. Wake me if anything happens—*before* anything happens."

"You're pissed at me." That husky voice, again.

He didn't respond. Yeah, he was pissed, but that would pass, along with every other illogical reaction.

"I didn't fake it, for the record," she said.

"Which part?"

"Any of it. I saw an opportunity and took it. Heat of the moment."

"Uh-huh."

He yawned, so wide it pulled his wound. He was done debating, and the jackhammer had started back up in his head. He zipped the pistol into the backpack and sunk a few painkillers. What a messed-up twenty-four hours. By daybreak it'd be all over. She'd be on her way without finding out his dirty little secret and he'd return to being the mercenary he was paid good money—mediocre money—to be. He stretched out as best he could on one side of the truck, his head on a sack of grain. The home straight.

"Tess?"

"Yeah?"

"I already knew you didn't fake it."

She laughed, softly. He couldn't stop a smile, dammit.

TESS LAY ON the dusty floor, the lumpy backpack for a pillow. Her right sock snagged on dried blood and pulled at her scab. She winced, exhaling away the sting. She didn't want to even look at that mess until she was somewhere reasonably sanitary.

She could still smell the bitter reek of mice crap. Once in Djibouti—if that was where they ended up—she'd toss her clothes and borrow money from Flynn for new ones. Surely he'd have access to funds at the French base? Then what? Hire a car and recover the spare dossier? She wouldn't recruit a crew, couldn't risk more lives. Flynn would be safe once he was back with the legion.

After a few minutes his breathing evened out. She'd expected him to insist she sleep first but maybe she'd got the hero-complex theory all wrong.

Interesting that he was no longer bothering to hide his Australian accent. Why pretend to be French in the first place? Could she do a background check on him when it was safe to access the internet? Not that she knew his surname—and it was probably fake. The only solid information he'd revealed was that he'd joined the French Army nine years ago aged twenty, and her bullshit radar had pinged at that. If he was faking his identity and nationality, smaller lies would slide out like honey.

Had Hamid sent Tess's note to Quan? He'd see it was bogus, written under duress. He'd know the story had legs, even if she died before she could deliver it. Her best chance of success—and survival—was to give him a package ready to go to air with the evidence to back it up. Incontrovertible. Authoritative.

Flynn stirred, muttering. Maybe he'd sleep the whole way, leaving just enough time for an awkward good-bye. Well, good. Because the alternative was to jump his bones. And then she'd convince herself it was okay to drop her guard, because *this* guy was worth it, yada, yada. And then one day he wouldn't return home—or would go home with another woman. Not the life she wanted. The very life her mom had warned her about when they'd last been together, welcoming her youngest brother home from Iraq.

Kurt was never the right guy for you, her mom had said, crossing her arms over her blue service coat as they'd waited in the hangar near Fort Bragg. *I will never regret the way things turned out with your dad, because without him I wouldn't have you kids. But we all could have used a stable figure in our lives, someone who anchored the family—not just physically but emotionally, too. That was never going to be me. And you're like me—you need to be out there doing things, you need to be flying. You need a guy who will be that anchor.* She'd thrown her palm up, as if expecting a protest. *I'm not saying someone who'll drag you down or hold you back. But someone steady, someone you can count on to always be there.*

Not a guy like Kurt. Or Flynn.

Several hours later, Tess was still feeling every rock and pothole the truck bounced over. About two hours in she'd crawled to Flynn, felt down his warm, rough forearm for his watch and lit it up, shading the glow. He'd sleepily unstrapped it and pushed it into her stomach.

Having long since given up trying to nap, she sat against the pallet toward the front of the truck, where the ride wasn't so bone jarring. Sleep would be a blessed relief from the horrors zapping through her mind, and the aching in her toes and back. Not to be. Anyway, every time she closed her eyes, she saw her cameraman's dying face, like he was haunting her—as he had every right to do. She certainly wasn't about to cuddle up to Flynn again, but she let her knee flop to the side so it grazed his thigh. Just a trickle of comfort but it flowed through her veins like a warm sedative.

Amazing how intimate contact could draw two people together while opening a chasm between them. No denying it—she was insanely attracted to him. *Insane*, as in crazy, mad, deranged. No way was she going there. Well, not again. But it was good he knew she hadn't faked it—that made it feel less cheap.

A vehicle rattled past, horn blasting—the first in an hour. Crap, he wouldn't boast to his friends, would he? He was too secretive, surely. The last thing she needed was another social-media explosion about her love life, or lack thereof. She massaged her calves through her pants. Tomorrow they'd be tight as guitar strings.

How good would Flynn be in bed—a real bed, with crisp, clean sheets? She'd seen and handled enough of his body to create a solid mental picture of him naked. *Very* solid. Honed, strong, with a dusting of blond hair on his tanned chest and maybe a few tattoos. Long muscular legs, a sculpted butt, a narrow waist sliding into a broad back that would undulate under her fingers as he moved against her. He'd give as well as take, if their brief encounter was any indication. Hell, the thought alone was getting her hot.

She straightened her spine. For God's sake. It wouldn't happen, so why torture herself? Her last romantic whim had ended when a colleague had spotted photos on social media of Kurt kissing a Zambian supermodel. They'd gone viral within the hour. Relationship over and out. She'd spent her career forging a reputation as a serious journalist, and which scoop drew the biggest audience? The one *about* her. She'd been deluged with offers to leave the field and present high-profile TV shows—even star in a reality show. And she'd been thoroughly trolled: she was a cold hard bitch, she was a ditzy lightweight; she traded off her looks, she was an ugly whore; she was a nymphomaniac, she was frigid…

She'd ignored it, or tried to. Soon, she'd give the world a story that mattered—and it wouldn't be about Tess Newell falling for a dashing legionnaire. Wow, how much would Flynn hate that attention? He thought *she* was nosy and relentless? She was a poodle next to the hyenas of the gossip media.

And the story certainly wouldn't be about a journalist beheading. Flynn had delivered her an immediate future and she would hedge that to buy long-term survival. Once the story was out, Hamid would gain no advantage in killing Tess. If anything, her death would give the story more credence.

The truck slowed. Solomon and the driver exchanged urgent words. She stiffened. The border post, already? They'd stopped for fuel earlier, so it wasn't that. Would the border guards search the truck? Shouts flew in from outside, some in English. "Stop!"

Solomon spoke, a terse instruction. The truck accelerated. Tess jammed her feet against the front wall and braced. Flames shot up from her toes. Not the border. Something clunked underneath the truck and it bucked like a bull. Flynn scuffled and banged on something.

"What's going on?" His voice was hoarse.

"Someone told them to stop."

He crept up on hands and knees. "They're not stopping."

A gunshot cracked. Oh man. Solomon yelled. Flynn scrambled for his rifle and passed hers over. More gunfire, peppering Flynn's side of the truck. He dragged a sack of wheat over, then another, and another, building a wall around them, like sandbags. The truck swerved, engine screaming, Solomon and the driver shouting to each other. Another round pelted out. The truck lurched, hurtling Tess into the front wall, driving the rifle barrel into her belly. She stifled a cry.

"We're under attack. *Shiftas*," Solomon shouted. On

the phone? "Fifty kilometers south of the border. They have guns. Yonas is shot."

"Shiftas," she whispered. "Bandits."

The truck was losing power, sliding to a halt. Another volley rang out, then silence. Men's voices filtered in from outside, speaking an unfamiliar language. A regional dialect? Flynn eased up to standing, his back against the truck's front wall, and peered out the window. He caught her gaze, shrugged, crouched.

"Stay flat, stay behind the sacks," he whispered, retrieving the pistol and shoving it into his waistband.

"What will you do?"

"Ambush these bastards back. Wait here and cover me. Don't shoot me."

The driver's door squealed open. Something thudded to the dirt. Oh God, a body? Would they hijack the truck?

"What if they're not bandits?" she said. "What if they're al-Thawra?"

"We'll find out pretty soon."

The ramp shuddered and began to move. Crap. Flynn cocked his rifle, the snap masked by metal scraping on metal. Tess did the same—she wasn't cowering like a princess. She could feel him sending her a dirty look. A groan rose from the passenger seat. Solomon was injured, too? She willed him to be quiet—if the thugs knew he was alive they might finish the job.

What was Flynn's strategy? Open fire straight off? Jump out? Shoot from the truck? Too late to ask. The men talked rapidly, tension crackling between them. One voice cut above the rest, high-pitched and staccato. Panicked. Maybe killing the driver hadn't been their plan. She fought to hush her breath. Whoever they were, they weren't going to mess up *her* plan.

FLYNN PINPOINTED THE enemy positions from their voices. At least four men. The agitated guy to Flynn's ten o'clock—maybe the shooter, defending his fuckup— the others at eleven, two and four. *Keep arguing, numbskulls.* Professionals or not, if they expected trouble they'd be quiet and focused, saving the debrief for later. They had at least two weapons, probably AKs. If Twitchy had one, where was the other?

Flynn shot Tess a look he hoped said "stay put"—if she could even see him. She seemed to be crouched over the backpack. Not that she'd comply. He'd have to neutralize the threat before she lined up a shot. Every life he'd taken haunted him, no matter how justifiable—she didn't need that guilt. Damn, he should have grabbed her ammo.

He backed up as far as he could, eyeing the growing space between the ramp and the top of the truck. Twitchy's voice was reaching a whole new octave. *Now.* He sprinted two strides and launched through the gap.

He got a scalp the second he landed, driving his rifle butt between Twitchy's eyes, midsentence. The guy crumpled. Flynn fanned his weapon. Where was the other shooter? Three enemy stared back—one older, two maybe teenagers. Too scruffy for al-Thawra. The young guys raised their hands as Flynn circled. Had the weapon been a sidearm, now pocketed? He could have sworn the shots were continuous.

"Don't shoot," said the old guy, waving his hands. "We go. We go now. That man…" He jabbed in the direction of the guy Flynn had taken out. "That man kill your friends. You keep him. We go."

The ramp hit the ground and silenced. "Where's the other rifle?" said Flynn. "You had two."

"No gun. That one, only one. He stupid. He kill your friends. Not me, not my sons. We hungry, sir—need rice, wheat. Famine here very, very bad." He started singing in his native language. The younger guys—his sons?—joined in, nervously. The tune was unmistakable: "We Are the World." Jesus.

Flynn noted a battered sedan pulled up across the road. It could have been yellow, once. The headlights lit up twin columns of dust. "That your car?"

"Yes, yes, sir. We leave him and we go. You give him prison. He very bad. Stupid."

Could Flynn call the authorities and get these guys picked up? This was murder. The old guy's gaze flicked up to the back of the truck, behind Flynn. "Change of plans, sir. My friend knife sharp. Sharp!" He drew a line across his throat. "He butcher. Usually camels, but human same-same."

Neck prickling, Flynn backed to a point he could see all the men and the truck. He swore. A fifth guy held a knife to Tess's throat, two rifles slung over his shoulder—Tess's M16 and another AK. Shit. He'd underestimated these twerps.

"Put your gun down or I tell him kill her. He already killed tonight. He good at killing."

CHAPTER ELEVEN

THE GUY HOLDING Tess yabbered at his mates, then spoke in English. "This is Tess Newell, reporting from Ethiopia." He laughed and returned to his own language. Flynn caught the words "al-Thawra." *Putain.*

"You," said the old guy. "Gun down, or he slice, slice like camel."

Flynn lifted the rifle sling off, lowered the weapon to the ground and backed off, but not too far. Hand in the game. A faint moan drifted from the cab.

"Small gun. Small gun. Take off."

Damn. Flynn tossed it. "Al-Thawra would be angry if you killed her," he ventured.

The old guy frowned. "New plan." He gestured at his sons to recover the weapons. "We take lady. You be good, we let you go."

Sure they would. One of the young guys wrestled Twitchy's AK from his shoulder. As he leveled it at Flynn, the man on the truck—the butcher—shoved Tess. She stumbled down the ramp and collapsed with a cry, clutching her ankle. She caught Flynn's gaze and dropped focus to her foot, lit by the truck's rear lights. A rectangular shape was stuffed into the sock. *You beauty.*

"Let us go before you get into more trouble," Flynn said.

The second youngster bent to retrieve Flynn's M16.

Tess slid a hand into her sock. The butcher pulled her rifle off his shoulder, examining his prize.

"I am boss now," said the old guy.

Not for long. Flynn sprinted at Tess. She pulled out the pocketknife and he grabbed it as he leapfrogged her. Before the old guy could react, Flynn had him locked down, the blade against his neck, his wiry body a shield. Half a shield. Tess scrambled behind them while the butcher juggled his rifles.

"My knife sharp-sharp, too," Flynn growled. "Drop your weapons." The old guy scraped Flynn's forearm with shaky fingers. Flynn squeezed his neck. "Drop them and go home. Three, two—"

The man gasped a few words. One son flung his rifle like it'd turned into a snake. His brother followed suit. The butcher got a hold on one of his rifles and aimed it at Flynn and the old guy. *Merde.* Flynn had counted on a bit of loyalty among bandits. He needed to lock the situation down, fast.

"Tell your sons to get in the car—and take their friend."

The man choked out instructions, gesturing at Twitchy and the vehicle. The boys backed away. After rapid-fire consultation, each took a leg and dragged the unconscious guy away, his head bouncing along behind.

"Now the butcher," Flynn said, swinging his hostage so he and Tess were better sheltered from the gunman. Not that the old man would stop many bullets. "Drop your weapons and go."

The old man spoke sharply, a thread of saliva dripping onto Flynn's arm. The butcher spit on the road, then tossed both rifles at Flynn's face. He stepped back and the weapons smacked into the old guy's legs. At the car, the boys opened the trunk and heaved Twitchy in.

Tess dashed out, grabbed her M16 and aimed it at the butcher. The old guy bucked but Flynn held firm. One of the boys disappeared into the driver's seat, the other into the back.

"Tell your butcher friend to get in the car."

The engine stuttered and started. The butcher didn't need the translation—he took off like an Olympic sprinter. Flynn shoved the old guy free and stepped on the AK barrel at his feet. "Go!" The car jolted. "Better hurry."

The old guy scrambled into a stumbling run, yelling, his trouser legs flapping. The butcher got to the car, wrenched open the passenger door and flung himself in. A rear door opened from inside as the tires spun.

Tess stepped in beside Flynn, weapon at the ready. The old guy sprinted, yelling. His hat flew into the air. He grabbed for it, missed, hesitated. *Boom.*

Flynn flinched, clutching his head. She'd opened fire. "The hell are you doing?"

"Encouragement."

"I think they're pretty motivated."

She shrugged. Jesus, she was a loose cannon. But no harm done, except to Flynn's ringing ears. The old guy dived into the car, his feet flailing as it fishtailed away.

"Keep an eye on them until they're out of sight," Flynn said.

He shoved the knife and pistol in his pockets and ran to the slumped figure by the driver's door—Yonas, his mate had called him. The light spilling from the cab confirmed he was well dead. Flynn skirted the hood. In the passenger seat, Solomon slumped forward. Flynn pressed two fingers into his neck. He groaned. For a dark-skinned guy, he was crazy pale.

"You're okay now, mate," Flynn said. "They've gone."

"You—?"

"Shh. I'm going to sit you up."

Bad idea. Blood gushed from a chest wound. Flynn took off his combat jacket and yanked out the foulard. Too thin. It'd get soaked through in a second. He tossed the scarf, balled the jacket and held it to the wound. In the darkness, Tess yelped.

"Tess?"

"Just stubbed my toe. The *shiftas* put rocks across the road." Something thudded as it landed on the stony roadside. She caught up to Flynn. "They've gone. The truck driver..." She glanced warily at Solomon.

"I know. Take over here a minute. I'm calling for help. Solomon, mate, where's your phone?"

The guy mumbled, his left hand flailing at the dash. On his ring finger, a gold band glinted.

"I see it," Flynn said.

"Knew..." the guy murmured like a drunk. "Knew you...hiding...in back."

Tess sidled in and took over with the jacket. "You knew we were in the truck?"

"Mmm." He said something that could have been "journalist."

"Take it easy, mate. We got you." Flynn grabbed the phone and backed out, around Solomon and Tess. "You know I have to do this?" he said to Tess. "Given the circumstances."

"Of course. And anyway, there's no reason for anyone to link this with us. But don't identify yourself— or me."

"Wasn't planning to."

Flynn dialed the last number Solomon had called—a Djibouti prefix. A guy answered after a single ring. After a second's hesitation, Flynn identified himself as Australian Army. Digging himself in ever deeper. He gave the barest details, hung up and pocketed the phone.

"A chopper's already on its way. They have a fix from the truck's GPS."

"I can't get a good hold on this," Tess said. "He's slumping too much. Can we get him out?"

Flynn's balled jacket was soaked. "Best if we don't, in case we do more damage. But maybe if I recline the seat a little." He squeezed in around Tess's hips and felt for the controls. "Actually, swap. I'll plug the wound, you lever the seat back. Then I can ease him down with it."

He slipped in beside her and held the jacket in one hand while propping Solomon against the seat. "Damn, this wound is pumping." How much blood could a guy lose? A single gunshot, in his right upper chest. What was up there? There was no sucking noise, so the bullet might not have blown through the lungs.

"Lowering now," she said.

"Easy. Just enough that he's not slumping."

Flynn transferred Solomon's weight onto the seat, trapping his hand under the guy's back. It was warm and wet under there, too. "The bullet's gone right through. We need something to plug the exit wound. There's a duffel bag between the seats—wanna check it?"

He jammed the heel of his hand over the hole in the guy's back. Tess ran around to the other door and climbed up, frowning at Yonas's body.

"Nothing we could have done, Tess."

"I know, but…" She opened the bag, wiping her forehead with her sleeve, leaving a streak of blood. "It sucks. Can't help thinking that if we hadn't busted out, they wouldn't have been spooked to leave the camp when they did, and, well…" She sniffed. "Here."

He grabbed the T-shirt she held out and stuffed it against the rear wound, shuffling his weight to keep pressure on both holes. She scooted along the seat and pressed two fingers into Solomon's wrist. She stilled awhile, her brow bunching. Mate, what if his heart stopped—could you do chest compressions on a gunshot wound? Flynn knew first aid but he wasn't a goddamn medic. What would Doc do? That was the bugger about having the best combat medic in the legion— probably the entire French military—Flynn hadn't needed to learn more than basic TacMed.

He tried to check the horizon for nav lights but couldn't see jack past the truck's headlights. Were they even facing north?

"How long do you think the helicopter will take?" Tess lowered Solomon's wrist and dug for a pulse in his neck.

"Guy on the phone said Djibouti Air Force were responding. Their base is in Ambouli. If we're fifty klicks outside the border, like Solomon said, we're talking maybe 150k. That's about a forty-minute trip, and they might have covered half that by now."

"Twenty minutes," she said, staring grimly at Solomon's gray face.

"You finding anything there?"

"I don't know if it's a pulse I can feel or just my hand shaking."

"Hover your cheek over his mouth and see if he's breathing."

She pulled her hair to the side and carefully lowered herself, screwing up her face. "Air's coming out, but it's faint."

"Nothing we can do but keep the plugs in."

She shuffled across to the driver's seat, leaning forward to avoid the blood seeping down the back. "You think those bandits will be back?"

"Doubt it. They'll figure we've called for help. You want to grab the chest wound? I'll check the pulse." He nodded at his top hand.

"Sure." She scooted across, leaned over and pressed her scant weight on the jacket as he slipped his hand out. His palm was sticky and crimson. "He's lost a lot of blood."

"Blood spills always look worse than they are. But yeah, it looks bad." Flynn pressed his fingers into Solomon's lolling neck. "There's something there, but..." He touched the guy's cheek. It felt as clammy as it looked. He'd seen too much of this bullshit. He was supposed to have been a bloody structural engineer.

"What if the bandits tip off al-Thawra? There could be a price on our heads."

"If they don't already have the phone number, that might take a while—it's not like al-Thawra has a website with a contact page. Can you find something to keep this guy warm?" He returned pressure to Solomon's chest as she slid her hand away. "I hate that we let those pricks go."

"So do I."

"We'll be out of here soon, Tess. It's nearly over."

"You think?"

"You don't?"

She wiped her bloody hands on her T-shirt and dug into the duffel bag. "Al-Thawra won't let me go this easily."

"*This easily.* Right." Because busting out of a dungeon, running through a minefield and several rounds of hand-to-hand combat was a stroll to the emergency exit. "You'll be safe soon. We'll be touching down in Djibouti within the hour. I'll take you to the French base—you'll be secure there, until..."

She looked up. "Until?"

Until you walk out of my life and give me a chance to think about something other than the things you do to me—the things you might do to me. "Until you decide what to do next."

She pulled a thin jacket from the bag. Flynn raised his elbow so she could lay it across Solomon's chest. The guy murmured.

"Doing good, mate," Flynn said. "Cavalry's coming. Hang in there."

"Anything else I can do?" she said, like she already knew the answer.

"I wish."

She stared ahead a minute, then frowned and popped the truck's nav unit off the dash. "If this thing has a history, we could check where we've come from, figure out where Hamid's base is." She pressed some buttons, waited, waited some more. "We're in Ethiopia, on the road to the Djibouti border. Looks like we passed through the towns of Dire Dawa and Harar overnight." She pressed her lips together as she searched. Minutes passed. An animal howled, so close that Flynn flinched. Wild dog, drawn to the scent of blood? Not a hyena—

they made a gravelly whoop. "Bingo." She held out the unit, pointing to a kink in a road. "Hamid's camp has to be there, east of Harar. Though I guess they'll be moving out, now it's compromised. That's one of al-Thawra's greatest skills—disappearing."

She switched off the internal light, then the headlights. Solomon's faint rasping became the only sound. *Just keep breathing, mate.*

As the minutes ticked by, the darkness abated. Flynn could make out—or maybe imagine—a separation between the black earth and the charcoal sky, way out on the horizon. It was so flat they could be at sea. Tess hunched over the wheel, biting her lower lip. Planning her next move? What? The French base was safe, but safety was relative when al-Thawra wanted you dead.

Not your concern, soldier. He shook his head, which just made him wince. His headache was setting back in behind his eyes. At least at base he'd have access to serious painkillers.

"What's the time?" he said.

She started, as if he'd dragged her mind back from somewhere far away, and pressed the button on the watch at her wrist. Its blue glow lit her face. She still looked hot, goddammit, despite her sunken eyes. Just looking at her drooping eyelids made his want to close. "Nearly six." She unclipped it. "You'd better have this back."

"Hold on to it, until we get on the chopper."

She stared at it a second, then leaned over, slipped her hands under the jacket and delicately fastened it around his wrist.

He straightened. "Listen."

"I can't hear…" She looked out the windscreen. "Wait, now I can. The helicopter?"

Flynn squinted. "Can you see it?"

"Just above the horizon."

She switched on the headlights and fumbled for the hazards.

"Not long now, mate," Flynn said to Solomon. The guy drawled something incoherent, like sleep talk. "Keep dreaming, dude. Stay in that happy place."

Tess gripped the door frame and eased herself to the ground, avoiding Yonas's body. "You're home free, Lieutenant. Thanks for everything."

She disappeared into the darkness. "What? Tess!" *Merde*. That sounded like a goodbye.

The headlights picked up her slight figure as she jogged around to his side. He twisted to face her. Her eyes gleamed with a new energy. "I was never here, okay? You lost track of me after we left the compound. Better yet—a land mine got me. Blown to smithereens. Poof."

"What are you talking about?"

She pulled herself onto the step and planted her hands either side of his head. "Seriously, Flynn. Thanks—for *everything*."

"You're not—"

She pressed her lips to his, soft and lingering. With his hands trapped he could do nothing. A goodbye kiss? Turned out he didn't want a goodbye kiss. The chopper thudded closer. She drew back. "And I mean *everything*." She dragged her thumb over his bottom lip, inhaling as if she were about to go underwater. "Take care of yourself. I have no doubt you're very good at that." She retreated into the shadows behind the truck.

"Tess, get back here. You're coming with me." No

reply. "Tess! Enough of the conspiracies. Don't be so bloody stubborn."

Silence. Goddammit. What would she do—walk across the desert? Hitchhike? He'd saved her life ten times over and now she would sacrifice herself to the hyenas, the bandits, the land mines, the desert, al-Thawra...

He called for her until the chopper drowned him out. It hovered down on the road in front, pelting stones onto the windscreen. An Mi-24 flying tank—they were prepared for trouble. A second after it touched, two figures with FAMAS rifles dropped out and scooted out of the perimeter of the blades, doing a recce.

One soldier sheltered his eyes from the glare of the headlights and pointed out the fallen driver. They split up, one each side of the truck. *Stay in the shadows, Tess. No fast moves.*

"Raise your hands," the nearest soldier shouted in French, then English.

"I can't," Flynn yelled.

"Hands in the air!"

"I do that, this guy's gonna spout blood like a geyser." Did the soldier even know that much English? He'd rather not give the game away by speaking French. Give *Tess's game* away—this wasn't his fight, so why was he risking his neck? Hell, why was he doing a lot of things he hadn't signed up for?

"He's been shot by bandits," Flynn yelled. "*Shiftas.* He needs a medic...*infirmier*! *Auxiliaire sanitaire!*"

The soldier closest to him approached, rifle leveled. He was dark-skinned, wearing desert camos with brown splodges—definitely Djiboutian. Crap, they wouldn't think Flynn would kill the guy, call it in and stick around to be captured? Flynn stayed rigid, maintaining eye contact and what he hoped was a nonconfrontational expression. In his peripheral vision he counted two more figures exiting the chopper. They'd better have a medical kit.

The soldier trained his weapon on Flynn's chest and ordered his mate to check the cab from the other side. Flynn's blood ran hot. He heard Angelito's voice in his head: *Du calme, Flynn.* These men were professionals. They'd figure it out, as long as Flynn stayed still and didn't do anything threatening. And as long as Tess didn't emerge from the shadows with an M16. No, she was a lot of things—*a lot* of things—but stupid wasn't one of them.

The second guy circled the back of the truck and approached Flynn. Flynn swallowed. The guy lifted the pistol and knife from Flynn's pockets and passed them to his mate, then patted him down. "He's clear," he said, in French. He shouted over his shoulder for a medic. Hallelujah.

"Bon—" Flynn began as the medic neared, eyeing him suspiciously. "Gidday."

"Hello," the guy replied, in a thick accent.

"You speak English?"

"Yes."

Flynn tipped his head toward Solomon. "Single gunshot wound to the right upper chest," he shouted, above the blades. "AK-47. Gone straight through. The driver didn't make it. *Shiftas.* Bandits." To make doubly clear. "They've gone. I guess they freaked out and took off."

The medic frowned, taking in Solomon with quick, dark eyes, and shouted to someone out of Flynn's view to take care of the driver. He eyed his mate's weapon, still trained on Flynn, laid his medical bag on the road and lifted the bloody jacket for a look. Flynn raised his hand a second. The guy nodded, reaching for a pulse. "Has he been conscious?"

"He's muttered a few things. He'd lost a lot of blood before w—before I got to him."

"You found him?" said the medic to Flynn. "Or shot him?"

"Found. *Found.*"

His gaze flicked down Flynn's cammies. With the blood and dirt, they'd be unidentifiable, and a khaki T-shirt didn't mean shit. "Where are you from?"

"Can't tell you that, sorry. Black ops." He forbade his gaze from flicking to his jacket, which would incriminate him in seconds, bloodied as it was.

Another guy jogged up, with a pop-up gurney. *"Le conducteur est mort."*

The medic grunted and addressed Flynn. "You are with a team? Where are they?"

"They dropped me here. We heard about the call for help and responded." Mate, why was Flynn lying— again—for a woman with a death wish? He didn't need to be any deeper in this. He'd come clean about his identity once they were in Djibouti—once *he* was in Djibouti.

The medic pulled out an IV kit and yelled to a soldier to load the driver into the chopper. "My colleague will take over from you now," he said to Flynn. "What happened to your head?"

"Long story." Flynn eased away, holding his jacket in a tight ball so the ID patches didn't show.

"Do you need a carry to the hospital?"

Flynn should say yes and get in the damn helo. Instead, he slowly removed Solomon's phone from his trouser pocket and held it up. "I'll contact my unit. See if they're still in the vicinity."

As the medic got to work, Flynn backed away, pretending to dial. No one followed but the soldier's rifle stayed trained on his chest. Another guy stood back, monitoring the road. They probably had door gunners, too.

Flynn stopped at the rear corner of the truck, within view so they had no reason to follow. "You there?" he said softly, making out he was speaking on the phone. A shadow moved in the back of the truck and Tess's face came into view. "We have a lift out of here. Let's get to safety and then figure out the next step."

She crouched, close enough that he could reach out and touch her—or shake some sense into her.

"I'm not going," she said.

"What do you think these guys will do—call al-Thawra?"

"Al-Thawra, the authorities, the marines—anyone could be a risk. Besides, I have another plan."

"What?"

"I'll tell you if it works."

He kicked the closest truck tire—what was left of it. A bullet had ripped the rubber clean off one side. "You're going after the dossier."

"I can't not see this through. Until it's in the public domain there's a price on my head. I'm done running."

"And how were you planning to get there?"

She held up a set of keys.

"You're gonna steal a truck from a charity?"

"I'll be doing them a favor, Mr. Moralistic. They leave this truck out here and it'll be stripped or gone by lunchtime."

Flynn pinched the bridge of his nose. *Merde.* Maybe he could at least get some painkillers from these guys. "So where are we headed?"

She stilled and swallowed, eyeing him like he'd spoken Russian. Why so guarded?

"When did we become a 'we'?" she said.

"I have no idea—maybe when we got imprisoned together, when we busted out, when we took on Hamid's thugs, when we nearly got blown up by a mine, when we fought off a gang of bandits and saved a man's life." *When we did whatever that was back in the ranger grave?* The gunman took a few casual steps in his direction. Mate, he needed to put a lid on his tone. Could he carry her kicking and biting to the chopper? Would he even survive that?

"Flynn… I'm grateful, okay? This has been the craziest twenty-four hours ever and I owe you my life, several times over. But I do this next bit alone."

"I think we've demonstrated you need a bodyguard." Jesus, why keep digging himself in deeper?

"I can hire one."

"No one as good as me—not out here."

"You have a high opinion of yourself, Lieutenant." Her tone had lightened—she was teasing him, trying to end the discussion.

Ha. A high opinion? She couldn't be more wrong—and he planned to keep her ignorant on that point—but he couldn't walk away until this was done. When did he get so bleeding-hearted? "When it comes to survival, yeah, I do. I've earned it."

"Shouldn't you get back to your unit?"

The medic and his mate lifted Solomon onto the gurney, the IV bag swinging from a pole. Still the gunman kept Flynn in his sights. "I'm officially MIA. I figure that gives me an open-ended leave pass." Though if he turned down safe passage back to base, was he technically AWOL?

"Don't you get it, Flynn? I don't want you with me. I don't want to be responsible—"

"—for my death."

"Yes. It's been happening to people around me."

"I can take responsibility for my own death."

She smiled thinly. "Laughing out loud. I'd rather not share that responsibility—and I can look after myself."

"You got kidnapped."

"So did you."

"I got myself out. I got *you* out."

"And I am grateful but I don't need your help anymore."

And why was that not enough to sway him? She didn't want help, he didn't want to help. Perfect. He wanted to leave on that bloody helicopter.

The medics rolled the gurney away. The soldier backed off, lowering his rifle. "You come now!" he shouted, gesturing. *"Vite!"*

"Go," said Tess. "I'll be fine."

The rotors whined to a higher pitch. "I'm not leaving you here. What kind of man would I be?"

"A rational one. This isn't your fight. Fly away and forget all this. At the very least, you need to get your head looked at."

"No kidding, I do." He swiped the phone screen like he was hanging up and walked toward the chopper.

"At least leave me the phone," Tess hissed. "Flynn!"

He pretended he hadn't heard.

CHAPTER TWELVE

FINE. TESS DIDN'T need the phone. She couldn't call anyone, anyway, and she had the nav unit for a map.

She shivered. Her blood-soaked T-shirt was cooling. The soldiers' shouts petered out, replaced by the crescendoing chop of the helicopter blades. It was good Flynn was leaving. Very good. He'd be safe, and she could concentrate on her goal.

Dirt billowed out behind the truck as the chopper lifted. Couldn't be long till dawn—she could clearly make out the landscape, not that there was much to see. It was as bleak and pitted as the moon, with about as much life. Dust coated the back of her throat.

Adieu, Lieutenant. She never did find out his surname. How strange that she'd never see him again, after such an intense experience.

What now? Her stomach dived. No. She would not let herself feel lonely. It didn't get lonelier than waiting for death in an underground bunker. This was nothing.

Her fingers were coated with Solomon's blood. He'd be okay now, right? She retrieved the wipes from the backpack and scrubbed her hands, the wipe reddening in seconds. When this was over, maybe she could record a piece about him and Yonas. Shot by bandits while doing an honest day's work for a charity—the kind of thing people should know about.

There was a story in Flynn, too—the secretive legionnaire who rescued a woman from terrorists and seduced her. Or had she seduced him? She attacked her nail beds with the wipe. She'd leave out that part. The Kurt fallout had been damaging enough.

Flynn had left surprisingly easily. She'd been prepared for a longer argument, had worked out all the answers to his protests. And then he'd wheeled and walked away, pretending to hang up the phone as if declaring the conversation over, their connection severed. Leaving her feeling...feeling...

Fine. Great, in fact. Just a little...empty. Which was understandable given recent events. Maybe that PTSD thing again? That was probably why a small part of her wanted to peep out the window and watch the chopper until it was a speck on the horizon, and then nothing.

She pulled out another wipe. Really she needed a head-to-toe decontamination shower. Flynn would be getting that soon—or at least a regular shower.

Crap. That gave her a mental image of him naked, again. She grunted. Time to focus. She was over being the pawn—bullied by Hamid, led by Flynn. *Distracted* by Flynn. Now she was the queen. She sat straighter. Back in charge of the chessboard, and damn that felt good.

The strange hollowness in her belly was hunger, obviously. She burrowed into the backpack, unearthing another granola bar.

Eat the bloody thing. I'm not having you flaking out on me.

Yep, he was a charmer.

"Maybe that's what the attraction is," she muttered as she unwrapped it. *"Was."* Flynn was a soldier through and through but otherwise he was the opposite of Kurt. He wouldn't say all the right things and open doors and send flowers before breaking her heart. He'd probably skip straight to the heartbreak.

Flynn was honest, and unapologetically himself— if that wasn't a weird thing to say about a man whose entire life was evidently a lie. But there was a sexiness in his bluntness. He was a real hero—not a superhero pinup like Kurt but a what-you-see-is-what-you-get guy whose actions spoke louder than his citations. Like when he'd shielded her from the land mine. A medal-worthy act he'd never seek a medal for.

She forced down a dry mouthful. Enough thinking. The chopper noise had faded. Time to—

Something thudded. She froze. Another thud, and another. Crap—footsteps, even and unhurried. Had the bandits been lying in wait, like vultures?

Tess reached for Flynn's M16—the one weapon she'd managed to grab before the soldiers had confiscated them. The footsteps paced along the side of the truck, headed her way. She raised the rifle, chest tightening. A tall, broad figure strode into sight. Her breath hitched.

"Put that thing down. Jesus, sunshine, yesterday you were all leftie greenie live-and-let-live and now you're a regular Rambo."

Her lungs filled with cool relief. "You scared the skin off me."

"You really thought I'd leave."

"I hoped you would."

"I wish I could have." He rested a boot on the side of the ramp and retied the lace, tugging it so tight she winced. "Looks like you're stuck with me."

She felt five pounds lighter. So maybe she wasn't

ready to be alone just yet. "It's your hero complex, isn't it? You should see someone about that."

"Right after I get my head examined. Chuck me those wipes, would you? I don't want to think about what I've got on my hands."

She couldn't help smiling as she tossed him the packet. Damn, she was like a teenager who'd scored a date to the prom. "So you never intended to leave?"

He took out three wipes and pocketed the packet. "I did, for several glorious seconds. But then I found myself telling the guy I was good for a ride, that my team was on the way. Don't ask me why because I really don't know."

"I know why." She slung the rifle over her shoulder and leaned against the side of the truck, crossing her arms. "Because I've turned you into a leftie greenie tinfoil-hat wearer."

"Hell, no! Because..." He paused in his scrubbing and stared at his hands as if the answer was written there. "Because I couldn't get it out of my head that you couldn't change that tire yourself."

"What tire?" She stashed the rifle and jogged to where he was standing. "Oh. That tire. Can you fix it?"

"You're asking if I can change a tire? I can change a tire."

"You're a regular breakdown service." She bit her bottom lip. So he'd stayed to change a tire? "I've changed a tire before."

"On a sixteen-tonne truck?"

"On an OB van, about this size."

"OB?"

"Outside broadcast. A TV truck. Like an overgrown RV with a satellite dish."

"You tell me this now." He stood, threw the dirty wipes in the back of the truck, then froze, casting her a sideways look. "You changed this wheel alone?"

"I...had a little help."

He raised his eyebrows.

"Okay, so I read the manual and supervised. But I've been living in Africa awhile, you know. I would have figured it out. I'm not a suburban princess."

"I would never accuse you of such a thing." He tucked his fingers into his belt loops. "Happy to sit back and watch, if you want to prove your *G.I. Jane* credentials." Was he flirting? Hard to tell—his tone was more pissed than playful.

"No, no, go ahead. It'll be good for your hero complex. But I'll have to drop you off somewhere safe and cozy afterward because too much macho pride will drive me up the wall. Or into a wall. I'll take you to the border."

"Or I could let you go ahead and satisfy your savior complex on foot."

"My what?"

"Your savior complex. Your compulsion to save everyone."

"Like who?"

"Me, the world, Huey, Dewey and Louie. You think everyone's safety is your responsibility and people like me can't be trusted to make our own choices."

"I do not." *Do I?*

"Good. Because I'm coming with you," he said. "On one condition."

"Why should you get to make conditions? I should make conditions, seeing as it's you inviting yourself along."

He crossed his arms, making his biceps bulge. On purpose, no doubt. "And what are your conditions?"

Number one: stop making me like you so much. Number two: stop making me picture you naked.

"Tess?"

"I...don't have any yet."

"I'll go first, then. My condition is that you don't ask any questions."

"That's it? That's your condition? Why?"

"That was a question. Three, in fact."

"What, no questions at all? Not even, 'Shall we turn left here or right?'"

"You know what I mean." He appraised her coolly, his chin lifted. "No nosy questions. No journalist questions. No digging."

She slipped her hands into her rear pockets. "Wow. What *are* you hiding?"

"Question."

"I can't even wonder aloud?"

"Question."

"It has to be something big—something that made you turn your back on your country."

His jaw tightened. "I'm serious, Tess. I'm getting you to your dossier, and that's it—I'm out." He swore. "Okay, I'm getting you to the dossier and then to safety and *then* I'm out. In the meantime, no questions. Promise."

Hmm. She could always draw him out some other way. He hadn't contradicted her about abandoning his country, for starters, which all but confirmed his worst-kept secret: he wasn't French. What could be bad enough to drive him out and make him lie about his nationality, but not bad enough to make him wanted by

Interpol? Bigger than a misdemeanor, but smaller than a major conviction—the modern legion didn't take serious criminals.

Something bad enough to make headlines? She pressed her dry lips together. Was that why he looked familiar—whatever he was running from had drawn international media coverage? Yes. That was lighting up neurons. She swallowed. And it was making her nervous. Why? God, this was driving her nuts, like watching a movie and trying to figure out where you'd seen the actor.

"Earth to Tess…"

Crap. "Fine. No questions."

"*And* I get to use this." He pulled Solomon's phone from a pocket. "I'll be careful," he added, as she started to protest. "Just…" His gaze flicked down and up her body, making the morning suddenly a few degrees warmer. His Adam's apple wavered. "No dirty tricks this time."

She hoped he couldn't see her face flaming, along with other parts of her anatomy. "It wasn't a dirty trick."

"Seemed pretty dirty to me."

"Well, it wasn't a trick. I told you, I made up a plan as I went along. Look, let's get this straight so we can forget it ever happened. I kissed you because…" She frowned. Because it was true what she'd said—he was *fucking sexy.* She sucked in a breath between her teeth.

He lifted an eyebrow. "Because?"

"Because of the phone. And it's still not a good idea." She reached for it. He held it away. She exhaled and lowered her arm. Not that routine again.

"Hear me out. First we prioritize getting out of here,

in case those bandits come back—or al-Thawra comes looking. Then I'm getting a message to my CO."

"I don't like it."

"Sunshine, I don't like any of this. I don't like the fact that terrorists are after me—or whoever those bastards are. I don't like being grilled like I'm on the news. I don't like that I'm not halfway to a decent meal and a hot shower."

Don't mention hot showers.

"And most of all..." He slipped the phone into his back pocket, right where she didn't want to go. "I don't like that I still don't know whether my buddies are alive, and I'm going to find out, conspiracy theories or not. You gotta trust me on that, Tess."

She screwed up her face and looked at her blood-splattered boots. Of course he wanted to know about his friends.

"Look." He stepped closer, his voice lowered to a gruff murmur, and lifted her chin with his finger, forcing her to meet his gaze—which just made her want to stretch up and kiss him. Damn, she'd so nearly been rid of him, rid of *this*. "Somehow we became a *we*, and it looks like we'll be a *we* until you're done with this suicide mission, whether you like it or not. Whether *I* like it or not, because I don't know what I'm doing even standing here. Meantime, I'd like to think I've done enough to earn your trust. *Oui?*"

She squinted up at him. He wanted her trust but he didn't trust her enough to tell her more than age, rank and serial number—minus the serial number.

"Really?" He stepped away, groaning. "Not even a little bit?"

"I've known you for one day—and for some of that

you were unconscious." So why did it feel like she'd known him for years?

"And in that time have I done a single thing to make you doubt me?"

"You've been very secretive."

"I swear to you, Tess, my life history has no bearing on what we're doing here, so please stop asking. Anything else?"

"I don't want to put you in danger."

"Like I say, I can make my own decision there, and I have. You got anything else?"

"I guess I… I don't normally let my guard down easily." *In any of the ways I have with you.*

"Oh, believe me, sunshine, neither do I. But this…" He threw his hands up, gesturing at a world of gray stone and milky-blue sky. "This is far from normal."

Good point. Well, hell, it wasn't like she was trusting him with her heart—she wasn't that stupid. Just her life. And this might all be over by tonight. "Fine. You can send this secret message, but I have right of veto if I think it's not secure enough."

"It'll be secure enough."

"That's the first of my conditions—you only make contact with the world if I am comfortable with it."

"Agreed," he said. His forehead creased. "Wait— the *first* of your conditions? Why do you get more than one?"

"You made two conditions—the questions and the phone."

"Uh-huh."

"And your first condition is a hard one for me. I'm a journalist—I ask questions for a living. It's second nature."

"Consider it a personal challenge. I'm going to find the tools."

He thumped past her and leaned into the cab. Metal squealed as he pushed the seat forward. He rattled around and emerged with a long bag and some wooden blocks.

"Could you get to work on putting the cab to rights while I do this?" He unzipped the bag and dragged out an oversize jack. "Punch out the glass in the driver's side window so it looks open rather than broken, find something to cover the blood on the seats. I'll clear those rocks off the road."

Translation—"I'm over talking." She itched to get moving, anyway. She'd have to figure out the route and switch off the nav unit's transmitting function. He crouched, pulling out tools. Why had he come back, exactly? For the same reason she was secretly pleased he had? God—did she want to admit that even to herself? She could make out a few freckles across what was visible of his face, between the stubble and the dirt. They made him seem boyish. She scoffed.

He looked up, his face locked into pissed mode again. She started. She'd been staring.

"I'm going," she said, raising her palms.

As they worked in silence, the sky became bluer and the sun broke over the horizon, lighting up ridges in the stony ground like a choppy sea, and turning the gray into a pale, dirty terra-cotta. When she was done, she wandered back to Flynn. He was under the truck, fitting the blown tire into a large box.

"You're pretty handy at that," she called, leaning against the side and crossing her arms. "Were you a mechanic in your past life?"

"I don't have a past life and that was a question." He scooted out. "Plenty of calls for truck maintenance in the legion. Not that I'm answering you."

"I found you a T-shirt." She lowered her voice. "And there's toothpaste."

"Is that a hint?"

"Not at all." She liked the taste of him just fine. She held out the T-shirt, her mouth watering. Actually *watering*.

"You take it," he said, stretching.

"It's a little big. And you're twice as dirty as you were before."

He took it and slapped it over his shoulder with a sly half grin. Crap. She needed to stop using the word *dirty*. He replaced the tools, wiped the grease from his hands and pulled his old T-shirt over his head. *This should be good.*

She gasped. No surprise to see several fresh bruises around his ribs and stomach, but the small scars dotting his abs, chest, shoulders... Dozens of them.

"Are those cigarette burns?" The words slipped out.

His gaze snapped to hers, his eyes narrowed. Not pissed this time. Defensive...*vulnerable*.

He yanked the clean T-shirt on and strode around to the driver's door. Suddenly he didn't seem so bulletproof. All this time she'd been teasing him about his secrets, his past life, assuming he'd run from something he'd done. She yearned to ask, but for once in her life the questions wouldn't come. The hydraulics clunked and the ramp began moving. She shivered. No wonder he'd been so guarded.

She took a dusty breath and followed him. He was examining something in his hands. As she neared, he held it up. The old bandit's cap, a bullet hole through the lid.

"And I thought you'd missed," he said, back to normal levels of cynicism. Was this standard practice—prickling like a porcupine when anyone got too close to the truth of him?

"Like I said, I've done some skeet shooting. When will you stop underestimating me?"

He shrugged, tossing the cap. "You ready?"

"Yep."

She stepped to the open driver's door just as he did, and pulled up a half inch from collision. He was standing so close she had to crane her neck to meet his gaze.

"This is my operation, soldier," she said.

"The CO never drives. Did you get any sleep before, in the back?"

She grimaced.

"Sunshine, this isn't some chauvinistic thing. It makes sense—I'm feeling fresh, and I'd rather not survive terrorists and bandits and land mines to die in a road crash."

Thing was, she was also feeling fresh—remarkably so. Despite the lack of sleep and food, and the pains shooting around her body, her brain was firing. Even her skin seemed to buzz. She was never happier than when she was chasing a hot story. The feeling had nothing to do with the hot guy in front of her. Nothing.

"You see?" he drawled, waving a hand in front of her eyes. "You're so tired you've fallen asleep standing up."

She blinked hard and stepped back. Gawking, again.

"Besides, this way, you can be in charge of the phone." He slipped it from his pocket and held it in his palm like an offering. "Because I trust you—see how easy that is?"

She took it quickly. "You trust me, yet I'm banned from asking you anything."

He tilted his head. "I didn't hear a question mark in there, did I?"

"Rhetorical."

"I trust you enough to want me not to get killed, which will have to do." He pulled himself in and shut the door. "Coming?"

Her feet ached as she walked to the passenger side and climbed in. The truck growled to life. Compared with the darkness of a few hours ago, it was positively noonday sun. That was the equator for you—the sun rose fast and dropped fast. No sluggish sunrises or lingering sunsets.

Flynn's clean blue Global Food T-shirt made him look even more rugged from the neck up—unshaven, bloody, dirty… And why was that not a turnoff? He was layer upon layer of sexiness and intrigue—and now, vulnerability, too.

"So where are we going?" he said, the engine idling. "Where's this evidence?"

"Back the way we came."

He banged his forehead on the steering wheel in mock frustration. At least, it looked mock. "I'd figured that much. When are you going to let me in?"

"It's need-to-know. Right now you don't need to know—and it's better for both of us if you don't, in case something happens."

"If something happens to you, wouldn't you want someone to help get your story out?"

She smiled thinly. "Just drive, soldier."

"Oui, Capitaine." He settled back on the seat and turned the truck, empty wheat sacks crackling under him. As he accelerated, he leaned forward and switched on the music player. It blasted a high-pitched tremulous voice, caught in the climax of a song. He hurriedly switched it off.

"I *love* Ethiopian food. I'd eat it every day, every meal. But the music…" He shivered like he'd licked a lemon. "Nails down a blackboard."

She laughed. "And what did your country give the world—Olivia Newton-John?"

"Edith Piaf."

"Sure it did."

He grinned. "Well, this is more like it, huh? A good old road trip." He grabbed a grubby cloth from his door pocket and wiped a streak of blood from the steering wheel.

CHAPTER THIRTEEN

FLYNN NODDED AT the phone in Tess's hand. "Tell me when you get enough coverage to get on the internet."

"The internet? You're not going to make a phone call?"

"You want me to make a call?"

"No."

"Didn't think so."

She switched it on. No lock screen. Damn, that would have settled things. "Nothing at the moment. What do you want to do on the internet? We have to be careful—any keywords could be immediately flagged."

"So I'll wear a tinfoil hat."

"I'm serious."

"Too serious. Don't worry. I won't use naughty words—and I'll even let you type them."

She laid the phone on the seat beside her, untied her boots and eased them off. Wincing, she unwound the filthy, caked bandages. When she got down to the last blood-soaked layer, she paused, swallowing. It would not be pretty.

Here goes. She ripped off the stuck cotton, suppressing a cry, and waited for the shot of pain to pass. Crappity crap. She rummaged around the cab for a plastic bag, stuffed the socks and bandages inside and tied it tight. If only she could do that with all her clothes.

And don't go thinking about showers because you know where that leads.

"I stink, don't I?" she said.

He grinned. "Don't sweat it."

"Most guys would just say no." She liked that he didn't.

"Hey, I've been on the road for weeks before without a shower, with some seriously rank guys. One trip we ran out of baby wipes on day three and had to conserve all our water to drink. That was a low point. You're a walking rose petal."

She leaned back in her seat. A road trip with a cute guy. Oh, for those carefree days. Wait—what carefree days? She'd spent her late teens and early twenties studying, and chasing stories for whatever newspaper would print them. Sure, she'd had road trips with guys but they were her brothers, and being in close confines with three farting, cursing, pranking Energizer Bunnies as the family moved between bases was never relaxing and far from pleasant. She smiled, gazing out the window. Aside from the road itself, the only indication human life even existed was a plastic bag caught on a prickly bush, being tugged by a breeze like it was trying to free itself.

"You've gone all serene. Did you find some interesting drugs in that kit?"

"Just high on the novelty of being alive—and knowing my story might actually get out." She leaned over and grabbed the last of the wipes. Just enough to clean her feet.

"Is that why you do your job—the thrill of the chase?" He made it sound distasteful, like she cleaned sewers or embalmed people.

"Yeah, I guess. But it has to mean something. I hate celebrity interviews—they actually make me a little sick, like I'm not just buying into the bullshit, but feeding it, creating it. I guess that's why I like working in Africa—besides Bono and Angelina Jolie and Prince Harry, you don't waste time chasing celebrities and other crap. It's stories that matter."

"How do you know what matters?"

She paused, midwipe. Odd question. *Loaded* question? "It matters if the story can change things for the better, even in a small way, even for one person."

"Ah, your savior complex."

"That's so not a thing."

"I'm making it one. You want to save the world."

She tsked. "I don't know about that, but a good story... It has to right a wrong. Out here, there are plenty of wrongs—just not enough airtime to do all of them justice."

He locked gazes with her, his expression inscrutable. "Right a wrong," he repeated eventually, refocusing on the road. "What if you hurt people in the process?"

"Most of the time they deserve it." He made a scoffing sound. She'd hit a nerve. Why?

"Sure, there are exceptions." She looked out the window, deliberately keeping her tone offhand. This could get interesting. "Some people are launched into the public eye through no fault of their own. But the people I go after are usually guilty as hell."

"What if they've just made a mistake? And making a big deal of it means they're never able to escape it, make up for it?" His tone had hardened. He wasn't talking hypothetically—this was personal.

"What kind of mistake?"

"Something that—" His eyes narrowed. Shutting down. Damn. "Forget it."

"Is that why you left Australia?" she asked gently. "Some youthful misdemeanor you were hounded for?"

"One more question and I'm calling for a medevac on mental health grounds."

Not a no. She ached to ask about his scars, but if anything was guaranteed to shut him down… "You don't have a high opinion of journalists."

"Does anyone?"

She gave a curt laugh. "Harsh. Most of us do it for the right reasons, you know."

"Are you saying you've never dumped someone in it? You've never treated anyone badly?"

"Hell, I've made mistakes. Who hasn't? But I'd like to think I've learned from them and I'm not making as many these…" Her heart dropped. Except to get her crew killed. And there was Latif. And Solomon and Yonas. Sheesh.

"Tess?"

"Okay, sure. Sometimes people pay a price they shouldn't." She looked down—and picked up the phone. "We have internet. Signal's weak, but we could have a go."

"Great. Get onto Facebook."

"Facebook? That's your top secret communication strategy?"

"Hiding in plain sight—the last place people think to look, like the burkas."

"I don't like this."

"I'll talk you through it. You'll see. Log in as 'Priscilla Kenny.'" He gave her the details. It loaded so slowly she could almost hear the phone creaking. Priscilla Kenny, it turned out, was a blurry woman in her fifties, with a bunch of middle-aged female friends. "Go into the Shopping Alerts group."

A secret members-only group. She read the description: "'A heads-up on designer bargains.' Seriously?"

"Read me the posts."

She scrolled down. "The most recent is from Henrietta Lamont."

"When was it left?"

"Yesterday. God, I don't even know the date today."

"Oh, thank fuck." He closed his eyes a second.

"What does it mean?"

"My CO—Angelito, the guy I said you could trust. That's him. What does he say?"

"'That sweater Flo was eyeing is down to $9.50! And I'm defo getting that little red dress—forty-four bucks! Bargain. Both two-thirds off!'"

"Show me." He narrowed his eyes at the screen. "They're in Hargeisa."

"How—?"

"Longitude and latitude. The $9.50 means 9.5, and two-thirds is 66.7, so that's 9.5667 latitude. Likewise, the forty-four bucks translates as 44.0667 longitude. That's in Hargeisa. We always memorize the coordinates of the places we're posted to. Write, 'Hi, ladies,' for now, and post it. Read me the other recent stuff."

She posted the note, and read aloud a scroll of posts and comments which could conceivably be what they appeared—a conversation between a network of keen shoppers. The banality of it and its relative invisibility in plain sight…genius.

"Anything from Dora McDonald in the last couple of days?" he said.

She scrolled. "Nothing."

He hissed out a breath.

"Is that bad?"

"My buddy—he got shot when I got kidnapped."

She opened her mouth to say something comforting, then shut it. Empty words wouldn't help. She knew that worry too well.

The phone beeped. "A message from Henrietta," she said. "'Hi, stranger! Haven't seen you round lately.'"

"Tell him I've been busy with work, 'not like you lazy ladies.'"

She complied. A reply popped up almost immediately. "'LOL. Sounds like you need retail therapy, Pris.'"

"Okay, Tess. This is when you tell me where we're going."

"Flynn…"

"We don't know how long we'll have a signal."

"I don't want to drag anyone in—I didn't want to drag you in. Like I say, people around me have a habit of dying."

"Well, these guys are my best chance of getting out alive, if that makes you feel any better. And you can trust them to keep their traps shut."

"And how about the people they answer to, and the people those people are connected with? If word gets around—"

"It won't. No one even needs to know I'm with you."

"A few hours ago we were locked up together in an al-Thawra dungeon. It'll be a reasonable assumption that if you broke out, we both broke out."

"They might assume that I've left you to your fate."

"I doubt that very much."

"Okay, look, we can go dark, keep this on the down

low. Just my guys, no one else. They'll be under orders to get me out by any means possible, and if that means going quiet, they'll do it."

"You can't make that call," she ventured.

"My *capitaine* can—Angelito. Once you have your evidence, they can help us get out of town and back to the French base at Djibouti. Somehow."

"Flynn—"

"These guys are commandos—some of the best soldiers in the world, and the best guys I know. Believe me, you want them on your side."

She stared at the phone. More people to put in danger.

"Screw this," he said, swerving to the shoulder and braking hard. "Tess, look at me."

She turned, her neck muscles creaky and reluctant.

His eyes sparked. "I want to see this through. I'm on your side and I want you to win. But I don't know what more I can do to make you trust me. I'm clean out of ideas. All I can do is look you in the eye and promise I won't do anything to mess this up."

The truck shook as it idled.

"You want to keep me safe, right?" He lowered his voice to gravelly. Guaranteed to get to her every time.

"Of course."

"This is the best way."

She dropped her gaze. What if she said no and got him killed?

"Tess," he whispered.

"Harar," she said, swiping the phone. "We're going to Harar."

A pause. "That's maybe a hundred and fifty klicks from Hamid's HQ."

"I know. Too crazy?" A beam of sunlight picked up

his eyes, making them look translucent. Would he refuse? Then what?

His mouth softened into an almost-smile. "Nah, it's perfect."

"How so?"

"They won't be expecting us to be driving in from this direction. We'll look like a supply truck headed to the camps, like all the others."

"Hiding in plain sight."

"Yep. And if we need to hide you again on the way back out, I have the perfect place."

"Which is?"

"The spare tire box. It'll be bumpy but safe enough just to get us past any checkpoints. I should have thought of it before. Hell, we could both fit, if we…you know…"

"I'm not sure if I do know." And there she went, smiling again. The single most chaotic day of her life and she was grinning and flirting like a prom queen.

"My guys could drive us out. Enemy's looking for a French man and an American woman. They wouldn't find either. Shit, sunshine, this could actually work."

She frowned. "It could." She and Flynn and the dossier, safe and *very* cozy. The phone beeped. "Henrietta," she said. "'You still there, doll?'" Tess typed, reading aloud: "'Still here, babycakes. Just grabbing the deets.' Okay?"

Flynn nodded, jamming the truck back into gear. She sent it.

"Won't it look obvious if a team of legionnaires suddenly arrives in Harar?"

"We'll tell them to dress down." He pulled back onto the road. "Where in Harar could we meet, where tourists hang out, where Hamid wouldn't expect us to go?"

"Um, the markets? No, too public, too busy. Rimbaud's house."

"Rambo's house?"

"Arthur Rimbaud. Very famous French poet who lived in Harar. It's an old house, now a museum. I'd have thought you'd know him, being… French."

"Poetry's not my thing. Think you can Google the coordinates and figure out our ETA?"

"Sure."

With the teeth-grindingly slow internet, it took a while to look everything up and code and send the message—with a warning not to tell anyone else about the "secret sale." A minute later, a reply flashed up.

"He says, 'Fab, we'll be there shortly after you.'"

She read aloud as she typed: "'Look forward to catching up, sweetie. Hugs.'"

Flynn tsked. "Thank you. You can shut off the phone and put your tinfoil hat back on."

"Never took it off. I'm just going to check the news headlines, see if word's got out about our escape." She punched in the URL of her TV network. Better that than Googling her name. "You know, that's not a bad communications scheme of yours, though you'd have to be careful not to use any devices that could be traced back to you."

"You want to get a message to your family?"

"Absolutely not. I have to assume anything that comes in or goes out of their emails or computers or phones will be monitored. How about your family in Australia? They must be worried." She pretended to be fascinated by the loading icon.

"Yeah," he scoffed. Hastily, he added, "I don't have family in Australia."

"Sorry, I meant Corsica."

"None there, either. *Legio patria nostra*."

"Meaning?"

"The legion is our fatherland."

"So no family at all."

"Is that a question?"

"It's a statement I'm using to try to provoke you into a response. You didn't make that a condition."

"I'm making it one now."

"Too late. Contract negotiations are over. I get to make provoking statements."

"Suit yourself. I just won't get provoked."

After forever, the headlines came up. She scanned them. "Nothing on here about us getting out." An update on the search for her sat about ten stories down. She resisted clicking on it, to avoid leaving a trail, and kept scrolling.

"Crap," she said.

"What's up?"

"Story about US and allied air forces amassing in Djibouti. The perfect place to launch air strikes on Somalia."

"Could be bluster."

"All it takes is a nod from the top, and it's on." She swore. "They say my kidnapping is the last straw—they're using me as an excuse to launch their war."

"Well, that's ironic."

"Ugh. I think I'm getting car sick."

"You want me to stop?"

"I want you to go faster."

"Yes, ma'am."

She focused on the horizon. A bird of prey sliced through the pale sky. This just got more urgent—and

Djibouti just got more dangerous for her. She exhaled, loudly. Which brass had gathered there—the ones she was about to destroy? She scrolled down. Another story focused on an internet fund-raising campaign to send a mercenary force to free her. Spearheaded by... *Kurt.* She grunted.

"You're killing me here," Flynn said, deadpan.

"My ex wants to come and rescue me."

"Too late! I already rescued you. Who does this guy think he is?"

"Captain America."

"He's military?"

"Very."

"Ah." He grinned, his eyes bright. "You have a thing for military guys."

"Not anymore."

"Ouch. What went wrong?" Was that genuine interest in his tone?

"I'll tell you something about me if you tell me something about you."

"Depends what you want to know."

Her gaze dropped to the outline of his abs, under his T-shirt. "Those scars. They're cigarette burns, aren't they?"

The lightness dropped from his face. "It was too much to hope you'd let that go."

"From when you were a kid?"

His mouth tightened.

"Parents?"

Silence. "Father," he eventually offered. "My mother...died, when I was nine."

My mother...died. Why the pause?

"So, Captain America, huh?" he continued, not quite pulling off a casual tone.

"Wait, that's all I get—you had a prick of a father?"

"It's more than most people get."

Heck, from him it was a three-volume memoir. "Captain America—not his real name—is a certified war hero. With a trademarked action figure."

"No shit...*that* guy? He's like the meme king. What's his name—Kirk something?"

"Kurt."

Flynn whacked the steering wheel. "*La vache*, seriously? You fell for that tosser? And I was just beginning to respect you."

She threw a wipe at his smug face. "Don't be horrible! He broke my heart."

"Nah. You're too smart to let a guy like that screw you up."

"Apparently not." She couldn't keep the defensiveness from her tone. She pretended to find something interesting to look at out the passenger window.

"Hey." His voice softened. "Tess." She risked a look. His head was tipped to the side. Still half grinning, still looking bemused, but also a little...sympathetic. "I'm sorry. It's just—"

"I know—it was stupid. You don't need to say it. I fell for the wrong guy and it was humiliating."

"I didn't mean..." He reached across and tucked a stray lock of hair behind her ear. "Tess, promise me you won't let a numbskull like that mess you up for good. You're awesome and he's...*une tête de con*. You gotta get over him."

She giggled, partly because Flynn's gentle touch was messing with her nerves. And partly because, well:

you're awesome. Crap, she really was falling under this guy's spell.

"Don't worry," she said as he turned back to the road. "He didn't break my heart, though it kinda felt like it at the time. He just broke my trust and my hope and my…pride."

"And I guess it was reported in the media? That must have hurt."

She waited for the dig about the irony of her being media-shamed, but it didn't come. "It did hurt, actually. More than I would ever have expected. I thought I had a thick skin, that I was used to the trolls, but this… It was a whole new level." She crossed her arms. "And that's why next time I'm dating a very reliable accountant who's lived his entire unblemished life in a charming small town. Someone the media will find so unremarkable they will move on from the story within the hour."

"You have this guy lined up?" Was that tension in his voice—or wishful thinking on her part?

"Not yet. It'll be my number one priority after saving the world."

"You know there are probably tens of thousands of women who are dating accountants and fantasizing about Captain America?"

"And if I could, I would sit down and have a serious chat with each one."

"Why an accountant? You want someone to do your taxes?"

"I want someone I can trust to always come home to me."

"Oh, come on. You've had one bad experience with a loser soldier. Don't write off the rest of us."

The rest of us. He was including himself in that?

Overthinking.

"It's not just that," she said. "Throughout my life, I've lived with the possibility that anyone in my family will be killed on the job at any minute—plus half the kids I grew up with. I have enough people to worry about. I guess dating Kurt drove that fear home. Maybe that's why I never let myself fall in love with him. Luckily."

"Do you know that fishermen are way more likely to die on the job than soldiers?"

"Good to know. I'll add them to my list of men to avoid."

"I bet accountants die at work all the time. Heart attacks at their desks from all that sitting around doing taxes."

The man doth protest too much. "I'll take that risk."

"To be fair, most soldiers don't screw around and don't die. One bad experience, Tess…"

"Huh."

He tilted his head. "It's not just one bad experience, is it?"

"My father was a war hero who cheated on my mother and died in action. So, yeah, there's a pattern here I don't intend to repeat."

"Ah. I'm sorry. How long ago did he die?"

"I was in my early twenties. Home from college."

"Knock at the door?"

"Yep. My parents had been divorced for years but Mom was still listed as next of kin. And even after how bitter it'd got, his death broke her. I think it was that finality, you know. She hides it, but I know she's terrified of it happening again. Every time there's a knock on the door you can see her looking around with these wild eyes and calculating—where are the boys today, which one is it? Seeing my mom like that… That's not the life I want."

"Ah, jeez, Tess. That's tough."

She pressed her palms into her eyes. Way to break the sexual tension. She'd enjoyed the respite from the stress. Too much. She picked up the phone. Another story covered the fury in France. The teaser confirmed Flynn remained an "unnamed French soldier." Al-Thawra's photo was horrendous—he looked washed out, shabby, filthy. She stole a sideways look. Well, he was shabby and filthy, so why did that not put her off? And scarred, inside and out, and now she had an idea why. Last thing she'd do was pull a guy like that into her crazy public life, no matter how loudly he proclaimed he could look after himself. They probably only had a few more hours together. She'd enjoy his company while she could.

You're awesome.

Yeah, and that was the kind of flattery that'd made her fall for Kurt. People always assumed she was superconfident because she appeared that way on screen, but she craved approval as much as the next person.

Farther down was a piece about a joint news conference with the secretaries of State and Defense, defending their efforts to rescue her. As far as she knew, they weren't in on the conspiracy, but they'd be getting pressured by Denniston's political cronies to go nuclear.

She closed the tab. Facebook was still sitting there. She stared at it awhile, chewing the inside of her cheek as an idea formed. A risky idea but her choices were few.

Yes. This way she could get her story out without a trip to Djibouti and before an air strike began. Before she got anyone else killed.

CHAPTER FOURTEEN

TESS TAPPED HER lips with one finger. *All risk is relative.* "Could I use your Priscilla account to send a message?"

"You would trust a message to the internet? You're not scared that Facebook will send out a missile to blow us up?"

"I could get a note to Quan, my producer, in Addis. I'll need his help to get my story to air."

"You'll send him a message?"

"Not directly—too dangerous. But we share the same housekeeper, and she's glued to social media. I could send her a private message on Facebook to show him, without using my name." Tess searched for her. Bingo. Go Generation Z. Or the Millennials, or whatever they were called. "He could send someone to Dire Dawa by plane and then Harar by taxi. He'll know where to find me there. If I record my story and save it onto a flash drive, it'll be easy enough for a local to smuggle it out, even under al-Thawra's eyes."

"Will he believe it? You've told him there's no story." She looked up blankly.

"The note Hamid made you write."

"Oh, he'll know that's bull."

"Sounded authentic to me."

"Depends on your grasp on punctuation."

He hit a pothole and tightened his grip on the wheel. "What?"

"I left out the apostrophes."

"So?"

"I never leave out apostrophes."

"Even under torture?"

"Never."

"And he'll pick up on that?"

"Hell, yes. I break many rules but never grammatical ones. I took a stab that Hamid wouldn't pick up on it."

"Wow, you guys are nerds. I bet your texts are all grammatically correct and shit."

"What, yours aren't?"

His face relaxed into a grin. She could get used to seeing that expression. It warmed her up in all sorts of places.

"Lieutenant, how can you possibly make yourself understood without apostrophes?"

"You know you're fighting a lost cause?"

"That's what I do best."

He laughed. She swiped hurriedly and reread, checking she wasn't missing anything, checking it wouldn't raise any flags. *Send.*

Too impatient to stare at the phone, she looked up, blinking to ease the dryness in her eyes. The sun wasn't even full beam and already it was burning her retinas. "Man, I haven't seen proper daylight in a while."

"I saw sunglasses in the glove box. There are baseball caps around, too. Don't want that sun to go lighting up any blond hair." As she rummaged, he leaned forward, peering up to the lightening sky. "Bet some shit's going down at Hamid's compound."

She handed him a Global Food cap and sunglasses,

and put some on herself. "And in a few other places around the world. She'll have some explaining to do."

"If she's even told them—she could be trying to contain it." He grabbed a water bottle. "So what do you know about her? What's her story?" He took a swig.

"What is this, *60 Minutes*?"

"Laughing out loud," he said. "You said she was a marine?"

"Yep. She joined up after she was rejected by the FBI Academy."

"What for? Being a psychopath?"

"Pretty much. The official reason was that she couldn't keep up academically—she has a brilliant mind and speaks half a dozen languages, but has learning difficulties. Dyslexia. It's haunted her confidence throughout her life—still does. But my colleague has a source there who said that in the FBI psych evaluation she scored off the charts for antisocial personality disorder, and that was the real reason she didn't make the cut."

"So she joined the marines. Because that's just what the military needs."

"Yep. That's where she met Hyland. He was her CO, and word is they had an affair for years. Possibly still are. In her early thirties she was recruited by the CIA and sent to Africa, but my sources say she wasn't fond of following orders and didn't play well with others. At some point she began secretly moonlighting for Denniston, where she felt she'd at last found recognition for her talents, her intelligence. That's where my paper trail goes cold, but I know she was with the CIA until a few years ago."

"About the time al-Thawra popped up."

"Exactly. My source says—said—she gets off on

the power, as you will have seen. And with her buddy Hyland in the Oval Office…"

"This is some crazy-ass shit."

"Can I quote you on that?"

He evil-eyed her.

"At ease, soldier! I'm joking."

They fell into silence. She watched him out of the corner of her eye—tall frame leaning back in the seat, sharp eyes scanning the road, arm slung over the wheel. His head turned and she snapped her gaze away—only to catch sight of herself in the wing mirror. She swore.

"What's up?" he said.

"I saw something terrifying."

"Where? It's all stones and dust to me."

"My reflection."

He laughed. "You look like one of those teenage movies where they try to make the babe look bad so they can give her a makeover and surprise everyone with how pretty she is."

"Doesn't strike me as the kind of movie you'd watch."

"Hey, I had a big sister once."

"*Once?* Did something happen to her?" She bit down on her lip. Precisely the kind of question to make him clam up, just as his wariness was easing. *Idiot.*

Sure enough, his jaw locked.

"I'm sorry. I shouldn't have asked." Wow, *that* wasn't something she said often.

Anyone else would have responded with "It's okay" or "You weren't to know" or would have volunteered an explanation. Flynn stared out the windshield, his silence shutting down the conversation. His knuckles whitened around the steering wheel. Had he run away to the legion after a tragedy—something that still haunted him, something that made a kid who'd watched corny movies with his sister into a cynical tough guy? Maybe his mother and sister died in the same incident, leaving him with an abusive father? That would give her a place to start searching. A crime or an accident would have made the papers.

Sheesh, how much of a betrayal would he consider that? But it wasn't because she wanted to do a story on him. She wanted to understand him. Because…she cared. She felt it like a rope tugging on her heart. He was hurting and she wanted to…what? Heal him? Wow. That wasn't her style, as much as he might think she had a savior complex. She wasn't the type who was attracted to a broken man, thinking she could fix him. Sure, she empathized with people who'd had tough lives—she met them every day and tried to do justice to telling their stories. Sometimes that helped them; sometimes, sadly, it didn't. But in her love life she'd learned to steer clear of complications. *You need a guy who will anchor you.*

Flynn rubbed a hand over his face, looking as drawn as his al-Thawra mug shot. She yawned in sympathy.

"Get some sleep, sunshine. We got a whole lot of nowhere to drive through. I'll wake you if anything fun happens."

Her eyes watered at his mention of sleep. Why not? She was in a place of relative safety, and by the look of Flynn, he could use a break from shoring up his defenses. This time yesterday she'd woken to him leaping off the mattress as if he'd found himself cuddling a scorpion. He'd been on alert ever since. He was right—she should rest. By the end of today, her story would be broadcasting everywhere. She needed to be sharp.

She checked the phone. "Response from the house-keeper. Quan has my message and is working on it."

Game on.

AFTER FLIP-FLOPPING ALL OVER the cab, Tess ended up sleeping curled across the seats. Her palm had come to rest on Flynn's thigh, where it remained, burning a hole in his combat trousers. He should have removed it, but almost immediately she'd stilled, falling into a deep sleep. Stupid truth was, he didn't mind the contact. Okay, he *liked* the contact.

Yep, this wasn't a normal mission. Or a normal road trip. He slowed as he caught up to a lumbering green truck, with thorns stuck to the back. Hitchhiker deterrents. His last road trip before joining up was with a goddess, too—and a journalist, though he didn't know that at the time. From the cattle station at Shitsville, South Australia, where he worked—okay, *hid*—in his university holidays, to Sydney for his final year. Endless flat arid land and arcing blue skies, a lot like this. He kept his head down at uni, shit-scared of being recognized, of someone seeing through his fake name, but when you're a hormone-drunk twenty-year-old and hot Katie the "psych student" comes on to you, hard, you make an exception and screw her, repeatedly. Because you're a dickhead.

And when she suggests she fly up to Shitsville to join you for the three-day road trip back to uni, you say, *sure.*

Because you're a bloody dickhead.

Three days. Plenty of time for her to draw out his life story, in between hot, dirty sex. He pulled out and accelerated past the truck. Journalists. Screw them all.

Yeah, and screwing a journalist is what got you screwed in the first place.

After her scoop came out he'd been fucked over so bad by the media and vigilante groups that one morning he'd walked out of a lecture, packed a bag, left a month's rent on the table for his flatmates and boarded the first flight to Paris, without telling a soul. Because who would give a crap? Certainly not Katie, the one person he'd let in since bolting from his hometown.

He'd walked down that flight bridge feeling more alone than ever, his stomach churning with the knowledge that he was a coward and a quitter. Within seconds of taking his seat, a passenger had recognized him, and by the time they touched down at Charles de Gaulle, he was surrounded by empty chairs. Mothers spent the entire flight gripping their daughters. Hell, they did him a favor. They steadied his resolve to walk under the stone archway of Fort de Nogent. He'd practiced his introduction so much on that flight it'd become a meditation: *Je veux rejoindre la Légion Étrangère.* God knew how the guard understood his attempt at French.

It was during his recruitment medical that he'd first begun to understand what had happened to him as a kid, that all those one-sided "play fights" he'd dreaded and hated weren't just his dad messing with him, toughening him up, teaching him to survive, like his dad had claimed. The scars, the badly healed ribs that in his recollection now had ached for years but his dad had dismissed as growing pains... The legion doctor hadn't asked any questions, hadn't made any comments, just explained the irregularities on the X-rays. Suddenly Flynn had understood what his defense lawyer had been on about. He'd thought the guy had been grasping at any old loophole to get his client off. Though, mate, what'd happened to Flynn was nothing compared with his father's real victims. He'd walked out of that doctor's office, slammed the door on that old life and thrown himself into the new one. He'd worked his arse off to survive basic training and hadn't looked back.

Years later, he'd read on the internet about his dad's death in prison. Every report had speculated on Flynn's whereabouts but none had hit close to the mark. Every now and then a "sighting" would spark a burst of media speculation, but as time passed and he distanced himself from that young *imbécile*—in age, looks, naïveté—he'd begun to believe he'd erased the past. Then, a couple of years ago, he'd looked in the mirror and realized the gut-churning truth: he was turning into the old man— the weathered skin, the cold eyes, the hard set to his jaw. A matter of time before someone made the connection.

Tess murmured and changed position, her hand climbing up his thigh. He eased it back to safer ground. A matter of time before *she* made the connection. Yep, he'd bogged down in hostile territory—a minefield was nothing next to the threat she posed. What had she said about the people she exposed? *Most of the time they deserve it.*

Would she think he deserved it? Hell, he did deserve it. But being sprung in the media would screw up his career. The brass wouldn't want that kind of attention on a military that had fought to the death for the world's respect since its wild early days. And he'd be in deep shit for going AWOL for a crusade that was turning more personal by the minute. At best he'd be demoted to grunt, lose his place in the commando unit. Worst, he'd be kicked out, lose his French citizenship, be deported. Then what—become a security contractor for hire? At least the legion pursued something bigger than profit. He might not have Tess's noble views, but he wouldn't kill people to line some bastard's pockets. Nope, he'd worked his Outback arse off for a European passport and he wasn't going back.

He swerved to avoid a cardboard box in the road. And yet, here he was, some numbskull with a *hero complex*, unable to do the sensible thing and walk away. That bloody tire. It was the first seed of doubt—how would a half-starved, injured woman change a wheel that weighed more than she did? And in the time it took to walk from Tess to the waiting soldier, a montage of disturbing images had come to mind. What if next week he saw footage of her body being dragged through some street in Somalia, like that of her translator, provoking the war she was prepared to die to prevent? How would he feel then?

Too many evil things had happened to women because of him—he wasn't about to add another face to the slideshow of victims in his head. This one he would deliver to safety. It wouldn't make up for the others but it was something.

He passed half a dozen women trudging along with sticks strapped across their shoulders and babies strapped to their fronts, their skinny limbs gray with dirt and dryness. Going from nowhere to nowhere, as far as he could tell. He pulled his cap lower, ignoring the complaints from his injured head.

If only Tess would stop with the questions. If only he could find her curiosity switch and flick it to Off—and switch off his dick at the same time.

Because, mate, she was hot. Fiery, smart, driven,

brave, funny. As she'd washed herself with those wipes, he'd pictured himself sponging the dirt and blood off her entire naked body—slowly.

He smoothed away a clump of her hair that had escaped its knot. She looked like her bones would shatter if she tripped, but she might well be made of titanium. How many people would risk their lives to protect people they'd never met? She wasn't doing her job for the fame, like Katie. No, Tess had discovered a wrong and she wanted to right it. And despite his carefully honed survival instinct, he wanted to help her so much his chest knotted. Not because he found her seriously sexy—well, not only because of that—but because it turned out he liked to see justice done, too. Yep, he was a hypocrite. Or just a bonehead with a boner.

He drove for hours, passing few vehicles—a battered car the color of rust, a dusty bus piled with sacks, a van with chickens tied to its roof, wings flapping from panic or the wind or both. A rusted railway track snaked in and out of view. Closer to Dire Dawa, the road got busier. He grabbed his foulard from the floor of the cab, tied it loosely around his neck and ducked into it, as if keeping out the dust. Out here, the sight of a white person was still enough of a novelty to arouse curiosity. Despite the spreading heat, he put on Solomon's jacket to hide more of his skin. It was only bloody on the inside.

The town was surprisingly orderly—tree-lined streets, squares, fussy colonial buildings, squat concrete blocks painted in dirty peach and green. At an intersection, a guy in dreads that covered his eyes and a sack over his shoulder approached Flynn's window, tapping his fingers to his mouth. Flynn dug into the backpack and gave him the first random MRE packet his hand touched. "Good luck with that," he muttered.

At the outskirts, the town dissolved back into scrub. As he rounded a corner, a rickshaw shot out in a blur of blue and white. He stomped on the brake and Tess tossed forward, her spine crunching on the dash.

"Crap," he said. "Sorry—one of those motorized rickshaw things. You know, like a scooter with a roof. What do they call them here? Not a *tuk-tuk*…"

"Bajaj," she groaned. She went to push herself up.

And then he saw it. He shoved her down, his hand on her bony shoulder. She dived nose-first into his lap but that was the least of his problems.

Fifty meters ahead, five guys in black fatigues manned a military-issue portable roadblock. Mercenaries. An M16 in every pair of hands.

CHAPTER FIFTEEN

SHIT. FLYNN SHOULD have put Tess in the tire box. He hadn't expected a checkpoint this far from Hamid's base.

"What is it? Why are we slowing? Why are you looking like that?"

Flynn neutralized his expression, for her as much as the soldiers. "A roadblock. Private security contractors. Now, what would they be doing out here?"

She slid off his lap and into the footwell, her face paling. "One guess."

"They've come to rescue you?"

"Would you set up a roadblock if you're looking for someone you plan to help?"

He sucked on his front teeth. Fair call.

"I'm not saying the world revolves around me, but Denniston has a whole lot of muscle at its disposal, not just al-Thawra. Can we turn around?"

"Too suspicious. We're committed." He checked his mirror. "And boxed in. Most of their resource is focused on the other side of the road. We might get lucky."

He hated relying on luck.

He squinted into the sun. They'd stopped a white Land Cruiser heading the opposite direction and were pulling two people from a car—including a skinny blonde.

With three contractors occupied with the Land Cruiser and one surveying traffic banking up behind it, only one guy, wearing a Yankees cap, was focused on their side of the road. He cast a loose gaze their way, casually shouldering his weapon.

"Let me go! You have no right to stop me," the woman said, in English with an accent that could have been Swedish. "Who are you?"

The guy in the Yankees cap glanced at the *bajaj* driver, then up at Flynn. Flynn ducked his face into the foulard and lifted a couple of fingers from the steering wheel in a casual, bored acknowledgment. Lucky he hadn't got all the grease off his hands after changing the tire. Nothing unusual in a Global Food truck driving through Dire Dawa at this hour, on its way to the camps. And they wouldn't expect him and Tess to be heading back into the red zone, seeing as it was so incredibly stupid.

An American voice carried over from the Land Cruiser. "Ma'am, we're just doing our job. If you'll do what we ask and show us some ID, we'll have you on your way lickety-split. If you are who you say, we have no…"

As the *bajaj* approached the barrier arm, Flynn changed down, too quickly. The truck jerked, the crunching gears drowning out the conversation, which was evidently getting heated. Yankee strolled to the arm, all military swagger, like he was packing a grenade between his legs.

Flynn drew his pistol from his pocket and held it out of sight—lucky the Djibouti soldiers had grudgingly returned it. The M16 was lying across the footwell, next to Tess. These guys would be well drilled, ex-military, eager to prove themselves worthy of their big bucks—possibly even working for a reward. He should have hidden Tess. He should have talked her into going to Djibouti in the chopper.

He changed into Neutral and rolled on, forcing himself to lean back in the seat like he expected to pass through without incident. Tess picked up the rifle and smoothly cocked it. He coughed to cover the click.

His attention on the confrontation, Yankee lifted the barrier and the *bajaj* passed through ahead, engine straining like a lawn mower about to go into orbit. Five more meters...

"Ma'am, all I need to see is—"

"Not until you show me your authority—"

The guy holding the woman swore, threw her to the ground and forced her hands behind her. "You want to feel my authority?"

Bastard. Flynn went to jam on the brakes, then stopped himself. The woman would be okay—she wasn't Tess and she'd be able to prove it. If he leaped in to help, they'd find their real quarry.

Behind them a siren wailed. Police? Whose side would they be on? The barrier stayed open. Flynn shoved the truck into gear and rattled through. The voices trailed off.

"Stay low but I think we're good," Flynn said.

Tess slumped, puffing out an exhalation. "What was that about? Who was that woman? What were they doing to her?"

"An aid worker who looked a lot like you. Nothing she won't be able to talk herself out of. But we'll have to be careful getting out of Harar again. That tire box is looking more and more appealing."

"I don't plan to get out."

"I'm not finished with my shitty life yet, sunshine."

She flipped the safety on. "I mean I don't plan to leave until my story's out. Then they'll have no reason to kill me. You can have the box all to yourself."

"We can pick up your stuff and sneak you out. You could do your story in Djibouti, where it's safe."

She scoffed. "Where are we?"

Changing the subject? He couldn't leave her unprotected with this kind of muscle on her tail. But wasn't that exactly what he'd intended to do all along? And somehow, here he was, still with her.

"Just leaving Dire Dawa," he said. "You can sit up but suit up with the cap and sunglasses. I'm thinking we're good to Harar, since this is the only road in or out."

The terrain changed as the road climbed out of the plains, from clumps of pinkish dirt studded with wiry bushes, to more bushes and less dirt and the odd cactus, to *chat* plantations clinging to hillsides. Endless rows of glossy green leaves gleamed in the midmorning sun.

Tess stretched her neck, digging her fingertips into her shoulder muscles.

"Good sleep?"

"I had a nightmare that I was stuck in a desert with a cranky soldier, and several armies of bad guys were after me. Oh no, wait…"

"You should be a comedian."

"I hope that woman's okay."

"She will be—she's not you."

He felt Tess's gaze on him, long enough for it to burn a line up the side of his face.

"Thank you," she said faintly.

"For what?"

"For staying with me. I would have got caught back there."

His chest expanded. He reached a plateau and accelerated. "At last some credit." Could he tie and gag her and force her to evac with them?

"I do appreciate what you've done, but I don't want you getting hurt on my account. Or anyone else."

"Tess, if I die—and I don't plan to—don't blame yourself. I've made my own decisions and your colleagues did, too. They knew the risks but they decided the cause was worth it. They believed in you."

She smiled, sadly. "Maybe they shouldn't have."

"I believe in you." The words came out before he had time to think, but they were true. He'd ride shotgun on any crazy plan she hatched. He believed in her—in this—like he hadn't believed in anything for a very long time. Just a lost kid looking for a cause.

"I wasn't fishing for compliments."

"I don't give compliments. I was stating fact—I wouldn't be here if I didn't think you were doing the right thing, and you were capable of seeing it through. So now we make sure your friends didn't die for nothing."

He figured by her stillness that she was staring. After half a minute he glanced over. Yep. Staring. She looked away.

"Right," she replied faintly, as if to herself. Her teeth toyed with her lip.

Ah, those lips. He could still feel their softness when she'd kissed him goodbye. Had that helped sway him to stay? It should have had him leaping in the chopper before the blades stopped spinning. It wasn't like the kiss in the wasteland, where she had an agenda. It was slow, meaningful. There was no reason for it, except—

Shut it down, soldier. She's not for you.

TESS ROLLED DOWN the window, inhaling the fresher, wetter air of the highlands. If oxygen was supposed to get thinner as you rose, how come breathing seemed so much easier up here?

The traffic eased as they climbed an escarpment and passed through a marshy area. Cows chewed on reeds and a man leaned on a staff, picking at his teeth with a splayed stick.

"Flamingos," Flynn said, nodding at a cluster of angular pink shapes in the distance.

"This is the *best* road trip." As the scenery rolled by, her anxiety lifted. It was unnerving, this buoying effect he had on her. *I believe in you.* Another thing she could too easily get used to.

As Flynn predicted, they reached the shabby outskirts of Harar without incident. Tess reluctantly eased her socks and boots back on, biting down so hard against the pain that she tasted blood.

"You'd better duck down again, just in case," he said, as she loosely tied the second lace. "Where is this Rambo house?"

She slid into the footwell. "In the old walled citadel, at the far end of town. Stick to the main road and it'll lead us to the gates."

Cars revved and honked. Diesel fumes wafted in. A dog barked, the call answered by several more. Under his sunglasses, Flynn's eyelashes flickered. Scanning for threats. Maybe that was the attraction of a military guy—you knew he had your back. Behind him, powder blue sky filled the window, interrupted by sagging strings of power lines, rusty tin roofs, buildings scaffolded with bamboo, domed mosques, soaring minarets. A few days ago she'd wondered if she'd see blue sky again. Now she was hours from finishing this.

Time for her to drive the action. She'd hide at Samira's family's guesthouse in the citadel while she put the package together. Samira could quietly buy a video camera at the Smugglers Market, and a couple of flash drives. Tess would film her piece-to-camera and edit it on Samira's laptop, interspersing screen grabs of the documents— deliver something Quan could put straight to air. She wasn't the ace editor he was but speed was more important than polish. She'd also give him the crucial raw evidence from the dossier for the network's website. It had to be watertight. How long would it take him to get someone here to collect it—a few hours? She'd ensure nothing could be traced back to Samira. She'd failed to protect Latif. She wouldn't fail the woman he'd loved.

"So," Flynn said, shifting down and slowing, "we meet my unit, we get your dossier, we get out."

"We find your unit and go our separate ways. I can take it from here."

"So you keep telling me. But somehow we keep ending up *dans la merde*."

"Meaning?"

"In the shit."

"Oh."

"You asked."

"I told you, I'm not dragging anyone else in."

"These are the kind of guys you want to drag in."

"I'll be fine, Lieutenant." He looked down at her, his sharp eyes visible underneath the glasses. "From here it's an ordinary day at the office." Nerves crunched in her stomach. Her biggest-ever day at the office.

"You'll be *fine*. That's another thing you keep telling me."

Something clunked under the floor. Flynn braked and she braced, jamming one of her toes against the seat. She hauled in a breath as the pain settled.

"Sorry—pothole. First thing we're doing is getting our medic to look at your feet."

"I'll worry about that later. I'm not planning to do any more running."

"I'm not suggesting you check into a hospital. Let him take a look, give you some drugs. Two minutes."

She chewed the side of her mouth. It was tempting. She might need to lie low at Samira's after her story went out, and it'd make sense to avoid local doctors in case flags went up.

"Does he carry antibiotics?"

"You think they're that bad?"

She winced. Every touch belted fire up her legs. She didn't have a fever, though, so if she had an infection it'd be localized, for now.

"They're that bad," he muttered. "You should've said something."

"And you'd have done what—given me sympathy?"

"He'll have antibiotics. Combat medics have plenty of experience with festering toenails."

"You make it sound so pleasant." Man, could she feel any less sexy? She felt like she'd been dipped in blood and sweat, rolled in dirt and gravel, and left to dry in a sandstorm.

At least in her current state her attraction to Flynn was easy to ignore—no way did she want anyone touching her. Even the thought of subjecting some poor medic to her feet… She shuddered. *Please don't let him be young and hot.*

Maybe she should do her piece-to-camera before cleaning herself up, for that ring of authenticity? That'd give the network's makeup artists a fright. Whenever they dolled her up for studio work she always felt like a piece of toast being smeared with peanut butter. Avoiding that was one of the many benefits to reporting from out here. But then, half the responses to her work were criticisms of her appearance. *That color washes her out. I liked her hair longer. She looks tired.* Her male colleagues could have sweat-drenched armpits and wispy gray comb-overs flapping in the breeze and it just added credibility. Pity smell didn't transmit through airwaves—that'd give the trolls something real to complain about.

"You're smiling," Flynn growled.

"You sound suspicious."

He'd pushed up Solomon's jacket sleeves, and the low sun lit blond hairs on his tanned forearms. What would he look like after a shower and shave?

Good grief, woman, stop thinking about him in the shower.

"It's good to be getting back to normal programming," she said. "For the first time in a week it feels like this could all work out. Or is that tempting fate?"

"I don't believe in fate."

"Of course not."

"You've created your own luck and you get to take full credit. Fuck fate."

If fate had dumped Flynn in the dungeon, all kudos to it. As cell mates went, he'd proved useful. But perhaps fate should have delivered her a less sexy companion. What *was* it about his type? Perhaps if she could figure that out, she'd be less susceptible. She'd thought she was attracted to Kurt—okay, she *was* attracted to Kurt, because what woman wouldn't be, at least initially— but this feeling was so much stronger. Like right now, she felt she could slake her thirst by staring at the sharp contours of Flynn's face. She could feel his finger pads on her skin just by looking at them. She could feel his hands deftly—

Not helping. She grabbed her water bottle. Maybe it was the circumstances. She'd never been in a life-or-death situation with Kurt—they'd hung out when he was on leave or on his "victory tour" through the US. Perhaps this we-could-die-at-any-minute thing inevitably created a bond—the adrenaline getting confused with desire, one cranking up the other in an endless cycle. Would the attraction dissolve once the danger passed?

Luckily, she wouldn't find out. Thing was, she'd been in plenty of stressful situations with male colleagues and hadn't felt anything beyond the urge to get the job done and get the hell out.

Flynn swore. His focus fixed on something in the distance.

She straightened, bumping her head on the glove compartment. "Oh God, what now?"

"Another Global Food truck, on approach. Can't be too many of them plying this route."

"Maybe they won't recognize our truck."

"They'll know it. I know every vehicle in my regiment."

"Anywhere to turn off?"

"Nope." He pulled up his scarf and pushed down his sleeves. "No choice but to pass by."

"Maybe they haven't heard about Solomon and the driver?"

"They'll have heard—their bosses would have had to warn them of the risk. Here they come."

He half raised a hand from the steering wheel in a greeting. She held her breath.

"Did they see you?"

"Yep." He flicked his wing mirror to a different angle. "And the passenger was reaching for his phone."

"He might be calling the police. How far are we from the citadel?"

"I think I can see the walls up ahead. They'll have to get to the next roundabout before they can turn around. That gives us a few minutes."

"We have to ditch the truck."

"I can outrun them. We need the truck."

"No. We can't risk a confrontation or a run-in with the police. We don't want to draw any more attention to ourselves or put anyone else in danger. We have to bail."

"We bail, we lose our best chance of getting out of here again."

"Like I say, I'm not leaving. But you'll find another way. You're good at winging it, remember?"

CHAPTER SIXTEEN

STAYING LOW, TESS started loading the backpack. She found the driver's wallet and took the cash, wincing. She'd figure out a way to repay his next of kin.

"The driver has kids," she said, running a thumb over a photo of him with three little girls. "Had. Wonder if they know yet."

"That sucks. But maybe Solomon has kids and we gave them a chance to play football with Dad again."

She stared at it a minute longer, then slipped the wallet into the glove compartment. "Do we take the M16?"

"Leave it. It's too big to hide, and nearly empty. But take the clip, in case someone gets to the truck before these guys. Don't want any hyped-up street kids playing soldier. Is the gate we're looking for a dirty yellow, with a photo of some guy at the top?"

"That's the one. Has the other truck caught up?"

He checked the mirror. "No sign yet. Shall we drive in?"

She hesitated, trying to picture the layout. A pale green medieval-style tower came into view, its crenulated top tipped with burgundy. "No. Hang a right and follow the city walls around. There's a quieter pedestrian gate to the south. We can ditch the truck and disappear straight into the alleyways. It's a maze in there."

"Oui, Capitaine."

"I love it when you defer to me in French."

She could almost feel her blood pressure rising as Flynn nudged the truck through the streets. *If we're stuck in traffic, they will be, too.* Loud chatter ebbed and flowed, the crow of a rooster, a horn that sounded like a goose call. The truck shuddered as they left the asphalt. Then the road smoothed and quieted. The top of the wall rose above Flynn's head, terra-cotta stone bricks warmed by sunlight. On her side of the truck, trees appeared. The noise faded. He slowed.

"There's a hole in the wall," he said. "Like a hobbit hole. Is that it?"

"No. They're for the hyenas."

"Hyenas?"

"Wild hyenas. Harar's famous for them. They have to get out somehow."

"Wouldn't the holes let them in? Hang on, I see it. Big stone archway, next to an old guard tower. Kind of castle-like."

"That's the one. See anywhere to hide the—"

He spun the steering wheel, lurching her sideways, and jammed on the brakes. She thwacked her head on the door.

"Sorry—goats. This'll do. We walk away nice and quiet, a couple of aid workers taking a break from saving the world." He killed the engine, glancing at her T-shirt. "You'd better wear Solomon's jacket," he said, shrugging it off. "You look like you just got out of surgery."

She slid onto the seat. "There's a market near Rimbaud's house. We can buy new clothes."

He tossed the keys in the glove box, grabbed the backpack and pocketed the handgun. At least he wasn't fighting her about the truck. As they crossed the road, Tess could manage little more than a hobble. Her feet felt swollen to basketballs, her quads and calves threatening to snap. A man in gray rags, no fatter than a stick figure, sat against the wall, smoking and staring.

"You're walking like a pregnant ninety-year-old," Flynn said, slipping an arm around her waist and lifting her as she stepped.

"I think my feet were less painful when we were running."

"Probably because the adrenaline was masking the pain. Be grateful for the pain. It's a sign you're safe, that your brain and your instincts don't feel like they have bigger problems to freak out about."

He adjusted his grip and they settled into an awkward rolling gait.

"You're a regular self-help guru," she said.

"It's my bright and sunny nature."

They followed two women under the towering gate, their turquoise, red and yellow dresses and head scarves dazzling against the stone and dirt.

"Gidday, mate. Welcome to Harar. How are you today, Crocodile Dundee?"

A man jumped up from a bench within the gate, wearing pants the same dusty brown as the ground, and a green-and-yellow-striped soccer shirt. What was it about touts that they could immediately pick your nationality? Which was further proof that Flynn was 100 percent Australian.

"We're not tourists," Flynn growled.

"Where are you going?" said the tout, in a heavy accent. "You want to see old town? I am licensed guide.

Take you to private homes, only I know. Only forty dollar US for whole day."

Flynn ignored him, his hand tightening on Tess's waist.

"What do you want to pay? Thirty? Cheapest in Harar. And best."

"Not interested."

"Tell you what. You are first customer of the day, so special price. Eighteen dollar. I make no money on that, no money."

"Lekek argeng," Tess snapped. *"Hid. Police etaralew."*

The guy held up his palms. "Okay, lady. *Chegerellem.* No problem. Be happy." He backed away, his eyes already seeking his next target.

"That worked," Flynn said, as they crossed a dirt path to a stone wall. "What did you say?"

"I think I told him to go away or I'd call the police. Amharic."

"I think he did, too. Know your way to this poet place from here?"

"If we keep walking uphill and hang to the right we'll come to the main market. It's not far from there." She glanced behind. No blue baseball caps or police uniforms.

As they navigated the rough cobblestone paths, Tess's tension ebbed and her muscles eased. It was a relief to be sheltered in the familiar narrow alleyways, between crumbling walls of mud and stone and brick, and doors of intricately carved wood or wrought metal. So many places to disappear.

"This doesn't feel like Africa," Flynn said as they passed the powdery-pink plastered facade of a tiny mosque. Its miniature domes, crenulations and towers were painted white, the whole effect like a marshmallow castle. "More like the Middle East. Or the Middle Ages."

"I don't know if it's comforting or scary to be in a town that's older than your entire nation—and by several centuries."

"Hey, France is pretty old."

"I meant your other nation."

He smiled. At some point, his questionable nationality had become a private joke. He hadn't acknowledged his lie about being French, but he was no longer defending it, either. Maybe because he was about to lose her.

She ran her hand along a wall, its indigo paintwork crumbling to dust under her fingers. If it weren't for the satellite dishes and cobwebbed power lines, they could have walked right into the Crusades.

"Makes our lives seem insignificant," she said.

"You're about to do something very significant. Not many people get that chance."

He pulled her aside to make room for a woman leading a donkey, its saddlebags stuffed with bamboo. The woman's hips swayed in time with the animal's.

"And your dossier," he said as they continued walking. "It's hidden somewhere in the citadel?"

"Flynn, it's better if you—"

"Yeah, yeah, need-to-know basis. Forgot about your paranoia."

They lapsed into silence as the twisting passages became busier—women with jangling bangles, their swirling bright dresses making Tess feel even more drab and dusty; men with foaming green mouths sitting on doorsteps chewing *chat*; an old man in white robes and a lacy skullcap picking his way through with a staff; kids sprinting around blind corners or dashing out from doorways, stopping before Tess and Flynn to yell *"farangi, farangi"* or "you! you! you!" or demand "whereyoufrom?" In clearer alleyways she caught glimpses of hazy blue mountains over roofs of rusted iron weighed down with rocks and bricks, and birds circling cobalt skies. Roasting coffee beans scented the air, cut in with charcoal and incense. Sweat trickled down her spine but she kept the jacket pulled tight.

Eyes met hers everywhere she looked. Maybe they were just wondering why Flynn was keeping such a tight grip on her, or why she stank so bad. *You're basically a walking rose petal.* Hardly. The best she could hope for was eau de baby wipes.

Eventually, they rounded a curved wall and emerged onto a wider path. To one side a man sat before a whirring antique Singer on a treadle table, concentrating on running up a seam, his leg a blur as he pumped the pedal. A dozen more tailors lined the passageway.

"Machine Alley," Tess said, relieved. They'd emerged farther north than she'd intended but she could pretty much smell her way to the market from here.

At the market, they navigated around sacks of spices in shades of red and orange and yellow. Women on tarpaulins and rugs shooed goats and children from pyramids of oranges and piles of garlic and onion and potatoes and toasted nuts and tomatoes and limes and withered herbs. A woman crushed tiny chilis into a bowl with the heels of her palms. Just the sight made Tess's eyes water. From a hole-in-the-wall drugstore a TV droned.

They stopped at a jumble of clothes piled on a tarp.

The fashion boutique. Tess dug through and found a long floral wrap skirt with pockets at the sides, a couple of T-shirts and a scarf. Flynn grabbed some clothes and two baseball caps. She left him haggling the price like a seasoned backpacker as she hobbled into an underwear stall in a tin shack.

After a few more purchases, the smell of toasting corn got the better of them and Flynn bought them a cob each, her first fresh meal in a week. She tossed the spent cob to a goat, but a young boy got to it first and sprinted away, loudly pursued by several other kids. She and Flynn washed down the corn with tiny cups of thick dark bitter coffee. She could almost feel the caffeine hitting her veins.

As they pushed back out to Machine Alley, Flynn's hand brushed the small of her back. He stooped and pulled a battered Lonely Planet guide to Ethiopia out of a pile of dusty books.

"Good idea," she said. "We'll go from aid workers to tourists."

"Ten years old but it's an old city, right? Things wouldn't change quickly."

A few lanes uphill, the Rimbaud museum could have been in another city, another continent. Always the way with Africa—manic one minute, tranquil the next. The alleyway was deserted except for a man pushing a tire in a squeaky wheelbarrow, speaking loudly on a mobile phone. He didn't look up. Behind a whitewashed wall a baby cried out—or maybe a goat.

"Is this it?" Flynn said, as they walked under an archway into a dirt courtyard. To one side, an elegant two-story building towered, its upper floor all stained-glass windows of green, mustard, blue and burgundy, carved wood panels and latticework. As they gazed up, a woman threw open a pair of shutters. A shard of sunlight glinted off a window into Tess's eyes. She closed them tight until the pinch of pain passed.

"Tess?"

"My eyes are freaking out. Too much light. Yes, this is it."

A creak and bang echoed out as the woman moved on to the next shutters.

"We're early. Let's go in before anyone sees us." He caught her waist and guided her to a set of stone steps leading up to the veranda, as naturally as if they'd been a couple for years. "This is good. Hamid won't expect us to be sightseeing."

"Still, I don't want to hang around here long. If your guys don't come soon, I'm going, drugs or not."

"They won't be far off—and they'll have a solid evac plan to get me out. You might want to hear it before you go charging off."

"I'm good with my plan."

"Give them half an hour."

"Ten minutes."

"Fifteen."

"Fine." She lifted her plastic shopping bag. "First, I'm finding the ladies' room."

They paid the entry fee with their stolen birr, the banknotes so worn and soft they could have been cloth, and nodded their way through the manager's introduction. Tess's bladder stung now that relief was nearby. If the woman noted their disheveled appearance she didn't let on.

In the bathroom, Tess cleaned up as best she could, flushing wads of blood-and dust-colored toilet paper.

Soap, running water, a toilet, toothpaste—what outrageous luxuries. She changed into a T-shirt and the skirt, and stuffed her old clothes and boots in the plastic bag. She ripped the scarf into strips and wound them around her toes. It'd do until she saw the medic. The pain was shooting up to her knees.

She ripped the tag off a pair of flip-flops and eased them on, wincing. If she could superglue a sole onto her skin she would.

Even clean, the face staring out of the mirror looked like a badly Photoshopped version of herself, with wrinkles and purple smudges encircling bloodshot eyes. Her skin looked thin and the dull yellow of a sepia photo— where it wasn't grazed or bruised. There was even a fetching red scrape on the tip of her nose. Broken capillaries spiderwebbed across her cheeks. She ran a finger over a protruding cheekbone. Her teeth looked too big for her shrunken face. She shuddered. It was like looking at her own death mask. How could Flynn have wanted to kiss that?

A knock on the door. She started.

"Tess? You okay in there?"

"Coming."

She pulled on her new cap and tucked her hair into it. Ugh, too severe, like a skeleton wearing a hat. She pulled out a couple of tendrils and finger-curled the strands, but they hung limp and greasy. Who was she kidding? She pushed them back in, sighing, and dumped the plastic bag in the trash.

Flynn was waiting outside the door, leaning back on a sage-painted wall, the color echoed in his eyes. His crossed arms made his muscles bulge from the sleeve of a black Nirvana T-shirt, the sunglasses slung from its neckline. Charcoal chinos pulled tight across his thighs. A bolt of attraction hit her in the chest.

She swore. She looked like she'd been dead three days and he looked like a rock star.

"What's wrong?"

"Nothing. I think you got a size too small."

He tilted his head, the beginnings of a smile on his lips. "I've never seen you clean before."

"Wow, you know how to pour on the compliments."

He pushed off the wall, tugging his black cap lower. "Told you, I don't give compliments." He offered his elbow. Without thinking, she wrapped her fingers around his arm, the hair-roughened muscle somehow reminding her of their…episode…in the wasteland. It seemed like weeks ago.

"So, what now?" she said.

"We pretend to give a crap about poetry? We're gonna look strange if we stare out the window the whole time. Come on. How bad can this stuff be?"

They circled the ground floor, her flip-flops slapping on tiles. From outside came the *tap-tap-tap* of a ball being bounced, happy shouts, laughter. Basketball. The normality of it made her want to laugh.

"Come on. I'll show you something cool." She tugged Flynn to the circular central atrium and pointed out the pale-pink-and-mint fresco ceiling.

"Just when you think you have Africa figured out," he said.

"I don't think you ever figure out Africa. The more you learn and see, the more confused you get."

"True that. Bit like the Middle East. Or America."

He held her gaze a beat too long. She broke it and studied a patched black-and-white photo of the poet as a boy. If only they *were* tourists. They could run away and spend the next ten years backpacking through Africa until the world forgot them. Wow, how was it she could totally picture a future with a guy she knew nothing about? Maybe it was that blank slate—she could fill it with whatever she liked.

A few visitors lingered, speaking in a museum hush. She made a point of not meeting their eyes. Flynn stopped beside an information panel.

"'*Le dormeur du val,*'" he read.

Really? Flynn speaking French, just as she was fantasizing about running off with him? "What does that mean?" Damn her squeaky voice.

"'The Sleeper in the Valley.' It's a poem. Wish I was asleep in a valley right now."

A woman approached, her arms linked behind her back. Tess tucked into Flynn's side. He smelled of soap but a trace remained of the gravelly scent that seemed to belong just to him. "Read it to me."

"Seriously?" he said quietly. "You want me to read you poetry? Like saving your life ten times wasn't enough?"

She looked at him through lowered eyelashes and faked a sweet smile.

"I know you too well to fall for that." But he began to read. Not in the rough, hurried voice she'd expected, but slowly and hushed. Behind her, the woman stopped. Eavesdropping, and why not? As if this week could get any more surreal, Tess was being serenaded by French poetry. As his words trickled over her, *into* her, she dropped her head and closed her eyes, the lip of her cap shielding her face. For all she knew, he could be reading terms and conditions for a plumbing contract, but she ordered her mind to quiet and let his deep voice brush over her, catching at those throaty *R*s, rising with the inflections. *Take me now, Lieutenant.* She caught a few familiar words: *rivière, soldat jeune.* He trailed off on the last word: *tranquille.*

She opened her eyes and cleared her throat. "Something about a young soldier and a river?"

"Yeah. He's sleeping beside it, smiling. The sunlight is...kind of raining on him, but he's cold." He bent slightly as he reached the bottom of the panel. "There's one more line." He read the few words aloud. She picked out *"deux"* and *"rouge."*

"Two red...?"

"Holes. In his side." He tapped his heart, twice. "So I don't wish I was sleeping in *that* valley." He studied the poem, his smile lost somewhere between sad and sardonic. "No one can ever be happy in poetry, right? It's a rule or something."

The woman padded out, leaving them alone. Tess liked that he didn't shrug her off. The reprieve from danger settled into her veins like an anesthetic, like that glorious moment after being ill when you realize you're well again, and vow you'll never again take health for granted. Flynn kept reading, silently. This could be the nearest they had come to normality. Was this the real Flynn behind the gruff facade: funny, charming, even... tender? Damn, she had it bad.

"He wrote it when he was sixteen."

"Bit morbid for a teenager."

"Aren't they the most morbid of anyone?" With his free hand, Flynn pointed. "The date says 1870. France would have been at war with Prussia. Some kids grow up too fast."

She pictured the cigarette burns on Flynn's stomach. "Like you."

His biceps tightened. "Here's another poem." He stepped clear of her. Her heart thunked. As if he'd heard it and felt bad, he looked back, grabbed her hand and pulled her to the next board, though the set of his jaw confirmed he was ignoring her comment. "He writes about wanting to hide from the world, block out the monsters and wolves."

"I can so relate."

"No kidding. I'm guessing he's a little older because he's fantasizing about kissing a woman's neck like a crazed spider running all over her." He hitched an eyebrow. "Is that what it feels like for you?"

"No." She let out an awkward giggle even a tween would be embarrassed about. Kissing Flynn felt way better than that. Man, she'd like to have his lips exploring her neck—and everywhere else. "Keep reading," she said throatily.

He studied her with that half smile for so long she had to kill the urge to squirm. When would his unit turn up? Did she want them to hurry or take their time?

"So she orders him to find the spider, and he says it's gonna take a long time because he's gonna have to chase that thing to a lot of places before he catches it."

"Cute."

"I don't think *cute* was what he was aiming for."

They laughed. Yep, actually laughed—quiet, but genuine and soul soaring. His gaze dropped down her body, as if he expected to see a spider crawling under her T-shirt. She shivered. At the thought of a spider, or him chasing it?

Unhurried footsteps tapped and squeaked toward

them. A local guide, relating the history of the house in English to two couples, rolling his *R*s like butterflies had invaded his mouth. One of the tourists replied in an American accent. Tess stiffened. Flynn leaned in, pulling her close so his shoulder hid her face.

"What's wrong?" he whispered. "Don't like spiders?"

Her grin pulled her skin taut. She should have bought moisturizer. As the group strolled around, she let her head fall onto his shoulder, further obscuring their view. Just two lovers having a moment. He slid a hand around her waist, dug under her T-shirt and flicked his fingernails over her skin. She flinched, shrieking.

He shushed her, laughing. "I'd like to be that spider, if that woman was you."

Oh, and I'd like you to be the guy chasing it. She slipped her arm around his torso and nipped him, regretting her stubby fingernails and his impenetrable muscles.

"Hey!"

"Some spiders bite."

He glanced behind them and kissed the crown of her baseball cap, winding both arms around her. It was nice, this pretense. This would be the end of their journey together, whether he accepted it or not. Was that why he seemed liberated from the bitterness he carried like a burden—because he was about to disappear back into his macho comfort zone? This was their happy ending.

Might as well make the most of it. She buried her face in his collarbone, her cheek brushing the soft new cotton of his T-shirt. Taking advantage—and why not? Her cap flicked off and he caught it. He pulled them chest to chest, one hand cradling her head. They fit

like they'd come in a pair. She felt like she was floating off the floor.

"Must be some good poetry," a man drawled, in a
Southern US accent.

"Oh, eet eez," Flynn replied, looking over Tess's
shoulder. *"Très bon. Très romantique."*

Melt.

"Ah, enjoy it, enjoy it while you can," the guy called
back, his voice and footfalls receding as the guide's
commentary faded toward the staircase. "It all passes
so quick. Just make sure you never ruin it by having
children. Right, honey?"

A woman laughed. The stairs squeaked under the
man's heavy tread.

"We definitely won't be doing that," said Flynn,
still speaking in a French accent. He lowered his voice.
"Right, *honey*?"

He pulled back far enough to tip up her chin. Her
face warmed. Having their bodies flush together was
one thing. Having their faces so close she could feel the
heat of his was another. He pinned his focus on her, like
he was imagining all the things he *would* like them to
be doing. Or maybe that was just her.

Her peripheral vision registered the last of the
group—a woman—studying a poem, in no hurry to
catch up. Flynn lowered his head and nibbled the side
of Tess's neck. A joke, of course, but desire zinged right
down to her mangled toes. How good would it be to take
him to Samira's, block out the monsters and wolves and
travel all over him?

Lucky it'd never happen. *What goes on in the mind
stays in the mind.* But, man, she ached to feel his lips
on hers one last time.

Hell, why not? She shot a glance around the room. The woman leaned forward, engrossed in a display. Flynn relinquished Tess's neck and looked left and right. Checking the room, too. Her stomach flipped. For the same reason?

"You know," he said, his eyes drilling into hers, "you're an incredible woman. I'll look forward to seeing that pretty face on TV, bringing those bastards down."

He leaned in, focusing on her mouth. *Yes. Finally.* His warm breath tickled her cheek. She angled up, meeting him halfway, and their lips touched. He groaned, threading his fingers through her hair as he hardened the kiss. She closed her eyes and sank her hands into his waist, let herself melt into him, let down all the barriers, let the tension wash away. No games, no tricks. This thing between them was real. Temporary, yes—even bittersweet—but real. She could kiss him for hours, lose herself in the warmth that cloaked her. Safe. Adored. Wanted. It didn't get better.

He froze and jerked away. She stumbled backward, the room swirling in and out of focus. Crap—he'd drawn his gun. His gaze fixed on the doorway leading to the foyer.

Her pulse pummeled. "What is it?"

He held the pistol down, arms locked straight. "When I say run, run," he whispered. "Downstairs and out. Go straight to your friend's house. I'll hold them off."

Her cheeks went cold. "Them?"

"We're being stalked. Run!"

CHAPTER SEVENTEEN

TESS BOLTED THROUGH the doorway, her brain registering a blur of movement. Several men. Big men. Security contractors? Oh God. Pain shot through her feet.
Footsteps sprinted after her.

"Stop!" The voice was right behind, heavily accented, calm, commanding. Shouts echoed through
the building, their meaning not registering. Another
language.

She upped her pace. Her flip-flop slid out and she
slipped sideways. Strong hands closed on her arms from
behind, pinning them to her sides and lifting her clean
off the floor, leaving her legs kicking air.

"We're not going to hurt you."

Her attacker wrapped one arm around her torso and
caught her thighs with the other. She bucked but he
held firm. He had to be three times her size. Shit. He
wheeled, spinning her with him. Three men restrained
Flynn from behind—one with a headlock, the others
capturing an arm each. His gun was on the floor. Her
mouth dried. She'd dropped her guard, with the end in
sight. They were screwed.

One of Flynn's captors laughed and said something
she couldn't make out. They released him, throwing
him forward so he had to stagger to retain his balance.

Tess kicked out but the behemoth tightened his grip.

Flynn bent double and rested his hands on his knees. He spit out a few breathless words, in French. The other men laughed. One slapped his back.

Huh?

Tess's assailant let her go. She spun to face him, sizing up her options, her chest heaving. He held up his palms as if to calm her. Like hell. Options? Was she dreaming? With injured feet she couldn't outrun him—hell, even with her regular feet she'd be no match. Screwed, screwed and more screwed.

"Flynn, perhaps you could reassure your friend," the guy said, expressionless, in an accent that could be Eastern European.

Flynn? He knew Flynn's name?

"Tess, stand down," said Flynn, straightening. "This is my unit. *Gorilles attardés*, the lot of them, but we're safe."

A man with a thick brown beard let out a long, low whistle, imitating the swooping squeal of a falling bomb. Did Flynn just call them gorillas? She swallowed, looking from one man to the next. They were overgrown and muscular, dressed in T-shirts, shorts or jeans, sunglasses, baseball caps, a beret. One wore glasses with heavy black frames; a few carried dusty backpacks. These were French Foreign Legion commandos? They looked like the Giants' defensive line gone hipster.

The woman who'd been in the poetry room scurried past, giving the men a wide arc.

"Morning, ma'am," said the bearded guy. "Just playin' a little joke on our friend here. Nothin' to worry about."

"You could have used the signal," Flynn said. "I thought you were—"

"You lowered your guard," said the behemoth, glancing from Flynn to Tess, his eyes narrowing. She felt herself blush, goddammit. "I told them to test you. You failed."

"Good to see you, too, Angelito." Flynn surveyed his friends, one by one. "I note it took three of you to bring me down."

Angelito—the guy he said she could trust. Flynn's *capitaine*, right? Her neck cracked as she looked up at him. Well, thank God he was on their side—he was like Lurch but handsome. Like Flynn, he had a few days' growth on his strong jaw, but was darker in coloring. Two gray-green amulets hung from leather cords around his neck—one small and smooth, the other large and rough.

"Only a precaution," said the guy wearing glasses, in a thick accent. Scottish? "Any fewer than that and you might have injured yourself, princess."

Angelito sent a tall Scandinavian-looking guy out to watch the doors, and spoke to Flynn in rapid French.

"Nothing that a bit of fancy stitching can't fix," Flynn replied, pulling off his cap. Fresh blood was trickling into the ruby-colored clumps matting his hair. The Scot stepped forward. As Flynn bent his head for inspection, the guy spoke in French.

"Speak English, guys," said Flynn, glancing at Tess. "Enemy is looking for a French soldier." He frowned. "Where's Okoye?"

"Back at our ride," the bearded hipster drawled. Now, that was a familiar accent. Texan?

"And Levanne?" Flynn's voice caught.

All eyes trained on Angelito. He gave a grim shake of the head.

"Dead?" Flynn said quietly.

Angelito gave the slightest of nods, his expression inscrutable.

Flynn linked his hands behind his head, then flinched and jerked them away. He stared at the smear of crimson on his palms and swore. His nostrils flared as he fought to keep his battle inside. Tess gulped, her eyes watering. The guy he'd told her about, who'd been injured in the ambush?

The Scot gripped Flynn's shoulder. "I'm sorry, mate. He didn't give up easily, but there was nothing any of us could do. Nothing you could have done."

Flynn spun, facing away. *"Putain de merde,"* he said with quiet fury, his neck muscles cording. Angelito and the Scot exchanged a tight-lipped look.

God. She ached to go to Flynn, thread her arms around his back and hold on. But she knew guys. He wouldn't want that, not in front of his buddies. He'd want to zip up the anger and pain, for now. Later, maybe, when they were alone, she could offer him a refuge to grieve.

No. There wouldn't be a later.

The Scot fixed a blue-eyed, black-framed gaze on her. "So you're Tess Newell."

"I am." She paused, waiting for him to offer his name. The silence stretched out. "And you are?"

"Your hero and savior," he said, the rolled *R*s making the words twice as long.

"I'm thinking Flynn's already taken that job," said the hipster. Unmistakably Texan. A Latino Texan in the Foreign Legion? That had to be a good story.

"I'd say you're right," said the Scot, still focused on her. "You can call me 'Doc.' And this here's Grumpy."

He pointed to the Texan. She got it—Doc was deflecting the attention from Flynn, giving him a chance to recover. "You've already met Lieutenant Grumpy. And that guy next to him? That's Captain Grumpy."

"Watch it, Doc," Angelito growled, without a flicker of humor.

"Don't mind him. The *capitaine* here is about a century behind on popular culture. We haven't started him on Disney films yet."

Despite Doc's attempt at levity, the atmosphere was charged with tension. They were all grieving, all hiding it. There was a guy missing, a space where there should be a person. They were relieved to see Flynn, no doubt, but with none of the hoo-ah bromancing of her brothers and their buddies.

"Tess needs attention, Doc," said Flynn, turning. His eyes were rimmed with red, but his voice was certain. He met her gaze and she gave a grim smile, hoping it communicated sympathy. "Al-Thawra ripped out her toenails."

Wincing, the Scot dropped his gaze to her feet. So he was the medic? Relatively young and definitely hot. Damn.

"Flynn's head takes precedence," she said, pulling her hair back and knotting it. What had happened to her cap?

Doc nodded curtly. "I'll do my prettiest seam. How the hell did the two of you get away from al-Thawra?"

Flynn stooped to collect his pistol, stepped in beside Angelito as if assuming his natural position and gave a brief, whispered rundown—playing down his heroics. "Did you see militia or contractors on the way in?" he asked, as he finished.

"Many," Angelito replied. "Roadblocks in and out of Jijiga and into Harar. A few likelies around here, too. Good thing we ditched our SUV in Hargeisa and got a civilian van."

"We're gay backpackers," said Doc. "Here on a pilgrimage for the poetry."

"You guys would have to be the world's least likely poetry buffs."

All four pairs of eyes trained down on her, none but Doc's looking even close to friendly. Outsiders not welcome, evidently. She straightened, fighting the urge to shrink. Flynn was with his pack now, back with his alpha.

"Gonna be tough to get her out past all that muscle," said the Texan. "Airlift?"

"You don't need to get me out. I'm stay—"

"You want to draw an RPG-sized target on the chopper, Texas?" Flynn said, as if Tess hadn't spoken.

Texas. Original.

Angelito glanced at Flynn. "A US Army chopper was shot at this morning, along the Ethiopia-Somalia border. They recovered. Airlift's still our best bet but we'd have to be careful. Keep away from urban areas."

Flynn frowned. "What was an American helo doing over there? Looking for Tess?"

Angelito shrugged. "There's been a lot of movement in the last twenty-four hours. We have no official orders yet but the US are in talks with our brass, and my bet is that they're gearing up for something. That's what the media's saying, too." He glanced at Tess, as if holding her responsible.

She pressed her lips together. Gearing up for a strike on Somalia?

"So we get outta town by road and catch the helo on the outskirts, somewhere defensible," said the Texan.

"Possibly," said Angelito, assessing her with a dark stare. Yes—that was what this felt like: an assessment. "Standing orders are to deliver her to the US Navy at Lemonnier, should we find her."

Her breath caught. "Your bosses know I'm here? That we escaped al-Thawra?"

"Only immediate chain of command know we're in Harar. We're on black ops. Our mission was to find Flynn and they figured you'd be with him. Obviously we haven't had a chance to confirm that."

"Well, don't," she said.

Angelito glanced at Flynn. "Your photo's everywhere, *Lieutenant*—the one al-Thawra took."

Flynn threw his head back as if in pain. *"Putain."*

"So far, no one's ID'd you," added Angelito. "You looked like a sixty-year-old *clochard*."

"Thanks, man."

"As far as anyone knows, you're regular French. No one outside the company knows it's you." He returned his focus to Tess. All other gazes followed. "Except her."

"Hey, even if I wanted to spill his secrets, I have no idea who he is or what those secrets are. I don't even know his last name."

Flynn looked at her as if she'd said she didn't know the world was round. What was that about?

"Mademoiselle, I know of a navy SEAL unit looking for you," said Angelito. "I can get a message to them, if you—"

"No! You can't tell anyone I'm here. No one."

He frowned.

"In fact, you didn't see me, you didn't find me. You only found Flynn. Take him out of here and tell the US I died. Blown apart in a minefield—not even a fingernail left."

Angelito looked at Flynn as if to say, *What is she on?*

Flynn shrugged. "Can I have a minute with her?"

The *capitaine*'s gaze flicked to the entrance, where an Ethiopian couple were entering, hand in hand. "Only one. We've wasted enough time." He ordered the other men to step away.

Flynn steered her toward the staircase, his hand gripping her biceps. "Get your dossier and come with us. I can figure out a way to keep it on the down low, keep you away from the US authorities, if that's what you want."

"You heard them—I leave town, I'm toast. You will be, too, if we remain together."

"Not with these guys on our side." He'd leaned in so their foreheads nearly touched, his voice dropping so low she had to freeze to ensure she caught every word. "Tess, I've just lost one of my best mates—and I don't have many mates. Right now I want to keep the few people I give a shit about where I can see them."

She dropped her gaze to his Adam's apple as it moved up and down. He was including her in that— the people he gave a shit about. And, sure, she'd rather stay within sight of him, but she couldn't. "I'm not putting anyone else on the firing line—I don't care how good they are at defending themselves. I'll do what I need to do right here in Harar. You can walk away. No one knows who you are. Hamid doesn't know who you are. Hell, I don't know who you are."

"As long as you're with us you're safe, Tess."

"No, I'm not and neither are you. If al-Thawra wanted one French soldier for their snuff movies, they wouldn't think twice about mowing down an entire unit. And I'm not going to risk your bosses handing me to the US— or risk you or your friends getting in trouble for hiding me." She touched his bristly cheek. "Get rid of this and no one will connect you to the guy in the photo." She flattened her palm, suddenly reluctant to lose contact. "Go. Get word out that I'm dead—that's the best way to help me. I'll feel better if I know you're safe."

"That goes both ways."

Near the door, Angelito cleared his throat, pointedly. She snatched her hand away.

"You're coming with us long enough for Doc to get a look at you," Flynn said.

Angelito eyed them grimly, like he was Flynn's older brother and she was a corrupting influence. Flynn had to be stalling, holding the medic card over her as a delaying tactic. Well, hell, temporarily hanging with five guys who were brawny, presumably armed and on her side—or, at least, not shooting at her—would make a comfortable change. As would drugs. Her burning feet made the deciding vote.

"Fine," she said, shaking her arm free.

"And don't ask questions of these guys," he hissed. "Especially not Angelito."

"Why," she said, forcing a cheeky grin, though she didn't feel much like teasing. "What's he got to hide?"

"I don't know—I never asked," he said, too quickly.

"See, now you've got me interested."

"No questions, Tess. I mean it."

"I'm joking. I have no interest in your secret fraternity." *Liar.*

He laid a hand on her lower back, the light pressure urging her to start walking. As they passed Angelito, he held out her cap, casting a loaded glance at Flynn. Those two shared more meaningful looks than lovers in a silent movie. Had Flynn crossed some line? Flynn muttered in French. It sounded dismissive, like he was denying something.

Angelito followed. "You know where the Shoa Gate is?"

"I know it," she said. "That's where we're headed?"

"Yes. If we get separated, look for a white van with a green stripe. But don't lead any likelies to it. Flynn, you walk ahead with Doc. Nice and slow, like tourists. Stick to the alleyways. Texas and Thor will bring up the rear." *Thor.* The Scandinavian. Why, of course... "I'll take the woman."

Angelito looked sideways at Tess, as if she were the threat. Trust issues for, well, Africa.

FLYNN JOGGED DOWN the museum's front steps beside Doc, easing his cap back on. He felt ten kilos lighter and fifteen kilos heavier. Having his unit at his six was like being back in familiar surroundings. But Levanne... He swore softly.

"You did what you could for him, Flynn."

"I got nutted on the skull. I didn't even see it coming. What happened after that?"

"Chaos. They backed up a truck and chucked you on it. We got a couple of their guys, but it wasn't enough. The others gave chase while I worked on Levanne but we lost them. And him." He shook his head, his jaw clamped shut. Calling time on the *sergent* must have cut him up. "When the *capitaine* got that message from you this morning… *Merde.* He practically did a backward triple somersault."

"Sure he did."

"I'm serious. We're gonna sign him up for Cirque du Soleil when he retires next month."

"You're full of crap." Angelito would have raised one eyebrow, tops. "Mate, losing a guy on his last mission—that must have hurt."

"At least he didn't lose two. That'd destroy him."

Flynn bowed his head. Angelito was about to go off the grid, try a regular family life. If he took that kind of baggage along he'd never get the peace he deserved.

"So what's the story with you and the girl?" Doc said. If he was trying to lighten things up, he'd chosen the wrong topic.

"No story."

"Sure looked like a story. She's pretty."

Pretty didn't begin to do her justice. "She's not my type."

"Too right—she has far too much class."

"Don't I know it, Doc."

Sometimes it was best to take the razzing. He sure as hell deserved it. Jesus, the mental image of chasing that spider down Tess's neck and into her cleavage and beyond… Temptation had almost overridden his instinct for danger.

He let Doc navigate. The alleyways were getting busier as the sun got higher—zombified men swaying to some *chat* beat only they could hear, kids begging for "Bic" or "baksheesh" or "youtakephoto," women plowing through with blackened teapots or baskets of live chickens on their heads, donkeys and goats and dogs and cats and every other bloody thing.

Being confined by endless curving stone walls was making him antsy, like being stuck in a maze. Just people getting on with their simple lives but he couldn't shake the feeling of being watched. He kept a hand close to his weapon. Despite the reinforcements, his stomach twitched like it was filled with click bugs. He had to talk Tess into evacuating with them. No way would he leave her here unguarded. What if her report didn't show up on TV? Better to be under fire than waiting for word on a buddy who was.

When had he ended up caring about her? He'd spent a lifetime watching out for no one but himself and, in recent years, his unit. He was no hero, just a regular coward who was usually good enough at surviving to pull the guys around him out of the crap at the same time. If he got credit for that, it was misguided. So why wasn't his survival instinct kicking in to get him safely away from Tess?

At last, they squeezed through a crowd at a stone arch that looked like a mini Moorish castle and picked their way around a market sprawling onto a road. The van was parked at the edge of the chaos. The headlights flashed—Okoye, in the driver's seat, indicating it was safe to approach. Texas hung back by the gate, pretending he was taking a photo on his phone, and Thor wandered over to a woman cooking on a charcoal stove.

Forget it, Flynn. She doesn't even know your name and it has to stay that way.

Flynn and Doc crossed the street, avoiding a whining flock of *bajajes*. Doc made out he was watching traffic but he was checking for threats, as they all were.

Doc opened the van's rear door and tipped his head. "After you."

The back of the vehicle was an empty metal shell. Flynn climbed in and took off the backpack. Through fly-spotted net curtains, he watched Angelito stroll out of the gate with Tess, her cap drawn low, sunglasses on, walking slowly to disguise her hobble. Next to the *capitaine* she looked like a child, which was probably a good thing. He caught a whiff of mold and piss.

"Where'd you get this piece of crap?"

"A Somali in Hargeisa, after we sent a *caporal* back to Monclar with our SUV and rifles," replied Okoye from the front seat, in his Nigerian accent. "But, *mon ami*, you are not in a state to judge anything on its appearance."

Flynn scratched his chin. "True that."

"Let's get you cleaned up," said Doc, tossing his fake glasses and hauling his medical kit from a rucksack.

"Sort her out first," Flynn said, nodding at Tess, who was being ushered across the road. "She won't let on but she's in a lot of pain."

As Tess and Angelito neared, Doc pushed open the rear door. She clambered inside, taking off her sunglasses, her gaze darting between the men. Too many people knowing her business—that was what she'd be thinking.

Angelito leaned in. "Flynn. Shave off that beard. I don't want you recognized."

Doc pulled an electric shaver from his bag. Flynn met Angelito's gaze, a question in his eyes. The *capitaine* knew he hadn't been clean shaven since the day he saw the old man staring back from the mirror. His father had always been closely shaved, probably to make him look more boyish and less psycho killer.

"If al-Thawra recognizes you we're all in danger,"

Angelito said. "There's nothing we can do about your hair—or that crevasse in your skull—but getting rid of the fuzz will help."

And if she recognizes me, I'm screwed.

"C'est un ordre, Lieutenant," Angelito added.

An order. Flynn sensed Tess's eyes on him. He could almost hear her curiosity radar bleeping.

"Pour sa sécurité."

For her security. Right.

"Pour leur sécurité." Angelito nodded to Doc and Okoye.

Screw it. Angelito was right, as always. The risk of Tess recognizing him wasn't their biggest problem.

"And then, *il faut qu'on parle.*"

Angelito shut the door and leaned back on it. He took something out of his jacket pocket—an orange—and started peeling it. Damn. Last thing Flynn needed was a "talk" with Angelito. The air crackled and a call to prayer wailed from a mosque's loudspeakers nearby, echoed within the minute by several others across the citadel. Men began standing up, pushing off walls, moving off.

Flynn snatched the shaver from Doc and switched it on. Maybe he'd get lucky and she wouldn't recognize him. Shame he didn't believe in luck.

CHAPTER EIGHTEEN

"BETTER YOU EARN his wrath than me," Doc mumbled, jerking his head to Angelito's tense frame. "Here, these might help—with the pain *and* the interrogation." He popped a couple of capsules from a pill tray, dropped them in Flynn's palm and swiveled to face Tess. "Now, my lady, let's take a look at those toes."

As Doc got to work, Tess trained her gaze on Flynn. He figured she just wanted to look anywhere except her feet, but it felt like she was waiting for the exposé. With no mirror, he shaved on feel, taking off the bulk of it first.

Okoye rummaged around in the front and chucked Flynn a pink plastic bag. "You're messing up my van," he said in French, stabbing a finger toward the fallen hair.

I'm messing up my life.

They fell silent as the shaver buzzed. Flynn paused to coax a window open. Was the expression on Tess's face changing? A narrowing of her eyes, a tilting of her head...

Paranoid, much?

"How's that?" he said, running his hand down a cheek he hadn't felt for years.

She touched her chin. "A patch there."

He found it and buzzed it off. A warm breeze brushed

his jaw. The skin prickled, like it'd forgotten what wind felt like.

"That's got it," she said hoarsely, her forehead still lined. She flinched and turned her focus back to Doc.

"Hang in there, *mademoiselle*. I'll be finished soon."

Flynn wiped down the shaver and tossed it on Doc's bag. Better to get the inevitable grilling from his CO than sit here watching the dots connect in Tess's brain. Then the disgust would set in, like it had all those years ago with the last girl he'd attempted to have more than a fling with, before Katie. She'd actually vomited, and when he'd tried to help her she'd screamed like he was murdering her.

Avoiding Tess's eye, he let himself out and leaned on the bumper. Angelito handed him half the orange. Inside, Doc's lilting voice murmured.

"You caused a minor diplomatic incident back there at the border," the *capitaine* said quietly. "The Djibouti Air Force is scrambling to find out what the Australian Army's up to in Ethiopia."

Flynn broke off a wedge and popped it in his mouth. The sweetness exploded on his tongue, creating ten times more saliva than it warranted. "I hope no one explained."

"The colonel at Monclar denied any knowledge but he immediately contacted me. A lone Australian soldier suddenly popping up? Had to be you." He threw the orange peel to a scattering of skinny goats guarded by an equally skinny girl. "You're damn lucky."

"You don't know the half of it. There were a couple of aid workers got shot by *shiftas*. One of them died, but have you heard anything about the other guy?"

"Being operated on. Word is this mysterious Australian soldier saved his life, so I guess he's gonna be okay. Does your new friend speak French?"

"Non."

"Can she be trusted?" Angelito switched to French.

Ah, mate. A conversation Angelito didn't want Tess to understand wasn't a conversation Flynn wanted right now. Still, he continued in French. "In what sense?"

"You know what I mean."

"She's a journalist—I wouldn't go confessing your secrets."

Angelito shot him a dark look—at least Flynn figured it was dark, beneath his aviators. The two of them probably had more to hide than the rest of their unit put together. "I hope you've been watching your tongue. A woman like that…a journalist… She could be dangerous for you."

"Like she said, she doesn't know my full name—not even the fake one. Stop looking at me like that, *mon Capitaine*. I'm not an idiot."

"I wasn't so sure, back at the Rimbaud house."

"We were putting it on, for the tourists."

"The tourists weren't watching."

Flynn focused on the last wedge of orange in his hand. Busted. He put it in his mouth.

"She could be a risk to all of us," Angelito continued.

Across the road, Texas was fending off a toothless old woman who was evidently angling for him to take a selfie with her—for baksheesh, no doubt. Thor was eating a samosa, his arctic stare enough to deter the most shameless of hustlers.

"Believe me, I know the risk," said Flynn, chewing.

Aside from Angelito's history, he didn't know the stories of the guys in his unit and they didn't know his, but he could assume there wasn't a single picket fence among them. Like him, most went by false names, which told him all he needed to know about their reasons for enlisting.

And the *capitaine* had even more to hide now, with an American girlfriend whose history was none too spotless, from what Flynn could tell. He didn't know what subterfuge Angelito had used to get her a French visa, but he gathered Holly had secrets she'd rather keep that way. Which made her as perfect for Angelito as Tess was wrong for Flynn.

"I'm telling you straight, as your...friend," Angelito said eventually. "I understand the attraction, but she's famous. You don't want that attention."

Friend. Was that a first? "And I'm telling you straight—I'm not involved and I'm not getting involved."

Angelito eyed him a long while. Was it a lie? Even he didn't know.

"You're involved," Angelito said. "Don't get caught out. Things can happen quickly in a situation like this."

You're telling me. "It's nothing I can't handle."

"You want to take her with us."

"Can we do it without handing her to the US?"

"Those are my orders."

"That could endanger her life." Mate, he'd really bought into her conspiracy theories. "I kind of promised her."

"You know better. Would coming with us be more of a risk than al-Thawra recapturing her?"

Flynn crossed his arms. "As far as I can tell, she has good reason to believe that people close to the US government want her dead. She's doing this big investigation. It's not my story to tell but I'd…like to see it get out."

"Why not leave her here, like she wants?"

Flynn gritted his teeth. "I'm not walking away."

"From her story or from her?"

Flynn stared at a guy carrying a swaying stack of twenty pillows on his shoulders. Who the hell knew? For the hundredth time that day he went to shove his fingers through his hair, pulling up as he touched his cap. Even that pelted pain into his skull. He hadn't realized it was such a habit. Those painkillers weren't doing shit—or maybe Doc had given him happy pills. Either way, not working.

"She needs protecting, that's all," he said.

Angelito's silence told him everything. "You should know," he said, eventually, "I've recommended you for promotion."

"For your job?"

"The *commandant* has started the paperwork. I figured it's what you wanted."

Too bloody right. The legion was all he had, and a promotion to *capitaine* would take him one big step further from his past. "Better than answering to some arse-licking French officer-school graduate."

"It's a done deal, Flynn, unless you do something to screw it up."

Like get your past splashed through the media. "Noted." As if he didn't already have enough to lose from his kamikaze liaison with Tess. It was rare for a foreigner to become an officer, let alone a *chef de section.* "When would we evac, and how? Tess has something she needs to collect from somewhere in the citadel—it's important, for her story."

A pause. The guy with the pillows tossed them on the dirt beside a row of gaudy foam mattresses, like the one Flynn had shared with Tess.

"Will that take long?"

Flynn inhaled. Angelito was accepting the change in subject, for now. "I don't think so. It'll probably take longer for me to talk her into leaving with us."

"We can leave as soon as she has what she needs, if she wants to come. We can hide her or disguise her." Angelito pushed off the back of the truck. "No one in command would need to know she's with us. It stays in the unit. I'll wear the consequences."

Flynn gave a sharp nod, the tension dropping from his shoulders. Big call for a guy about to take an honorable discharge. "And if al-Thawra found her on our way out?"

"The roadblock we passed through was manned by five soldiers. We'd need to neutralize them before alarms are raised, but it'd be a fair fight."

Flynn cricked his neck. "Not for them."

DAMN, TESS WISHED she spoke French—though she didn't need an interpreter to pick up on the tension in Flynn's tone, humming through the side of the van. Or figure out what Angelito had meant by *femme dangereuse*. Flynn had used the words *journaliste* and *secrets*, so they probably weren't discussing Hamid.

Heck, eavesdropping wouldn't get her anywhere but paranoid—and she was over being paranoid. Better to dig information on Flynn's history out of Doc while she had the chance. Purely for curiosity's sake.

"So you're Scottish?" she said.

He snipped a length of gauze. "Japanese."

"Really."

"I know—crazy, right?"

"So Flynn's Australian and you're…Japanese…and your mate is from Texas and you talk to each other in French?"

"No, ma'am," he said, wrapping the gauze around a newly disinfected toe. "We're all Japanese and we talk to each other in Sasquatch."

She sighed. "Are you all like this?"

"Is who all like what?"

"Legionnaires. No one gives a straight answer to a straight question."

"Is that right?"

"Oh, for the love of…"

He laughed, applying tape. "You've spent too much time with Flynn. He wouldn't reveal his drink order at a bar when he's blootered."

"Blootered?"

"Japanese word. Meaning *drunk*."

"Of course. You must be relieved he's okay."

"That bastard? He could shake off a nuclear bomb and remain as miserable as ever."

"Does his family in Australia know he's okay?"

His blue eyes studied her from under thick black lashes. "You know they warn us about people like you, in training?"

"People like me?"

"Journalists. Curious people. People who ask questions."

"You mean, humans?"

"Them, too."

He secured the dressing with a thicker tape. He was far more relaxed than his comrades. Despite his wariness, he didn't seem to carry the weight on his shoulders that Flynn and Angelito did. So what had drawn him to the legion? Not the promise of a European passport. Why not join the British Army? She knew better than to ask.

He sat back and checked his handiwork. He'd made the dressings snug and streamlined but not painful. She no longer felt like she had tennis balls stuck to her toes.

"So," he said, "it looks like you bandaged your feet too tightly, and when they swelled you got into trouble. That one's infected, so take care to keep it clean and covered. I'll give you a course of antibiotics. Air them when you can do so without them getting dirty."

"Without getting them dirty. Right."

"Yeah, okay, so that's going to be a challenge out here." He scooped up a pile of rubbish and dropped it in the plastic bag. "The dressings should be fairly waterproof, unless you decide to go for a swim." He put a thumb under her jaw and tilted her cheek, investigating the grazes. "Anything else worrying you?"

"Nothing your kit will fix."

He released her. "That's you done, then. I can give you some iron pills if you'd like. You look a little anemic."

"Thank you."

"No trouble at all." He rapped on the rear window. "Next!"

So that exchange had given her exactly zero new information.

As Flynn climbed in, he cast her a sideways look. And there it was again—a tremor rolling up her spine when she looked at his face. Why? She scooted across the van, giving him the space beside Doc. Without his beard he looked even more annoyingly familiar. Her neurons were a hairbreadth from connecting.

"I'll leave you to it," she said, pushing up to a crouch. Her quads protested.

"Stay," said Flynn, with a hint of reluctance, removing his cap. "Keep out of sight as long as you can." He slumped into an uncomfortable-looking position and focused downward while Doc got started.

"Who applied the suture strips?" Doc met Tess's gaze. "You?"

She nodded, sitting back down. She'd be on her way soon enough.

"Not a bad job." He pulled a sealed plastic pouch from his kit. "How's the pain, mate?"

"Bitch of a headache. I might need something stronger than paracetamol."

"I can try all sorts of fun stuff on you. Do you remember what happened?"

"I can still hear the clonk when they smashed whatever it was into my head but that's all."

"A good old-fashioned rock, I believe. Know how long you lost consciousness?"

"Several hours. But I'm pretty sure they drugged me. They drugged Tess."

"Stay still." Doc gripped Flynn's jaw and shone a penlight into his left eye. "What happened next?"

"If you're thinking I have amnesia, I don't. I remember every second since I woke in that bunker."

Doc switched to Flynn's other eye. "Have you been thinking straight since then?"

Flynn shot a sideways glance at Tess. "Several lapses of judgment but nothing I can blame on my injury—unfortunately."

Tess bit down a smile.

"Dizziness, vision problems?"

"A little when I came to, but nothing since."

"Loss of feeling, weakness, speech problems, numbness, tingling, nausea, dyspraxia?"

Flynn shook his head until Doc reached the end of his list. "Dys—what?"

"Has your mind been in charge of your body?"

Flynn raised his eyebrows. A giggle bubbled up in Tess's chest. She killed it. Nerves.

Doc continued. "Like, when you throw a punch does it land in the place you intended?"

"Always."

"I'd ask if you've been irritable, but that's like asking a bee if it's been buzzing."

"Real funny, Doc."

"Any other injuries?"

"Nothing that won't take care of itself."

Doc wrapped a cuff around Flynn's biceps. The skin on the lieutenant's jaw was several shades lighter than his forehead. He'd had a beard awhile. He was breathtakingly handsome without it, even with his lumpy, asymmetrical nose. So why did she automatically tense when she looked at him? Her instinct was flapping like a pinned butterfly, trying to point her attention to… something. Any minute now she'd start believing in past lives.

"Your blood pressure is high," said Doc, unwrapping the cuff.

Flynn eyed Tess again. "I'm not surprised."

She rolled her eyes, earning a hint of a dirty grin from him that made her heart skip. Pathetic. She drove her knuckles along her aching quads. Yeouch.

Doc dug around in his kit. "Still, that's not a bad thing, in the circumstances. If it was low, it might signal a problem." He cleaned the wound and tore open a sealed packet. A syringe and needle. Ugh. "The bad news is that your brain appears to be functioning as normal."

"You know I outrank you, right?"

"When I'm about to inject this into your scalp, I think I'm technically in charge. Hold still."

Tess hugged her knees, looking at her neatly bandaged feet. Anything but watch.

"Tess, I've squared things with Angelito," Flynn said. "We'll get you out on the quiet."

Not that again. "And what about his orders to hand me over?"

"We can avoid that."

"I'm not taking that chance—and I don't want you or your friends captured by al-Thawra or landing in front of a military tribunal. You can leave with your unit, I'll record my story here and Quan will send someone to collect it. Then we'll all be safe."

"Tess, you'll be just as saf—"

Doc tugged on a suturing needle, the thread making a rasping sound as it passed through Flynn's scalp. Flynn gripped his thighs. "Easy, mate."

"Suck it up, princess. I've only just begun."

Damn, when had she started watching again? She dropped her gaze to Flynn's hands, which led her to his thighs, which led her to other parts she needed to stop thinking about. Was his silence a tacit agreement? Not that she needed his permission, but she'd like his confidence.

"Okay, then," she said, shuffling to the door. Why

was she feeling deflated when everything was working out? Maybe she *was* anemic. "I guess I'll be going."

Flynn shot out a hand and grabbed her ankle. Doc swore.

"Flynn, I just need to get to my...friend's house and then I'm safe."

He frowned, tilting his head. "You hesitated."

"What?"

"Before 'friend.' You paused."

"No, I didn't."

"This 'friend'—you don't know if you can trust him?"

"Her." She tugged her foot but his grip held.

"What are you not telling me? Are you going to be safe or not?"

"She *might* blame me for getting her fiancé killed."

"Your translator? Or the cameraman?"

She glanced at Doc, who had suspended his surgery. "The guy who died in the drone strike. I know it's hard to keep up with all the people I'm getting killed. Don't worry—it'll be fine. She can help me get everything I need to record my story and I can lie low until it broadcasts. Meantime, you can put out the word I'm dead."

"I'm worried that'll become the truth."

"What, so now you believe in karma?"

He groaned. "Touché."

"Flynn, somehow I've managed to survive for thirty-two years without your protection."

"Barely."

"This is the safest solution all round."

He paused. "For me, you mean. I can take responsibility for—"

"—your own death. I know. But what about your

unit? This is the best way to ensure they get out without more casualties." He winced at the word *more*. "If I'm not with you, you'll breeze through al-Thawra's checkpoints. If they find me—and they probably will—"

"We'll deal with it."

"This is not a negotiation, Lieutenant. You have no hold over me." She looked at her ankle. "Not legally or morally, anyway." The fact her muscles seemed reluctant to take that last step out the door—that was nerves, again. She'd be fine once she set out.

He released her with a sigh. "You know we could take you, whether you like it or not? Those are our orders."

"And you know that there are several laws against...?" She threw up her hands. "Ah, who am I kidding? Like military forces take any notice of such trivialities as laws and human rights."

"I'm staying with you, then."

Oh God, yes. "No. Your unit will never leave without you, right? If you stay, you'll force them to stay. You'll put them in danger. You'll jeopardize their careers. Is that what you want? Flynn, you don't need to protect me anymore."

He swore. He'd lost the argument and he knew it. She reached for the door handle.

"Wait." He hissed out a breath through clenched teeth. "I'll escort you to your friend's place, make sure you're safe."

"I'll be fine," she said, for what felt like the hundredth time today.

"Humor me. After all we've been through, I don't want you getting captured by al-Thawra the minute you're out of my sight. This will only be a few more minutes, right, Doc?"

"You realize this is minor brain surgery? It's like asking da Vinci to hurry up on the Sistine Chapel."

"Michelangelo," she corrected automatically, earning eye rolls from both men.

"Doc," Flynn said, "while you're there, could you take out the part of my brain that gives me this compulsion to protect annoying, self-righteous vegans with death wishes?"

"I'm not a vegan." *Oh, why bother?*

"Happy to give it a go, sir. Might need a longer scalpel."

"Tess, please." Flynn's voice dropped to a guttural plea. "Let me escort you and then I'll tell everyone you're dead, like you want."

"That sounds like blackmail."

Flynn swore. Doc yanked him back by his shoulders. "Technically, it's bribery. It'd be blackmail if he said, 'If you don't come with me, I won't tell everyone you're dead.' A fine line, but there you go."

"Tess, just a few minutes," said Flynn. "We'll make sure your friend's house is safe—and that she'll let you in. Then you can get on with doing your story without having to worry about the door falling in. I won't need to take responsibility for your death and you won't need to take responsibility for mine."

Out of the corner of her eye, she caught Doc exchanging a look with the driver. Wondering where Flynn's head was at?

Granted, the prospect of Flynn and his team escorting her to Samira's eased the tension in her chest. And if it meant she'd be rid of him… Sitting in here was driving her nuts in several ways. The longer she back-pedaled, the more she itched to get her story under way. Her mind was already firing with possible ways to intro it, the structure falling into place. Very soon, she'd be back in control, free of distractions and threats, and doing the job she was trained for.

"Okay, fine," she said. "But I need to get going."

"Doc?" Flynn said. "You nearly done?"

"Sure. I'll just stuff your primary somatosensory cortex back into your skull and pour some superglue on your head, shall I?"

Flynn tapped the door with his boot. *"Mon Capitaine!"*

Angelito opened it a crack and leaned in.

"Tess wants to be left in Harar."

The two men eyed Tess, Flynn looking pissed, Angelito blank. The guy would be great at poker, but it didn't take an MRI scan to determine he'd be happy to be rid of her.

"Permission to escort her to safety?" Flynn said.

"Denied. You'll stay here with Doc, out of sight. The rest of us will take her."

Flynn stilled, then gave a tiny, sharp nod.

Angelito swung his gaze back to Tess. "Where are we heading?"

"You need coordinates?"

"I need a rough idea, in case my men get lost." He exchanged an impatient look with Flynn, who shrugged. At least, she figured it was impatience. Impossible to tell.

She sighed. "It's a guesthouse called Anaya, a short walk downhill from the Starburst Café, which is in the alleyways behind Machine Alley—Makina Girgir. It's kind of hard to explain." She looked at Flynn. "Might be in your Lonely Planet. Bright violet wall with a yellow stripe, with steps up to an old wooden gate. Can we go now?" *Before I change my mind about walking away?*

"Can we have a few minutes alone first?" Flynn directed the request at her, not Angelito, but the *capitaine* jerked his head.

"Doc, Okoye, out."

Doc grabbed his bag. "I'll get that medication ready, Tess. Don't worry. I'll send your TV station an outrageous bill."

In two seconds the van was cleared. She swallowed. "If you're planning to change my mind..." She sounded nervous, dammit.

"That's not what this is about." Flynn spoke just above a whisper. He inched forward, took both her hands and held them to his chest. The air in the van suddenly felt stifling. "You've made your decision and there's not a damn thing I can do about it." He stroked the sensitive skin between her thumbs and forefingers, making her breath shudder. "I have to let you go. But not without doing this, one last time."

He released her hands and cradled her jaw instead, his eyes pinning hers. As he leaned in, her stomach somersaulted.

CHAPTER NINETEEN

TESS CLOSED HER EYES, her hands drifting to either side of Flynn's waist. At first their lips touched so gently her overstimulated nerves might have imagined it. He sniffed in a breath and pressed his mouth to hers. Heaven. She groaned into him, let her mouth fall open and surrendered to the respite, from fear, from doubt, from anything but the surety of his touch and the buzz of being connected to someone so freaking awesome. The kiss wasn't a buildup to something else; it wasn't a promise of more to come—it couldn't be. Just a sweet, sad acknowledgment that this was something beautiful that could never be. No pretenses anymore—he liked her and she liked him, despite all the friction. Simple... but...so not. Her chest ached even as her body lit up. Their last, last, *last* goodbye kiss.

Too soon, he pulled back and rested his forehead on hers, panting. "I wish you would come with us," he whispered, "but I respect you too much to talk you out of it. Just...take care of yourself. No crazy risks. I'll be watching TV every minute until I see you on air."

"I'm safe now. You've seen to that."

"You have a story to get out." His tone rung with finality, but he made no move to release her.

She stroked the sides of his waist. "Maybe when this is over we could—" *What?* This wasn't the life she wanted, pining for some guy who was never around until one day a couple of officers in dress uniform knocked on the door, hats—berets—tucked under their arms.

"Bad idea." They said it at once.

She caught the flicker of a grin.

"That might be the first thing we've agreed on," he said.

"Goodbye, Flynn." She let her hands slip away.

He pulled back and smiled, a rare full smile. "Funny, I've heard you say that before."

"We're like boomerangs. We keep circling back to each other." *But not this time.*

"I wouldn't know what that is."

"Of course not."

She touched her lips to his one final time, allowed her chest to fill with tingles and let herself out, without looking back. *Au revoir, Lieutenant.*

FLYNN WATCHED ANGELITO cross the road with Tess, the sound effects from Doc's stitching grating in his eardrums. From the back they looked like different species, Tess swallowed by Angelito's shadow. Hell, maybe they should have folded her into Doc's rucksack. Okoye, strolling ahead, disappeared through the gate first, fingers looped through his belt—half a second away from his concealed pistol. The *capitaine* instructed Texas and Thor to follow, using hand signals that would go unnoticed by anyone else.

Flynn watched until Tess and Angelito disappeared into the fortified gate, their backup trailing at a distance. His fists closed. It should be him going.

She was officially out of his sight and out of his control. Control. Huh. As if he'd ever had any—over her, over his reaction to her. Angelito was right to separate them, for so many reasons. He rubbed his index finger along his lower lip. He'd sure left some unfinished business.

"She didn't take her backpack," Doc said.

"She doesn't need it. There's not much in there. How much longer, Doc?"

"A few more minutes. So…no story there, you say— with you and the reporter."

"The reporter is a pain in the arse."

"A perfect match for you, then. *À bon chat, bon rat.*"

Flynn groaned. A good cat for a good rat. Doc had a bad habit of asking personal questions, probably from when he'd been a real doctor, before the legion. Lucky Tess didn't know that story. Hell, all Flynn knew was that some colossal screwup had made a hotshot surgeon abandon everything to play battlefield nurse to a brotherhood of outcasts.

"Never seen you so worked up over a woman. Come to think of it, I've never seen you worked up over a woman at all."

"I'm not worked up. I'm stuck with a med-school reject stitching up my skull, so yeah, I'm a little worried I'm going to end up looking like Frankenstein."

"There's an idea. I'm sure this van has a few loose bolts."

In the distance a horn blared. Flynn let his shoulders relax, his gaze following a camel's lazy stroll. The last thing he wanted was to be grilled on shit he couldn't figure out himself. Perhaps he did have a brain injury— lapses in judgment, irritability, weakness.

Maybe when this is over we could…

Hell. He'd been thinking the same thing. But a future for them—a smart, fiery media star from a family of all-American heroes, and the bitter son of a criminal, hiding under a fake identity? On the bright side—he was pretty sure she'd ruined him for other women.

The camel burst into a trot, at the urging of the man leading it. The guy darted a glance at the road behind. Panic? The noise had changed—sharp instructions, shrill calls. Everywhere there was movement: people whipping donkeys, women sweeping their wares into buckets and cloths, men hoisting sacks over their shoulders—all of them looking nervously along the road.

"Doc, you sensing something here?"

A white Ford Ranger screamed to a halt, right where the woman with the stove had been sitting a minute ago. A chicken flapped from under a front wheel. Four men piled out and ran through the gate, dressed in gray camo gear and holding M16s. People scattered. The driver got out last and leaned on the door frame, shouldering a rifle.

"You think they're after her?"

"Gotta be." Flynn touched the pistol in his pocket.

Doc reached into his rucksack. "I'll call Angeli—"

"No," said Flynn. Christ, her skewed perception of the world was catching. "No phone calls. We go in."

"They'll be looking for you, too."

"I'll take that risk. We have to warn the others."

"If they recognize you, they'll know she's here, as well."

"I'm guessing they already know that." He leaned forward. "Cut the threads, Doc. I'm wearing different clothes, I'm clean—relatively—I've shaved, I'm in different company."

Doc hesitated a second, then snipped. The street was nearly deserted. Flynn put on cap and sunglasses. At least his scalp was numb—he wasn't looking forward to the anesthetic wearing off.

"Your boots," said Doc, indicating Flynn's legion-issue desert boots. "Dead giveaway." He drew a pair of running shoes from his rucksack. "Wear these."

Flynn pulled the guidebook out and chucked it at Doc. "Look up the guesthouse Tess was heading to—what was it, Alaya, Anaya? Figure out our quickest route."

He kicked off his boots and grabbed the sneakers. A horn blared. Another Ranger roared in. Same routine as before—four guys went in, one remained.

"It's not in here," Doc said. "What about the café she mentioned?"

"Sounded like Starbucks. We might have to try another gate."

Doc flipped a few pages. "Starburst. We could drive to the… Buda Gate? It's the next one around the old town, anticlockwise."

"Let's do it. You drive. I'll stay back here."

"Oui, Lieute." Doc skidded into the driver's seat. The van started with a squeal of worn belts. "Can you shove my stuff into my rucksack? I'd rather I had my kit with me."

"I'd rather you did, too. And don't go speaking any French while we're in there."

Doc crunched into first gear and moved off, nice and easy. "Bonza, cobber mate."

"What was that—Swahili?"

"Would you prefer Scots?"

Flynn packed the last of Doc's things and pulled the straps tight. "Top o' the morning to ya."

"Completely wrong country."

"Och, aye."

"May a Loch Ness monster strike you down."

"I don't believe in monsters." Flynn shook out the contents of Tess's backpack and pocketed Solomon's phone.

"Well, I don't believe in kangaroos."

"Neither do I," Flynn said. "Those things make no sense at all. They can't even freaking walk—they're all jump, jump, jump." Really, he was scared shitless for Tess, and Doc knew it. Every soldier covered for the tension in different ways. Doc's defense mechanism was bad puns. "Got any spare nine millimeter ammo?"

"Rucksack." Doc swerved, forcing Flynn to brace. "Side pocket. There's a shoulder holster in there, too. Levanne's."

Levanne's. *Sorry, buddy.* Flynn fitted the holster and grabbed the ammo, then tried to get a fix on the guidebook's tiny map. It was like trying to make sense of a cobweb. If he could get them to Machine Alley...

"One enemy, outside a wee hole in the wall."

"That's not the gate but it'll be coming up." Crap, al-Thawra had this figured out. A fortress was all well and good until you got surrounded. He took a swig of water.

"Here's the gate now. One enemy."

Through the windscreen, Flynn noted an identical Ranger parked outside the stone gate, the sentry leaning against the inside of the arch. The Global Food truck had gone—to the correct owners, hopefully.

"Your call, *Lieute.*"

"Pull over nice and easy. We'll play dumb tourist, act like a sentry with an M16 is nothing unusual."

"Shall we ask for directions to McDonald's?"

As they crossed the empty road to the gate with forced nonchalance, Flynn kept his head in the Lonely Planet, relying on peripheral vision to keep the guard in check. The shoes he'd borrowed from Doc were too small, crunching his toes together. Nothing next to what Tess was dealing with. She'd better be okay in there.

"She-it, I can't get my head around these streets." Flynn settled on aping Texas's accent. "What do you make of this, Carl?"

Doc scratched his neck. "Well, heck, I don't know. Let's just go wandering. I need breakfast."

By the guard's posture, Flynn figured he was looking their way, but keeping the barrel at ease. They neared the archway. Footsteps jogged toward them. Flynn didn't dare look.

"Australian! Australian! Gidday, mate!"

Damn. The tout, coming up fast. Flynn didn't slow. Nothing unusual in a tourist ignoring a tout, but he should have used a bloody Queensland accent a minute ago. The soldier didn't move, but he'd be watching.

"Australian! Mister! You must not go in there! Terrorists are in there!"

The tout pushed Flynn's chest. "Oh. I am sorry, sir. I thought you were someone…" He peered closer. "No, you *are* him. You shaved your beard, yes? You look different but I never forget a face. Where is your girlfriend, the American? Not in old city, I hope? There are many terrorists. You must not go in. It is not safe."

Shut. The. Fuck. Up. "I'll be okay," Flynn said under his breath. The soldier better not understand English.

"No, please, sir. I am serious. Terrorists. You must stay away from Jugol, from the old city. I take you to another place. You want to see Harar Brewery? Best beer in all of Ethiopia."

"Stop! You in the black cap, stop!" The guard's heavy boots pounded behind them. Damn. That answered the language question.

TESS DIDN'T EVEN try to talk to the *capitaine* as they wound through the alleyways. She was mapping out her story in her head, and she guessed he was happier scanning for threats than maintaining light conversation.

She ducked as a woman in a rainbow robe and tangerine head scarf swept past, a huge basket of green and yellow oranges poised on her head. Her mouth watered. Around them, people haggled over the price of vegetables, and gossiped. Life as usual.

She could almost imagine that the last hideous month hadn't happened, that she was starting this over, on her way to Samira's grandmother's guesthouse to meet Latif and trawl through the documents he'd stolen from Denniston. She'd promised to keep him and Samira safe and he'd promised to stay put, stay low, while Tess verified the evidence. Latif's forbidden relationship with Samira had been a secret he'd kept from everyone he knew, so he was safely off the radar in Harar. What had drawn him out of hiding?

Tess rounded a corner and had to skip to avoid a portable stove with a coffee jug steaming on top. A car horn blared from beyond the city walls, long and shrill. Shouts rose, bouncing in from somewhere beyond the narrow alleyway, the direction impossible to decipher. Angelito stiffened. Ahead, the man they'd called Okoye

crouched and tightened his shoelace. As she and Angelito passed him, the *capitaine* gave an instruction in
quiet French. Okoye bounded to his feet, skirted a bun-
dle of rags on the ground that could have been a sleeping person and disappeared. Tess looked up at Angelito,
her chest tightening, but he gave nothing away. More
shouting, in Arabic. This time she made out words. She
stopped, grabbing his forearm, ice in her veins.

"They're talking about soldiers coming, about The
Revolution. I mean—" She'd used the English translation. "About al-Thawra. They're here. Al-Thawra's
here."

"They're coming after you?"

"They must be."

"How would they know?"

She shook her head. The legion?

"Could they know about this guesthouse?"

"I can't imagine how, but…"

"Are we close to it?"

"Very."

"We keep going."

Fast footsteps approached, from around a blind bend.
Someone running. Angelito swiveled, turning her with
him, and continued walking, fast. He jerked his hands
in quick movements, like sign language—signaling to
Thor and Texas as they approached. Texas turned, to
walk ahead of her and Angelito. Thor swept past them
the other way, hand at his hip, as the footsteps neared.

A skid of braking feet behind her. A man shouted in
Arabic, "Al-Thawra is coming, with guns. Hide. Hide!"

The street spun into panic. People grabbed belong-
ings, donkeys, children. The man kept shouting.

"He's saying they're coming in everywhere, every gate, every direction," she told Angelito.

How stupid was she, to feel safe with a guard of four men? How stupid to drag them into this. They might be gods by human standards but they'd be outnumbered many times over. And what about Flynn? Al-Thawra could already have him.

"You have to leave!" she said to Angelito. "They're not after you. This is not your fight."

"It is now," he growled. "We need to get off the paths."

"You need to get your unit out, and find Flynn. *They're* your priority, not me. Just walk back out the gates."

His massive jaw tightened. Well, crap, two could play at stubborn. If this was how her life was to end, she wasn't taking anyone else out with her.

As FLYNN SPUN, the sentry snatched his cap off.

"It *is* you. You killed my brother."

Oh man. The soldier he'd trussed by the minefield, a red egg of a bruise on his forehead. The guy backed up, raising his rifle. *Too slow, mate.* Flynn shoulder-shoved the barrel, grabbed the handle and slammed a kick into his nuts. Textbook. Rifle in hand, Flynn covered Doc, who caught the guy from behind, forearm tight on his throat, hand jammed over his mouth. The tout unleashed a torrent of indecipherable words.

"Get him to the van," Flynn said, checking their surroundings. No other witnesses, at least.

"You are not tourists, I think," said the tout.

"Get out of here," Flynn snarled. "You didn't see anything."

"Nothing, sir. Nothing. Just blue sky. Beautiful day today."

Doc dragged the guy into the van and Flynn climbed in behind, shutting the door.

Doc drew his pistol and shoved the muzzle against the guy's temple. "You want me to shoot, bonehead? Keep struggling."

The guy stilled. Fast learner. Doc pulled out cable ties and secured him, then patted him down. He found a mobile phone and chucked it to Flynn, who followed Tess's lead and destroyed it.

"Why is al-Thawra here?" Flynn said, removing the rifle's clip and shoving it in Doc's rucksack. As handy as an M16 would be, he didn't want to look any more obvious in there. He grabbed the guy's sidearm from a holster.

"No English."

"Bullshit. A minute ago your English was fine. Why is al-Thawra here?"

Silence, but the guy was close to hyperventilating. Doc holstered his pistol and pulled out his medical kit.

"Talk."

"No English! No English."

Doc pulled out a scalpel and syringe, holding one in each hand, his normally calm eyes coming over all mad scientist. "Answer my friend's questions and you'll get to have a little sleep. Refuse, and I'll slit your throat. I know how to keep you alive just long enough to watch all the blood drain out."

The guy's wild gaze flicked between the men. Gunfire burst out from within the walls. *Putain*.

Doc tossed the syringe into the bag. "He's no use to us if he doesn't speak English. Hold him down, *Lieute*." He grabbed a dirty towel from the floor and held it up. "For the blood," he said, eyeballing the guy. "There will be a lot." Jesus, for an ex–brain surgeon, he made a convincing psycho killer.

Flynn grabbed the guy in a headlock, exposing the side of his neck to Doc. "Make it quick. We're wasting time."

"No, not quick. Slow."

The guy bucked but Flynn clamped down. Doc pressed the scalpel against his throat. Blood dribbled onto the blade, pooled and dripped onto the floor. Flynn screwed up his face. A wet stain spread across the guy's crotch.

"Last chance," Flynn said, doing a recce of the street through the netting.

"Mrs. Hamid found out the woman was here," the guy said. "An hour ago."

"From who?"

"I don't know. I am just soldier."

Right. Just a regular jihadist. Doc held up the blade so the guy could see the blood. Amazing how you could have a gun barrel in someone's temple but it was the tiny scalpel and teaspoon of blood that made them piss their pants.

"How many soldiers are here?" Flynn said.

"Twenty, thirty trucks," the guy said. "Hundred, hundred-fifty soldiers."

"How did Hamid know?" Flynn nodded at Doc, who pressed the blunt side of the blade to the guy's neck.

"Someone rang Mrs. Hamid—I don't know who. She gave us orders—barricade Harar and search old town. She know she find woman in Harar but not know which house. Others are coming, from all around. Number one priority."

"Where is Hamid? *Mrs.* Hamid?"

"Coming. From Dire Dawa. I am just soldier. I don't

know." More gunfire. It seemed to boost the guy's motivation. "She plans to execute journalist today."

"Where? Where will she do it? Harar?"

"I don't know. Really."

Doc pushed the scalpel. Blood oozed from the tiny
existing cut.

"I don't know. I would tell you. Please. I have wife.
New wife. I don't know where, just know she will do it
straightaway, today. Please."

"Syringe," Flynn said to Doc. They'd wasted enough
time. He pinned the guy as Doc injected, averting his
gaze. He'd seen plenty of bloodshed—too much—but
needles turned him into a wimp, every time.

In a few minutes the guy was drowsy.

"It's safe to go," Doc said, repacking. "He'll take a
few more minutes to drift off entirely. He'll be out for
four hours, tops. Let's hope they're shite at keeping
head counts."

"Are you even allowed that sedative shit?" Flynn said.

Doc hoisted his backpack on. "I still have contacts in
low places. Anytime you want some Viagra…"

"Save it for yourself." Flynn opened one of the back
doors and jumped out. "If we're quick, we can bring
Tess and the others out this way before al-Thawra real-
izes the gate is unguarded."

"You killed him, sir?" *Merde.* The tout was standing right next to the van.

"I told you to get lost," Flynn said, striding to the
gate, with Doc following.

The tout jogged alongside. "You are going in for your
wife? You will need a guide."

"You want to join him?" Flynn gestured to the van.

"I guide you for free. Terrorists in there, everywhere.

I know secret ways, all of them. We go fast. Where do you need to go?"

Flynn picked up his cap from where it had fallen and warily fixed it in place. Quick and secret would be good. And they'd look more like tourists, with a tout. He caught Doc's eye. The medic shrugged—why not?

"You know where the Starburst Café is?"

"Of course. I can take you. This is my city—my people have lived here a thousand years. We do not like invaders."

"Okay, take us there. But if you cross us..." He tapped the gun in his holster.

"I am honest man."

Flynn raised his eyebrows. His scalp pulled.

The tout tipped his head. "Even honest men have to make a living."

"What's your name?"

"Dawit."

"Lead on, Dawit."

As they passed under the gate, a vehicle thundered along the road outside. Doc eased in behind Dawit and Flynn as it pulled up just out of their view. Doors opened and closed. Footfalls, shouts. *Merde.* A second vehicle engine rumbled, approaching from the same direction.

Flynn kept his head down as they crossed open ground and made for the nearest alleyway.

"These are your soldiers?" Dawit said, breathless.

Flynn's jaw tightened.

"I am thinking 'no'?"

The second engine silenced. The hand brake ripped up.

"What does this mean?" the tout said quietly.

"It means we won't be getting out easy."

The alleyway was longer than most, ending in a
T junction—too far ahead. Behind them, still out of
view, a dozen footsteps smacked the ground. Even if
they sprinted they'd be mowed down before they got
halfway. Three-meter stone walls, wooden and metal
doors along each side, resolutely shut. They'd run into
a shooting alley.

THE ALLEYWAY OUTSIDE Samira's guesthouse was deserted—recently, going by the black coffee running
from a smashed cup into rivulets between the cobblestones. Shouts rang out on a nearby pathway, followed
by gunfire.

Tess skidded to a halt outside Samira's gate and
knocked on the wood. Angelito pulled up beside her,
with Thor taking point duty at the spot the purple-and-
yellow wall curved around the corner. Texas watched
the other direction. As bodyguards went, they were as
hard to shake as Flynn. Hero complexes all round. More
gunfire.

"Warning shots?" she asked Angelito as she thumped
the gate.

"That round was my *sergent-chef.* Diversion. Confusion. The good thing about a maze is that no one knows
where anyone is, enemy included."

Okoye, she guessed. She went to knock again when a
face appeared at the tiny peephole. Wrinkled eyes narrowed. Samira's grandmother—not Tess's biggest fan.

"Seulam," Tess said, her Amharic deserting her.
How did you say "Help me, please"? "Ah, *ehbakish
erduny,"* she ventured, cringing. She'd probably asked
for a potato.

A door banged farther up the alleyway, out of sight. Tess jumped. Shouts, in Arabic.

"They're coming," Thor muttered.

Crap. Without her, Flynn's unit could stroll away. *"Please."*

A woman called out from inside.

"Samira!" Tess hissed.

Something clunked behind the gate and it swung open. Samira stood holding a mobile phone, mouth open. Collecting herself, she spoke quickly in Amharic and hung up.

"Tess Newell," she said, blinking rapidly. "Oh my God, you're alive. You're free." She looked at her phone. "*That's* why al-Thawra is here."

"Hi. Yeah. I didn't mean for this—"

"They ransacked my cousin's house, searching for you." Samira gestured at the phone, gold bangles clattering. "Every room, every cupboard. They are coming this way. I thought, 'Well, thank God she's nowhere near here.'"

"Samira, I'm sorry. I—"

"People don't know me by that name here."

Crap—Tess had forgotten that. A month ago it'd seemed like a ludicrous precaution.

Samira took in the large figures flanking Tess. "*This* is your new TV crew?"

"Ah, kinda bodyguards. Self-appointed."

"I can't hide four people—there is nowhere." She tugged at her shirt collar, her voice hitting a desperate note.

"These men don't need to be hidden—al-Thawra doesn't know about them. Just…me? I'm sorry. I would never have come if—"

Another gunshot, closer. More yelling.

"Get in, quickly," Samira said, grabbing Tess's forearm and hauling her inside. "Quickly!" The three legionnaires backed in, Samira drawing the gate closed behind them and dropping the iron latch. She spoke rapidly to her grandmother, who disappeared inside. Angelito gave Texas a signal, and he took up a position by the gate, sheltering behind a large metal drum.

"They're armed?" said Samira, paling. "Who are they?"

"Long story."

"Capit—" said Texas, the remainder of the word silenced by a glare. "We gotta hurry this up."

"Can I take a look around, ma'am?" Angelito's words were clipped but calm.

"You can leave now," Tess said. "Walk away. They'll never make a connection."

"Not before I know you're safe," he said, with a finality that indicated negotiations were over.

"Come with me," Samira said, making the deciding vote before Tess could argue. She hurried across the square courtyard to the main house, its carved wooden doors yawning open. "My guests are not here. But there is nowhere I can hide Tess. It's a very simple house. They will search."

"We'll figure it out," Angelito said, pushing Tess inside.

A rap at the gate, and a shout. Crap.

Samira swallowed. "I will try to delay them."

"Don't take any risks," Tess whispered.

Samira's forehead wrinkled. Tess knew what she was thinking—*too late*. Tess had already taken the risk. And Samira, Flynn's unit, her mom... They would pay.

CHAPTER TWENTY

FLYNN TRIED THE handle of an old metal gate. Locked. Doc tried a door. Also locked. No time to test every door and gate along the alleyway. Voices and footsteps closed in.

"We'll have to go over a wall," Flynn said.

"You come," Dawit whispered. He ran five meters uphill and pushed a green metal gate. It creaked open. "Come!"

Gladly. They sprinted into a courtyard flanked by a horseshoe-shaped whitewashed building. Closed doors on all three facades. Only a slight improvement. Dawit eased the gate closed and dragged a plant pot in front of it, just as the footfalls reached the path outside. Chest heaving, Flynn ducked under a laden washing line and flattened against the compound's wall. He could hear a guy breathing in the alleyway on the other side.

A hammering echoed down the passageway, sounding like a rock on metal. Shouts. A door groaned open. Footsteps. Another knock. A gunshot. Flynn's eardrums burned. More voices—orders, protests, a yelp. The plant pot wouldn't hold the enemy for long.

"They're searching the houses," Dawit hissed, his fingers digging in the gray dirt of the planter, which didn't look like it'd seen anything green in years.

The whole property wasn't much bigger than a double garage. It was dwarfed by the satellite dish on its roof. Short on hiding places.

Dawit pulled out a rusty key. "Ah," he said with satisfaction. "This has been here since I was a little boy. Come." He eased it into one of the doors, twisted it, jiggled it, rattling the whole door. Flynn winced. Too much noise. Dawit turned with an apologetic shrug. "No one changes locks here—usually." An argument rang out next door. "We cannot wait."

"Any other ideas?"

"I take you on tour, like I promised."

"What?" Maybe the guy was mad, just a regular *chat*-head?

"We will just need to climb over the top of this house."

A thumping made Flynn start. Their gate. The alternatives had run out. Flynn linked his hands beside the wall of the house and gestured at Doc to go first.

Once on the roof they crawled across the scalding tin. As they jumped onto the neighboring building, something behind them crashed. The planter? They dropped into a courtyard that opened into another alley.

After that Flynn lost track. It wasn't a tour they could have got from the Lonely Planet. Instead of winding around the maze of lanes, Dawit took a direct route, right through any house, mosque, church or school in the way. He seemed to know all the unlocked doors and secret knocks and hidden keys. The number of people who saw them made Flynn nervous—wide-eyed kids chanting the Koran in squeaky falsetto, women rushing to cover their hair, muezzins giving Dawit hushed updates on enemy positions, glassy-eyed men sitting around chewing *chat*. But none blocked their way.

As they emerged from a courtyard into a narrow alleyway, three armed enemy stepped out of the house opposite. Eyes met. Flynn dipped his head, pulling the Lonely Planet from his pocket and opening to a random page. The wooden door slammed shut behind them.

Dawit spun and laid his hand on the door. "So you see this home was excellent example of traditional Harari architectures. Hundreds, hundreds years old." Doc pulled his phone from his shorts pocket and zoomed its camera in on a pattern carved into the wood. "City goes back fourteenth century, tenth century, even eighth century. No one knows for sure. You are Christian? You are Muslim? Does not matter here. We have peace. Beautiful, yes?"

Full marks to the tout. But the soldiers weren't moving on.

One stepped closer. "You see this woman?" He held a phone up to Dawit.

The tout peered. "Yes…oh yes, definitely."

Shit.

"Blonde American, yes? I see one like that leaving, leaving in *bajaj*. Maybe half hour, maybe hour. Harar Gate."

Flynn eased out an exhalation. *You beauty.*

"And this man?"

The soldier swiped to another photo. *Merde.*

"Yes, yes, he left with her. I recognize the beard. Her husband, I think, yes?"

The soldier spoke to his buddies, and the trio's footsteps retreated downhill.

"No, sir," the tout called. "Sir! *Harar* Gate. Quicker that way." He pointed up the slight slope.

Silence, and then the men strode past Flynn and Doc.

"Nice work," Flynn said, rolling the guidebook into his hand.

"Now *we* go this way," the tout said, leading them downhill. A few turns later and he announced they were at the Starburst Café, which was a concrete bunker all of two meters wide, with a fair attempt at the Starbucks logo painted above the door.

Doc took out an American twenty-dollar bill but the tout waved it away. "Free, free," he whispered. He took Flynn's hand in a death squeeze. "Just get the terrorists out. They are bad for business." He spit on the ground, narrowly missing a rooster, gave a half bow and strolled away, hands linked behind his back.

"She said this place was downhill from here, right?" Doc said.

They rounded a curve in the path. Flynn pointed out a purple-and-yellow wall. Inset into it was a wooden gate, swinging open. Loud voices burst from within. Al-Thawra. They checked for eyes and crept closer. In a courtyard beyond the gate, a small old woman crouched before an herb garden, cloaked in lime green. She squinted at Flynn and called to someone inside. Flynn gestured to Doc to advance along the wall with care, while he flattened against it, hand on his gun. Had they already captured the others? Something crashed, probably inside the dwelling.

Shoes scuffed on flagstones. A light tread. Doc, who had a better sight line, held up a palm… Wait. A younger Ethiopian woman in jeans appeared at the gate. She took in Doc and Flynn with quick brown eyes.

"You are the soldier, the one who was kidnapped," she whispered.

So much for looking incognito.

She glanced behind. "Come quickly. I will get you in without them seeing."

Like the compound they'd climbed over, this one was laid out in a horseshoe. The woman grabbed Doc's elbow and pushed him to a closed door along one side of the courtyard, her eyes never leaving the bigger central doors.

"They have already searched this room," she whispered. Voices rose in pitch. A thud. "Hurry! It is not locked."

The door led to a small, simple bedroom. White-washed walls, a large bed on a platform. Mosquito net, tied up. Bathroom. Two windows faced the courtyard. Doc checked the bathroom while Flynn locked the door and took up position next to one of the windows, protected from view by a white net curtain. The wall was cool against his back. Thick bullet-stopping stone.

A guy in gray stepped out of the central door. Flynn checked his breath for fear of moving the curtains. He signaled to Doc, who stole across to the other window.

The old woman picked an herb and calmly laid it in a basket next to her, as if a terrorist with an M16 wasn't standing a meter away. Loud laughter rolled out of the house. Flynn swallowed. Texas?

A smattering of voices. Another three soldiers tumbled out the main door and crossed the courtyard, one kicking over the woman's basket. She glared at him, mouth pursed. They left and she sprang up and closed the latch.

The younger woman appeared in the central doorway and the pair exchanged words. Her gaze rested on Flynn's window and she beckoned, resting a finger against her lips. Doc and Flynn let themselves out. Uphill, a fist hammered at a door.

They silently crossed the courtyard to the main door and walked straight into a living area. Thor lay on the highest of three seating platforms arranged like terraces at a football game. Texas sprawled on the next one down, clutching a green plastic bag with a leafy plant in it, and Angelito sat on a suitcase on the floor. Two people short.

"Du calme, Flynn." Angelito's teeth were coated in green mush. All their mouths were. Just backpackers hanging out at their lodgings chewing *chat*. A sweet peppery scent floated around the room. "I Hate Myself for Loving You" was playing over a speaker system.

"Thor, gate," Angelito said.

The Scandinavian gave a crisp nod and left.

"Où est Tess?" Flynn asked Angelito.

"Elle est en sécurité. We may keep her there."

A muffled cry came from somewhere in the room, then a dull knocking. The house was like the ones he'd raced through with the tout—a chaos of decorations his mind hadn't been able to absorb. The walls were covered with stuff—round red baskets, black frying pans, Turkish-style rugs and a TV, with books and urns and pots in whitewashed alcoves. More rugs on the floors and platforms. Pain pinched behind his eyes. No Tess.

More knocking. He traced it to the rigid suitcase under Angelito, a smile pulling at his mouth. No way.

"And Okoye?"

"Doing recon. He's the least conspicuous of us. You're supposed to be in the van."

"Thought you could use a little help."

"You could have jeopardized the operation."

"I couldn't not…" He stared at the suitcase. How the…?

"Est-ce qu'elle mérite que tu meures pour elle?"

Flynn snorted. Was she worth dying for? *"Je t'ai*

posé la même question une fois." I once asked the same of you.

Angelito's eyes flickered with annoyance.

"Want some?" said Texas, offering the plastic bag. Playing peacemaker, as usual. "Some kinda herb. Much better than the real thing—maybe it'll catch on."

"Besobela," said the young woman, appearing in the arched doorway. "Sacred basil. My grandmother was about to dry it for her *berbere*."

Saliva flooded Flynn's mouth. Whatever that was, he wanted a heaped plate of it, stat.

"Let me out!" Tess's voice, reedy and stifled.

"What do you think?" said Angelito, bouncing a little as Tess evidently whacked the top of the suitcase. "She is safe there."

"Shoot, you know, I think I hear them coming back," Texas said. "We better keep her there a day or two just in case."

"You know I can hear you, and you're speaking English?" came the muffled response.

Flynn sat on the lowest platform and took off his cap. Doc stepped up and Flynn felt a feathery touch as he examined the wound. The music switched to "Piece of My Heart."

"No respect for craftsmanship," said the Scot.

"Flynn!" More knocking. "Are you there?"

"I think she wants you, *Lieute*," said Texas, smirking.

"I think she does, too," said Doc. "Hold still, Flynn." He swung his rucksack off and climbed to the middle platform.

Angelito rose, flicked a few latches and opened the suitcase. Tess was all folded up, like she'd dislocated several limbs to get in. She ignored Angelito's offered hand and pushed up to sitting, stretching her neck side to side. She met Flynn's gaze and closed her eyes for a second. Relief. Maybe annoyance. Somehow they'd failed at splitting up, again. But somehow they'd survived another hour.

"I do yoga," she said as she climbed out, in answer to his raised eyebrows.

"Evidently." He didn't want to think about the implications of that.

Too late.

"It was her idea," Angelito said, "for the record. Perhaps they're searching all the towns and villages around here. We wait till they clear the old town and move on. Then we go."

"Hamid knows Tess is in the citadel," said Flynn, gritting his teeth as Doc got back to work. The local was wearing off. "She's on her way to Harar. She'll assume I'm here, too. We thought we had an escape route, but…"

"Crap," Tess said, pushing her knuckles into the small of her back and arching.

Angelito swung around. "Hold on—*she*'s on her way? I thought you were talking about Hamid Nabil Hassan."

"Long story, *Capitaine*." He gave a rundown on their encounter with the soldier at the gate and a 101 on Hamid and al-Thawra, while trying to ignore the tugging on his scalp.

"Putain de merde," Angelito said under his breath.

"So when this guy comes to," Flynn said, "Doc will be on the hit list as well, and they'll be on alert for others."

"I should have come alone," Tess said. She looked up at her friend's stern face. "I shouldn't have come at all. But I definitely should have come alone."

"It's lucky you didn't," Flynn said.

She narrowed her eyes at him. "Ever thought you guys might have led al-Thawra to Harar?"

Flynn frowned. Ah, jeez.

"Who did you tell about us coming here?" She directed the question at Angelito.

Doc whistled. No one demanded answers from the *capitaine* in that tone.

"The legion doesn't give away secrets," Angelito replied darkly.

He towered over her, but she straightened and held eye contact. "Except to the US authorities?"

Angelito frowned.

"It's possible, right?" she said.

"It's not likely. Yes, the French share intel with allies, but we're treading carefully here. Our priority is rescuing Flynn. The nature of the mission gives us leeway."

"We don't have time to waste on blaming," Texas said. "Question is, what now?"

"Could we call in reinforcements?" Doc asked.

"And effectively invade Ethiopia?" Angelito said. "The bosses would never go for it, not for..." He glanced at Flynn.

"One soldier. I know."

"Besides, the collateral damage could be intolerable. We will get her out alone. We can arrange an airlift once we're far enough away."

"It'll be obvious if we try to leave now," Flynn said. "The city's gone dead quiet. They'll be waiting to see which rats leave the sinking ship. I might get away, but she won't."

Tess sat on the lowest platform, a meter from Flynn. "The plan doesn't have to change. You guys stroll out, nice and quietly, before that soldier wakes. I hide here and do my story. Once it's out, finding me will be the least of al-Thawra's priorities." She filled her friend in on the plan to get the story out on flash drive. She'd evidently accepted that Flynn's unit could be trusted, at least.

"Hamid will toss this town until she finds you," Flynn said.

"They've just come through here—it'll take them a while to loop back."

"Tess, I don't like—"

From above, Doc clamped his hands on either side of Flynn's head, straightening it. "For God's sake, Flynn, keep still. I'm almost done. Next time I'm using a general anesthetic."

Tess's friend pushed off the archway. "It may pay to wait a few hours before you leave, until the *chat* delivery comes into Harar." Flynn couldn't pin her accent. It had the rich songlike quality of Amharic but with an American curve to it. "It's chaos in town then—trucks of the stuff screaming in, women rushing to sell it, men rushing to buy it. Even the goats get high. And the children will have just got out of school. The whole place erupts." She threw up her palms. Her hands were dyed with swirled, precise henna patterns. "Every day without fail—people everywhere. I can't imagine even al-Thawra could keep a lid on that. If you want a safe time to slip out…"

"Let's work up a plan," said Angelito, crossing his arms.

Tess stood, straightening her skirt. "Can I talk to you in private, Samira?" She crooked her head toward an internal door.

The woman—Samira—nodded, her wavy black hair bouncing. They left, closing the door behind them.

"Capitaine," Flynn said quietly. "What if I stayed here with Tess, and you guys left?"

"That's not our orders," said Angelito, an edge to his voice. "You do that, I can't dig you out. You know how this works—if we have a clear path out, we have to take it."

"I know the consequences of disobeying an order."

"We came here to pull you out. I want to pull you out."

Doc pressed something onto Flynn's head. "Mate, there could be repercussions for all of us if we don't get you out when we have the chance," he said.

All of us. Meaning, Angelito's honorable discharge and his life after the legion.

"Think carefully, mate," Doc said.

Putain. Doc was right. Flynn had a choice: Angelito's future or Tess's safety.

TESS PERCHED ON the edge of Samira's carved wooden desk. "You should leave, too," she said. "Go with Flynn and his unit—or just jump in your car and drive. If you're caught with me, Hamid will... Not that I intend to get caught, but I haven't intended for a lot of things to happen. You've sacrificed enough for this."

Samira leaned against the opposite wall, studying her with clear brown eyes, flecked with the same shade of amber that hung on a pendant around her neck. "Too much," she said, almost to herself. "So much there is nothing else left. This is not much of a life but I have nowhere else to run. I will stay."

"He would want you to be safe."

Samira's eyes flashed. "Don't tell me what he would want. He would want his death to save others."

"And it will, but you getting hurt won't save anyone." Tess noted the photo of Samira and Latif that had sat in a frame in the corner was gone. Too risky to have on display? Tess's chest ached. If she'd got the story out earlier, would he still be alive? "I'm truly sorry for bringing this on you. I know we haven't talked much since Latif died but—"

Samira held up a henna-painted palm. "You didn't bring this on us. Latif knew there could be consequences. *I* knew. I'm sorry for earlier, when you arrived. I was…shocked. Seeing you again…" She turned to the tiny window, the diffused light from the net curtain brightening her cheek to a smooth caramel. "Latif would want me to help you. And I want to help you." She turned back, delicately crossing her arms over her crisp navy shirt. "My friend, I live in darkness already."

Tess looked at the rippled whitewashed ceiling, her eyes watering. Now was not the time for tears.

Samira stepped to the desk, pulled out a drawer and felt around behind it. She retrieved a small plastic bag and handed it to Tess.

Inside was a flash drive. The copy of the dossier that Samira and Latif had kept. Tess closed her fist around it, feeling like she could breathe properly for the first time in too long.

"What else do we need?" Samira said.

Tess rattled off a list of equipment. "I'll do everything off-line so it can't be traced to you." She bit her lip. "And I might need to borrow some money for it all."

"Eshi." Okay.

"I'll need a good computer—do you have one?"

Samira raised an eyebrow.

"Sorry, dumb question."

"You can use my laptop. It's a quad core i7. Sixty-four gig."

"Um… I take it that's good?"

"You Luddites are so cute." Samira smiled creakily, the creases in the corners of her eyes deeper than Tess remembered. She was still striking but had aged five years in six months. "It's very good—not that I get to use it for anything but gaming these days. *Off-line only*," she added grimly.

Tess frowned. Like Latif, Samira was a computer security expert. Playing housemaid to tourists had to be killing her. So to speak. "Once Hamid and Hyland are brought to justice, you can return to your life."

Samira made a ticking noise, as if to say, "What life?" "I can buy everything from the Smugglers Market. It'll be counterfeit but should work."

"I hope they're still trading."

"They're probably selling fake iPhones to al-Thawra as we speak. That's everything?"

"Yes."

Samira pulled a purse from the drawer. "Now tell me about this Flynn. There is something going on? The way you looked at each other, when you climbed out of the suitcase. He was *very* worried about you."

"*Nothing's* going on."

Samira's eyebrows arched.

"Not really."

Silence. Crap, she wasn't going to let up, was she?

"Oh, I don't know." Tess rubbed her eyes. "There shouldn't be, that's for sure."

"He is married?"

"No! But he's a soldier, and I don't want to take the risk that…" Her cheeks went cold, then hot. "I'm sorry. I didn't mean—"

"The risk that he won't come home." Samira sharply drew breath, making a faint "ow" sound. Amharic for *yes*. "Believe me, I understand that…but one thing I've learned from losing Latif? You must treasure life while you can. I wish I had taken more opportunities when I had them. It was nice to see the way Flynn looked at you and remember…" She blinked twice and straightened. "I should get going. I will also buy food, to make it look like a regular shopping trip."

"I'd feel better if one of the guys went with you…?"

"*Eshi.* I have texted my guests and arranged for them to stay at another guesthouse, outside the old town, so it will be just us here for today."

They rejoined the others. Okoye had returned, and Angelito assigned him the shopping trip.

"Everyone needs a token black man," Okoye said, winking at Tess.

Flynn sought Tess's gaze, a question on his face. She opened her palm, revealing the flash drive. He nodded.

Samira picked up a basket. "It'll take maybe an hour." She looked from Tess to Flynn and back again. "While you wait, you two might want to clean up."

Flynn looked down at his clothes. "I thought we already had."

"That's your idea of clean? I'm surprised al-Thawra hasn't tracked you down by smell. You can use the room off the courtyard."

Tess's scalp itched, on cue. A shower. Holy cow, she could have a shower.

"Appreciate the honesty," Flynn said.

Angelito lifted the suitcase. "Take this. In case they return."

"The room has a *well*-stocked bathroom," Samira said. "Use anything you wish. See you in an hour."

As she walked past, followed by Okoye, Tess detected sly grins. Her cheeks warmed.

The way you looked at each other... It wasn't that obvious, was it? Though, granted, since Flynn had turned up she'd been fighting competing urges to drive him against a wall and kiss him, and toss him out the gate.

His hand grazed her lower back, making her jump. "Guess we'll go and get...cleaned up, then," he said.

Oh man. *Flynn* and *shower*. They'd spent most of the last two days alone together, and much of it in confined spaces, but suddenly the prospect of being together in a real bedroom made her breath catch. She followed him through the living room and courtyard, staring at the ground, like she already had a guilty conscience. He pushed open the heavy wooden door and stood aside, clearing his throat. When he closed it behind them, the hum and whir of the outside world muted.

"Oh my God, Flynn. A real bed."

Her body felt weighted, like something was pulling her toward it. She stumbled a few steps, slipped off her shoes and flopped onto the crisp white bedcover, staring at the rough whitewashed ceiling. Her bones practically groaned.

Flynn's lips curled up, making her belly somersault all over again. "Guess I'm having first shower?"

"Guess you are." She shut her eyes. From head to toe her body ached and tingled. "Turns out ninja yoga is not a good way to follow a half marathon."

"Ah, Tess?"

"Mmm-hmm?"

"There's no door to the bathroom."

She cracked open her eyelids. The showerhead was indeed straight ahead through an archway. "You choose now to be a prude?"

He chuckled and grabbed a white towel from the end of the bed. The reminder of their earlier encounter heated her up from the inside.

"I won't watch," she said.

If she had the energy to cross her fingers, she would. He pulled up his T-shirt, easing to slow motion to get it over his head wound, and took off his gun and a holster. This time it wasn't his scars and bruises she noticed, but the tanned ridges and bunches of muscle. A tattoo looped across his upper back, accentuating the knots that dipped in to meet his spine. A word, in cursive letters. *Sans retour.* Suddenly, she wasn't feeling so tired. Suddenly, breathing wasn't so straightforward. He balled up the T-shirt and fired it onto a chair.

You must treasure life while you can.

"You're watching," he said.

She lifted her gaze to his face, which had cracked into his trademark asymmetrical grin. Liquid heat simmered between her legs. She swallowed. "Am I?"

He tipped his head. "You know, they probably don't have much water out here. It would make sense to conserve it." He stepped to the edge of the bed and held out a hand.

Good grief. She didn't move—couldn't move. Neither did he. His sexy grin didn't waver; his hand didn't budge; his heavy-lidded eyes didn't leave hers.

Like he already knew she'd say yes.

CHAPTER TWENTY-ONE

"WE SHOULDN'T." TESS'S whisper sounded as half-hearted as it felt.

"Probably not." Without taking his eyes off hers, Flynn planted his hands either side of her thighs and leaned over. "You know, usually, in a situation like this—not that I'm saying it happens all the time—I might use some bullshit about how good we are together and how this could be the beginning of something beautiful."

"Usually?" She licked her dry lips.

Like a predatory big cat, he crawled—prowled—onto the bed, his knees brushing the outside of hers. So close and yet so far. He had her pinned by a single strand of hair under his right hand. "But I'm the kind of guy who might not come home." He sank to his forearms, bringing his lips an inch away but still not touching her, *anywhere*. So why was her every nerve buzzing? "I can't hide how much I like you, but I can't get involved with you, either."

"Your dark secrets."

That tantalizing flicker of a grin. "I don't have secrets, remember? I have a very average regular past that I will not bother going into because it's so dull. Sunshine, I'm so tedious I can't date anyone in case her soul shrivels and dies from extreme boredom." He spoke in

a hoarse growl that brought to mind his throaty French
R, every word raising the heat in her body. "Seriously,
that happened with my last girlfriend, and I have too
much of a hero complex to do it to anyone else. There,
that's my dirty secret."

"Sure it is." She touched his smooth cheek with a single finger and stroked it along his jaw, down his neck,
over his collarbone.

"So we're cool with this being a one-off?" His voice
was getting huskier by the second.

"Right now, I'll agree to anything." She scraped a
fingernail over his nipple, biting her lip as his pec tightened.

He grabbed her wrist, leaving his torso balanced on
one arm. "Tess, I need to know we're on the same page. I
like you too much to want to leave you…disappointed."

I like you too much.

She swallowed. "A one-off." Something clunked in
her chest. *No.* No regret. She was going to enjoy this.

"A one-off. Just sex. Just fun. Just an escape."

"We'd better make it good, then." It was meant to
sound sexy, but it came out squeaky.

He released her wrist, returning his forearm to the
bed. "We'd better make it awesome."

She slid her free hand down his abs—rigid from the
strain of taking his weight—and around his muscled
hip. "Seeing as I'm already close to exploding, I think
we're okay there. From my perspective."

He flicked his gaze down her body as if expecting
to see the heat pulsing volcanic red through her skirt.
"Hey, if you're okay, I'm okay. Guaranteed."

And still he didn't touch her. *Come on.* This was
not a time to drop the Action Man act. "Flynn." If her

breasts got any heavier they'd grow enough to reach him—and that was saying a lot.

"Yes?" His gaze returned to hers.

"You'd better touch me before something happens spontaneously that makes me look embarrassingly desperate."

"Really?" He lowered just close enough for his chest to graze the fabric covering her bra, squeezing a squeak from her throat. "I'd like to watch that. You're making abstinence sound fun." His warm breath coasted across her face.

"Good grief, Fly—"

He pressed his lips to hers, sinking onto her—his chest crushing her breasts, his stomach on hers. At. Last. With his knee, he nudged her legs apart. The wraparound skirt gave, falling open, and he settled between her thighs, pressed hard against her. *Hard* against her. He cradled the sides of her head as his tongue explored. Hell, an hour with Flynn had to be the equivalent of a lifetime with her dependable accountant.

And, man, now was not the time to think of her accountant. Sure, her future would be with a regular guy, but today she'd settle for a god. She bent her knees up and wriggled her hips to free the skirt and get him in *just* the right spot. She groaned. *Just* the right spot. She grabbed his butt cheeks and wrapped her ankles around his waist. Yay, yoga. Yay, wrap skirt. He got the memo and ground against her, settling into a tempo that could end only one way. Her breath quickened and shallowed as he moved, his chest kneading her breasts, his lips and tongue devouring her mouth. Heaven.

When she could no longer get enough oxygen through her nose, she broke the kiss, panting. Laughing, he eased his chest off hers, slipped a hand under her T-shirt and palmed her breast. His lips touched her neck, and he kissed and licked as he flicked her nipple through the scratchy lace and kept up the tormenting rhythm below. *Who said men couldn't multitask?* she thought, dimly. Crap. This was it; she was going to come, fully clothed, like some teenager groping in the back of a car. He pushed harder. Yikes. She dug her fingertips into his shoulders and rode the sweet flow of magic, gasping as she built and built and built and... splintered. Heat flew through her lower body, fiery and quenching at the same time. Her vision pinpricked as the fire bloomed, ebbed and, gradually, slid away. He eased into stillness, panting into her throat, his hand cupping her breast.

He chuckled, the movement vibrating through her. "You are *so* easy."

"Not normally, believe me."

"Just with me, right?"

"Yeah, because you need the ego boost."

He slid onto his side, his head propped in one hand. "Hey, don't bite the hand that gets you off."

He leaned in and began kissing her in slow, hot strokes. She palmed his stomach, slid over his waistband and cupped his fly.

"Hell," she said, breaking the kiss. "You are *so* easy."

"You see how much of a saint I am for letting you have your way every time?"

"*Every* time? Twice."

"Why stop there?" He rolled away and reached for the drawer under the bedside table. "Jackpot," he said, holding up a condom packet. "Free condoms everywhere on this continent, and finally I get to take advantage of it." He jumped off the bed and held out his hand. "Shall we see if we can double your score? But you know, Tess…" She let him pull her to her feet. Her knees wobbled. "I'm a little bit tired of you taking advantage."

"It is getting a little predictable." Unable to tiptoe with her toes bandaged, she slid the fingers of her free hand to the back of his neck and pulled him down for a teasing, nibbling kiss. This was…fun. Fun was not what she'd expected of this week. Flynn wasn't what she'd expected.

He backed into the shower, taking her with him, kissing all the way. As his back hit the wall, she coasted a hand over his shorts. He grabbed the bottom of her T-shirt and lifted, as she dived for his fly. Their arms crashed. She giggled.

"You first," she said, raising her arms. He pushed her T-shirt up and over her head, sending it flying blindly back into the room, and fumbled with her bra clasp. It'd be much easier if she could push a button and get them naked.

"Damn, this thing's a bitch." He spun her around and caught her waist with a jolt, like some graceless ballet. She pictured him bending to navigate the clasp. Her skin shivered at the sudden absence of his touch—and the anticipation of it returning. "Got it."

Kissing her neck, he slid his hands under the loosened bra and caught her nipples between his fingers, lighting her up all over again. His erection jammed into her lower back. His chest was smooth and warm against her spine. *More, more, more.*

She dropped her head back, giving him more room to nuzzle her neck, while his hands slid to her waist.

Her skirt had come so loose it fell away with hardly a touch. Half a second later it flew overhead, a swirling flag of colors.

He shoved her panties over her hips so fast she gasped. She wriggled them to the floor. Blessedly efficient. He returned one hand to her breast, pulling and teasing the nipple, while rubbing the heel of his other palm into her red zone. Heck, she was in danger of losing the use of her legs altogether. Somehow it'd become all about her again. He gripped her between her legs and lifted her clean off her feet just long enough for her to kick the panties into the room, his fingers *so* close to slipping in right where she needed him.

When she regained her balance, she swiveled. As nice as all that was, she wanted to watch him, wanted some control, wanted to give back. She dived for his mouth and shuddered her fingers down his abs to slip under his waistband. As she fingered his silky, wet tip, he moaned. A charge of anticipation shot between her legs. She released his lips and he tipped his head back onto the tiled wall, panting, his eyes half-closed, like opening them was beyond him. "So fucking sexy," she murmured as she undid the button, kissing the salty hollow above his collarbone. As her hands worked the zip, she trailed her lips and tongue down his chest—the light V of hair between his pecs, a flat brown nipple, the ridges of his abs. Skirting his bruises, she diverted to the knotted muscles at one hip, grinning as they tightened.

"Holy shit, Tess."

"*So* easy. I haven't even started."

"Fuck me." His words were barely audible.

"I plan to. Condom?"

"Uh, back pocket."

With a nudge, the fly fell away. Straightening, she wrapped a hand around him, watching his eyes roll back and his mouth drop open. Oh yes, she would enjoy every sweet second of this. He slapped his palms against the wall and held them there as if the earth were shaking. She let him go long enough to retrieve the condom and push his shorts and underwear to the floor, then sank her fingers into the muscular flesh of his ass and kissed him, her hunger building. Bliss. Dirty, no-strings-attached bliss. He kicked his clothes away and pulled her in tight, his hands exploring her back and butt, his erection pushing into her stomach. His body felt hard and rough and demanding. He broke the kiss, panting, and fumbled at the wall beside him.

She let her gaze drop over him. "You look exactly how I thought you would."

"You pictured me naked?"

Heat stung her cheeks. "Uh…"

"Don't sweat it. I totally imagined you naked, too. But it was nothing compared with this."

"To," she murmured.

"What?"

"Compared t— Forget it."

Cold water spurted from the showerhead above his shoulder, blasting her cheek. She gasped. Karma? For correcting his grammar?

"Sorry." He reached under her butt, hoisted her and spun them, his tongue slippery and demanding in her mouth. Her back touched the cold tile. She arched, but the chill was a welcome change. She wrapped her legs around his waist and clung to his shoulders. His erection pushed against her, sending need throbbing through her. Warming, the water ran down his hunched back and trickled onto her chest, creating pools in the dips between their bodies.

"Much as I'd like to take this slowly, sunshine, I—"

"Oh, take advantage, please."

He held her steady with one hand while he tore open the condom packet with his mouth. Desire ripped through her. Somehow he managed to roll the thing on while holding her up. Pretty fucking ninja, all right. He guided himself to her entrance and pushed into her with a groan.

"Oh." Magic.

He gripped her ass, kneading her cheeks and pulling her into him with each thrust. His mouth searched, hitting her chin and the side of her mouth before she turned and took him in, hot, wet kisses slamming into her with the same urgency as his hips. Water slicked them, its warmth nothing next to his fiery heat, and the cool tiles. Raw desire took over. He hoisted her and drove in harder.

"This okay?" he whispered, breathless.

"Oh hell, yes."

"Good. Because…fuck."

She laughed. French poetry be damned. That was *exactly* how she felt.

"Don't. Laugh."

He silenced her with his mouth. She wrapped her fingers around his nape and kissed him greedily as the pressure and heat built. All sound gave way to the roaring in her head. She rose, and rose, and rose, her head spinning like it was separating from her body. She squeaked. Pleasure ripped through her, his mouth absorbing her cries. He grunted and pushed deep before stilling, then coming apart himself. She gripped his butt as he crested.

They stayed put a minute, panting, and then he gently lowered her feet to the floor, her legs quivering. He touched his forehead to hers, closing his eyes. She let hers shut, too, exploring the ripples of his back as he hugged her tight. The water washed down his spine. She could just melt into him.

As their breathing returned to normal, as the fire between them gave way to the merciful lukewarm of the shower, he reached up and grabbed a bottle from an alcove. He squeezed out a clear gel, rubbed it between his hands and stroked down the sides of her neck and over her shoulders, lifting her breasts, massaging her back, rubbing her thighs and calves like he knew how they ached. Silently, slowly, he washed her top to bottom, like a ritual. She leaned against the wall, lapping up the exquisite luxury of being worshipped. Two days ago, this was not where she'd have expected to end up. A day from now she'd wonder if it ever happened.

No. Don't think about tomorrow. Don't think about anything but him, and this. No monsters and wolves, not yet. Just this—the gentle insistence of his touch, the feeling of being...yep...loved. Even if they both knew it wasn't that. In time, he moved up and washed her hair, his clear gaze so intent on his task, it freed her to study his face. He looked boyish, liberated from the darkness that cloaked him. The shudder she'd felt earlier had gone. Whatever instinct had triggered her doubts had been overridden by this—the urgency and release of sex followed by the bliss of being looked after by more than his protective streak.

Her chest twisted. How much harder would it be

to watch him walk away now? If only she had time to get to know this side of him, to give him a permanent place of safety where he could shed his defenses and heal his scars and be this generous, loving man. Where she could retreat and love him without fear.

Not to be. But the memories of this would last a lifetime. Better to watch him go today with a sweet pang of regret than have her heart ripped apart later. One day she would remember him with a wistful nostalgia, smiling to herself about the happy secret that was all her own. No suffering awkward questions from relatives. No third degree from her brothers, or knowing sympathy from her mom. No friend saying, "Whatever happened with that guy, anyway?" No women's magazine "scoops" about her broken heart. No anger, no humiliation, no grief. The delicious beginning of a relationship, with no fraught middle or bitter end. A secret oasis, which she could return to in her mind whenever she needed.

So, oh God, why did she want to wrap her arms around him and tell him things she shouldn't tell him and nestle in like it was forever?

CHAPTER TWENTY-TWO

FLYNN WATCHED TESS dress while he rinsed the soap from his body. How could a moment rock and suck at the same time? The long buildup since their encounter in the wasteland had been worth the wait—the reverberations were still shuddering down his legs. Jesus, the thought of it had him ready to go again. And then soaping her up afterward—what was that even about? It'd seemed like the natural comedown. He hadn't wanted it to end—he'd wanted to own her, or something. Like any guy could own Tess Newell.

She cautiously dried the dressings on her toes. They'd held. Good. If they'd had to fess up to Doc, he'd guess exactly how it'd happened, and Flynn wasn't ready for that interrogation. At least sex had stopped his nerves from banging on about his throbbing head and the bruises that had pretty much joined up to form a ring around his torso. He patted his crown. Doc's handiwork seemed okay.

Halfway through tying her skirt, Tess froze and stared at him like she'd figured out something. "Oh crap."

His gut churned.

"I don't even know your surname."

He exhaled. False alarm. "Yeah, you do."

She frowned.

"Flynn," he said.

"Wait—" She pulled the ties tight. "That's your *sur-name*? I've been calling you that all along."

He shut off the water and grabbed his towel. "It's what everyone calls me."

"What's your first name?"

He wrapped the towel around his waist. "Does it matter?"

"After what we just did? Yeah, it does."

Ah, what harm could it do now? "Errol."

She frowned, computing. *Wait for it...* Her shoulders slumped. "Way to make a girl feel cheap."

"It's the name in my passport."

"You're so frustrating." She snatched up her towel and began to squeeze the water from her hair. "Okay, so it's your legion name. What's your real name?"

He stepped into the room, strapped on the holster and pulled his T-shirt over top. His real name was two fake names ago. It meant nothing. "That's a question."

"Don't you think I've earned a bit of honesty?"

"What, so this was a fact-finding mission?" He knew it wasn't—that shit was real, on both sides.

She dropped onto the bed, the towel falling across her lap. "I don't think it's unreasonable to want to know the name of the guy I just slept with."

"Errol Flynn. My legal name."

Rolling her eyes, she returned to rubbing her hair.

"I'm not being rude, Tess. As far as I'm concerned, Flynn is my name. No one's called me anything else since I was a teenager."

Her eyes crinkled with...*pity*. Shit. He should never have told her about his mum and sister dying. "Wait." Her expression changed, to her *60 Minutes* face. *Here we go. She's figured it out.* "No one's called you anything else since you were a teenager?" She spoke quietly, like she was playing the words around in her head. "But you said you joined the legion after first serving in the regular army and graduating officer academy. You would have been well into your twenties."

Bloody hell. She was a dangerous woman to lie to. "Leave it alone. It doesn't concern you and it makes no difference to this thing between us. My name is Flynn, end of story."

She chewed a fingernail, evidently unconvinced. "I know you're not being straight with me about a lot of things, for whatever reason, and I'm trying to tell myself that it doesn't matter—but it does. Honestly? It's kind of doing my head in to try to figure out how much is truth and how much is a lie."

"Well, stop trying to figure it out. Enough." Ignoring the sting of guilt, he strode to the end of the bed, pushed her shoulders until she was lying on her back, eased on top of her and kissed her. She moaned, sliding her hands around his neck. He pulled away slightly. "From now on I'm doing this every time you get nosy."

"You know that's only going to make me nosier." Her blue eyes had darkened. "Like a lab rat getting rewarded for doing tricks."

"Sunshine, you've probably figured out that I left my old life behind a long time ago, for some very good reasons. Believe me when I say you don't want to know."

She stroked the sides of his neck with her thumbs. "You know, you are like an Australian Errol Flynn. Swashbuckling, lady-killing, heroic…at least in your head."

"Errol Flynn *was* Australian."

"No way."

"Dead set."

"Dead what?"

"Never mind."

"So…you're not denying you're Australian now? That's a start."

He nudged her lips with his.

"Did you choose it—the name?"

He kissed harder. She giggled, opening her mouth, and he flicked his tongue across hers. Silky and sweet, like other parts of her he'd like to spend a lot more time exploring.

"The recruiting officer chose the name. He had just done the paperwork on an American he named John Wayne, so he figured he was on a roll. I didn't care, as long as…"

"As long as you could leave your past behind." She wriggled up the bed. Getting more comfortable. Good. Because he wasn't nearly finished with this thing they had going. He followed, settling his legs between hers and sliding his arms under her shoulders.

"Is that what *sans retour* is all about?" she said.

"Yeah. No going back."

"To what?"

"Tess, I really like you. I like hanging out with you. I like the things we talk about. I like that you stand up to me and push me around and don't take any of my crap. I like how you chew your lip when you're thinking. I like the way you groan when you're about to come. Actually, I fucking love that. But stop with the interrogation. My past isn't important. Hell, my future's not important. All I give a damn about is this moment, because

I swear it's one of the best in my life—or it would be without the endless bloody questions."

She laughed, looking as fresh and bright eyed as if she'd spent a week in Hawaii—if you overlooked the bruises and scrapes, including one cute graze right on the tip of her nose. "I guess…" She touched a finger to his bottom lip, swallowing. "I wish you felt you could share more with me. Whatever happened back then has made you the man you are today."

"That's the problem."

"I mean that in a good way. Your protective instinct, your thirst to see justice done—maybe you're compensating for whatever happened when you were young."

Mate. A timely reminder of how dangerous she was.

She slipped her hands up the back of his T-shirt, her palms heating his lower back. His dick all but twanged. "Whatever you did in the past, it can't be that bad. You had to have been cleared by Interpol to get into the legion."

"Question."

"Statement. No question mark."

"So you don't expect me to respond."

"Hey, look, no hidden microphone. I wouldn't sleep with someone for a story."

"Yeah?"

Lines bunched around her eyes. "Seriously? You think that poorly of me. What have I done to deserve *that*?"

He raised his eyebrows.

"That thing with the phone? I've already told you—I hadn't planned it to go so far." She broke out her sexy changing-the-subject smile. "I can't help it if you drive me crazy."

"In bed or out of it?"

"Both. Look, Fly— Erro—" She shook her head like a fly was buzzing her. "*Flynn.* I get you've got a secret, and I'd love it if you could confide in me. But if you can't, fine. I trust you that you wouldn't seduce me if it wasn't…appropriate."

He dropped his gaze, focusing instead on her shoulder, the bone sharp under her T-shirt. Appropriate? Way to make him feel like the lowlife he was. Would she figure out the connection one day and despise him? Should he come clean—make this thing they had going mean something?

No. It was too late for the truth—and too soon. Like there was ever a good time to say, "My old man was a serial killer, and I stood by and let him do it because I didn't want to bring down my world, messed up as it was."

She slid a hand off his back and stroked the bridge of his nose, firing up the skin like she was charged with electricity. "There's a sadness in your eyes, even when you're making a joke. It's always there. Like you've seen too many things you wish you could forget."

Mate, she had a talent for striking close to the mark. "I have, okay? Things happened, when I was a kid, a teenager. They will always haunt me. But please, let me leave them in the past, where they belong." He swallowed. "I'm into you like I've never been into anyone else. You're smart. You're strong. You're so way out of my league you could be on another planet. If things were different, who knows? But they're not, and neither of us can change that. This right now? This is awesome. Very, very soon we leave all of it behind—but I'll be taking some fucking good memories with me."

She laid her finger on his lower lip, pulling lightly on it. "Or some good fucking memories."

He laughed and captured her finger between his teeth. That was another thing he liked—the way she caught him off guard. "Dare you to say that on live TV," he mumbled.

This time he made the kiss last, exploring her gently and slowly. Building up again. His body hadn't got the message this was a onetime thing and their time was done. He moved his lips down to her neck and slipped his hands under her T-shirt.

She sighed. "What was I saying, just before?"

He bunched the T-shirt and licked one tight nipple through her lacy bra, grinding into the paradise between her thighs. Good thing he hadn't fully dressed. And now he got to strip her all over again. "You were saying you're ready to go again."

"Mmm."

He pushed down the lace and sucked her nipple into his mouth. His dick throbbed. How had he not found the time to do this before? So much unfinished business.

"Yes, that's what it was…exactly." She arched into him, her voice husky. Yep, that right there was going to be a good fucking memory. She clutched his shoulder as he teased, her fingernails digging in. He reluctantly released her to pull her T-shirt off and smoothed the messy, damp hair off her forehead. Her pupils were dark and big and steady, her light blue irises thinly ringed in navy. She looked younger, untainted by evil and worry, like they were regular lovers having a regular encounter in a regular place.

"Sunshine, there are many things in my life I want to forget. But this I intend to remember."

FOR THE SECOND time since her shower, Tess located her strewed clothing and hurriedly dressed. As she fastened her creased skirt, Flynn checked his watch.

"How long have we been in here?" she said. Surely someone would have knocked if hell had unleashed.

"An hour."

"Seriously?"

"I know, right?" He sauntered up and caught her hips, forcing her to tip her head back to maintain focus on his face. "If you'd told me it'd been four hours I would have believed it in a shot."

"Me, too."

He smoothed a lock of her hair between his fingers. "You know, I thought your hair was naturally a dirty-blond color."

"No, that was genuine dirt." Not that the blond was genuine.

"You were filthy, weren't you?"

"You weren't so fresh yourself."

He laughed, wrapping one arm then the other around her back, and bowed his head to kiss her crown. She rested a cheek on his chest and wound her arms around his waist, her lungs filling with the bliss of this sanctuary, however temporary. The last hour had felt like one of those rare times where life tipped and rearranged, creating a new center of gravity, jumping to a new track.

But it hadn't. It was just a very pleasant blip. An oasis in the craziness. Neither of their lives would change. They might have detonated the physical barriers between them, but the emotional ones remained. Yet, she felt as if more had joined than their bodies, like her heart had jumped out of her chest and fused a little with his. God, she wasn't supposed to feel sad after the best sex of her life. Sated, uplifted—sure. But sad?

She smoothed her palms onto his hips and reluctantly pulled back. He took the cue and released her.

"That was a beautiful thing, Tess," he whispered.

"It was. Thank you." *Beautiful* was a good word— an unexpected word from him. Not *mind-blowing*, not *stupendous*. Sure, it was all that, but so much more.

He held her gaze with those pale eyes, that slightest of smiles. So now she knew—everything she felt for him, he felt for her. And something held him back, just as her doubts held her. It was too risky, all round.

He caught her hand, threaded his fingers through hers and squeezed. "Ready for the monsters and wolves?"

FLYNN STROLLED ACROSS the courtyard, his palm skimming Tess's lower back. The top of her butt shifted with her every step. That was another place he'd like to chase a spider into. Too late. Back to business, back to reality—and reality was a hot and hazardous place. Thor, on lookout, acknowledged them with a jerk of his chin, his face parked in neutral, as usual.

The smell of spices and coffee curled through the air. In the main house, Angelito and Doc, seated on the lowest platform, didn't look up from the map spread between them. Texas had pulled up a chair beside the door, where he had a sight line to Thor. A whistle flew in from the gate—the theme from *2001: A Space Odyssey*, the unit's code green. In the courtyard, Thor lifted the latch and the gate creaked open. Samira's rich accent floated in, lilting and rolling. Maybe she'd studied in America?

"You will have to eat before you leave," she was saying as she walked in, a basket balanced on her head. "My guests might not return for a while, so we have plenty of food."

Plenty of food. Magic words.

As Okoye hauled the overstuffed shopping bag inside, Samira swung the basket from her head. She dug under a heap of red onions and capsicums and brought out a box advertising a "Sonny" brand camcorder.

"China's finest fakes," she said, handing it to Tess. "I got you an Android phone, in case it doesn't work. And a prepay card. Oh, and I have a new number. Quan and I ditched our burners and got new ones when you were kidnapped, just in case our numbers were on your phone."

"They weren't but good thinking," Tess said.

"Sit rep?" Angelito asked Okoye.

"Buildup of enemy, four or five at every gate, armed with M16s. Some contractors, some in al-Thawra gray. They're stopping all white people, checking ID. And still going door to door inside the walls."

"We will need ID for you," Angelito said to Flynn. "We all have our pre-legion IDs, or fakes."

Flynn nodded. They'd learned long ago that it could be handy to have alter egos when on black ops.

Samira handed Tess several packaged flash drives. "No sign of local police. There is talk they're being held by al-Thawra. Even if that's not true, they don't have the resources to take on al-Thawra alone. Word is that the Ethiopian Defense Force is on its way."

"No," Tess said under her breath. She cleared her throat. "That's what al-Thawra wants—to escalate this as much as possible. That could goad Ethiopia into having another crack at Somalia. And this old town is a World Heritage site, a holy city to Islam. An outright battle here would be up there with destroying the Buddhas of Bamiyan in Afghanistan." She met Samira's gaze. "Except with large loss of life."

Flynn grabbed Tess's elbow and drew her aside, putting his back to the others. "You can't stay here."

"I have no choice. If I leave with you, I'll endanger you and your whole team. And someone will trace them back to Samira. I can't risk being handed to the authorities—" She raised a palm as he went to protest. "You can't guarantee that won't happen."

"We'll disguise you. You heard what Okoye said. They're only stopping foreigners. We dress you in a full burka and send you out with him. The rest of us can—I don't know—create a distraction and cover you while you get out."

"It's not worth the risk. We've been over this—my best chance is to wait this out. Any minute, someone will be here to pick up my story. A couple of hours after that, I win this. I just need to stay out of sight until then."

"I'm not leaving you here."

"Yes, you are."

"Then I'm staying with you."

"No!"

Flynn tensed. The room had quietened. Damn. He turned slowly, releasing her. Yep, all eyes on them. He rubbed his face. "I'm staying with her."

"Flynn, no," Doc said. "You know what this could mean."

Tess crossed her arms. "What could this mean?"

Flynn shot Doc a shut-the-hell-up look.

"Doc?" Tess said. "What could this mean?"

"The end of Flynn's career. Demotion at best. And the legion is the only thing that *connard* has got. Not to mention it'll put a cloud over the *capitaine*, right when he doesn't need one."

"Shut it, Doc," Flynn said through clenched teeth.

"She's not stupid, Flynn. She has a right to know the consequences of what you're doing on her behalf. You heard the lady—she'll be fine here. Your judgment is clouded, and you have a head injury that needs an MRI and monitoring. You won't be much use to her if you have a bleed in your brain."

"Okay, *du calme, du calme*." Angelito stood, parking himself between Doc and Flynn. "*Mademoiselle*, putting my orders aside, there is a good argument for taking you with us, if you want to spare this town. If you're seen to leave, it could draw away al-Thawra's attention. We can get a chopper to Djibouti from outside the city."

Tess started, her eyes sparking. "I hadn't thought of that." She looked up at a corner of the ceiling. Thinking. "If I'm seen to leave." She returned focus to Angelito. "Once in Djibouti, I could announce my 'rescue' on social media. Not before, for all our safety. We would need to keep it very quiet."

"That would be wise," Angelito said. "We can maintain black ops until then. And my communications with command would be contained and coded. No chance of a leak."

She nodded, slowly at first, then vigorously. "Yes. Yes, that could work."

Hallelujah. A hand clapped on Flynn's shoulder. Doc, standing beside him, his head slightly bowed. An apology, of sorts, for his outburst. The medic might be 95 percent clown, but he gave a damn and wasn't scared to let it be known. He'd stand up for anyone—and to anyone—if he saw the need.

"All good, mate," Flynn said quietly.

"I'll record my piece here and leave a copy for Quan's courier," Tess said quickly. "Then we'll leave when the *chat* trucks come."

Samira pulled a packet of potato chips from the grocery bag and passed them to Okoye. "I don't know anyone who wears a burka, but I could get one made at Makina Girgir—there are still some tailors out. And I know a safe place you could land a helicopter. Give me a minute to get this stuff sorted and I'll show you."

Tess looked at the box she was holding. "I'd better get to work."

Flynn sat on the middle platform and leaned back, tipping his head to stare at the thick wooden beams running across the ceiling. Everything was going to work out.

Right?

CHAPTER TWENTY-THREE

FLYNN FOLLOWED TESS back to their room. *The* room, now. Their moment together was over. The sun burned into his neck even in the few steps across the court-yard. "So you're seriously coming with us?" he said as she opened the door.

"Yep." She walked to the bed and began ripping at the camera box.

"You're not worried about the US picking you up at Djibouti?"

"By then I'll have my piece recorded and on its way out to the world, so…" She scanned the room as she pulled out the camera. "*Que sera, sera.* Can you move that lamp over beside that chair?"

"That was a pretty quick U-turn on the whole stay-or-go thing." For a woman as stubborn as a bulldog with a bone. "What happened to your fear of putting my guys in danger?"

"You're trained to deal with danger and you're armed. Your *capitaine* was right. These people…" She swept her hand around the room, indicating invis-ible masses outside the walls. "Are not. This city has stood for nearly a thousand years. I will not be respon-sible for its destruction and the deaths of thousands." She stepped to a window and pushed across the net-ting, spilling a rectangle of light into the room. "It's my savior complex. Anyway, I thought you wanted me to come."

"I do. I'm just trying to get my head around your change of plan." He dragged the lamp over and found a socket for it, as she examined the camera.

"You were right, Flynn—is that so hard to believe? I should take the safer option here and come with you. Winging it, see?"

"Sunshine, it's not hard to believe I'm right. It's hard to believe you accepting that."

She shoved a chest of drawers into the middle of the room. "Because you know me so intimately?" she said, lowering her tone to sex-factor nine.

"I know you well enough that when you start flirting like this you're deflecting."

"Not everything I do has a hidden agenda." She picked up something shiny from the floor—a condom wrapper. "Better keep this out of shot."

He sighed. Whatever the truth was, she wasn't letting him in on it.

"Are you going to help me or stand there doubting?"

He shrugged. He should be grateful for the easy out. Risk his future by staying here with her? Why the hell had that seemed like a good idea? *Hero complex, my arse.* Rack it up as a lucky escape.

"Sure, whatever," he said. "You're filming it in here?"

"The background's neutral enough not to be recognizable and the lighting's okay." She plugged the camera in, rested it on the drawers and fiddled with it, angling it toward the chair. "I'll have to get you to focus it for me. I'll do a quick test and then start shooting. It won't be Scorsese but it'll pass." She fitted a microphone into the camera, unraveled the cord until it reached the chair and sat. "Welcome to show business. Tell me when it's rolling."

"O-kay."

"The big red button is usually a good place to start."

Once he figured out how to focus and record, she launched into a children's rhyme, the kind of thing that would have a normal person tied in knots, but it flowed from her as cleanly as if she were reciting the alphabet. She watched over his shoulder while they played it back, her breath on his neck messing with his concentration. She made some adjustments, recorded again, checked again.

"Let's do it," she said, sitting on the chair.

"You're just going to launch into it? Don't you need your dossier?" Wasn't that what they'd risked their lives for?

"Not for this bit—I'll fold that in during editing. Believe me, I've had plenty of downtime to think about what I'm going to say. I wish I had interviews on camera but…" She shrugged. "I'll get the evidence uploaded to the network's website so people can read the documents themselves. Don't want anyone discrediting this as a wild conspiracy theory."

"Now, why would they think that? Here we go…"

She took a couple of deep breaths, paused and began speaking. "The story I'm about to tell has very nearly cost me my life. It's cost the life of the brave whistle-blower who gave me the damning evidence I am about to share with you. It's cost the lives of two of my dedicated colleagues. It will reveal who was really behind the Los Angeles terror attacks. It will reveal a criminal conspiracy involving many people in power today—in the United States, in Britain and in Europe, in governments, in corporations and in the military. As I speak, these people, and their paid mercenaries and militia forces, are trying to locate me, to silence me. Everything I am about to tell you is true and I have the paper trail to prove it.

"A week ago, I was traveling in an unmarked Land Rover in Somalia, with a translator and camera operator..."

Flynn had pieced together most of Tess's story but he felt himself getting sucked in by her voice, clear and calm as glass, as she relived her capture, her interrogation, her torture, and launched into the allegations about Hamid, al-Thawra, Denniston and their cronies—while glossing over the details of her escape. To protect him?

Mate, she was cool. Through the viewfinder she looked pale and fragile, almost girlish with her hair brushing her shoulders. But her quiet tone commanded attention, better than any *sergent-chef* shouting at a recruit, and her battered face backed up her dead-serious voice. She spoke for twenty minutes without a hesitation or slip. A woman sitting in front of a white wall, just talking, but when she described her toenails getting ripped out, he clenched his fists in anger, like he was right there with her.

So this was her comfort zone. He'd march for a month without rations before he'd get up and speak in front of ten civilians, and she spoke to millions like it was nothing. She wasn't even wearing makeup. She wasn't in it for the glory or fame, like Katie. She was in it because she saw an injustice and refused to stop until it was fixed, no matter how many people were trying to kill her. He'd seen bravery—guys taking bullets to save strangers or running toward bomb blasts when everyone else was bolting. This was a whole other kind. *So* way out of his league.

Sure, she was stubborn and manipulative and she wound him up so tight he could combust—but she fired him up in a whole lot of good ways, too. And not just in bed...or the shower.

He scoffed, silently. Here he was, thinking about sex, and Tess was calmly outlining a conspiracy that'd blow Roswell into, well, outer space.

"If, after this, I am captured and beheaded, you will know it's just to keep me quiet. Consider it further proof that I'm telling the truth. Please do not seek retribution— seek justice."

As she wrapped up, Samira quietly opened the door, holding a laptop. Doc pulled up next to her. They watched until Tess told Flynn to switch off the camera.

"Wow, that was cool," Flynn said.

Tess blew her hair out of her eyes. "It's nice to do something I'm actually trained for, after all this running and fighting."

"You didn't mention the senator. Hyland. I thought he was behind it all."

"We don't have enough evidence to incriminate him—yet," said Tess, standing and stretching. "But there's enough in here to bring down Denniston and a dozen other key figures. Hyland's been careful. I'm hoping once the dominoes start to fall the momentum will take him down. This is just the beginning."

"Let's hope," Samira said darkly. "I look forward to watching it." She crossed the room and laid the computer on the bed. "Food is ready—I suggest you move quickly because your colleagues have already begun."

"I'll keep working," Tess said, moving to the bed. "I need to get this edited."

Samira widened her eyes at Flynn, with some message he couldn't decipher. Worried about Tess not eating? He shrugged. Like a word from him would pull Tess away from her story for a technicality like sustenance.

Doc tossed Flynn a plastic tray of pills. "One every four hours. I can give you something stronger when we're out of danger. For now, we need you alert."

Flynn nodded. "Tess, I'll bring you some food."

She grunted but didn't look up as she opened the laptop. Already concentrating. Flynn followed Samira and Doc across the courtyard.

"You need ID," Samira said over her shoulder. "I have a British driver's license a guest once left behind. He didn't want me to entrust it to the post. You might have to scratch up the photo but…" She shrugged, turning back to Doc. "All blond Western men look the same, right?"

"I get them mixed up all the time," Doc said, shoving his hands in his pockets. "Flynn told me about your fiancé, Samira. I'm sorry. That's rough."

She looked up at him, blinking, her pace slowing. "Thank you."

"When was the wedding?"

Another pause, like she wasn't used to being asked about it. She swallowed. "We hadn't set a date. I'm not sure we would even have been able to marry—he was Muslim and his family wouldn't have approved unless I converted, which I didn't want to do, and he was struggling to…" She shook her head. "We were keeping our engagement a secret, which turned out to be a good thing, for my safety, at least. If al-Thawra had known about me…"

"You've been in hiding?"

"Yes. But not for much longer, I hope. I'd like to be able to see a future beyond all this, even if I'm not yet ready to live in it." She cast her voice back to Flynn. "You know, when I met Tess I thought she was crazy, with all her warnings and theories."

Flynn gave a curt laugh. "Me, too."

"Ow," she breathed. "I will be happy to see her story get out. To think Latif died for nothing…"

Doc rested a hand on her shoulder as they reached the living room. She wasn't kidding about the guys diving in. They were surrounding a raised round basket set up as a small table and shoveling handfuls of curry into their mouths, wrapped in ripped pieces of *injera* flatbread.

Samira muttered something in Amharic. "I'll ask my *sayt ayat* to prepare some more for Tess."

As she left to find her grandmother, Flynn sat on the lowest platform, next to Angelito. The music had moved on to "We Don't Need Another Hero." "Rafe," he said quietly. "What was the name of that shady senator, the one you had dealings with over Holly?"

Angelito swallowed a mouthful of curry and wiped his mouth. "Hyland. Why?"

"Looks like he might be even shadier." Flynn leaned forward and ripped a piece of *injera* from the platter. "Tess thinks he's involved in this conspiracy she's trying to bust."

"Are you serious?"

Flynn dipped the spongy pancake in a mound of

reddish curry, elbowing Texas out of the way. "It's a long story."

"*Putain de merde.* That's Tess's big story? Wow. If anyone deserves to go down…"

Flynn nodded, his mouth lighting up at the novelty of eating tasty, real food.

"Is this why you're so eager to help her," Angelito continued, "because of her story?"

Flynn swallowed. "Yeah."

"But it's not the only reason."

Flynn ripped off more *injera* and shoveled mince onto it. "No. But don't worry—this is as far as it goes. I'm not stupid." He stuffed the food into his mouth, feeling Angelito's eyes on him.

"I know," the *capitaine* said, his voice a low rumble meant only for Flynn. "*Lieutenant,* I was hard on you earlier. I know what you're putting on the line here, more than anyone, and I'm not about to stand back and watch you screw it up. But I can see that you believe in this, in her, and that's not something I'm used to seeing from you."

"Me, neither." Flynn kept his gaze on the food. It wasn't Angelito's usual all-business pep talk. But then, the guy had changed a lot lately.

Mate…was Flynn following him down the same path?

"I can't stand in the way of that." Angelito shifted back on the platform. "Just, first, tell me it's not the head injury talking."

Flynn laughed, looking up again. "It's not."

"*Mon ami,* you once took a risk for me, for a woman you didn't know. I will do the same. If I can do anything to help…"

"You already are. Getting out of this place won't be easy."

The *capitaine* grinned. Also something Flynn wasn't used to seeing. "When have we ever had it easy?"

TESS PULLED THE flash drive from the laptop, tossed it in the air and caught it. Boom. Done. It was good. Solid. Now to get it out to the world. As long as Quan got someone in and out this afternoon, he'd have it legaled and on the air tonight. *Ready and waiting, Quan.*

Meanwhile, it wouldn't hurt to quietly check the headlines. She set the web browser to incognito and punched in the address of a news network. More on the buildup of troops in Djibouti, more talk of a Somalian invasion. A photo of Hyland, accusing the president of being spineless, urging him to use military force. As far as the world knew, she was still captured, though there were rumored sightings of her in "remote parts of Africa."

Before she knew what she was doing, she clicked on the search bar. Her fingers hovered over the keyboard. There was one thing she could look up without Hamid possibly connecting it to her. She slid off the bed and padded to the door. The courtyard was empty except for Thor, leaning against a wall on sentry duty. Voices murmured from the main house. Her pulse quickened. A quick search. She probably wouldn't find anything, and Flynn would never know.

She inhaled. The air was heating up—it'd look suspicious if she closed the door, but she'd hear if anyone approached. She pushed open both windows, settled back on the edge of the bed and pulled the laptop onto her knees. Australia's most wanted, she typed. Worst-case scenario, of course. She opened a recent news story and scrolled down a gallery of mug shots. Some seriously scary-looking men but none vaguely resembling Flynn. She exhaled, in a rush. *Well, what did you expect?*

She tapped her fingernails on the laptop casing, then typed. Australia's worst criminals. The top result opened to a list of about a hundred names, but it was no use without photos. She glanced at the doorway. No time to search each one separately. She returned to the results list and opened the next hit: Australia's most notorious gangsters. She scrolled. Nope. She clicked the back button. The screen froze. *Come on.* She tapped some keys. It stuttered back to life and she accidentally loaded the next result. Australia's worst serial killers. Hell, she wouldn't find him there. She moved her finger to the mouse pad, but her gaze snagged. She froze, icy cold creeping up her face. Her breath stalled. *What the—?*

Flynn's face stared out. With hair curling around his neck, but it was him. Robert Karl Koegansen. Her stomach pitched. That was why Flynn looked familiar—she'd seen that mug shot a hundred times. He'd made headlines worldwide. The face of evil, all the more shocking because of his boyish good looks. But how could...?

She read, the letters diving into each other. He'd killed his wife and daughter and twenty-seven teenage girls between the years of...

No. The timeline didn't work. Obviously. The heat prickled back into her face. Flynn would have been a child when it started, a teenager when it finished. The guy had died in prison several years ago. False alarm, but...crap, the resemblance...

Swallowing, she plugged the name into the search bar and added son. The screen filled with media hits.

Son of Koegansen spotted in Bondi. Serial killer's son lives it up in Hawaii. Neither story fit—Flynn would have been in the French military, assuming he'd told the truth about the dates. She scrolled. Spawn of Koegansen disappears. Son of murderer gets taxpayer scholarship. An older story: Koegansen accessory case thrown out: victims furious. She clicked on that one.

A photo loaded of a much younger Flynn—unmistakably him, broken nose and all—next to a shot of Koegansen. There were differences—the nose, most obviously, and Flynn had a shaved head. But the Flynn in the photo had since morphed into his father in many ways—his face had become thinner and more angular, his eyes keener and edged with wrinkles. She chewed her lip. This was what he was running from?

The story was thirteen years old, several years before Flynn claimed to have enlisted. She forced herself to read, her shoulders growing heavier with every word. He'd been sixteen at the time of the final murder, was charged as an accessory and ordered to be tried as an adult because of the seriousness of the crime. Holy cow. The story alleged he'd intended to change his plea to guilty but the case was thrown out for lack of evidence, because of a police technical error, and because his father admitted to physical and emotional abuse. An accessory. There was a quote from the mother of the final victim.

"I don't care how young he is. He was older than my daughter. He knew what was going on and he could have stopped this. My precious girl died because he didn't speak up. We can't have this in our society. Justice has not been done today, but justice will catch up with this animal."

Her eyes pricked. No wonder Flynn was guarded. His father had abused him and murdered his mother and sister—the girl he'd watched chick flicks with. His countrymen had loathed him; people had devoted themselves to tracking him down. She covered her mouth with her palm. What had he done to be charged as an accessory—covered for his father, *helped* him?

No. Not Flynn.

She loaded the story about the scholarship, biting a knuckle. An investigative piece, written around the time he'd become a soldier. The reporter had tracked him down to a university, where he was studying under an assumed name. A photo showed him leaning back on a sun lounger, looking into the camera with the edge of his mouth curled.

Holy shit. It was the way he looked at Tess when he was flirting. Younger, more arrogant perhaps, but still with that intimacy and suggestiveness that implied he was picturing the photographer naked. The pic was credited to a Katherine Miller-Harrison. Tess's gaze flicked to the byline. Same name. His girlfriend? Oh man. *That* was why he'd gone weird when Tess had said she wouldn't sleep with someone for a story. This woman had.

A sound from the doorway. Crap. She slammed the screen shut and turned, her forehead prickling. Flynn stood frozen, a food tray in his hands, staring at the closed laptop. Wide eyes, clenched jaw, heaving chest.

CHAPTER TWENTY-FOUR

TESS GULPED. HOW could she not have clicked to the resemblance? Now all she could see in front of her was the mug shot of Robert Koegansen. And she'd slept with…

Jesus.

Flynn's gaze drifted up from the computer, fury flashing in his eyes. Or maybe hurt. Or both. She'd been so stunned she'd forgotten to watch the door. Her mouth dried.

"Flynn, I—"

"Did you find a juicy scoop?" He dumped the tray on the drawers and pivoted.

She leaped up and caught his arm. "Flynn, I… I…"

His muscles tensed from neck to jaw, his Adam's apple working. She dropped contact, backing away. Her hand shook. It wasn't Flynn's face anymore. It was the face of evil, the face she'd seen and shuddered at.

He made a ticking noise at the back of his mouth. "I should have known. People like you, you can't help yourself, can you?"

Bile burned a path up her throat. She dropped her gaze. *People like you.*

"You can't even look at me now, can you?"

"It's not that… I just…"

"It is *that*." He turned to leave.

"Flynn, no, please, I can—" *Explain? How?*

He reached the doorway and stopped, then spun. "You think you're the first person to look at me like I'm evil?" He stepped toward her, a finger raised accusingly. "It used to happen every time. I could see the reaction in people's faces as their brains figured it out. Recognition, confusion—the best you get is pity. But most people just grab their children and run. Sometimes they spit in your face. Once, a woman threw up—projectile vomited right over my T-shirt. It's the survival instinct. Which reaction are you going to give me?"

"No. Flynn, I…"

"Ah—pity."

"No, I—"

"Don't!" he shouted, making her shrink. "Don't go all 'Oh, Flynn' on me. I don't want to see that look, not from you. I don't need it and…" His voice dropped to a dismissive whisper. "I don't deserve it."

"Your broken nose. That was him, too? He beat y—"

"Stop. It wasn't like that for me. He was my dad. He wasn't the perfect dad, the dad my mates had. But when he wasn't being… Sometimes he kicked a ball around with me, you know? I wasn't a victim, so do *not* pity me."

"You were a victim. You might not have lost your life, but… You were a kid."

"You have no bloody idea what I was. You're disgusted—I can see it—and you should be. I should have told you, before we…" He looked at the shower. "But I'm a coward."

"Flynn, you are many things, but not—"

"I've been a coward all my life. I knew since I was a kid he was up to some shit. I finally figured out what just before his last kill—finally admitted it to myself.

The cops caught him with the body. When they came to find me, I already knew—where he was, who he was with, what he must be doing. I should have..." He trailed off, his focus fixed well beyond the walls. "But I didn't. I sat there, staring at a wall, a phone in my hand, and I let a girl die because I was too scared to face the truth." His mouth turned down so far the corners nearly reached his chin. "Is *that* what you so badly wanted to know? Happy now?"

"You must have been terrified."

"*She* was terrified. I don't get to play that card."

"He'd hurt you. He'd killed your mother and sister. Wait—did you know that then?"

His eyes glossed over. "Why don't you look it up?" His voice cracked. He swiveled to go.

She caught his hand. "Stay a minute, please. I looked it up because I care about you. No other reason." Was that even the truth? She had to stall him. This could be the end of things between them—she couldn't leave it like this. "I'm sorry, Flynn. I shouldn't have... I just wanted to know what haunts you. I wanted to *know* you. Because I care. Stay. Talk to me. You can't go back out there this wound up."

He dropped his head, looking at their hands. She had him there, at least. A minute passed, maybe two. She could almost hear the battle in his head between opening up, and clamming up and walking out. Her heart splintered—for that scared kid, for the adult who still suffered under all that bravado. And she'd betrayed him. She ached to thread her arms around him. Instead she wound her fingers through his. To her surprise, he let her. He sniffed loudly.

"Let it out, Flynn. Let it go. I'm a safe person."

"Are you?"

"You know I am."

Silence.

"It's not something I talk about," he said, finally.

"Maybe you need to. With someone who…cares."

He seemed to deflate in front of her eyes, a slow, imperceptible leak. She waited until she sensed the fury had ebbed and coaxed him to the bed, where they sat side by side, thighs touching. More silence.

"He told me they'd drowned, in the river," he said eventually, pulling her hand onto his lap and cradling it in both of his, like an injured bird. "Told everyone. Said he'd tried to save them. By the time their bodies washed up, they'd been in the water too long for anyone to figure out what happened. I don't know if I suspected anything at the time. I guess I didn't want to think it was possible—he was all I had left. But when he was arrested after that last kill, he confessed to all the murders, like he needed to get it all out. Ever since then, I've replayed that day at the river, over and over, trying to figure out what I really knew. It's not there. Wiped from my brain." He stroked her palm with his thumb. "I don't know why he kept me alive and I never got a chance to ask him."

"What—you never spoke to him again?"

"I couldn't face him. Didn't want to hear it. Just wanted to run and hide, and I did. Still am."

Part of her wanted to circle her arms around him, cradle his head, kiss him. But she felt repelled, too, like they were opposing magnets. He was right—she could never look at him the same. She was in shock, right? Any minute now the feeling would pass and they'd be back to…

Normal?

"They charged me. Did you read that?" he said, his deep voice quaking.

"Yeah."

"I was going to plead guilty. I was ready to go to jail, even just to give those families a little comfort, but the judge threw the case out. The choice was taken away from me—I couldn't lock myself in prison. And with Dad put away, I became public enemy number one. I was big for my age and I looked kinda tough, so people didn't see the scared kid trying to hold it together. They saw this heartless skinhead with this dead look in his eyes." His fire had burned out, leaving an exhaustion she could feel behind her own eyes. "Even thought about killing myself but I didn't have the guts. So I worked my arse off to finish school a year early, changed my name, moved as far across Australia as I could. Was stupid enough to think that would keep me safe. But with the number of girls he killed, everyone in the country seemed to know someone who knew someone… And his face had been everywhere—still is. Every time a serial killer strikes, anywhere in the world, there's his name again, his photo. The World's Top Ten Serial Killers. The World's Most Evil Criminals. Every time, like it's a competition."

"You were going to be an engineer?"

"Yep."

"What kind?" Anything to keep him talking, to give him the safe outlet she guessed he'd never had. She might not have the strength to cross that heavy physical space between them, but she ached to understand him, to let him know it was okay to hurt, to share some of that great weight. To help him heal. To fix him. So maybe she *was* that kind of woman—a woman with a savior complex.

"Structural engineer." She waited. Muffled voices filtered from the main house. "The town I grew up in had one building higher than two stories—and that one was three stories. Tall buildings fascinated me. Now I work in places where the buildings are propped up with sticks."

"You didn't get to finish your degree."

He shook his head.

"That's when you joined the legion?"

"Yeah. That story I fed you, about transferring from *l'armée*—it wasn't true, like you guessed all along. I dropped out of uni and spent my last money on a flight to Paris. The legion was perfect because you walk through that gate and your history is wiped. When you're a recruit everyone looks at you like you're shit. That makes a lot of guys crack but I was well used to it. And as the years went by and I worked my arse off, people stopped looking at me like I was shit, and started looking at me like I was *the* shit. No one asked, no one cared."

"None of them knows?"

"Angelito knows the basics. Like I said, he can be trusted. Not that the other guys can't but they have their own demons." He dropped her hand and pushed to his feet. "What are you going to do now?"

She stood, her muscles feeling wobbly. "What do you mean?"

"Write a story? Expose me?"

"You're not serious!"

He shrugged.

"Katherine Miller-Harrison. It's because of her you don't trust me."

"Hey, I have good reason not to trust you. But yeah, she gave me an early lesson."

"That's on her, not you. She seduced you and betrayed you."

"*Seduced* me? Give me some credit—that was a trap I happily walked into. And fuck me if I haven't gone and done it again. I knew I shouldn't have trusted you."

"You didn't trust me, Flynn. You still don't."

"Tell me you wouldn't have done the same as she did. She thought she was doing this great public service. A lot of people still think I have questions to answer. Hell, they're right—I do, but I still haven't figured out the answers." He lowered his voice. "You would have done the same if you'd met me back then. Written the article, I mean—maybe not the other stuff."

"No. *No.*"

"Really? So, shit-hot journalist that you are, you would have told yourself, 'Nah, let's give him a chance. He's a poor dumb kid.' You would have walked away from the scoop that would set up your career."

She squeezed her burning eyes shut. A flat denial would be a lie, and she couldn't lie to him. If she looked at the facts, if she distanced herself from the man she knew, divorced herself from her personal feelings like the good journalist she was... He *did* have a case to answer—he said so himself—and there *was* a question mark hanging over him, though she knew in her soul he was a good man. It *would be* in the public interest, and her job was to serve that interest. She should do the story now, though of course she wouldn't—she couldn't.

How far had this Katherine gone? Had Flynn been

in love? The way he'd looked at her in that photo… But no, he'd given Tess that look and he sure as hell wasn't in love with her.

"There's a great story here, Tess—that's what you're thinking, right?"

"You seriously believe I'd do that."

He gave the slightest shrug.

"Oh God, you do. I couldn't do a story. There's a…a conflict of interest, for starters." To put it mildly.

"So if we hadn't screwed, you'd be filing a story by now?"

"No." Would she? She couldn't think straight.

"But you could tell one of your journo mates and they could write it."

"No, Flynn, I wouldn't. Not after…everything we've been through, everything *you've* been through."

His mouth twisted. "Ah, crap."

"What?"

"Pity. There." He pointed to her face, like an accusation. "You feel like eating?" He waved his arm blindly toward the tray.

"Huh? No." Food was the last thing on her mind.

"Thought not. I'm sorry. I shouldn't have screwed you. A lot of things have happened that shouldn't have happened."

"Don't apologize. I don't regret anything."

Footsteps beat a path across the courtyard.

"Only because you haven't had time to absorb it. Look at you—you're shaking. You can't look at me without flinching. I bet you feel sick in your stomach. Tess, I know I haven't been straight with you and I don't deserve your respect, but I'm begging you—walk away after this and forget about me, forget about my past. I'm not like you, with your nuclear family and your career and your confidence and nothing to be ashamed of. I might not have much of a life, but please don't mess it up any more than it already is."

"I wouldn't," she croaked. She was losing him. She'd screwed everything up. "I wouldn't."

He raised his eyebrows.

"Seriously, Flynn? I thought you thought better of me than that."

"I did. But then." He jerked his chin toward the laptop.

Angelito darkened the doorway, stooping under the arch. His focus flicked from Tess to Flynn and back. "You finished?"

"We're finished," Flynn said, in a tone that stabbed her chest.

"We move out in fifteen. Briefing, now." The *capitaine* left.

Tess swallowed. "You're not a coward, Flynn. And I do respect you—more than you could ever believe."

He scoffed, deep in his throat. "Because you know me so well."

"Stop shutting me down. Yes, I screwed up just now, but don't shortchange me. You think you need to self-administer your punishment because the judge didn't? Lock yourself away from the world? You did, and you've done your time. You've atoned—if you ever had anything to atone for—by becoming the man you are. It's time to forgive yourself."

He crossed his arms. Defensive. Shutting her out. "Quit acting like you've known me all my life. You've known me two days, and like you say, I wasn't even conscious for all of them. For all you know, the Flynn you know so well is my brain injury making me act weird."

"But it's not, is it? This is the real you. This brave, smart, caring guy."

"Sunshine—"

"Flynn, at any time, you could have dumped me in this and walked away."

"Oh, I tried."

"But you couldn't. Maybe if you were still that same person, that same scared kid, you would have walked away. But you would never do that again. Am I right?"

"You're a dreamer. You're seeing what you want to see."

"You are not the coward you think you are—exactly the opposite. You're like me—you see an injustice and you can't stand by and let it happen. That's the man you are. That's what drives you—and maybe it's because of what happened back then. Maybe it's your way of atoning."

He snorted.

"It's true, Flynn, and if you'd stop hating yourself for one minute, you might come to realize it. And, yes, I might have done a stupid thing, but I'm glad I know why you're the way you are. I just wish you could see yourself the way I see you." Her voice hitched. "And I'm sorry for the hurt you must carry."

"Don't," he whispered. "Don't give me pity."

"Of course I feel pity. Why is that a bad thing? What reaction do you want—a shrug of the shoulders, a bad-taste joke? You know why I feel pity? Because I care. What *should* my reaction be? I Googled it because I wanted to know what haunts you, what you couldn't tell me."

"Bollocks. You Googled it because you wanted to be nosy. It's not that I *couldn't* tell you. I didn't want to tell you. I didn't want you to know because I'm a dickhead like that. Big difference. If you cared that much, you would have respected that I didn't tell you because I didn't want you to know. And now you know, and you'll never look at me the same. Which is not a problem because very soon you won't have to look at me at all."

"I don't know if I want that anymore," she blurted. She gaped. She didn't usually open her mouth without knowing exactly what she was about to say, but…suddenly she knew it was true. It made no sense, but it was true. Despite the risk of falling for a man like him, the thought of watching him walk away without a backward glance speared her through the heart. She cared about him, more deeply than she'd cared about any guy. And it was too late. She'd already lost him—given in to temptation and broken his trust, the one thing he'd needed from her. *Please let me leave it in the past, where it belongs.* Her eyes stung. *Idiot, idiot, idiot.*

"It's how it has to be." He blinked, hard, and walked out the door. Without a backward glance.

FLYNN DROVE HIS fingernails into his closed fists to reclaim some control. In the main house, Angelito and Doc were back to studying the map, while Texas leaned on the doorway to the courtyard, cleaning his pistol. Tension hummed in the room. He needed to focus on the mission, on getting out of Harar, but his mind wanted to fix on one thing: *I don't know if I want that anymore.*

On the TV, some local version of *American Idol* was playing. Muted, thank Christ. The dull thud of fatigue was setting in as the painkillers and sex hormones wore off. He needed to get out of here, get out of his head, get away from *her*.

Angelito planted a finger on the map and looked up at Flynn, all business. "Thor's gone to find Okoye. Then we'll get started."

Tess's footsteps tapped in behind him. He walked to the basket table and mopped up the last of the *injera* and *wat*. After the guys had dealt to it, it looked as appetizing as a stained dishcloth, and eating it just reminded his stomach that it was nowhere near full. He'd been planning to share Tess's platter. Fucked if he'd be sharing anything with her anymore.

Samira leaned out from her office, holding a mobile phone to her chest. "Tess? Can I speak with you?"

Tess brushed past, leaving behind her a scent of plain soap. It was the smell of washing her clean, washing away the dust and the hurt. What a fool. Samira shut the door behind them. He caught the murmur of hushed voices and strained to listen, but they were being careful. Too careful. His tongue toyed with his back teeth. How much would Tess tell her friend about their... What would you even call it? A fling?

You didn't trust me, Flynn. You still don't. Too bloody right. He'd been so careful for so many years, and one slip of the accent, one too many loose words, one lapse of self-control, and he could be right back where he started.

Doc walked across the room and tore open a box of water bottles. "Heads up," he said, firing one at Texas, then Angelito and Flynn, leaving two aside for Okoye and Thor.

Any of them could have searched the internet, found Flynn's father's photo. But they hadn't, because they respected that some things were private. Flynn chugged back the water. The pressure of gravity made his skull thump. The room took a dive. He rested his hands on his thighs.

"Stronger painkillers, Flynn?" Doc said, checking his watch.

"Nah, I'll hold out."

"Though to be honest, your head's probably not worth fixing. Might be best to amputate."

"Bad taste, mate."

"Too soon?"

"Flynn!" Texas said, pointing at the TV. A photo of Tess had popped up behind a newsreader, with an Amharic script curling across the bottom of the screen.

"Tess! Quick." Flynn grabbed the remote and unmuted. The newsreader was speaking Amharic. "And Samira!"

As the women entered, the screen switched to footage of a thin older blonde hurrying across a tarmac, the newsreader narrating. A built twentysomething guy overtook her and lifted a hand to the lens. Between his fingers, Flynn made out the outlines of two more guys.

Tess swore.

"What is it?" Flynn said.

"My mom. And my brothers. Samira…?"

"They're in Addis Ababa." Samira narrowed her eyes at the screen, her head tipped, listening. "Lobbying authorities to find you. You're still thought to be held by al-Thawra."

"Oh no."

"You want to get word to them?" Angelito said.

"No. Al-Thawra and its allies will be expecting that, will be monitoring their communications. They'll get word, soon enough—the same way the rest of the world will. I just hope they…stay safe." She cupped the flash drive in her palm like it was treasure.

The screen blinked to footage of an airstrip, a B-1 roaring past on takeoff. Samira's jaw dropped. "Fighter planes and troops are assembling in Djibouti and other bases around the Gulf of Aden."

The newsreader moved on to another story. The guys went back to their map and their posts. Tess kept staring at the screen, gray as death. Samira rubbed her back and the two exchanged a dark look. Was Flynn missing something?

He couldn't not ask. He muted the TV. "Tess, what is it? You look worried…more than usual."

She shook her head.

"Tell me," he growled.

She looked at him, defeat in her eyes. "You know how Hamid said she'd discovered my source—not Latif, the other one—and was preparing to kill her?"

"Your *mother*? She's the source?"

"Maybe this was Hamid's plan—to use me to lure her here."

"Your mother would be careful, right—about who she trusts, about her security?"

Tess managed a weak smile. "Where do you think I got my paranoia? She knows how the flow of information works. But—" She looked at the TV. "Now Hamid knows she's here."

The gate creaked. Texas froze, eyes trained outside. Someone whistled—the *2001* theme. Texas gave the all clear.

Flynn went to put his arm around Tess and stopped short. "Nothing you can do," he said. "Except…"

They looked at the flash drive in her hand. She squared her jaw and nodded.

Okoye walked in, followed by Thor. "The streets are getting busier," he said. "Looks like al-Thawra are starting their search over again. A woman is in charge."

"A woman?" Flynn said, exchanging a glance with Tess.

"Tall, thin, brown robe. Does that sound like Hamid?"

Flynn nodded.

"And the van is gone from where you left it," Okoye added.

"Gone?" Doc said. "As in stolen or taken by al-Thawra?"

"I wasn't about to ask around. But we'll need alternative transport. And Doc's cover might be blown."

Doc shook his head. "He wouldn't have woken yet—but he won't be far off."

Angelito stood. "Did we leave anything in the van that could point to us?"

"Tess's backpack," Flynn replied. "There's nothing much in it but Hamid might recognize it."

"It won't tell them anything new," said Tess. "Except to confirm that I have help. They'll know I couldn't have overpowered and sedated that guy."

"We'll factor that in," Angelito said. "Wasn't planning to travel as a group anyway. Let's do this."

He outlined the game plan, as Flynn had heard him do a thousand times. Next time it could be Flynn directing traffic—if he stayed alive that long, stayed out of the media. At least now that Tess was coming he wouldn't have to go AWOL to protect her. He could still have a career at the end of this, even if he couldn't have her.

The *capitaine* relayed Samira's information that

the busiest gate at *chat* time was the Erer, to the east. "You've scoped it out?" he asked Okoye.

A nod. "Seven enemy. Less than at some of the other exits."

Flynn grunted. "What about these hyena holes—the smaller cutouts in the walls?"

"Two men at each and more in whistling distance. The narrow gap and less foot traffic would make them a risky choice."

"Could we go over the walls?"

"Not without being seen."

"Eastern gate it is," Angelito said. "Me and Thor first, then Okoye and Tess, with Flynn, Texas and Doc behind."

"We're just walking her out?" Okoye said.

Samira lifted a plastic bag from the floor. "I have the burka. With you next to her..."

Okoye smiled. "Token black man, I know."

"It's an unjust world," Samira replied.

"Will you come with us, Samira?" Doc said, frowning.

Samira clutched the plastic bag to her chest. "I'll be safer here."

Angelito continued the briefing. Once through the gates, Doc, Flynn and Texas would pick up Samira's car from where she kept it. With the van out of contention, the others would take taxis—Angelito and Thor in pole position, Okoye and Tess in the middle, Flynn and the others following.

"We can't risk getting an airlift around here—too much firepower on the ground, and we know from Flynn they have RPGs. But Samira has a relative with a coffee plantation forty klicks from here." He tapped the map. "With the terrain, we'll have enough cover to get a chopper in and out. I've arranged it directly with the colonel. The chopper should arrive at the LZ when we do. All going well, we'll be in Djibouti in just over an hour."

"Roadblocks?" Doc said.

"We can assume there's at least one, here." Angelito pointed. "If they catch Flynn or Tess, we neutralize them before they can raise the alarm." He outlined the tactics.

The room fell silent. Far above, a bird cawed.

"Questions," Angelito said, folding the map.

Flynn glanced sideways at Tess, waiting for her objection. She just pressed her lips together. Thank Christ.

Samira held up the plastic bag. "I'll help you get into this," she said to Tess, casting a look at Flynn he couldn't decrypt. Had Tess shared details of their encounter? "I had him make the sleeves long to hide your hands. You can wear long socks underneath to hide your feet and borrow my ID. And of course you'll stay silent."

Angelito checked his watch. "Five minutes, people."

The guys started moving, checking weapons and supplies. Tess took a step toward the office and swiveled, looking up at Flynn, chewing her lip, like she had something to say. *Don't back out now, sunshine.*

"Tess?" He and Samira spoke at once.

She'd frozen. He imagined himself reaching out and pulling the words from her mouth like a clown pulling out a scarf. What was she hiding?

Her eyelashes flickered down. "Be careful, Flynn." She turned and left. Whatever she'd wanted to say, it wasn't that.

Samira emerged a few minutes later, zipping her laptop into a neoprene sleeve. She closed the door behind her. "She's almost ready. Would someone mind carrying my computer for her? She may need it yet."

Doc stepped forward. "Sure. And listen, if you need any help from us, if you have any problems..." He patted his pockets and looked around. "I'll give you my details."

Samira narrowed her eyes as if trying to decode the gesture. Doc had too much class to hit on the woman so soon after her fiancé's death. This was just him lowering the comedy routine long enough to let the real Doc through, the one who gave a damn, who couldn't stand by when someone was hurting.

Frowning, Samira fished a pale green business card and a pen from a box on a shelf. As Doc scribbled on the back of the card, she studied him with curiosity.

"The phone can be a little hit-and-miss but I check the email as often as I can," he said, handing her the card and taking the laptop.

She thanked him, slipped it in her jeans pocket and left, pulling the office door closed.

Any second, Tess would come out and declare she'd changed her mind. But after a few minutes she emerged, the smoky-blue burka brushing the floor, her arms tucked into her sleeves like a priest, head bowed. He could make out nothing behind the mesh covering her face. She would still stand out—he'd only seen a couple of women in Harar in full burkas—but not as much as a blonde. He slipped his sunglasses on, adjusted his cap and checked the holster hidden under his T-shirt. If they found her, he'd be ready.

CHAPTER TWENTY-FIVE

IT WAS AN EFFORT for Flynn to walk casually with every tendon in his body snapped tight. Samira was right that the craving for *chat* would outweigh the fear of al-Thawra—everywhere men were on the move, though there were no other white faces. Okoye and Tess blended in so well it was difficult to keep them in sight in the labyrinth.

Flynn and Doc walked side by side, with Texas ambling behind. Crap—Spartans didn't make convincing backpackers. In front, Angelito and Thor were head and shoulders above the crowd. Twice they passed al-Thawra thugs, one lot tossing a house and being lectured by an old woman, another searching a mosque. Flynn kept his head down and let the crowd jostle him along. Best way to help these people was to get out word of Tess's escape.

She seemed to be walking normally again, at least, though her dragging robes threatened to trip her.

"*That's* the gate?" he muttered to Doc as the path straightened. It was more like an oversize shack set into the wall, with a multicolored river of people pushing through. Outside the gates, a horn blared. A man in jeans and a football shirt brushed past Flynn. "This'll be cozy."

"I count three enemy," Doc said. "They're being shoved around as much as anyone."

"No respect for an M16 these days."

A guard watched Angelito and Thor pass but didn't stop them. In this crowd, the enemy would have to pick their fights. They passed out of view. Beyond the gate, they'd be loitering as planned, ready to step in if there was trouble.

Now for Okoye and Tess. Flynn swallowed. Okoye didn't drop his stride as he pushed through the crowd, Tess sticking behind him like a shadow, clutching the back of his T-shirt with a cloth-covered hand. Flynn lost sight of her among the roiling heads, Okoye's smooth scalp his only landmark. The guard scanned right past them. Flynn exhaled. Then the guy stilled and swept his gaze back. *Merde.* He shouted something.

"Heads up," Flynn said, quietly.

"I see it."

The guard strode through, shoving people left and right, eyes fixed on the space behind Okoye, shouting, weapon flailing. The crowd thinned long enough for Flynn to see Okoye sweep Tess to his side and turn, shielding her. The two men exchanged shouts, all but the bass boom of their words lost in the clamor of the crowd.

From the other side of the gate, another enemy began pushing through to Tess. Shit. Okoye hadn't seen him— he was still arguing with the first guy. Flynn upped his pace. Doc caught his upper arm.

"Use this as a diversion," Doc hissed. "Slip out while they're occupied with her."

Like hell.

The guard reached Tess, and then both dissolved into the surging crowd. Okoye had been dragged away to the left.

Flynn shook Doc off and resumed walking. "I'm not using her as a—"

"You jump into this, you'll endanger all of us. And her."

Okoye bellowed over the crowd, in English, warning the goons to leave his wife alone.

"You get to safety, we'll take care of it," Doc continued, keeping pace.

"I'm not about to—"

"*Don't* let your personal feelings screw this up for the rest of us."

"I don't have pers—"

"Then skip right past the queue. *Tu agis sans passion.* You can join the fight from the other side, but get out and get safe, first."

Flynn ground his jaw, scanning for Tess as they reached the back of the crowd. *You act without passion.* He'd sure as shit forgotten that rule.

"Any of us will give our lives for you," Doc said, grabbing his sleeve. "Try not to give us the opportunity. Keeping yourself safe is not cowardice—it's survival of the group. Don't be a hero. It doesn't suit you and you'll just mess everything up."

Survival. What Flynn had been best at, until now. Doc gave him a shove. Screw it, he was right. Flynn wasn't a hero. He was a survivor.

You're not the coward you think you are.

Oh yes, I am. Just watch me, sunshine.

Head down, Flynn fought his instinct and weaved through the crush, pelted around like a ball in a pinball game. He sheltered behind a trio of tall Sudanese as he brushed past the stone wall marking the right side of the gate.

Once spit out of the crowd, he scooted to the side, along the wall, behind a green mountain of *chat* leaves and squatting turbaned women in intense negotiations with male customers.

He pulled out the guidebook as cover to take a measure of the street. Two more enemy out here—arguing over a bag of *chat*. Angelito and Thor strode away across the road, hands in pockets. Didn't they know Tess was in trouble? Moving to a better fighting position? In this crowd they should be in close.

None of the others followed. Screw it, he had to go back in. He turned on his heel—just as Okoye's head bobbed through the floodgate. Flynn pressed back against the wall, crossing his feet, holding his breath. As Okoye cleared the crowd, Flynn saw Tess, jogging along behind. No enemy followed. Doc slipped out and ambled up to Flynn.

"What happened?" Flynn said as Doc caught up.

"No bloody idea. Heard them shouting for her to lift the veil, heard Okoye shouting back. Then suddenly she was moving out."

Texas sauntered through and stopped to buy a scoop of nuts from a woman crouching on the dirt. Doing a better job of acting cool than Flynn was.

Things went unnervingly to plan. They found Samira's white sedan right where she'd described. Doc drove, with Texas in front and Flynn in back. Beyond the gates, the town gave way to combed brown fields. Flynn sank into the seat. It was a relief to get a sight line farther than the next whitewashed wall.

Sweat had pasted his T-shirt to his back by the time they approached the al-Thawra roadblock. Tess and Okoye were two cars ahead, in the back of a circa-1980 blue-and-white Peugeot taxi. Another taxi had pulled up in the distance, beyond the roadblock. Angelito? Flynn pulled out his pistol and held it down. The others did the same.

Tess's taxi slowed and a soldier peered in at Okoye. He gestured to a mate, who strolled to the other side and tried the door. Locked. He mimed at Tess to roll down her window.

"Stay cool," Flynn mouthed, feeling anything but.

The guy reached in. The sun glinted on the rear window. Flynn couldn't see jack. *Come on, come on.* The guy stepped back and waved the taxi through.

"Wow," Doc muttered.

Flynn holstered his pistol and wiped his palms on his trousers. "All that muscle in Harar to find Tess, all these roadblocks, and they just let her through?"

Texas twisted in his seat. "Maybe they checked her ID and didn't look at her face."

"Look lively, lads," Doc hissed.

Flynn's throat dried as Doc wound down his window. The soldier bent double and looked from face to face. "ID," he said. "Passport. Drive license."

Flynn passed Doc the British driver's license. Doc pulled a card from his own wallet, and Texas dug a passport from his bag. The guy flicked through them.

Texas tossed up a nut and caught it with a crunch. "Hell, these are good." He thrust the plastic bag at Flynn. "Try one."

Flynn took two. The soldier peered into the backseat. The nuts went down his throat as smoothly as pinecones. He stifled a cough, his eyes watering behind his sunglasses.

The guy handed the documents to Doc and slapped his palm on the top of the car. Flynn almost hit the roof. He forced himself to look straight ahead as they rolled on, waiting for Doc's window to close. Too easy. "Think our pickup site has been compromised?"

Doc changed gear. "Why would they wait for us there, when we'd have extra firepower from the chopper? Better to take us on here or at the gate."

Ahead, Angelito's taxi moved back onto the road.

"Fewer civilians around?" Flynn said.

"You think they'd give a shite about that?" Doc adjusted the center mirror to meet Flynn's eye. "The most likely explanation? They messed up. People do that all the time. Hell, *we* do that all the time. We're home free."

"This is too easy."

"Be happy about that. *Lieute*, most of the time, things are what they seem."

Not this week they weren't. Flynn's instinct was going off like a siren. He just couldn't figure out why.

His gut hadn't unknotted thirty minutes later, when Doc rolled the car to a halt on a ridgeline between a stone hut that'd lost its roof and a dozen rows of raised wooden trays, with yellow-green coffee beans drying in the afternoon sun. Deserted, as Samira said it'd be. Doc had driven past the plantation gate twice, waiting for an empty road so no one would see them turn.

The Cougar perched on a clearing below, blades still. Flynn could kiss it. The crew, plus Angelito and Thor, were fanned out, weapons drawn, scanning. Flynn let his lungs expand as he climbed out. The air smelled like dirt and water and freedom.

"Where's Tess and Okoye?" he said.

Angelito nodded to a dirt path snaking through a field of green bushes. A dust whirlwind rose beside two walking figures, the breeze flattening Tess's burka against her front and billowing it out behind. Something flick-

ered on a field beyond. Just a buzzard. Nothing else bigger than a leaf moved for miles around. Flynn clenched
and unclenched his hands. He itched to talk to Tess—if
anyone would share his paranoia, she would. But hell,
if she was feeling safe, he shouldn't burst her bubble. It
always took a while to calm down after a stressful operation, to stop seeing threats in every twitch of movement.

Flynn, Texas and Doc fanned out, weapons drawn. Not
that pistols would do shit against M16s in this terrain. The
hot breeze was slow-cooking him. Angelito signaled the
pilot. The engine droned and the blades whooshed lazily
as if struggling to cut the thick air. The rhythmic thud
echoed through the valley but still nothing moved. *Tranquille*, like in the poem. So much had changed since he'd
read it to Tess, and yet here he was in the same position—
trying to get her to a safe place so he could walk away.
But now she knew everything about him.

I don't know if I want that anymore.

Mate, neither did he, but at least he'd had the restraint
not to admit it.

She kept her head bent as she passed Flynn, clutching
the neck of the burka in a cloaked hand as the downdraft
slapped it around. Okoye ushered her into the chopper,
which was whining like it was impatient to take off.
Flynn could relate.

Thor backed in, then the others, one by one. A crew-
man Flynn knew by sight high-fived him as he climbed
on. The chopper's seats faced inward in the otherwise
empty hull. The door gunners settled into position.
Flynn took a seat next to Tess, pulled his headset on
over his cap and repositioned the mic. She was wearing
her headset over the burka. She must be frying. The layers of fabric covering her lap rippled, like she was twist-

ing the cloth between hidden fingers. His own fingers twitched with the urge to find her hand and hold it. Did she intend to wear the burka until Djibouti? Hiding from the crew? She was getting more paranoid by the hour.

The chopper noise crescendoed and the machine lifted with a wobble.

"Décollage accompli." Angelito's voice crackled through the headphones as if he were in another country rather than sitting across from Flynn. "We have lift-off," he repeated, for Tess. She didn't look up. Flynn put an arm around her and squeezed her shoulder. She seemed less birdlike and fragile—or was that just his own confidence returning?

The chopper cleared the tree line and angled away. Angelito dropped his head back, closing his eyes. Out of danger, perhaps for the last time in his career, before retiring to the quiet life on Corsica. Thinking of the girlfriend and son he'd soon be heading home to, for good? How would that even feel? Flynn's gut wrenched. Longing, or dread? Or curry?

The team remained silent, leaving comms open for the crew. At some point the relief would hit Flynn, maybe when they were safely in Djibouti. How would that play out? Would the US be expecting Tess? What would he do if they were? He couldn't let them take her.

The chopper veered starboard. A pale green card fluttered from the folds of Tess's burka, onto Flynn's shoe. She lurched for it but her harness pulled her back. Flynn picked it up. The business card from the guesthouse. He flipped it. Doc's details. Why did Tess have it?

He caught a flash of skin as she retracted her hand. Blood shot through his veins. What the hell?

He grabbed a chunk of fabric. She lurched away. He

caught the end of her sleeve, reached in and found the hand inside it, fisted and pulling away. His breath stalling, he closed his fingers around the wrist and yanked her hand out. Brown skin, painted in whorls of henna.

TESS PERCHED ON the highest platform in Samira's living room, watching local TV on mute and picking at the tray of *injera* and *wat* Flynn had brought her, now cold and tasting of guilt.

She'd run out of things to do while she waited for Quan's courier. She'd gone back over her edited package on Samira's desktop computer and checked and rechecked the flash drive; she'd scanned the headlines on her Android, though nothing much had changed; she'd even cleaned her room.

Samira's grandmother had grudgingly consented to hide at a friend's place outside the old town, as a precaution, leaving Tess alone behind locked doors and a locked gate. The suitcase lay next to her. If the soldiers returned she'd have just enough warning to climb in.

Voices trickled in from outside. She froze. Scuffled footsteps, in no hurry. They trailed away.

Would Samira and Flynn be on the chopper yet? The TV had shown shaky amateur footage of al-Thawra searching Harar, but it hadn't got violent, as far as Tess could tell. More footage showed Ethiopian troops assembling in the capital.

It's okay. The plan is going to work. Samira had taken a lot of convincing but logic had won in the end. Without Tess, Flynn and his unit were far more likely to escape unscathed. And Samira was primed to log in to Tess's social-media sites from Djibouti to announce Tess's "rescue," complete with selfies of Tess to make it look credible.

If you're seen *to leave, it could draw away al-Thawra's attention*, Angelito had said.

Yep, and right then she'd realized that being seen to leave would achieve the same result as actually leaving.

A rap. Knuckles on wood. Tess lurched to her feet, sending the tray flying. Another knock. Hands fumbling, she unlocked the door to the courtyard. Al-Thawra wouldn't knock that warily.

"Tess?" a man hissed from beyond the gate. "You there?"

What the hell? She ran to the gate and opened it. Quan stared down at her, openmouthed, wide-eyed.

"You came in person?" she whispered. Half a dozen men stood at the curve in the wall, smoking and chatting. "I thought you were sending someone else. It's too much of a risk."

"I…" He blinked. His face grayed.

"Quan?"

"What are you doing here?"

"What do you mean? You told me not to leave—not that I'd planned to. Samira gave me your message."

Dots of sweat popped out on his forehead. He looked ready to faint. He screwed up his face, his gaze darting at the men. Maybe the stress was getting to him. Hell, it was getting to her.

"Tess," he whispered. "I tried to warn you."

Movement, to her right. The men were running their way. One pulled out a gun. More men closed in from the other direction. Also with guns.

"Get inside!" She grabbed Quan's arm.

FLYNN FORCED UP the burka's veil. Samira stared back, gaping.

"Samira? Shite." Doc's voice filtered into Flynn's

headset. Flynn ripped it off, the throb of the chopper closing in on his skull like a vise.

"What the—?" he said.

"I'm sorry." Samira spoke so quietly he had to read it on her lips. She said something else.

"What?" he shouted.

"Tess… She insisted."

"Why? What is she thinking?" *Merde.* He knew what she was thinking. "She wanted me out of the way. She never intended to leave."

"She wanted you safe—and me, and your friends. She knew you wouldn't leave without her."

"No shit."

"She figured there was more risk in her trying to leave than in her staying—to all of us, to Harar. Believe me, I tried to insist I should stay, but she was adamant. I think you know what she's like."

"Yeah. It's like she's out to save everyone but herself."

"This was for her safety, too. I'm to update her social-media accounts from Djibouti, saying that she is there, that she's been rescued, so the enemy will leave Harar. And I have a backup of her piece, and the evidence, just in case." She fished around under her burka and pulled out two flash drives.

Flynn shook his head, trying to piece it all together. "And you went along with all this?"

"It was the right decision," Samira said, straightening, her voice strengthening. "They lifted the burka at the gate, Flynn, when Okoye and I got separated. And then in the car I let them see my hand. Tess would have been caught. *Your* plan was doomed to fail. *Her* plan worked—is working."

Flynn pressed his knuckles into his temples. He'd had a bad feeling all along—now he knew why.

"And then," Samira continued, "after she'd made her decision, her producer texted me a message to show her, telling her to stay put, confirming he'd send someone to meet her. That sealed it." She fumbled under her robe and pulled out her phone, her long fingers shaking so much the henna was blurring. She swiped at the screen. "Here, see?"

He leaned over her and read. Fuck. "You showed her this?"

"Ow."

He grabbed the phone and held the screen to her eyes. "You showed her? You put the phone in front of her and she read it?"

"Flynn!" Doc lurched over and grabbed his forearm. "It's not her fault."

Flynn wrenched out of Doc's grip, his eyes not leaving Samira's.

"It's okay," she said, holding a palm to Doc. "I just told her the message—it wasn't complicated…"

Flynn's whole body was heating. "Didn't you wonder why he was suddenly texting, when we'd been using Facebook? Didn't Tess?"

"No. This is how I keep in contact with Tess—her producer and I keep burner phones, just for this. Believe me, we are very careful—we switch phones regularly, we never use names and we only contact each other in emergencies. It is much safer than your Faceb— Oh my God, what's wrong?"

"It's a code. Quan was warning her."

Angelito unclipped and leaned forward, headset in hand. "How do you know?"

Flynn showed him the message.

SHOW THIS TO T: Dont leave Harar. Its too dangerous.
A man will pick up you're package from there.

Angelito shrugged.

"The apostrophes—they're all wrong," Flynn
shouted. "Tess used the same code when Hamid forced
her to write a note to Quan. It's a warning that something's up. Hamid was probably standing over him as
he texted, telling him what to write."

Samira made a choking sound. She clawed the collar
of the burka, gasping like the oxygen had been turned
off. Shit, she was going white.

"Doc!" Flynn shouted.

The medic plonked to his knees on the floor in front
of her and grabbed her shoulders. "Panic attack?" he
said, coaxing her to look him in the eye. She nodded.
The collar tore.

"Keep your eyes on mine," Doc said. "Copy my
breaths, nice and slow. Let me do the breathing for you."

Doc steadied his own breath, exaggerating the sound
of his inhaling and exhaling. She grabbed his forearms
and stared at him, her chest heaving in time. Hell, Flynn's
own breathing synced up, which wasn't a bad thing. After
a minute she drew a big breath and sank back on the chair.

"Thank you," she said. "I'm so sorry. I…"

"Don't worry," Doc said, pulling up onto the seat beside her. "You make me look like a big hero."

"Tess's producer must have been compromised,"
Flynn said. "Or he was a traitor all along."

"No," said Samira, pushing back the burka hood.
"He is an honest man, and he and Tess are very close.
He would not betray her…willingly. I didn't think…
The apostrophes. I just thought he'd written in a hurry."

The housekeeper. Flynn could check with her. He grabbed his own phone and pulled up Facebook. No coverage.

The chopper bumped. Was that how they'd escaped Harar so easily—Hamid was waiting for them to leave? Had she orchestrated the whole thing? How had Okoye not noticed? He looked up, the question on his face.

Okoye shook his head. "She barely said a word, and when she did she used an American accent. I thought it was luck that we got through. *Putain.*"

Flynn was an *imbécile* to trust Tess. How had he not learned that?

"Flynn." Angelito pointed at Flynn's phone. Facebook had loaded. A message from the housekeeper. Flynn read, quickly.

"Bad?" the *capitaine* said.

"Bad."

TESS PULLED QUAN's arm but he didn't move. The men closed in. Behind them strolled a figure in a brown cloak. No. This wasn't happening.

"Come on!" She dug her fingers into his skin and tugged. At last, he pitched forward and she heaved the gate. Fingers clawed the edge of it, pushing it back.

"Quan! Help me!"

"It's hopeless. I'm sorry. There are too many of them."

She punched the fingers. They flinched but held. She shouldered the gate but it didn't budge. "I can't hold this!"

Quan just stood there, one hand over his face. Crying? After all these years, he chose now to fall apart?

"Quan!"

The gate lurched and flew open, tossing her sideways onto the flagstones. A dozen pairs of booted feet pounded in, surrounding her, running inside the guest-house, kicking at the locked guest rooms. Beside her, a thunk—a boot against flesh. Quan yelped.

The hem of the cloak swept dirt into her face. She looked up through stinging eyes, coughing. Hamid's mouth twisted into a victorious smile.

"I'm so sorry, Tess." Quan's voice cracked. "I had no choice. They have my wife, my kids."

FLYNN STARED AT the message. Pliz help. Men wiz guns in house. Shouting at lady and chidrens. Mister not here. I am hiding in cupboard. Help help.

Quan's family being held hostage? The message was left two hours ago, minutes after Flynn had last checked the phone. Damn. He hadn't expected another message. They could already be dead. A woman, children, maybe the housekeeper, too.

"What is it?" Samira clutched her robe.

"Quan must have been blackmailed to send that message to Tess. It was a trap."

"I will call her," Samira said. "We must warn her. I have the number. Her new phone." She was breathing so hard she could barely speak.

"Give me the number. I'll make the call," Doc said, pulling out his phone. "Just keep breathing, Samira. We'll fix this." He sent Flynn a look that said, "You hear me? Fix this."

Flynn turned to Angelito. "*Mon Capitaine*, I have to go back."

A WAIL FLOATED over Tess—the call to prayer, waver-ing out from a nearby mosque. Another call joined in, farther away. And another sound, bell-like. Crap, her phone, vibrating in her skirt pocket. Hamid's smile didn't falter. She gestured to her men to capture Tess.

Tess scrambled up and threw herself at Quan, shoving him to the ground and jumping on his stomach, the skirt hitching awkwardly. She shouted every insult she could think of, so loud her throat rasped. Still the phone sang out. Had to be Samira—only she knew the number.

Hamid laughed.

"Tess, I'm sorry, really."

She leaned down. "Fight me," she whispered through narrow lips. The muezzins' chants swam around, several of them now. The phone seemed to be getting louder. She leaned to one side, trying to squash it under her. *Hang up, Samira.* "Throw me over."

Quan blinked.

"Throw me!"

He frowned, but pushed back and flipped her. Her back punched into the ground. She screamed, masking the ringtone. She slid her hand into her pocket and gripped the phone. With her other hand she grabbed his shirt and hauled him closer. Still shouting, she slapped the phone into his stomach, making out she was punching him. He looked down. *Don't give it away.* His jaw dropped. He grabbed for the phone, his sweaty hand slipping against hers. The call to prayer was ebbing but the damn ringtone was still going.

"Samira," she hissed. "On the phone."

He blinked, twice. "I'm sorry, Tess," he shouted. "I held out as long as I could but there was nothing I could do—my family would have been killed unless I gave…" He was shaking. Oh God. This was no act—al-Thawra did have Xifeng and the girls.

"Unless you gave me up? Told them where I was?" Her shout rang through the compound. The nearest loudspeakers had silenced—as had the phone. Phew.

"The text I sent," said Quan in an undertone. "Hamid made me send it. I thought you'd figure that out."

"What?"

"I wish we'd caught that on film," said Hamid, stepping in. "As much as I'd like to stand here and watch you tear each other apart, I have more…dramatic intentions." She snapped instructions to her soldiers.

Crap. The flash drives. Tess should give them to Quan, too. She pulled them from her pocket but Quan was jerked backward, a gray-clad arm wrapped around his throat. The phone was nowhere in sight, thank God.

"It's going to be okay, Quan," Tess said. Empty words and he knew it. How old were his girls now— six and eight? Old enough to be terrified. They were Chinese citizens—if Hamid killed them she'd provoke China, too.

"Okay for his family, maybe, *if* he continues to cooperate," Hamid purred. "I don't want to have to murder an innocent woman and her children. But it won't be okay for you, my friend."

Hamid nodded at a man behind Tess, and she was searched. The guy smashed her fist onto the ground and retrieved the two drives—the dossier and her finished piece. Across from her, Quan swore quietly. Her last hope was the copy Samira carried—but Tess had told her to give it only to Quan, and only in person. And why the phone call—had something gone wrong? The goon handed the sticks to Hamid, then zip-tied Tess's hands in front of her.

At what point would Samira—and Flynn—realize

Tess had been captured? When Tess's execution went live? If Samira wore her disguise until Djibouti, as they'd agreed, no one would even know about the switch for another half an hour, at least. Tess needed to give Quan a chance to use the phone, create a diversion. But how?

Hamid flipped the sticks around her fingers like they were an agility game, studying Tess with a tipped head. The strips of kohl around her eyes were smudged, seeping into patches of purple underneath—the last two days had worn her down, too. Bluish bruises mottled her neck. Flynn's mark.

She crouched level with Tess, smoothing her cloak. "You know, I almost regret what I must do next. I admire your spirit, my friend. I admire that you live out here in a man's world and cower to no one. We need more women like you in the world. Sadly, we still live in a world ruled by men." She smiled benevolently, like a mentor giving advice. "The trick is to entice the men in charge to do your bidding even if they outrank you. This is something you will have discovered in your career, I am sure."

Several pairs of footsteps ran out of the guesthouse. "Nobody here," a man said, in Arabic.

Hamid ordered him to lead a search of the property. "I want every computer, mobile phone, storage device… Every last piece of paper. We must find out who knows what."

Tess swallowed. Samira would have good IT security, at least.

Hamid clicked her fingers, and men appeared either side of Tess, taking an arm each and hoisting her up.

"Where are we going?" Tess's voice wavered as she

was pushed past Hamid, the toes of her left foot scraping the flagstones.

"Not far." Hamid swept her gaze to Tess's feet as she was half carried, half shoved out the gate and down the steps. "You won't be in pain for long. You can comfort yourself that you'll become a famous and beautiful martyr, an inspiration to girls all over the world."

The alleyway was empty, the falling sun leaving one last strip of light along the cobblestones. Behind her, Quan stumbled out of the gate.

"I'd rather be remembered for the manner of my life than my death," Tess said.

"You are one of the lucky few who will be remembered for both."

Tess was dead, no question. But maybe if she went quietly, if things went to plan, Hamid would spare Quan and his family. And Samira could still get the story out.

"It is a pity I no longer have your pretty French lieutenant to play with. But never fear—you won't be apart much longer."

Tess twisted her head back. What did that mean?

Hamid strolled behind her. "You will soon be reunited with him and his friends—in the next life, if there is one." She swept a pair of sunglasses from the folds of her robe and slid them on. "You look shocked. Didn't you think I would find out about your little helicopter evacuation, given my contacts? Rest assured— like yours, their deaths will be quick and spectacular."

CHAPTER TWENTY-SIX

ANGELITO PLANTED HIS hands on his knees and stared at Flynn. "I can request permission for you to return but you know I won't get it. Our orders were to get you out. I can't let you go—"

"Sir, I'm not—"

"Let me finish, *Lieutenant*."

Flynn ground his teeth. Every minute they flew in the wrong direction took them several kilometers farther from Tess.

Angelito ordered the chopper crew who had taken off their headsets to put them back on. Containing the conversation, and giving them deniability. He returned focus to Flynn. "I can't let you go *alone*," he finished. "I'm not risking the other guys' lives and careers but I'm finished in the legion. You and I will go."

The objections from the others came swiftly and without exception. They all wanted in. Angelito held up a palm, silencing them.

"*Mon Capitaine*," said Flynn, "they could still put you in front of a tribunal, take your passport and your pension."

"I'll take that risk," Angelito said. "And if this works, they might overlook the…indiscretion so they can take the credit. That's been known to happen."

"If it doesn't work we'll be dead." *And your kid will be an orphan.*

"That's our Flynn," Doc said. "Always looking for the silver lining."

Angelito eyeballed Flynn. "You took a risk for me, not that long ago."

"It wasn't the kind of favor that needs to be repaid."

"I know. But I intend to."

The chopper swayed. Samira leaned over to check the phone in Doc's lap. "Out of service again. Why didn't she answer? She couldn't have missed the ring—it'll be quiet as a tomb in Harar by now."

"There could be a simple explanation," Doc said. "We can try again soon."

"I'm coming," said Thor, shrugging, like Angelito had suggested a trip to the pub. The others followed suit, Samira included.

Angelito leaned back. "As your commander, I must order you to return to Djibouti as planned. If you don't there may be consequences, especially if we fail. Is that understood?"

He was giving them an out. As if anyone would take it. He switched to French—intentionally locking out Samira? "Each man must make his own decision. But if anyone asks, you were following my order."

Flynn scanned the grave faces. Not a flicker of doubt among them. *La mission est sacrée, tu l'exécutes jusqu'au bout et si besoin, en opérations, au péril de ta vie.* The mission is sacred, you carry it out until the end and, if necessary, at the risk of your life.

"Samira will need to be escorted to safety," Angelito continued. "She has been compromised and should not return to Harar until we can guarantee her security. That task could also involve risks and consequences."

"I'll do it," Doc said, looking at her.

She frowned. "You are talking about me?"

"I'll fill you in shortly, ma'am," Doc said in English.

"Are we going back for Tess?"

Doc laid a hand on her forearm. "Just sorting that out. I'll tell you everything in a minute."

"Doc, you have to keep her away from all authorities as well as safe from al-Thawra," said Flynn in French. "We can't trust anyone until this is sorted."

"I understand the risks. We all do. None of us wants to see bad things happen to good people."

Grimly, Angelito slipped his headset on and began relaying orders to the pilot.

As Doc briefed Samira, Flynn leaned back in his seat and exhaled. What was he dragging these guys into? Angelito had too much to lose. As for the rest of them, himself included, the legion was the only life they had. Their sanctuary and their purgatory. Without it, they'd be tossed into hell.

TESS'S BREATH RASPED as she was shoved through the alleyways, to the wide-eyed stares of locals. A few shouted at Hamid's thugs or stepped to help Tess but were swiftly shoved aside.

Samira and Flynn and his unit couldn't be dead yet. Samira had just tried phoning Tess. *Their deaths will be quick and spectacular.* Future tense. Quan would know to warn her but he needed a chance to use the phone.

Ahead, two thugs flanked Quan as they squeezed past a street stall, its sacks of grains and spices taking up half the alleyway. Tess had to find that diversion.

Trying to run would last all of five seconds. Yelling and screaming would just get her gagged.

The sacks were open like tins of paint in shades of brown, gray, yellow, orange and red. Tess scanned them as she approached. Lentils, grains, pasta…*spices*. Behind them a woman in a green hijab crouched, eyeing the soldiers. Tess bit the inside of her cheek. Her gaze landed on a brick red powder. *Berbere*. Next to it, a paler orange one. *Mitmita*.

She stumbled and pitched sideways, shooting her bound hands into the sacks as if to break her fall. *"Yi-kuhrta,"* she mumbled to the woman in apology, as fingers dug into her armpits and hauled her up.

The maze messed with Tess's bearings. They left the landmarks she knew and began to pass unfamiliar walls and gates. The people thinned out until only al-Thawra soldiers stood at every turn, snapping to attention as Hamid approached. Outside a green gate set into an indigo wall, one of Hamid's goons shouted. It squealed open and Tess was shunted across a courtyard so quick she could absorb only the barest details—a dome with peeling turquoise paint, a towering minaret, grass sprouting through cracks in the tiles, rubbish blown up against walls, the stench of rotting animal flesh. An abandoned mosque?

She was pushed into a whitewashed room. One wall was covered with a huge light blue cloth stamped with a white star. The Somali flag. Sitting on a chair in front of it was a pale, freckly young woman in gray camouflage gear. A tuft of carrot-red hair had escaped her black hijab. She blinked hard, taking in Tess and Quan, who was shoved to his knees beside her. The skin in the creases between Tess's fingers stung.

The redhead fixed her gaze on something over Tess's shoulder. Tess twisted to look. A TV camera balanced on a tripod, aimed at the chair. A curly-haired white guy in thick glasses peered into the viewfinder and focused like a pro.

"Is everything ready, Jamal?" Hamid demanded in Arabic, striding into the room.

"One minute only," a man replied in English, from a corner. Holy cow. Psycho's brother, the one Flynn had left bound in the minefield—and then in the van.

The cameraman locked the camera into position and followed a cord to a laptop, propped up on a low shelf with cubbyholes along one face. An old shoe cabinet. A flat-screen TV stood on another cabinet, screening the local channel she'd been watching at Samira's.

Tess tipped her head toward the blue-draped wall. "One flag won't convince the US we're in Somalia."

"Maybe not," said Hamid, stepping forward. "But a live video of your execution that appears to originate from an ISP in Hargeisa should help. And you and I know how badly the politicians want to be convinced."

They were bouncing the signal, somehow. That took technical expertise.

"You're webcasting it?"

Hamid nodded at the laptop, where the cameraman crouched, tapping keys. "To the world."

So the cameraman was doing the techie stuff? They needed him as much as the executioner.

"Please, Miss Newell, take a seat," Hamid said, with a sweep of her hand. "Ready for your final, most important broadcast. Hollywood will no doubt make a movie out of this. We will both become famous."

Tess's guard jabbed her tailbone with his rifle muzzle. The redhead scooted off the chair.

"You will be played by… Scarlett Johansson. Yes. Though she has tits and you don't. Hamid will be played by…what's the name… Idris something?" She chuckled, low and quiet. Her confidence was sandpaper on Tess's nerves.

Tess's guard dragged her to the chair and shoved her down. Orange dust puffed from her fisted fingers. The heat felt like it was spreading up her arms, her neck, coloring her face. He pulled off her cap and flung it against a wall. Crouching, he zip-tied her ankles to the chair legs, pausing to wipe his nose, with a sniff. If he lifted his head a fraction he'd see the telltale orange stain. The goon guarding Quan pushed him against a wall and pressed a handgun into his neck. Damn. She needed them to forget about Quan for a minute. The cameraman moved back to the viewfinder and made adjustments. Tess's guard took up a post a couple of feet in front of Hamid.

"Move toward the window, this far." The cameraman— an Englishman, going by his accent—held his palms parallel, ten inches apart. When nobody moved, he took his eye off the camera and gestured at Tess. "You! Move over."

"You expect me to help you set this up?"

"Do it, *Scarlett*," Hamid said.

With a frustrated sigh, Tess shuffled the chair to where the light fell from an opaque window, more diffuse and even. The legs scraped over the dusty concrete floor. As she settled back down, she let a curtain of hair fall over her face.

"Fix your hair."

She raised her tied hands. "I can't, obviously." Underneath them, her skirt was smudged with orange.

Through the blond strands, Tess watched the cameraman approach like a skittish dog. He stretched out a finger like she was contagious and flicked her hair. It flew up and settled back in front of her face. At last, a benefit to having lifeless straight hair. He crept closer, until his breath brushed the strands against her face, in pulses. She clenched her fists. One chance, all in the timing.

You create your own luck. Fuck fate.

As the guy lifted his fingers to her hair, she shot out her hands, knocked off his glasses and flicked a fistful of spice into his startled eyes.

SAMIRA GRABBED FLYNN'S wrist as they descended onto the plantation. "What do I do with the copy of Tess's story? She told me to give it only to Quan, if something happened to her. But we can't trust him now."

Flynn stared at her. If Tess had been captured, getting it into the public eye quickly could save her. But how?

No, not that.

He closed his eyes. Damn. *Yes, that.*

"Samira, Doc," he said, rubbing his jaw. "There's something I need you to do. Listen carefully." As he gave his instructions, they narrowed their eyes, committing them to memory. "Do it as soon as you land. It must be priority one."

Once they made that phone call, Flynn's carefully constructed world would crumble. And right now he couldn't bring himself to give a damn. He no longer wanted to walk away from Tess. And he was done with running—and hiding. Time to stand and face the truth, of who he really was, of what he felt for Tess—if it wasn't already too late.

He checked his phone. Back in coverage. One more long-shot call for help, and then the rest was up to him and his unit.

THE CAMERAMAN REARED. Tess lurched forward and smeared her palm across his eyes. Hamid shouted in Arabic. Tess unbalanced and the chair slipped, tipping her sideways. She braced a microsecond before her shoulder crunched to the floor. Her temple bounced on the concrete. Above her, the guy howled, clutching his face. Her nostrils burned; her eyes streamed. Hah— Ethiopian pepper spray, with a clove chaser. And salt, because eyes loved that. A sneeze built. She fought to swallow it, the scene in front of her misting. Hell, if this was how the *mitmita* dust alone affected her, the guy was screwed. Where had his glasses landed?

A watery figure flew into view, blocking light from the window. A boot shot toward her stomach. She lowered her arms for protection. Too late. A direct hit. She skidded backward, pain blasting her torso. Her attacker pulled her chair upright with her still attached. Its legs teetered and settled. She scraped in a breath, her gut burning.

She blinked her eyes clear as the goon—Jamal, she saw now—dragged her back to her mark, his rifle bumping her elbow. The cameraman groaned into his palms. Quan hunched against the far wall, forgotten, curled up like an egg, shielding himself with one arm, his back to the action. Making out he was too scared to watch, but she knew better. All other working eyes were on her. How much longer did he need? The cameraman gestured vaguely toward the redhead, asking for water. *Just you do that.* Water would make it feel worse. This had to buy Tess another few hours of life, at least. She bent double, as if still in pain from the kick—well, she *was* still in pain. Awkwardly, she wiped the palm of her right hand on her skirt and fisted her still-loaded left hand, tucking it against her belly.

The cameraman's glasses had landed a foot to her left. Ignoring the strain in her flaming abs, she transferred her weight into her legs, scooted over and stomped the chair leg on them. *Crack.* With her heel, she ground them into the concrete, for good measure.

"Looks like you're experiencing technical difficulties," Tess croaked, suppressing a cough as she lifted her gaze to Hamid, resisting the urge to look at Quan. "And you had *one* job. What will your puppet masters say when you have to admit another failure?"

Hamid took a step closer, teeth clenched. *Yep, keep coming, lady.* The redhead rushed back into the room, sloshing a bowl of water. Hamid's focus landed on Tess's left fist. Damn. She barked orders at Jamal. He pinned Tess from behind and forced her hand open, dumping the powder onto her skirt and the floor.

"You'll have to reschedule," Tess continued. "Your camera operator won't be opening his eyes in a hurry. That stuff is lethal."

"Not as lethal as me. There will be no delay."

Hamid leaned over the cameraman, her hand on his shoulder. Tess couldn't decipher their whispered conversation. At least Quan was still being ignored.

Straightening, Hamid snapped an order at Jamal, in Arabic. He clamped a forearm around Tess's throat as the redhead pulled her hair, like they were in a tug-of-war with Tess as the rope. Tess made a point of wriggling and struggling as the redhead tied a ponytail. The pain barely registered.

"You!" Hamid said, swiveling to Quan.

Crap. Hamid's guard grabbed his shoulder and spun him. Tess caught her breath. He flattened against the wall, holding his palms like it was a stickup. They were empty. Tess exhaled. Had he even used the phone? Maybe it hadn't been an act. Oh God.

"*You* will have to film this," said Hamid. *No.* Why hadn't Tess thought that could happen? Hamid nodded at the cameraman. "He will instruct you and you will follow his orders. If you try anything, I will let you choose which of your beautiful daughters will be tortured and killed. If you cannot choose, they will both die."

FLYNN HAD LANDED the short straw—sandwiched between Thor and Okoye in the back of Samira's car, rattling back to Harar. The lowering sun flashed into his eyes.

"This is where the roadblock was," drawled Texas from the driver's seat.

"Was?" said Flynn. They'd fallen into the habit of speaking in English. Though it was the first language for most of them and a close second for the others, it felt off, ratcheting the tension in his chest to near snapping.

Thor met his gaze, his face in shadow. "They located their target."

Flynn winced.

"Like he doesn't already know that," said Texas. He studied Flynn in the driver's mirror. "Don't worry, man. It means they're not expecting us."

A bead of sweat rolled down Flynn's neck. "Cheers, sunshine."

They reached the outskirts of Harar in silence. Near the eastern gate, a fight had apparently broken out between al-Thawra and locals. A woman was dragging away a chain of donkeys laden with firewood. A crumpled body lay by the side of the road, a stream of blood winding through the cobblestones. Shit. Two dozen al-Thawra thugs had a group of men pinned to the city walls. As the car passed, unnoticed, one kidney-punched a man in a long white robe. Flynn reached for his gun, blood boiling. Okoye stopped him with a look he knew well. We choose our fights.

You see an injustice and you can't stand by and let it happen.

When had that become his thing? Had he got himself wrong all these years?

"Maybe they've pulled soldiers from the other gates," Angelito said.

They swiftly revised the plan. Flynn directed Texas to the Buda Gate. Just before it came into view, Texas stopped to let out Flynn, Thor and Okoye, before driving on. A minute later the horn blared three times. Three enemy. While Okoye walked calmly along the dirt road, hands in his pockets, Flynn and Thor hugged the wall, hidden from the gate by the curve of the abandoned guard tower.

Flynn and Thor hung back while Okoye strode up to the gate. Once he was inside, they'd pin the guards from three sides. Across the road, a skinny gray cat sat on its haunches, closing its eyes against the setting sun. Somewhere behind the walls, music thumped. Flynn wiped his sleeve across his brow. The whine of a *bajaj* engine rose, approaching from behind. They eased up their posture as it rattled passed, its tinny radio squealing. Hell, now they wouldn't be able to hear Angelito's signal. Thor's jaw tightened so hard Flynn braced to hear the bone crack. Okoye rounded the tower, out of sight.

The cat snapped to its feet, stared at the gate and bolted into the trees. *Here we go.* The *bajaj* noise drifted off, replaced by shouts. Angelito whistled.

"We're up," Flynn said.

They took off, weapons pointed down. Okoye was wrestling a goon in the arch. One down. The two other guards rushed to help, oblivious to Angelito and Texas closing in from one side, Flynn and Thor from the other. Flynn shouted. The two guards looked his way, raising their weapons. Distraction accomplished. Angelito pounced from behind. Two down. The third guy shrugged Texas off and scuttled away through the gate. Flynn bolted after him, followed by Texas, as Thor covered. Okoye flipped his guy onto his stomach.

Flynn's quarry sprinted into the shooting alley, yelling. Halfway down, a dozen goats jerked up from a scattering of *chat*. Flynn fired into a wall beside them, the bullet zinging off the stone. The goats skipped and darted in twelve directions, cutting the guy off. As he slowed, Texas caught up and tackled him into the cobblestones with a thwack.

"Shot, *Lieute*," Texas said, zip-tying him.

Okoye and Angelito shoved their marks up the alleyway. Flynn pushed open the green metal gate into the compound where he and Doc had hidden. "In here." He pulled a sheet from the washing line. "We'll use this for gags and get out quick, in case anyone heard."

They navigated the maze without incident. The town

had fallen quiet again, the paths in shadow. Peak *chat* saturation. A few street vendors listlessly waved at flies. The alleyway outside Samira's was deserted, the gate creaking in the breeze.

In front, Angelito signaled. Flynn held back with Thor while Texas did a recce. Voices and clunks carried through the air—from the main house? The TV droned. Flynn forced a lid on his gasping breath. After a minute, Texas shrank back and signaled. They retreated around the corner.

"At least four enemy, maybe one or two more. They're searching the place, but casual-like," Texas whispered. "I'm guessing the boss ain't here."

"Which means Tess isn't here," Flynn said. "They'd have more security."

"Agreed," Angelito said. "But these guys might know where she's been taken. Weapons?"

"Couple of Glocks, at least," Texas said. "But they're more interested in tossing the place."

"We make this quick and quiet," Angelito said. He set down the tactics. The men nodded. A routine takedown but Flynn felt jumpy. He wasn't used to having skin in the game that wasn't his own. "Go."

Texas returned to the gate. On his signal, Flynn linked his fingers for a foothold and boosted Okoye onto the wall. He sheltered behind a huge satellite dish, giving him a clear view of the compound, and held up a palm. Minutes passed. Something heavy crashed, jump-starting Flynn's pulse. Finally, Okoye signaled it was clear. Texas scooted into the courtyard. He'd be hiding behind the big metal drum, as planned. On his signal, the others folded in. Flynn skirted a pile of boxes, papers, computer gear.

The first schmuck to emerge from the doorway succumbed to clean Scandinavian efficiency. Texas took
care of a guy in the guest suite, while Flynn and Angelito sorted out the next two to pop their heads out
of the main house. They carried all four, zip-tied and
gagged, into the guest room, leaving Texas standing
guard.

In a bedroom beyond the office, a guy out of their
sight line was speaking rapidly in a language Flynn
couldn't decipher. As they crossed the living room,
Angelito caught Flynn's eye and crooked his head to
the TV. Tess. Bound to a chair, in front of a Somali
flag. *Putain de merde.* Her eyes darted left. The screen
changed. The US president, his words dubbed into Amharic.

Flynn followed Angelito, walking on automatic.
Fuck. He flattened against the wall next to the office
doorway, avoiding the hanging baskets and pans. Thor
zipped into position opposite. The guy kept blabbing.
On signal, they stormed the room. Shit—the guy was
alone, talking on a mobile phone. Thor took him down
before he could think of reaching for his Glock. The
phone clattered to the floor. Flynn silenced the tinny,
panicked voice at the other end while Angelito pocketed the gun.

"We need to get out quick," Flynn said.

Angelito and Flynn checked the other rooms. When
they returned, Thor had dragged the guy into the living
room. He shoved him to his knees.

"Where is she?" Flynn hissed.

"No English."

Flynn nodded at Thor, who wrenched the guy's arm
back. He yelped.

"Speak English now? Where is the American?"

"No English, please."

The arm went back a few more degrees.

"He'll break every bone, one by one."

The guy shook his head so wildly his cheeks jiggled. Flynn looked at Angelito.

"Do whatever it takes," the *capitaine* said, for the guy's benefit. "We're off the clock."

"Shoulder," Flynn said. A dislocation would do for starters. As painful as a break, but easily reversible.

The guy's palm went for his shoulder. He knew English, all right. Thor jerked. He howled. Thor wrenched it back in. A trick Doc had taught them one sleepless bug-infested night in South America. Lasting panic without lasting harm. The guy panted, sweat popping on his forehead.

"Where is she?" Flynn said. "Where have they taken her? Tell me or he does it again—permanently."

"They no say."

Flynn hefted his chin toward Thor. "Again."

"No, please. They no say. They no say."

Flynn had a sinking feeling he was telling the truth.

"They said to call on the phone if you come. She say she want pretty one for TV."

Putain. "It's a trap. We have to—"

A whistle from outside. Okoye. Flynn swore. Thor headbutted the guy, who slumped, his eyes rolling back.

Outside, the gate was shut. Okoye crouched on the wall that separated Samira's compound from her neighbor. "Enemy approaching, all directions," he hissed. "Twenty at least. We can escape through these courtyards and houses." He gestured behind the wall, then held out a hand to pull up the nearest guy—Flynn.

In the alleyway, boots shuffled and scuffed. Twenty M16s against half a dozen pistols.

"You guys go," Flynn said, swallowing. "They only want me. Take my weapon."

"Solidarité, Lieutenant." Angelito released his safety, as if it was Flynn he was about to fight.

"They might take me alive, but not you. I'll hold them here while you get away."

Angelito's jaw worked.

Flynn stepped in close, dropping his voice. "You have to protect these guys, Rafe. You have to get home to your son. This is your best chance and you know it."

CHAPTER TWENTY-SEVEN

QUAN WAS STALLING. The guy could hook up an edit suite in seconds, in a decked-out studio or on the road with an ancient laptop and a one-bar signal. And this equipment was expensive and high-tech. The blinded cameraman had tied a scarf around his eyes and was shouting frustrated orders at Quan, who was acting flustered. Hell, Quan had good reason to be flustered but he was hamming it up, for sure. To buy time? For what—had he got hold of Samira?

He adjusted the laptop, turning the screen into Tess's view. Live studio software. The screen was split into sections—the largest screen, in the middle, was black. The live screen. Four other feeds were stacked on the left, ready to go live in a keystroke. Tess squinted to make out the top one. A familiar living area, a woman sitting on a sofa hugging two kids like she was trying to hide them. A hooded figure stood behind them, like Death. Ice rolled up Tess's neck. Why was Quan's family being filmed—to remind him to cooperate? Or because Hamid planned to make this execution bigger? Tess bit her cheek. If she died like a good little hostage, would they be spared?

The next feed was a wide shot of a stony landscape with a huge sky. Could be anywhere from here to Russia. A man walked into shot, lugging the unmistakable silhouette of a massive rocket launcher. He stared at a pale pink horizon, waiting. For what? The Somalian invasion?

The next view was of Tess, sitting on the chair. *That* she knew all about. The last one was urban—a town nestled into a hillside, with a turquoise-capped minaret in the foreground. The tower she'd spotted on the way into the mosque. The camera had to be on the roof above her head.

"You said you wouldn't harm Quan's family," Tess said.

"And I won't, if everything goes to plan. On the other hand, there are plenty more children where these came from."

"I'll do everything you say. But first, let them go free."

"You are quite the heroine. But you have no bargaining power. I am in control. I am the director and this…" She swept her hand toward the laptop. "This is my Hollywood blockbuster. Ratings gold, yes?" She crossed her arms, long fingers drumming on skinny elbows. "The challenge will be to do justice to all these elements."

"You can't take down a fighter jet with a rocket launcher."

Hamid turned to the screen, her frown easing into a smile when she saw what Tess was referring to. "Oh no, my friend. That is scene one—the fiery destruction of a French military helicopter as it approaches its base in Djibouti. I expect you will cry for your friends aboard. My thanks to you and your producer for leading me to Samira. I have been looking for her ever since her last phone call with the traitor. She was a loose end I needed to snip."

Tess's face iced over.

Quan moved to the camera and tweaked the settings.

He swore and spoke to the cameraman. Tess couldn't pick up the words. A loose connection? The guy shuffled to the camera, waving his hands like antennae. He caught it, homed in and felt around for something, calling the redhead to help. Quan glanced at his family on the screen and shut his eyes a second. When he opened them, his jaw was rigid, his gaze narrowed. He met Tess's eye.

"Do what you need to," she said, tears scalding her eyes. "Keep them safe."

"I will."

Something changed on the laptop. The main picture had lit up. The live screen. A woman, in front of a… Tess blinked. Crap, it was her, looking even more haggard and worried than she felt. Behind her, in the shot, stood a man in a black hood, a belt of bullets slung across his chest, like some jihadist cliché. The twin of the guy in Quan's family portrait. She turned her head. No blue-screen trick, unfortunately. The guy stood quiet as a shadow. He moved, and something scraped the wall. She glanced at the laptop. He was swishing a sword from hand to hand. The breeze fanned her neck. She looked terrified. Was this it? The screen went black.

"One of a series of teasers we're webcasting," Hamid said. "To make sure everyone's tuning in. Now we will watch the world go crazy."

Tess slumped. A reprieve, but for how long? Hamid told the redhead to change the TV channel. One of the breakfast sets of Tess's network popped up on the screen, the sound muted, the normally chirpy hosts pale and grim. After a few minutes of chatter, the screen changed to the clip of Tess and the swordsman.

"Oh God, I have to throw up," Quan cried. He dashed

toward an archway to another room. Jamal started after him, but Quan barely made it through before he roared and heaved. Whoa, he wasn't faking. He slumped flat on the ground, legs still in the room, torso in the next, his arms and head twisted out of sight behind the wall. Tess gagged as the smell reached her. Jamal laughed and leaned on the wall next to the archway, his boot on the back of Quan's knee. Quan whimpered. If that was a cover for using the phone, it was a good one.

He dry heaved a few times, panting heavily between attacks. Tess swallowed down her own stomach contents. After several of the longest minutes in her life, he crawled back in, wiping his mouth. He swayed to his feet, took off his jacket and laid it on the shelf next to the laptop.

Shouts bounced around the courtyard. A bearded man—one of the guards from Hamid's compound—flung the door open and shouted for "Mrs. Hamid" in Arabic, the door squealing closed behind him. Tess caught the word *Faransa*. France? Oh crap, what now? Loud voices, scuffling. The door opened again and a large figure staggered in, shoved by two thugs. Green eyes sought out hers.

"No." Her voice shook.

Blood streamed down Flynn's face. His head wound had reopened. He spit a gob of blood at Hamid's feet. Oh God. How had they caught him? Had they caught the others? *Killed* them?

"Flynn," Tess squeaked. He'd come after her?

"Flynn? That's his name?" Hamid said. "Not very French. I'd prefer Jacques or Pierre or Baptiste, but perhaps I'm old-fashioned." She shouted instructions and another chair was brought in. Tess was shuffled over and

Flynn was plonked next to her. His hands and feet were bound. Tess blinked away tears, clenching her jaw to stop her chin shaking. She ached to reach out and clasp his hand, tell him she was sorry, tell him… Too late. Who knew you could fall so fast, in such crazy circumstances? But she knew it. Right now, when it was hopeless.

The cameraman told Quan to widen the shot to accommodate Flynn. Without his beard, the world would recognize him as the terrified sixteen-year-old he'd once been.

Like his secret mattered now. Suddenly there were more guards in the room, holding M16s. By the archway, the executioner swished his sword like an actor practicing for his big moment.

"Well," Hamid said, folding her arms. "Isn't this a sensational twist—the love interest arrives too late?"

Tess blew out a shaky breath. She sensed Flynn's head turning and caught his eye. He looked more angry than sad. Defeat and guilt lay heavy in her body.

"Samira?" she whispered.

"On the chopper."

"Oh God. The others?"

"I see my matchmaking was a wild success," Hamid interrupted, waving her hand between Tess and Flynn. "The air between you is electric. It is a shame the viewers won't feel that." She stood back, folding her arms. "Or perhaps they will."

Tess kept her gaze on Hamid, aware of Quan fiddling with his jacket next to the laptop. She damn well hoped he was up to something. All other eyes were on Flynn and Tess. He wandered to the camera and tweaked something. Hamid checked a delicate gold watch. "Fifteen minutes to showtime." She rubbed her belly. "I can feel the anticipation. Can't you?"

In her peripheral vision, Tess caught a familiar signal from Quan. He was recording? Recording what? Sure enough, a red light had appeared on the camera. She checked the laptop. He'd widened the shot to include Hamid as well as Flynn. She caught his eye and he nudged his head toward Hamid.

A confession. Could she goad Hamid into a confession? Quan couldn't put it straight to air, with his family in danger, but if he survived… They could still take Hamid and her friends down. The woman was wired; it wouldn't be hard to get her talking, gloating. Tess breathed in and out through her nose. First rule of an interview—start with an easy question.

"Hamid, why are you filming Harar?"

"Because in precisely—" Hamid checked her watch "—seventeen minutes you will begin to see explosions everywhere. Just in time for the morning news shows in America. We're very media friendly in al-Thawra."

"You call this media friendly?"

"You see, this is why your death is so difficult for me. You are clever and witty. I like you." She sighed. "Suicide bombers—twenty-one of them. Very soon they will make their way to the markets, the bars, the tourist traps, the Christian sites. You chose the perfect place for the jihad to begin. A series of coordinated attacks, one after the other, culminating in the climactic moment." She sliced a palm through the air in front of Tess's neck. "You'll get to watch the show but not the denouement, I'm afraid."

Hamid snapped her fingers at Jamal and spoke in Arabic, too fast for Tess to decipher. He bowed curtly, turned to the redhead and whispered in her ear. She'd paled, her freckles standing out. With one finger he steadied her chin, then gently pushed her hair back under the hijab. She reached up and finished the job, their fingers brushing, shiny wedding rings glinting. He laid a hand on her lower back and guided her out a side door. What was that about? Tess caught Flynn's gaze. He shrugged.

"And do these suicide bombers know that none of it's real?" continued Tess, trying to sound genuinely baffled. "That al-Thawra's a fake terrorist group, that the jihad is a scam funded by Denniston Corporation, that Americans tied to the US government plotted the Los Angeles terror attacks?"

Hamid gave a smug smile. "You'd be surprised what people are happy to believe if it fits their view of the world. Of course, you'd know that, in your job. People on both sides want a holy war, so I give them a holy war. It's that easy. I'm not creating this conflict—it's been boiling on for centuries. I'm merely giving the two sides an arena in which to...*express* their frustrations."

"Where do you find them, these people who will blow themselves up for a false cause?"

"My friend, all over the world, people are dying to find their purpose in life, to be counted above the masses, to be remembered. Western world or developing world—everyone's the same. But people like Jamal..." She waved a graceful hand at the door he'd disappeared through. "He can't go to painting retreats or seminars about work-life balance. When you have few options, blowing yourself up seems like a good way to leave your mark—especially when your brother has just been brutally murdered by infidels. I merely offer people a purpose." She wiped a puff of dust from her cloak. "It's sadly not hard to find disillusioned people in this world—our country helps to create them, and sends them to al-Thawra in their truckloads. The trick is to give them a cause to martyr themselves to, to make them feel their pathetic lives are good for something, to make them feel part of a movement."

"There's one thing I don't understand in all this."

Hamid arched pencil-thin eyebrows. "Only one?"

"How many of al-Thawra's soldiers know that you are pretending to be 'Hamid'—you, Sara Hawthorn, ex-CIA, ex-marines, an FBI reject…an *American*? That there is no Hamid."

Hamid swept the room with her gaze. "If you're trying to turn these soldiers against me, don't bother. These men and women don't speak English, aside from my cameraman, and he is paid too well to share my secrets. They wouldn't believe you anyway. People believe only what they want to believe."

"Humor me. I'm about to die."

"This isn't some gentleman's execution. You don't get a last request. But no, very, very few people in al-Thawra—or even in Denniston—know that I am Hamid, that I am directing al-Thawra. You may be a gatherer of secrets but I am a protector of them, and a very good one. You are among the very few who knows the truth, and the only one with the evidence to prove it. Oh no, wait—look." She drew the flash drives from a pocket. "It's a great pity your story will never get out. It's almost as sensational as the one I'll soon be broadcasting to the world, except that yours is speculation and innuendo. Words, words, words—no one cares about words anymore. People don't want their news filtered by journalists. They want the raw pictures and video.

Not complicated conspiracies but explosions, death, war. Speaking of which…"

She shouted for Jamal, who appeared in the archway, buttoning a jacket over…a vest, with a series of tubes strapped onto it. A suicide bomb. Flynn swore under his breath.

"We are ready," Jamal said to Hamid, in Arabic. The redhead followed him into the room, her focus on the floor. As well as the hijab, she'd covered up in a floor-length *jilbāb*—over a frame that was much bulkier than before.

Behind them, the TV screen changed. A White House press conference, live. The president at the podium, flanked by key staff and supporters—including Senator Hyland. On the camera, the red light was still on.

"You may go," Hamid said to Jamal. *"Allah akbar,"* she added, as an afterthought.

Jamal and the redhead gave the response and left.

"No! Don't!" Tess called after them, scraping her chair across the floor. "It's for nothing. Jamal!"

Hamid sniffed, turning back to Tess. "You think they'll listen to you, over me? My friend, you're very smart to have figured all this out, but not as smart as me. In case you haven't noticed, it's you who is about to die, not me, and your death will trigger the deaths of many, many others."

"There's one other thing I don't get," Tess continued, grasping. She had to keep Hamid talking.

Hamid sighed but tipped her head, unable to resist, like Tess knew she'd be.

"How have the people pulling the strings managed to fool an intelligent woman like you into thinking you're in a position of power?"

"Whatever do you mean?" Hamid attempted a dismissive tone but her eyes flashed.

Enrage to engage. "You are their pawn. You have no direct access to anyone within Denniston, or the US military or government, and yet you do all their dirty work."

"Oh, I have access you could only dream about."

Tess gave a knowing smile. "No. You're nearly as powerless in all this as I am, and Denniston probably plans to kill you straight after you kill me. Like you say, no one knows you're Hamid. You're expendable."

Hamid straightened. "Oh, so this is your plan? Female solidarity? Pathetic."

"Thanks to you, *Sara*, I am thoroughly out of plans. I am forced to concede that you've won this. But I'm curious about how they've strung along such a smart woman."

"Oh, you are so wrong. Maybe you're not as dangerous as I'd thought." Hamid reached into her cloak and pulled out a phone. "On this are private mobile phone numbers for every member of Denniston's board, plus several American politicians and the heads of state for three other nations. I am indeed in control."

Bingo. Tess snickered, shaking her head slightly.

Hamid's face set like concrete. She swiped the phone and peered at it, holding it away as if she was long-sighted. "The names are all coded on here, of course."

"Of course they are," Tess said, sliding a sly glance Flynn's way. He narrowed his eyes, but managed a slight smile. Bemused but playing along.

Hamid's chest expanded and contracted as she let out a frustrated sigh, her gaze flicking to the TV, where the press conference was still broadcasting.

"Hamid—*Sara*—I know I'm going to die soon, but at least I'll die knowing that you're not as important as you think you are."

Hamid huffed. She tapped the phone and calmly reeled off the names and numbers of a Denniston board member, a senator and a prime minister. She switched to names only and read breathlessly down her list. Good grief. Quan better have got that.

"How do I know you're not making that up to impress me?"

"Watch the television." She tapped out something on her phone. A text?

"The presidential press conference—you're texting someone there, right as it's going out live?" Tess said, for the sake of the recording, which wouldn't have the TV screen in shot. Oh boy. She bit her lip, watching Hyland. But he didn't move. Next to him, a white-haired woman in a blue suit pulled a phone from her jacket and surreptitiously checked it. "You're texting the national security adviser, in the middle of the press conference?"

"Just confirming we're all ready to go, as we planned."

On the TV, the woman glanced at the president, then tapped at the phone.

"She's replying," Tess said. "The national security adviser is replying to your text." No need to fake her surprise. That was one scalp she hadn't counted on.

Hamid held up her phone. On cue, it beeped. She tapped it and read, "'Great. This idiot is doing all the things we want him to.'"

"The national security adviser just called the president an idiot?"

"Read it for yourself." Hamid held the phone up to Tess.

"How about Hyland? You got his number on there?"

The picture changed, back to the TV studio. Press conference over. The sunset call to prayer cracked from speakers around the city.

"Time to get this show rolling," Hamid said, adjusting her hood.

Damn. Interview over. Quan pressed a key and the main window on the laptop filled with the shot over the desert, tighter than it'd been earlier—a helicopter in view, lit by a blazing sunset. No. *No.* Samira, Angelito, Doc…

The TV flickered and the same scene filled the screen. The network was live-streaming it? A whimper escaped Tess's throat. A flash of light and the machine silently exploded.

"No," Tess squeaked.

The screen changed to her and Flynn. Hamid had moved out of shot. Holy shit. She caught Flynn's eye and he held her gaze grimly, his brow wrinkling. Maybe she could watch his beautiful face until this was over. His focus flicked over her shoulder, back to the TV. His jaw tensed. Oh God, what now?

She couldn't not look. Quan's family huddled together, Xifeng hiding the girls' faces with her hands. The executioner raised his sword.

"Hamid, no," Tess gasped.

"Who is in control now?"

"Don't do it."

"Calm down. That's just a warning to your friend Quan to play by the rules. Wait and watch."

"Tess, I'm here," Flynn said, his voice gravelly. "We're together in this."

The TV switched to the airstrip in Djibouti. A jet

roared off the runway. A ticker scrolled across: US and allies announce air strikes on Somalia.

The cameraman issued Quan a quiet instruction. Grimacing, he tapped the laptop, sending the rooftop shot of Harar live. A second later it appeared on the TV. Sunset flooded the citadel skyline, bringing its roofs and domes and minarets into relief. Smoke shot out from behind a building and billowed, like a small volcano. A boom shook the floor, wobbling Tess's chair. Quan dived for his jacket as it slid across the bench.

"The Catholic mission," Hamid said. "Watch, it gets better." A new scene—shaky footage from a low-res camera. The main market. The camera was following a woman in a black *jilbāb* and hijab. She glanced over her shoulder, nervously. The redhead. "This may be the first-ever suicide-bomber cam."

Tess looked at Flynn. His gaze was locked on the screen. He flinched. A second later the shock from another explosion rocked the building. In an adjoining room something crashed. He swallowed, blinking, looking more rattled than she'd seen him.

"I can't believe they screened that," he said.

"I'm sorry," she whispered. "I'm so sorry."

A sad smile flickered and died. "You may be the gutsiest person I've ever met."

Her face crumpled. If that was supposed to make her feel stronger… Another blast boomed out, closer. Her chair danced along the floor. Plaster rained from the ceiling. Outside, something thudded, shouts. Flynn held her gaze. "I'm here. And I'm glad I'm with you. It's where I belong, whatever happens."

She nodded, her throat too swollen to reply. She was looking at a future she'd never have.

"Keep your eyes on me," he whispered.

"This is tremendous," Hamid said to herself.

A scream. Quan. Tess turned. He charged toward the TV, a chair above his head. The screen shattered as it flicked to a shot of his family. He couldn't watch, and who could blame him? A loud sob choked out of her. Her world was disintegrating before her eyes, and all for nothing. The monsters and wolves had won.

Quan dived for the camera as if to tackle it. Through blurred vision, she watched two soldiers catch him and drag him shouting and crying to a corner. Oh no. No way would they let him live now. Hell, he probably wouldn't want to, if his family were dead. Hamid snapped at the cameraman, who pulled his blindfold off and forced his eyes open to red, streaming slits. He flailed his way to the laptop, peered close and clicked. The last shot. Her and Flynn. She slowly turned back to Flynn. His eyes were still on hers, as if he'd been waiting for her to come back to him the whole time.

"Yes, you watch him, my friend," Hamid purred. "This will be good. Oh, and, Tess?"

Tess refused to look.

"I've found your mother. She will die right after you, along with your brothers. Drone strike."

Flynn's green eyes swam in Tess's wavering vision. Oh God, she couldn't even process that. The end of her world, the end of everything. Footsteps passed behind her—the executioner, taking position. The sword whipped through the air, puffing loose strands of her hair against her mouth. He strode behind Flynn and lifted the sword. Flynn's Adam's apple shifted.

Last chance. Last desperate chance. With a cry, Tess tipped her chair over, knocking into Flynn's. Not hard enough. Who was she kidding? She didn't have the weight to push him over. Her chair teetered, then slid out, and she smacked cheekbone-first on the floor. The sword swished down. She cried out.

Boom! Her hearing blanked. Warm liquid and plaster rained down. Another bomb? Footsteps pounded the floor, reverberating through her skull. Men were running in from the archway and door, shouting. More explosions. No, not explosions—gunshots. She twisted her head up, unable to breathe. She had to know the worst.

Flynn was still sitting on the chair, in one piece. The flag was sprayed with blood. What? Behind him, the executioner slumped against the wall, ripping the flag down with him, then dropped forward, his sword slicing into his shoulder as he fell. The flag fluttered over his legs. He shuddered, whimpered and stilled, staring sightlessly at her.

The room blurred. Shouts, flashes, movement, cracks, thumps, gunshots. Sound muted until all she could hear was a throbbing in her ears. She shrank as a large figure loomed over her and Flynn, the sword raised. She bucked but couldn't move an inch.

Then Flynn was moving, slashing at his feet with... the sword. How...? He kicked his chair away and bent over her. She blinked up at the retreating figure behind him. Angelito? Angelito had used the sword to cut his bonds. Had he shot the executioner?

"You're shaking," Flynn said, his words muffled as he sliced through the tie at her wrists.

"No...shit."

She forced her eyes to focus as he freed her feet. Texas and Angelito were all action, taking on Hamid's thugs, alongside soldiers in desert khakis. Ethiopian de-

fense force? Quan wrestled the cameraman. She caught
a flutter of brown disappearing through the archway.
Hamid slipping out. The legionnaires were prioritizing
the armed men.

"Come on," she shouted to Flynn, lurching across
the room. She leaped over Quan as he slammed a punch
in the cameraman's stomach, caught her balance on the
far wall and staggered into the next room.

No one there. Just drifts of rubbish and the stench
of vomit. She pushed open a door and stepped into another courtyard, surrounded by high, smooth walls, the
minaret rising from its center. In the distance, sirens
wailed. Or maybe that was her ears buzzing.

"Flynn?" She swiveled. He wasn't behind her. She
hesitated, looking up. Hamid had to be in the minaret—
there was nowhere else. Tess just needed to guard the
entrance and make sure Hamid didn't escape before
Flynn arrived. She'd trapped herself.

Tess crept into the tower and peered up. Dust swirled,
lit orange by the last shards of sun. In the upper reaches,
a cloud of pigeons rose and flapped away through
the windows. Recently disturbed. Hamid must have
climbed out onto one of the tiny balconies that encircled
the tower. The air was smoky, with a chemical sting.

Tess sat heavily on a rusty metal step at the bottom
of the circular staircase, swaying like she had sea legs.
Thank God she wouldn't have to climb the damn thing.
Was she really alive? But her mom. Samira. Quan's fam-
ily. Those people in Harar. The bombing of Somalia.
And now what—war? She'd failed.

But Angelito and Texas had made it out. Perhaps
the others were okay, too, somehow. She looked up.
And Hamid had the flash drives. If Tess could retrieve

them, maybe justice could still be done. Maybe all those deaths would be avenged. Maybe the Somalia strikes would be called off.

A thumping throbbed around the roofs. A helicopter. She pushed up and stumbled into the courtyard. A small black chopper approached—the same one that'd chased them to the refugee camp? She backed up. Her spine hit the compound wall. The minaret leaned over her, looking as if one solid push would tip it. Hamid stood on the uppermost balcony, clutching the railing, her face obscured by a cobweb of power lines. She was waving at the chopper. Oh man. They were planning to winch her up?

"Flynn!"

The door swung in the breeze. Nothing but thumps and shouts inside. He evidently had more immediate problems. Tess was on her own. She charged into the minaret, the stairs clanging as she circled. Her head spun. She clung to the shaky railing, her chest tightening with every step, like she was climbing into altitude. The whole tower seemed to sway. Blades and blocks of amber light pierced the walls where stones had fallen or shifted.

She slowed as she reached the top, her throat wheezing. Crap—which side of the tower was she even on anymore? The wind from the blades whipped her ponytail into her face. She took a deep acrid breath and dashed out, smacking right into Hamid's back. Spinning, Hamid grabbed Tess's upper arms with a sinewy strength and headbutted her. Tess's skull bounced off the side of the tower. Lights sparkled in her vision.

"Where is your hero soldier now, you slut?"

Tess recovered her spinning eyesight in time to see Hamid lift her boot.

Not the toes. Tess jumped clear and shoved Hamid, calling for Flynn, her shout swallowed by the whomping blades. Hamid fell backward, her spine bumping across the balcony's metal grate floor. Tess jumped on her. The helicopter had moved to the other side of the tower—keeping away from the power lines? A shout from below. Flynn? She peered through the grating, her head whirling. The ground rose and fell away, like the sea under a lighthouse. She swallowed bile. They were way higher than she'd thought.

Below stood a figure. Not Flynn. Jamal, his jacket still buttoned and bulging.

"Mrs. Hamid!" he called. "Sara!"

Hamid pushed Tess away like she was a feather and pulled up to the railing.

"I sacrificed everything for you!" he shouted. "You killed my wife, my brother. For nothing. You lied to us all."

"How the hell…?" Hamid muttered.

"You told me it was jihad. It was just money and power for America."

The door to the mosque banged open. Flynn launched out of it, running at Jamal.

"No, Flynn!" Tess yelled.

Jamal darted into the tower. Tess curled up on the balcony, arms cradling her head. *You die or you don't.* A great thud, then the blast roared up the tower and smacked into her like a solid force. *Please, Flynn, don't die.* The balcony gave. Her stomach dropped first, and then the rest of her.

CHAPTER TWENTY-EIGHT

ALL FLYNN COULD hear was a distant, echoing roar. He cracked his eyes open to a slit. He was in a gray swirling cloud. Too much pain to be heaven. Could well be hell.

He pushed up to his elbows, his ribs pinching. What the hell just happened? He'd been following Tess outside when he'd tripped, the sword shooting from his grip. No, not tripped—he'd been ankle-tapped by Hamid's guard. The soldier fired his weapon but Flynn had already rolled. He grabbed the sword, leaped up. The guy aimed, but Flynn drove the blade into the side of the barrel. As sword and rifle went flying, Flynn spun and shoulder-charged, yelling from deep in his chest. They'd wrestled, the guy laying into Flynn, Flynn giving right back. Shouts from the next room, from outside. Tess—calling for him.

Then…what? Flynn rubbed his stinging eyes. He'd delivered the knockout punch, stumbled back, wiping blood from his mouth. Tess had yelled again, her voice higher, panicked. He'd run outside. Tess and Hamid were fighting, on the top balcony. A helicopter hovered, a cable swinging from it. The suicide bomber bolted into the tower. He'd spotted Flynn, panicked, detonated. Flynn had braced for pain and noise but there'd been none, not at first. He'd been tossed backward, weightless. The blast had gone upward. To Tess.

He rolled from his back to all fours, coughing like his lungs were trying to force their way out. There was pain now, all right. And sound. A whining, a thumping—the chopper lifting, the downdraft pummeling him with dust and debris.

Tess. He pushed to his feet and stumbled sideways, fighting to stay upright. He pulled his T-shirt to his face and sucked a breath. Through the haze he could make out the shape of the tower, leaning sickly, like it'd go down in the next sneeze.

"Tess?" he roared, though it came out a croak. He coughed, spit out dirt and blood. "Tess!"

The chopper noise faded. Shouts and thuds continued inside. Angelito and Texas were having trouble. Something was swinging in the wind from the top balcony. Not something, someone—hanging by the fingers of one hand, clawing for a grip with the other. Tess. He could faintly make out her cries. The balcony had sagged, bringing it inches from a power line that was slung from the top of the tower to the domed mosque roof.

"I'm coming," he rasped.

The tower groaned, like a death rattle. No chance of getting her from the outside. He stumbled through the archway. The blast had torn open half the tower and skewed the rest. The bomber was...no longer a threat.

An iron staircase wound up, the bottom of it melted but the rest largely intact. Outside something smashed to the ground. He flinched. The tower was coming down around him. He took a run up and leaped for the lowest intact stair. It fried his palm. With a shout, he let go and thumped arse-first to the floor. He grabbed a bloody piece of fabric—part of the bomber's jacket—

and tried again. Ignoring the heat pulsing into his palm, he hoisted himself up, got a boot to the step and launched. He scrambled, gripped the metal, pulled himself up and began to climb. The staircase grated and shrieked under his weight. He passed the first balcony. Hot dust burned his throat. The tower shuddered and banked, tipping his shoulder into the stone wall. The iron railing came off in his hand and he unbalanced and crashed down half a dozen stairs. Cold metal sliced his arm. He flailed, got a hold and hauled himself up, panting, every-fucking-thing hurting.

"Tess!"

No point calling out—he couldn't hear jack. For all he knew, she'd fallen the second he'd stepped into the tower. *No.* He had to believe she was still there, waiting for him. He passed the second balcony. The stench of pigeon shit stung his nose. She couldn't die, not after all this. He'd lived two years in two days—started out as a guy who'd abandoned the world and ended up as a guy who'd found something, someone, to return for. Gone from a guy whose future would be spent fighting someone else's wars, doomed to die in battle or grow old drinking bad wine, to a guy who wanted to grow old with a woman he loved. And maybe that woman was Tess. What he'd found, what he'd fought for, what he'd risked, would not be for nothing. It was worth it, all of it, to get that rush through his veins when she looked up at him with those blue eyes and that stubborn chin. The archway to the top balcony came into sight, just above him. She was right. He would fight for what he believed in.

An earth-shuddering crash, then a rush of air like a wave rippling toward him. The stairs lurched, grinding and scraping against the sides of the tower. The step under his feet swayed. He grabbed the lip of the archway just as the stairs fell away below him. His chin smashed into the wall. He swung his other hand up. Great—Tess was swinging from one side and he was swinging from the other. The staircase screeched as it concertinaed into a heap way below. He heaved up, tossing himself through the archway, and landed facedown on a metal grating. The balcony. Through it he made out the shape of a twisted body far below, clothes and skin gray with dust. Bloody hell. Next to him, Hamid's cloak was caught on the railing.

Damn. Was that what he'd seen swinging? Had he imagined it was Tess? He croaked out her name, crawling on hands and knees around the balcony as it swung and shifted.

He saw her fingers first, clutching a drooping railing. Even as he looked, the metal sagged, dragging her down. The fingers clawed tighter. He scrambled to her, taking in wild eyes, wild hair. She whimpered. Or maybe it was a scream. He steadied his balance, not trusting anything to brace against, and leaned over. His head spun. He fought the urge to vomit. His vision narrowed as he grabbed her wrists, clawing his way up to her elbows. Groaning, he lifted her over the balcony.

She wrapped her arms around him, shaking like a jackhammer.

"Oh God, Flynn," she said, her voice catching. *That* he wasn't imagining. The balcony lurched downward. She tugged him toward the archway. "We have to get down."

He caught her waist. "The staircase collapsed. We'll have to—"

We'll have to... She stared up at him, clutching his forearms like they were the only thing keeping her from falling. Which wasn't far from the truth. Trouble was, there wasn't a hell of a lot holding him up. *We'll have to...*

Nothing. He had nothing. The tower growled and shifted, throwing them against the curved wall. There had to be something. There was always a way out. Every mess he'd ever got into, he'd found a way out. Getting himself out of the crap was what he did best. *Think.* If they went down with the tower they'd be buried under twenty tonnes of stone. What was the alternative? Falling to their deaths like...

Hamid. That was Hamid down there. He'd thought it was... No, Tess was right here. He tightened his arms around her, checking his surroundings, forcing his brain to focus.

Yes.

"I have an idea," he said.

"What?"

"I'll tell you—"

"—if it works."

"Yeah."

It probably wouldn't. He edged around the tower, still clinging to Tess, praying that his shifting weight wouldn't be the straw that brought the whole thing down, and grabbed Hamid's cloak. He tested it. Thick, strong.

Something cracked. Something big and structural and essential. The balcony listed. They inched back to where Tess had been hanging. He doubled up the fabric, looped it over the power line, grabbed the ends, twisted them around his wrists, gripped the fabric in his fists. It was a big drop to the dome.

"Tess, I'm going to let you go, just for a second." He pulled himself up to sit on the edge of the swaying railing, letting the line take some of his weight. "Okay, nice and slow, you're gonna climb onto me and link your arms and legs around me, tight as you can."

He detected a slight shake of her head. Her gaze followed the sagging path of the power line down to the roof of the mosque, and then back up to where it was attached to a rusty metal loop at the top of the tower, beside a loudspeaker. Yeah, so it wasn't much of a plan. *It's all I have, sunshine.*

The tower heaved like a staggering drunk. He tightened his legs around the railing. It clung to the wall by a single staple.

"Tess!" he shouted. "Now!"

She clambered onto him, wrapping her arms around his shoulders and her legs around his waist, hanging on like a baby monkey. The line swung under the extra weight, pulling his back clear so he was hanging in space, legs still curled around the railing. Tess gasped, climbing higher onto him. He released his legs and went to push off, but slipped before he could gather momentum. A dozen rocks sheared off the tower and smashed into dust. She coughed.

"We'll just slide to the dome of the mosque, nice and easy." He was talking shit, of course.

They hung, suspended, the fabric clinging to the wilting line. Tess tightened her grip, silent and still. Holding her breath. At least if they fell he would land first, giving her a chance. He leaned heavily to the downhill side. They lurched half a meter but the cloak gripped the wire like it had a survival instinct. He leaned again, then back, coaxing the swaying motion into a swing.

The robe edged down the wire, first in fits and starts, then smoother, then gaining speed, the cotton shrieking like it was alive. Crap, the friction could burn through it. He clung to the cloak; Tess clung to him; hot air rushed past.

The dome was coming up fast. Too fast. The minaret rumbled. The line lurched. Flynn twisted his head just as the tower imploded, collapsing straight down like a demo job and unleashing a wave of dust. They were over the mosque, in danger of overshooting the roof and smashing into the stone wall two floors below. He let go of the cloak but it caught at his wrists. The power line lashed through the air like a whip. A ripping noise and they were in free fall.

Crunch. His back struck first, in the center of the dome. Mate, soon he'd have no spine left. They careered downward. He shot out his feet and his shoes slammed into the low wall at the edge of the roof, the blow shuddering up his legs. Tess skidded out of his arms. He lurched forward and caught her under the shoulders just before she went over the side. With a roar, he pulled her up and collapsed into the dip between the edge of the dome and the wall. He twisted to cover her as stones pelted them. If a rock fell on his skull, so be it. Tess's breath heaved and squeaked. He scooped his hands under her back and held tight. *Karma, come and get me. I'm over fighting you.* Like a downpour easing to drizzle, the roaring and the deluge subsided.

They were alive. Some-fucking-how they were alive.

IF TESS HAD any breath left, she'd be sobbing and laughing and shouting and freaking singing. As it was, she could barely hyperventilate. She talked her arms into releasing their death grip on Flynn's neck and ran her hands down his shoulders and around to his back. Solid. Alive. Her body ached, protesting at taking his weight, but she didn't care. He groaned—not in a good way.

"You okay?" she managed.

"Yeah," he rasped into her hair. "You?"

"Peachy."

"Cool."

Eventually, the crunching and pelting from the minaret and the buzz in her ears settled enough for her to make out voices in the building below. French. Calm, deep French. Her shoulders relaxed. She picked out Angelito's low growl and stilled as she counted the other voices. Texas? Quan? Far away over the roofs a woman wailed. Another joined in. Ululating. Her eyes stung, the tears failing to flush out the dust. How many were dead? How many injured? Faces flashed through her head—the woman crushing chilis, the kids who'd scrambled for her corncob, the tout...

Sirens blared, and voices rang out from mosque loudspeakers, reverberating too wildly for her to make out words. Not the lilting call to prayer—civil defense instructions? She spread her fingers over Flynn's back, soaking up his heat and strength. He'd returned for her, he'd saved her, as he had so many times in the last two days. Her boomerang. There was so much she couldn't take in, but right now, at least there was this—the two of them, alive.

Minutes passed. A raw, primeval cackle arced over them. She shivered. Hyena. After an age, Flynn groaned and eased off her. She could almost hear his muscles creak as he hinged into a sitting position on the lip of the dome. Blood and sweat dribbled down his face and neck, carving pink rivulets through the dust and dirt. He offered his hand and she let him pull her up beside him. Even sitting made her dizzy. In the distance, plumes of smoke rose as smudges against the skyline, lit in a red and blue strobe. Above the horizon, around a sliver of a new moon, the sky was turning from navy to black, the first stars pricking through. Lights were winking on through the town.

"It got dark," she said.

"Yeah."

"I can't believe we're alive."

He squeezed her hand. "Yeah."

"Guess that karma came round."

"Guess it did."

She turned to him, saying his name, just as he turned and said hers. Her nose brushed his chin. She blinked, tilting her head to look at his eyes. One was blackening and closing. Her chest filled up until it pinched. He raised his free hand and pushed a tendril of hair behind her ear. Nerves twisted in her stomach.

"You were going to say something?" he said, a grin curling the corner of his mouth. He raised their joined hands and linked his fingers through hers. Hard to believe that two days ago she found that smile infuriating. Now it melted her bones.

"You're going to make me go first?" she said, a smile catching her own mouth. "You choose now to be a gentleman?"

He shrugged. "You're the one with all the words. I'm more the action man."

She bit her lip. *Say it.* What was the worst that could happen? He would let her down gently and she'd never see him again? Wow, that was weird. Two days ago she was convinced the worst-case scenario was to love a man who might not come home. Now her biggest fear was that Flynn would walk away before she could even start to worry about him not coming home. Her breath snagged. *All risk is relative.*

"Screw it," he said. "I'll go first." He closed the tiny gap between them and touched his lips to hers. She soaked up the gentleness of it, like a balm after all the violence and fear. Cradling her jaw in one hand, he deepened the kiss, tangy and dusty and a little metallic. She slipped a hand up to cup his shoulder. Yep. This guy.

A hooting and hollering drifted up from below, topped by a very Texan "Yeehaw!" Good news, evidently.

They kissed for a long time. Night dropped thick and fast, cooling her, caressing her skin. She felt safe. Permanently safe.

When at last they broke off, she sank her forehead into the dip of his collarbone, feeling his torso gently rise and fall.

"Still believe I won't come home to you?" he said. His hand drifted to the small of her back.

Home? Oh God, that sounded very much like he *wanted* to be the man coming home to her. Was she a fool to want that, too?

"It's your turn, sunshine," he whispered into her hair. Sunshine. He'd called her that all along, but it no longer sounded like an exasperated insult. He said it quietly, slowly. Like he planned to call her that until they were a hundred. She could live with that.

She inhaled noisily and straightened so she could see

his face. "All right, I concede. Turns out you are pretty freaking ninja."

"Victory, at last," he said, laughing right up into his eyes. He scooped his hands around her waist. "And...?"

She brushed a snowdrift of dust from his eyebrow. "Turns out you're also a man I could very easily fall in love with."

He stared blankly. He blinked. Crap, had she read this all wrong? *I can't get involved with you.* He'd told her straight.

A smile broke over his whole face, genuine and un-inhibited, not one of his cautious half grins. "Go on, then," he said.

"Go on, what?"

"Fall in love with me."

Her soul left her body and did somersaults over the dome. She shrugged. "Okay."

"Okay...?"

"Yeah, okay."

"You're gonna fall in love with me."

"Just did. Just then."

He chuckled. Her cartwheeling soul giggled in reply. Any second it'd fall off the roof.

"And...you?" she ventured. This was where it could all come apart. She had—unforgivably—betrayed his trust just a few hours ago. And he had so much to hide.

He frowned. "You know..."

Her soul froze in midair and blinked.

"That," he said, "was a question."

She huffed out a breath. Would loving him always be this deliciously excruciating? He settled his hands on her hips like he was getting comfortable for the long haul.

"Truth is, I fell in love with you somewhere between

there—" He jerked his head in a direction she guessed could be east. "And here." He pressed his lips against hers, for a long, luscious minute.

"Um," she said afterward. "I don't want to spoil the moment—because this is a damn good moment—but how is this going to work? Us?"

"We'll work it out. Maybe you could come and work in France. Maybe I could leave the legion. Maybe I could be your permanent bodyguard because, mate, do you need one. I don't care about the how. I know I'm going to be with you, and that's enough. It's been a long time since I had anything to live for. And I kinda like the idea of having something to live for."

"But…someone might recognize you and you'll be—"

"Pretty sure it's too late for that," he said, wincing.

"What do you mean?"

He blew out his cheeks and stood warily, as if he doubted his legs would hold him, then pulled her up. "First, let's figure out how to get off this roof and go join the others. There's a lot we need to catch up with."

She swallowed, her throat drying. "Samira. Quan's family. My mom." Oh God, she was lying here kissing Flynn, soaking up the relief, and they…

"Come on," he said gently.

They found a ladder fixed to the side of the mosque—rusty, but sturdy enough. Once on firm ground, Tess waited while Flynn picked his way across the debris to check on Hamid. With a grim shake of the head, he returned, and they limped into the mosque, leaning on each other. She wasn't sure who was holding who up. No way would she be able to move by morning.

The others were crowding around the laptop. Ethiopian soldiers were hauling off the last of Hamid's thugs, and her cameraman. They looked only slightly less bruised and bloodied than Angelito and Texas, who had been joined by Okoye and Thor.

"Where's Doc?" she said.

"He's okay," Texas said. "In better shape than the rest of us."

Quan shuffled up, cradling his left arm. "You did it." He looked from her to Flynn. "Both of you."

"But, Quan, your family—"

"—are fine. Thanks to your...*friend's* quick thinking." He extended a hand to Flynn, who shook it, clapping his other hand on Quan's shoulder.

"I don't get it," Tess said.

"Let's get you caught up." Quan leaned over the laptop. "Starting with this." He moved aside to reveal his living room in Addis. His older daughter, Sying, sat on the couch, holding a tablet up to a man's face. A live feed.

"Oh, thank God."

"She's never happier than when she gets to show someone the new level of whatever game she's obsessed by," Quan said. "Keep watching."

Sying lowered the tablet and swiped at it. Tess clapped a hand over her mouth. Cooper. The man was Coop. Her single most annoying brother. She stared up at Flynn. He was smiling. He knew?

Angelito pulled out his phone and dialed. "She's here," he said, without introducing himself. "She's watching." He caught Tess's eye and nodded toward the computer, hanging up.

A large shape made a flying leap onto the couch, followed by another. Luka. And Nate. As her brothers jostled for space, squashing poor Sying into the arm, another body came flying onto their laps. Zhu, Quan's younger daughter. Two women filed in behind. Xifeng and…

"Oh God," Tess mumbled. "Mom." She grabbed Flynn's arm, her throat clogging up. "How?" Her brothers waved, grabbing the girls' hands and coercing them to join in, which they did, giggling.

Flynn moved behind Tess and circled his arms around her waist. "I kept in contact with Quan's housekeeper through Facebook. She hid upstairs when al-Thawra came. We needed a team we could trust—you could trust—to go in, and, hey, your family were in town doing nothing much."

"How did you…?"

"Mauricio Luiz, the Special Forces guy I told you about—the guy I knew from exercises. I contacted him and he got us in touch with your brother. Figured you wouldn't mind me breaking radio silence under the circumstances. Your family were only too happy to step in."

Tears slipped down her cheeks. That was one risk she was delighted he'd taken. "Oh, I'm sure they were. But the drone strike? Hamid said—"

"A bluff, I'm guessing."

Tess looked at Quan. "So when you smashed the TV, it wasn't because you couldn't watch. It was because—"

"I saw them arrive. I was concerned that if Hamid knew things were going wrong, she'd speed up your execution before reinforcements arrived."

"There's someone else who'll want to talk to you," Flynn said. "Rafe?"

Angelito skipped his fingers over his phone. He

waited for an answer and said, "Put her on." He handed the phone to Tess.

"Hello?" said a woman's voice.

"Oh God, Samira?" Tess said, almost dropping the phone. "I thought... You're safe?"

"*Ow*. I'm with Doc."

"But the helicopter..."

"I'm sure your Flynn will explain. You are well?"

Tess felt Flynn's hands on her hips. "Very."

"I can't talk long. It is wonderful to hear your voice. You have done an amazing thing. I am very proud, and Latif will be, too. *Would* be, too." Her voice broke. Tess heard a man's voice—words of comfort.

"Samira?"

"I am fine, truly. Better than I've been in a long while."

Tess swallowed back more tears. A crackle swept through the phone, like a sudden wind.

"I have to go—the helicopter's waiting. I am proud of you, my friend."

"Samir—" She'd hung up. Tess handed back the phone and sought out Quan. "But the helicopter... It exploded."

"I got a message to Samira that the chopper was in danger, that Hamid was tracking her. By that time they'd already ditched her phone and were using the medic's. They dropped off the other legionnaires in Harar and diverted."

"But the footage...?"

"A helicopter explosion from a YouTube clip. I spliced it in when no one was looking. Too easy. We kept Hamid thinking her plan was working while we dismantled it, piece by piece. Best. Workday. Ever."

"*We?*" Tess looked from face to face. "Was I the only one who wasn't in on this?"

Flynn rubbed her shoulder. "I'm sorry—I wanted to tell you. I could see how spooked you were but I couldn't risk Hamid hearing. And I wasn't sure the plan was actually working—we were kinda winging it, and I was about the only one who wasn't hooked in by Facebook or phone at the end. Of course, Angelito was supposed to get here *a little* sooner."

The *capitaine* laughed. "One hell of a last mission, Flynn."

"The suicide bombers…?" Tess said.

Angelito crossed his arms. "Mostly taken down with no lives lost but their own. Flynn came up with the idea of getting himself captured, to lead us to you. While we were quietly picking off al-Thawra's guards, we saw the bombers leaving and guessed what was happening. Texas and I had things under control here, so I sent Thor and Okoye after them—and we were in contact with the Ethiopian military, so we gave them a heads-up. Only the white woman caused casualties. Okoye caught the man she'd been with, tried to talk sense into him, dragged him to some café where there was a TV to show him the news reports, the truth of what was happening, but after that he got away."

Okoye shook his head, looking grim. "It was chaos."

Flynn jerked his head toward the minaret—the former minaret. "We caught up with him outside. No harm done except to him and the architecture, and Hamid. She's dead."

Tess frowned, trying to weave it all together. "How did Jamal find out the truth about al-Thawra? What was on the news?"

All gazes fell on Quan. "It's probably easiest if you get comfortable and enjoy the show," he said. On the laptop he flicked to her network's website and clicked the top story.

She gasped. A video began—her package, starting with her piece-to-cam. "Holy crap, I'm confused. How did that get out?"

"Samira and Doc took care of it," Flynn said.

"But who did they send it to? Quan was here, being watched. A file that big—"

"You're not the only one with contacts." A bitter note crept into Flynn's tone.

"Watch." Quan clicked on the next video. A gray-haired newscaster she'd known her whole career began speaking: "Spectacular developments today in the kidnapping of journalist Tess Newell," he said. "The French legionnaire who was captured with Newell has been revealed as the son of one of the world's most notorious serial killers. The story was broken by a journalist from an Australian network who…"

"Oh no," Tess said, twisting to look up at Flynn.

He shrugged. "It was the quickest way I could think of to get your story on air. I got Doc and Samira to call Katie—the journalist who…you know. She's a big shot in Australia now. I left them to transmit her the video and she got it straight on air, though of course it meant…" He inhaled with a hiss, like he'd burned his tongue.

"It meant revealing your new identity. Flynn, no…"

While the others watched the video, he took her elbow and urged her aside. "We needed your story to get out. The world needed your story to get out and I knew she had the balls to do it."

"But…" Whoa. This was all failing to compute. "But the legion—like you said, it's all you have."

"I'd like to think it's not all I have anymore, Tess." He cradled her cheeks. "That I have the hope of something else."

She swallowed. "Yes, of course."

"Too many years I've lived in fear that this will get out. But today I realized that I couldn't hide behind the secret and have a chance for a future with you—or any real future that belongs to me. I chose to have a future. I chose you, if you'll have me. The consequences of stepping forward can't be worse than the risk of losing you before we even have a chance to get somewhere. We have something here, you and me. And I'm counting on you to stand by me when the shit flies."

"Oh, Flynn. Of course. Always."

"Good. Because you're the kind of woman I want to have my back. Anyway," he said, touching the graze on her nose, "I'm pretty bloody sure the French military will want to take credit for all this, which might at least leave me with a job—if I want one, even if I get demoted. I don't care. You told me it's time to forgive myself, and you were right. But I can't do that until I stop and turn around and face this thing. I'm done running. This is where my life begins properly. Tess, it was worth the risk. *You* were worth the risk." His eyes fixed on the laptop, over her shoulder. "*That* was worth the risk."

She turned, to see footage on the laptop of soldiers climbing out of jets in Djibouti. A ticker read: Breaking news: President calls off Somali air strikes—Key political figures under cloud following Newell report.

"This is *great* TV," Quan said, as if it were a religious experience.

"And you thought *I* would do anything for a story," Tess muttered to Flynn.

Quan switched back to the edit screen. "It'll get even better when they pick up on our exclusive interview with the late leader of al-Thawra." He tapped some keys—sending the interview to the webcast—and picked up his phone. "The net is going off. We're everywhere. Every freaking network and news site and social-media site. I'm so handling the movie rights."

"You're loving this," Tess said.

"I certainly am. And now for the happy ending. Watch this."

"There's more?"

"Oh yes, this is my favorite part."

He swiped, and handed the phone to Flynn, who nestled in behind Tess and held it in front of them. It was her network's live stream, broadcasting the feed from the camera on the mosque roof, from earlier. Like Hamid said, it did look like some Hollywood drama, albeit a grainy low-budget one. None of it seemed real: the explosion in the tower, Hamid falling, Tess clinging on, Flynn rescuing her, the improvised zip lining—with her skirt hiked way higher than appropriate for a family show. It passed on the screen a lot faster than it'd seemed at the time.

Her jaw dropped as realization hit. "Oh man. The camera, the angle… It would have picked up…"

"Oh," Flynn said, his voice clunking. "That's bad."

"You didn't…?" Tess said, directing her words to Quan while her eyes stayed glued to the screen.

"Tess, it's a beautiful thing."

Flynn squeezed his arms around her. Her face flushed cold then hot, her stomach flipping all over again as she watched him grab her and kiss her on the screen, silhouetted against the night sky. Oh God—that was why his unit had cheered. They'd seen the whole thing on the live webcast, like a silent movie. The *world* had seen the whole thing. She'd just launched into another relationship in the public eye.

But it was a relationship with *Flynn*. A guy who fought for what he believed in. A guy who believed in *her*. And hey, it wasn't as if she needed to worry about being taken seriously as a journalist. After this scoop?

"I guess it's official," Flynn said, as the screen switched back to the newscaster. Holy cow, the guy was crying? Voice cracking, he began reading the next story.

"Told you it was a happy ending," Quan said as Flynn handed back the phone. "Ratings gold."

"I don't believe in happy endings," Flynn said, spinning Tess and tilting up her chin. "Just happy beginnings."

He leaned down and kissed her softly. She slid her arms around his shoulders, basking in the bliss rolling through her aching body. Her boomerang man, who would always return.

* * * * *

ACKNOWLEDGMENTS

WHETHER YOU'RE WRITING them or reading them, novels are an irresistible invitation to meet new people and explore new places and ideas. I've relished writing *Edge of Truth* because it's allowed me to create two fiery and flawed people and watch what happens when they're forced together under challenging circumstances. It's also enabled me to return to Ethiopia (at least on the page), a fascinating country I was privileged to experience as a volunteer aid worker.

This novel, and the adventures it bestowed, wouldn't have happened without the support of my writing village. A huge thanks to the following people:

First and foremost, my insightful editor, Allison Carroll, and the rest of the talented, hardworking and enthusiastic team at HQN Books. It's an honor to share this journey with you.

My unfailingly supportive agent, Nalini Akolekar, and her colleagues at Spencerhill Associates.

My beta readers, critique partners, cheerleaders and technical advisers, including Brad McEvoy, Christine Sheehy, Cassandra Gaisford, Mia Kay, Kari Lemor, Carrie Nichols, M.A. Grant, C.A. Speakman, Jean Barrett, Fiona Marsden, Tracy Brody, Gina Rochelle, Rosalind Martin, Caroline Ross, Tristram Clayton, Andrew

Potter, Adam Ray, and Elizabeth Otto and the Trauma Fiction group.

My writer networks, who keep me motivated, entertained, on course and sane—the Inkspots, the Dragonflies, the Fab Five and Romance Writers of New Zealand.

The United Nations High Commission for Refugees, for the unique and indelible opportunity to experience life in remote Ethiopia, which provided some of the inspiration for this story.

My uplifting friends who always turn up at the right time with the right balance of encouragement, good humor and wine.

My husband and sons, for their infinite love, encouragement and perspective, and awesome writing advice. (More fighting! More gun battles! No kissing—ugh! This *definitely* needs a galactic armada!)

Lastly, all the passionate readers, reviewers, bloggers, authors, librarians, journalists and booksellers who have been so encouraging about my debut novel, *Deception Island*. Book people are the best people. Your support means a great deal, and this one's for you.

FORBIDDEN RIVER

CHAPTER ONE

THE CHOPPER APPEARED on the horizon, hovering like a dragonfly over the slate-blue mountain range. Right on time. A second later the bass throb of its blades ricocheted around the valley, on air so crisp Cody Castillo felt he could reach out and snap it.

He hauled his kayak and paddle from a baggage cart parked outside the airport terminal, loaded with the few supplies he needed for a river paddle. Food, pup tent, sleeping bag, thermals, first aid kit, safety gear, wet weather gear. His gut fizzed. One night in an alpine hut—alone, hopefully—and then nobody and nothing for four beautiful days. Fuck right off, world.

CROOKED VALLEY AIRPORT, the sign read. Well, *Crooked Alley*. The *V* had fallen off the line of letters spaced along the roof of the squat hangar that passed for a terminal. The *Y* was on its side, the *T* just hanging in there. Way out here at the end of the world, if you needed a sign to tell you where you'd wound up, you were crazy lost.

He'd been to plenty middles of nowhere—Marfa in Texas, the Empty Quarter of Saudi Arabia, Camopi in French Guiana... Like this, they weren't the kinds of places you happened upon, pit stops on a road trip, derelict stations on a train line. Nope, it took full commitment to get nowhere. For him, in this case: a ride in a rattly legion Peugeot 4WD from his base at Calvi to Bastia, a ferry from Corsica to Nice, a flight to Paris and then Auckland, via Hong Kong. That sucked up the first forty-eight hours of his leave. Then to Christchurch and a two-day wait for a flight over the Southern Alps aboard a five-seater Cessna piloted by a farmer who might have learned to fly in World War II, going by his age and the way he dipped and dived like he was still dodging the Luftwaffe. Just one journey left—a chopper ride to the source of the legendary Awatapu River—and then he was on his own steam.

Cody laid the kayak on the deserted tarmac, grit scraping the hull. Yep, Crooked Valley/Alley was his kind of airport, where the arrival of a plane seemed to baffle the skeleton staff. No baggage carousels—just the cart pulled by a quad bike, driven by the ace pilot himself, once he'd shut down the plane. "Security" was a ninety-year-old unarmed guard in a uniform she might have worn for half a century, shrinking into it every year until it hung off her like a kid's costume. No gates, no announcements—more a bus stop than an airport.

The helicopter began to descend, surfing the clouds sloshing over the range. Ah, New Zealand. A throwback to the days when the biggest threat to aviation was a Canada goose. One-third the size of home—

One-third the size of *Texas*. A long time since Texas had been home.

As it neared, the chopper mutated from insect to bird to machine, the blades beating a different note from the engine. An older model Eurocopter. Not the armored, camo-painted Puma or Tigre he usually rode but a tidy little Écureuil. A squirrel. He shaded his eyes as the chopper kissed the tarmac and settled, late-afternoon sun bouncing off the windshield. The rotors slowed until the disc dissolved and the blades became distinguishable— twelve, nine, six, then the regular three as they whined to a stop. What was the pilot's name again? Cody squinted, trying to picture the address on the confirmation email. Tia, right? Tia Kupa.

The pilot's door hinged back and he stepped out. No, not *he*, not with those curves rounding out the tight blue jeans and that thick black hair swaying to her shoulders. *She*, and one hell of a she.

She swiveled and walked his way, shoving her hands in the pockets of a black leather flight jacket. The kind of woman his mom would call handsome rather than pretty. Statuesque. Square jaw, cut cheekbones, smooth skin a little darker than his own, dark brown freckles splattered across her nose and cheeks. Maybe thirty, so about his age. She had the commanding aura of an officer, someone who quietly assumed she'd be respected, and thus was respected. Māori, he guessed.

"You're my guy?" She pushed sunglasses off her face and looked him down and up. Her eyes weren't the brown he'd expected—not that he'd stopped to think about it—but a blazing green, almost hard to look at with the sun striking them. "The kayaker?"

"Yes, ma'am. Tex—I mean *Cody*." It felt weird to be that guy again—no one called him Cody anymore. But introducing himself as "Texas" felt off. His commando team had inflicted the nickname on him years ago but he didn't offer it around.

She assessed his shiny orange kayak, nose to stern. "You might want to ditch the price tag." She nodded at the ticket attached to a grab loop.

"Yeah. Easier to buy a new kit than transport it." Not that he needed to explain.

"If you have the money, sure, why not?" There was a bite in her voice. Yep, she had him all figured out. The kind of adventure tourist who bought new gear and chartered a helicopter? He wouldn't take kindly to that guy, either. But hey, who cared what she thought, as long as she dropped him somewhere remote and deserted. "I'm busting for a wee. Keep an eye on her for me." She waved vaguely at the chopper.

He looked left and right. Apart from the security guard, who was sitting slumped at a graying bench dragged up against the hangar wall, there was no life for several dead-flat miles. "You expecting a hijacking or a parking ticket?"

"Funny," she said, her tone indicating it wasn't. "Don't go any closer till I get back."

She flicked her sunglasses onto her nose and walked away, ruffling her hair, her stride lithe and confident. Owning it.

He knelt over his kayak and pulled a water bottle from one of the dry bags stashed in the hull. He'd been crazy thirsty since Hong Kong, like the flight had sucked the water from his body.

"Hey, Cody," Tia called from the hangar a couple of minutes later. "Give me a hand with these."

He stowed the bottle and strolled over, the sun warming one side of his face. She waited by a roller door. Two single kayaks were lined up in front of her, faded and scratched, one yellow, one green, paddles balanced on top. As he neared, she nodded at the nose grab loops while she grasped the stern ones.

"It's not meant to be a group tour," he said as they lifted. They better not be taking anyone else.

"They're for a couple of tourists who are climbing the glacier and crossing the peaks before doing the Awatapu. The conventional route."

Right. Because he hadn't earned the downriver kayak without first hauling ass uphill? Whatever.

"Glaciers are too slow," he said, walking. The kayaks were lighter than he'd expected—but then, the climbers would be carrying a lot of their gear. "When are these guys due at the river?"

"Tomorrow afternoon."

Extra incentive not to mess around. Not that people usually caught up to him on any river, let alone a fast one. They dropped the boats near the chopper and in silent accord returned for his kayak.

"You've kayaked before, right?" She knelt before the port skid and began fitting heavy-duty straps to it.

"Yep," he said, yanking off his boat's price tag. The elastic gave with a snap that made her head turn. He caught a hint of a smile. He'd taken it off so it wouldn't flap during the ride, but he stopped short of explaining.

"You know the Awatapu is a grade six? Messy rapids, waterfalls, boulder gardens, sieves that'll suck you under and keep you forever, snags to lose a battleship in…"

Tremendo. "Yes, ma'am."

"You know no one does it solo?"

"I do a lot of things solo. I like it that way." Not quite true. Not a lie. In a parallel life where things hadn't gone to shit, he'd have been standing here with his brother, racing to be first into her good books and maybe even her bed. In this life, yeah, he was a loner, outside the legion. The shine had gone out of chasing women, like it had a lot of things.

"You know there's no mobile reception, and no one passes by? These climbers are the only others up there." Her lips tightened. "The only ones presumed alive."

"You didn't think of talking me out of it *before* I paid you?"

"Hell, no. I need the money. But we've already lost four tourists on the river this spring and it'll be bad for business to lose a fifth. So just…don't die." Her tone caught somewhere between dry humor and genuine concern.

"Wait, *four* tourists? I heard about two, a month or so back."

"Another couple went missing a fortnight ago. The *tapu* had only just been lifted after the last pair."

"Tapu?"

"If a place is *tapu*, it's sacred or forbidden. When someone dies up there, it becomes *tapu* until it's blessed."

"When someone dies. This happens often?"

"There's a reason the river's called Awatapu. But I'm hoping like hell both couples are waiting for us up at the hut, living off eels and huhu grubs."

He noted her pronunciation—*Ah-wah-tah-pu.* Long vowels, a soft *T*, even stresses on the syllables. Not far off Spanish. "What's it mean?"

"The forbidden river, the sacred river. Want to lift your kayak and paddle up here, and I'll strap them?"

"And… Wairoimata?" he said, hoisting the craft, following her lead on the pronunciation, rolling the *R.* "That's the name of the town I'm getting out at, right?"

"Yeah. *Wai* means water, *roimata* is tears."

"Water of tears. Uplifting names. Did you fly them in—the missing tourists?"

She frowned as she strapped the kayak. "The ones from two weeks ago, yes. Danish couple. Experienced kayakers."

"But not the others—the first couple?"

"I didn't think they could handle the paddle. Both couples are officially still missing, but yeah, it's a safe bet they won't be walking out. We've had some late-season snowfalls so it's not a good time to be lost in the bush. Not that there's ever a good time."

He pictured the terrain he'd flown over—the Alps, subalpine scrublands, rainforest… "Guess it can be tough to find people out there."

She tugged at the kayak—it didn't budge—then straightened and dusted her hands on her jeans. "Yep. I was up there long days, searching. I'll be paying off the fuel for months."

"You cover your own fuel on a search and rescue?"

She picked up the remaining straps and walked to the other side. "I'm funded to a point," she said as they got to work. "But what am I supposed to do when the budget maxes out, leave them out there? And I took the second couple in, so… They're probably snagged in tree roots, caught in a sieve. They'll be flushed out soon, with the snow melting in the tops. The river always gives up its dead. The bush, not so much."

"I'm getting the idea these aren't the first people to disappear up there."

She gave him a sideways look. "How much research did you do on this river?"

"Enough to know it's one of the wildest kayaking runs anywhere."

"See, I'd have thought that would warn people away, but it just seems to attract them. I've never understood that urge to put yourself in danger."

"And yet you fly a helicopter."

"I fly it very safely." Her voice strained as she pulled a strap. "The lucky ones get airlifted out with broken limbs. Of course, by then they've usually been waiting awhile—hungry, dehydrated, hypothermic…"

"You trying to talk me out of it?"

She yanked. "Would you listen?"

"Yes, ma'am."

"Would you heed the warning?"

"No, ma'am. You're just saying that for the record, right? Covering your liability."

"Yep. That and the fact I'm not your mother. I take it you've been in a helicopter before."

"Many times."

A dimple in her cheek twitched. "Okay, we're good to go."

"I'm a soldier." Now, why did he feel the need to make that clear?

"You're a soldier." Not a question, more a sarcastic echo. She tipped her head and studied him like he'd blown her assumptions and she had to start over.

He laughed.

"What?"

"I can hear you thinking."

"You're a psychic, too? Wow." Deadpan again, like it was the end of a long day and she didn't want to encourage conversation. Neither did he, normally. Mindless chatter shriveled his soul. But she was fun. There was passion hiding in those eyes, a smile simmering under those lips.

"Yep," he said. "You're thinking, 'What kind of soldier charters a helicopter rather than hiking in?'"

That dimple again. "Yes. Yes, I am."

"'And what kind of soldier buys a new kit instead of stealing military supplies?'"

"Maybe you *are* psychic." She folded her arms. "Or maybe you're a rich-boy fantasist who thinks that because he's in some hick backwoods at the end of the Earth he can reinvent himself into anything he wants—like, say, *a soldier*—so the gullible local girl will trip over herself to fall in bed with him."

"Whoa."

"And maybe you're also a risk taker with a death wish," she continued, a twitch away from a smile. "You've done so many reckless things—out of rich-boy boredom, let's assume—that you've overridden your survival instinct and now it's only a matter of time before you make headlines and everyone says all that bullshit like 'He lived life to the fullest' and 'He died doing what he loved' and 'He'll always stay beautiful.' But you'll just be unnecessarily dead like all the other unnecessarily dead people."

Shee-it. She was ten kinds of cool. "You calling me beautiful?"

The smile broke through, curving her lips at an intriguing angle. An exasperated smile, but he'd take it. "Still, it's not a bad thing that fate weeds out the risk takers. Makes the herd stronger. Just try not to die in my country, on my river."

"*Your* river."

"My people's river. *Ko Awatapu te awa, ko Maungapouri te maunga.* Awatapu is my river. Maungapouri is my mountain." She jerked her head at the highest of the snow-crowned peaks jutting up behind the deep green nearer range. "I haven't always lived here but my *whānau*—my family—are anchored by these mountains and that river, guardians of them. So yeah, don't die on my watch because you've screwed up your wiring and death is the only challenge left."

Oh, he was getting a reminder that a very different challenge could still amp him up. He had zero time for women who were impressed by his uniform or his family's money. A pity legionnaires with death wishes didn't do relationships.

She walked past him, toward the cockpit. "See, to me, you look like a rich guy with too much time to spend at the gym."

Okay, so that stung—his fitness had come from hard work, self-control and self-loathing. Those he *could* take credit for. But it also meant she'd been checking out his body.

Guessing he wouldn't get an invitation, he circled the chopper and let himself in as she settled in the pilot's seat.

She raised her chin in cool appraisal, clipping on her harness. "What's your weapon?"

A test? "*Le Fusil à Répétition modèle F2.* Sometimes a Hécate II."

She hovered long, slender fingers over the dials on the instrument panel, eyes narrowed, following their path. Not taking chances, even though the blades had just stopped spinning. Overkill, but he'd tolerate that in a pilot. "That's the FR-F2, right? Sniper rifles."

"You know them?"

"Those don't sound like US military issue. So…

what? You're a mercenary? Sorry, I mean *security contractor*?"

"In a sense," he said. "Just not a well-paid one."

"Isn't that the whole point of selling out—making money?"

"Not for me. I'm a legionnaire."

She gave him that sideways look again, pulling on her headset and handing him his. "What, like the French Foreign Legion?" Her voice boomed through the intercom.

"Oui, Légion Étrangère, mademoiselle."

"You are so full of shit you could be a long-drop at a campground in January."

"No idea what that is, but it sounds bad."

She checked the panel above their head, again following her fingers with her eyes, and adjusted a lever. "Seriously? You're a legionnaire?"

"Yes, ma'am. *Caporal* Cody Castillo *du groupement des commandos parachutistes du 2e régiment étranger de parachutistes de Calvi.*"

She did a three-sixty check through the windows, and engaged the starter. *"Commandos parachutistes,"* she repeated disdainfully. "A parachute commando?"

"You know, most people are impressed by that."

"You'll never catch me jumping from a perfectly good aircraft."

"Afraid of heights?"

"Only of falling from them, which is totally rational and something you should be grateful for right about now."

"Yes, ma'am. That I am."

"Are you for real with that 'yes, ma'am' thing?"

"Habit. My *abuela* would have me over her knee if

I didn't show respect to women." Okay, so he might be hamming it up there. His grandmother controlled the family fortune from a laptop, not a rocking chair. Why haul your grandson over your knee when a withering stare was plenty scary?

As Tia worked the controls with deft fingers and sharp eyes, a muted whine filtered through the headset and the shadow of a blade glided across the ground in front, slowly pursued by another.

"Vous parlez très bien français," she said.

"So do you."

"Expensive education—and that's about all I remember. But you had an *abuela*?"

"My family's from Mexico."

"And you're not?"

"Texas—born and raised."

She gave a sharp laugh. "Right, so you're a legionnaire commando from *Texas*."

"Now, what have you got against Texas?"

"Nothing. It's just that you're not what I…" She shook her head. "It's just one of those places that seems, I dunno, mythical."

*You're not what I…*expected? Hell, neither was she. "Says the woman who lives in Middle Earth. But go ahead and believe what you want about me. I just care that you're a good pilot."

The seat underneath him hummed, as if the chopper were straining with impatience. He knew the feeling.

"The best," she said.

"Where did you learn to fly?"

She sighed, a scratch through the headset. "Would you ask me that if I was a guy?"

"Uh, yeah."

She increased the engine speed and the blades whipped faster. "I get asked that a lot and you know what? My male counterparts don't. I've checked with them. They don't get the question."

Shit. Was she right? *Would* he ask a guy that question? "Ma'am, I got total respect for all pilots—planes, helicopters, fucking hang gliders. Takes guts and brains and composure, and that's something few people have."

She scoffed, as if she wanted to be pissed at that but couldn't manage it. "Nice recovery."

The chopper lifted without a shudder and skimmed above the tarmac. He liked the way she talked. Sharp and combative but with enough humor that she didn't cross into mean or bitter. Sparring, not landing real blows.

"You don't mention on your website that you're a woman. You don't have a photo." Because he was damn sure it would've given him extra incentive to book her, on top of her stellar reviews and safety record. "Was that deliberate?"

"I don't say I'm a man, either. If people assume the wrong thing, that's on them, not me. I don't want my gender to help me or hold me back. I've had journalists wanting to make a big deal out of it. Even a publisher once, though she was more interested in…" She frowned. "I say no to everything. I don't want to be the 'plucky aviatrix keeping up with the big boys.'"

He got the feeling that'd happened before—and that it was the big boys who did the keeping up. They rose over a braided river, the shallow, bleached water in no hurry. The Awatapu's lower reaches. Around him the chopper felt weightless, a mosquito next to the albatrosses he was used to.

"I guess what I'm asking," he said, "is how a civilian pilot in probably the least gun-crazy country in the world knows her sniper rifles."

"Nine years in the New Zealand air force."

Ah. "Flying choppers?"

"Yep, though I started on transport craft—Orions, Hercules."

"They're still making those things?"

"The ones I flew were Vietnam relics. Of course I grew up with visions of racing Skyhawks, but by the time I enlisted they'd been sold."

"You didn't fly other jets?"

"We didn't have any."

"An air force without jets? You serious?"

"And our emblem is a kiwi, a flightless bird. Go figure." She activated the radio. "I'm just going to call in."

She spoke in clear, clipped shorthand. Phonetic call sign, position, altitude, direction, destination. Ahead, the last of the spring snow clung to the range's shadowy folds, in denial about the blue dome that curved above.

"To be fair," she said when she'd signed off, "all that *Top Gun* shit went out with the nineties. The future's in drones, which doesn't leave many options for real combat pilots. I'm not into that remote-control crap. If you don't have the guts to go to a place you have no business blowing it up."

"Where did you serve?"

"Samoa, the Philippines, hunting pirates in the Middle East… Took a bunch of scientists to Antarctica one summer. Mostly disaster relief and humanitarian missions, which is how it should be."

"Word. Though they can cut you up as much as combat. Why did you leave?"

Silence. "We had a...family crisis. My *koro*—my grandfather—he's lived in Wairoimata all his life, and he was struggling to get his head around it. And my brother and I needed to...get away. So we made a pact to come down here for a bit. Lie low, look out for Koro. Of course, Koro thinks it's us who needed him. Didn't mean to stay this long but it's one of those places that sucks you in. Besides, now I have this monster to pay off." She slid a hand across the top of the instrument panel. "So I'm here for a while, like it or not."

He got the feeling she liked it okay. There was more to her story, but if she didn't want to share, then all good. Who was he to pry? Happy families weren't his thing, either, not anymore.

"I know a guy you might know," he said. "Ex-legionnaire. Came to us from the New Zealand army."

"Yeah, because I know everyone in this country. We all went to school together. Or is this more of a 'You're brown, he's brown, so you must know each other' kind of thing?"

"Hey, I'm just as brown as you."

"So you should know better."

He laughed. He was almost sad it was such a short flight.

Way below, the chopper's long shadow flickered over green rock-strewn foothills, like some slimy black creature rolling and jerking over the land.

"Okay, Cowboy, what's his name?" Tia asked, the words rushing out, like she'd been trying not to ask.

"Austin something. Austin Fale—Falelo..."

She quietly swore, a whisper in the headset. "Austin Faletolu. He used to date my brother. I hate that."

"What, that he dated your brother?"

"No, that I know the random guy you're talking about."

"It happens a lot?"

"More than it should in a country this size."

They fell silent, he in awe, as the landscape got wilder. Barely tamed farmland gave way to rainforest, and trees in turn succumbed to a desert of jagged rocks and brown tussock. Along the edge of the range, fresh landslides left plummeting scars of scoria. A country on the move, tossing and turning and refusing to settle into sleep.

Man, he felt alive. Anticipation churned in his stomach and his skin buzzed. Not a wired adrenaline, like the start of an operation, but a lightness, a freedom. Escape in T-minus ten.

"You have travel insurance, a will?" Tia asked.

Aaaand bubble burst.

CHAPTER TWO

CODY SHIFTED IN his seat. "Yeah, I got a will." His father's lawyers had insisted on a succession plan for the business, though if they were smart they'd skip him. "But you think any insurer's gonna give a reasonable quote for this?" He could fund an evacuation anyway. Or the repatriation of his remains. "Don't worry. I'll see you're well paid for the search and rescue."

They cleared the seam of the range and turned south. The view switched to black and white, a rocky alpine plateau with fog filling the basins and dips. Farther into the mountains the ground snow thickened from tattered lace to a sheet to a blanket. In a valley between two craggy peaks spread a blue-tinted tongue of ice. The glacier. No sign of climbers.

He zipped his jacket higher. It was high-tech but lightweight, like most of the clothes he carried. Tia turned west and the sunlight bounced off the glacier, into his eyes. He shut them until the burn passed. Shame he wasn't getting on the water until 0600. He needed to blast off the nerves in his belly. He felt a nudge on his thigh. Tia pointed down. Carving around massive boulders was a river of milky turquoise, so vivid it seemed to glow.

"Estupendo," he whispered.

"Indeed. The Awatapu."

"Hell. I thought the photos on the web were doc-tored."

"Nope. Cool, eh?"

Tia followed the river's winding path. Final approach to Nowhere. As the altitude dropped, rock and snow yielded to tussock and thick khaki scrub. The river nar-rowed into boulder-strewn white-water corridors, flared into blue pools lipped with beaches of ashen stones, narrowed, flared, narrowed, flared, growing faster and wilder as more streams washed in. Man, he wanted a piece of that.

Tia navigated down into a clearing beside a red-roofed hut along the river, blond tussock flattening under them. If he'd closed his eyes he wouldn't have sensed the moment of contact. She radioed in as she shut down. He pulled off his headset. As the blades whined to a halt and the engine's white noise ceased, silence washed in. She stared at the hut. Well, *hut* was ambitious. More of a shed with a couple small windows and a chimney. Under a corrugated tin awning, a gray dish towel slumped from a rope. Could've been there months. Tia screwed up her face as she removed her headset. No sign of any missing tourists.

He spent the next ten minutes trying to equalize his ears as he helped Tia stash the kayaks under the awning. He could be imagining the rush of water over stones, but the bell-like bird chatter was real. The biting stench of avgas lifted, leaving the scent of clean air and distant snow. No better perfume.

She nodded at a craggy white peak in the distance. A bird of prey was riding a thermal. "A cold front is blowing up from Antarctica. You should be out before it hits, but if the weather turns, ride it out in the hut or your tent and I'll check on you when it clears."

"Sure thing." Like hell.

"Because that river's going to get high and fast superquick."

Even better. "Noted. Thanks."

She sighed, like she knew he was a lost cause. "Camp well above the water level—it can change quickly this time of year. Your best launchpad is down that track."

The "track" she pointed to was a slight gap between the prickly shrubs circling the clearing. "The river meanders for about a kilometer. Then you get your first challenge with a nasty, narrow little rapid. After that a big tributary joins and it really gets wild and pretty much stays that way. But the worst part, the part that makes it grade six, is the Auripo Falls, which you'll reach about midday tomorrow. Eighteen-meter drop— that's sixty feet to you—underwater whirlpool that'll hold you forever—"

"Yeah, I've read up on it, asked around. You've kayaked this river?"

"God, no. Just rescued enough people to know where they get unstuck. Or rather, stuck. I know it mostly by air—and my brother runs canyoning trips in the lower reaches in summer."

"Jumping off waterfalls? And you call me a risk taker?"

Almost a smile. "He's very safety-conscious."

"Like you."

"You say that like it's a bad thing."

"So your brother jumps off waterfalls—and throws other people off them—and you call him safety-conscious.

And I put only my own life on the line, and I'm a risk taker."

"He knows what he's doing. But yeah, once was enough for me. I'm happy just being his taxi driver."

"You canyoned? I thought you were scared of heights."

"Not heights, just falling, as every human should be. And it confirmed I was right to be afraid."

"So you just drop his victims to their fates instead?"

"I figure if you're determined to kill yourself, you'll find a way. It might as well benefit me." Her tone dropped *just* on the side of teasing. She wiped her hands on her thighs, like she was absolving herself of responsibility. "Right. That's me out."

"Last chance to talk me 'round."

She raised her chin. "You want me to talk you around?"

"No."

"Good. I could use another search and rescue contract to pay off the last one. Just make sure you die in a place I can easily spot from the air. And keep an eye out for those tourists. I don't like the idea of them lying…" She rubbed her eyes, as if trying to erase a mental image.

"I'll do that."

"Get off the river well before dark each day. When the light drops you can't see the snags."

"Yes, ma'am."

"That was a bit 'no shit, Sherlock,' wasn't it?"

Man, she was so close to a real smile. If he just worked a little harder… "It's nice that you care."

"You have someone waiting for word of when you

reach Wairoimata? Who can raise the alarm when you don't show?"

"No, ma'am."

Was she asking if he was single?

In your dreams, numbskull. Not that he was looking to hook up, but she'd be a fun vacation distraction.

"Got a mobile?" she said.

"Yep."

"It won't work until Wairoimata. You have my number—call me when you get out. If I don't hear by Wednesday, I'll start asking around."

"Will do."

"Got a distress beacon?"

"Yes, ma'am." He nodded to the kayak.

"A GPS one? Bought locally, not overseas?"

"Yep."

"Keep it on you. It's no use in your kayak if you get swept out. But don't use it unless you're dying. I don't want to fight my way up here at midnight in a cyclone to find you twisted your ankle."

"This happens?"

"Some people treat those things like Uber. If you can kayak out safely, do it. It'll make a better war story to boast about later."

"Noted."

She gave a sharp nod and walked away. Security briefing over.

"Well, thanks," he said.

Right. He checked his watch. A few hours before dark. He'd scout out the river, get sorted for the morning, then settle in with a freeze-dried dinner and his e-reader. He rubbed his belly. Food would fix that empty feeling. Damn, twenty minutes in her company and now he had to get reacquainted with solitude. Maybe when he called her from Wairoimata he'd ask her for a drink. Even a place that small had to have a watering hole.

"Hey, Cowboy," she called.

He killed his smile and swiveled. She was leaning into the helicopter, writing something on a clipboard.

"You got insect repellent?"

"Don't usually get bit. No malaria here, right?"

She looked up. "It's not the mosquitoes you need to watch for. It's the sandflies."

"I need to watch out for a fly?"

"You'll see." She pulled a spray bottle from a bag on the rear seat and lobbed it. He caught it one-handed. "I'll add it to the tab. Oh wait, you prepaid, didn't you?"

"You didn't give me a choice."

"On the house, then. And watch out for wild pigs."

"Pigs? For real? I fucking love this country. You're saying the most dangerous wildlife out there is flies and pigs?" He was crossing into flirt territory, drawing this out as long as he could. He wasn't even sure why.

She crossed her arms and leaned against the door frame. "Less Porky Pig and more a rhino crossed with a bull. I've seen boars up here twice your weight. There's also stags but they won't take you on unless you corner them. And chamois and tahr—wild goats—but the smell is the biggest danger there. At least they're herbivores."

"Unlike the sandflies?"

"Spoken like a guy who's never stood beside a New Zealand river at dusk." She pushed off the chopper. "And watch out for kea—big green parrots. Cheeky buggers. Don't turn your back on your dinner."

"Noted." He stuffed his hands in the back pockets

of his shorts. "Okay. Guess I'll go look at this river of death, then."

"Good luck."

"I don't intend luck to be a factor."

She nodded, again with that almost-smile. He forced himself to turn and walk away. Seeing her again would be his reward for surviving this paddle.

Of the ten wildest kayaking runs in the world, he'd kayaked numbers ten, nine, eight, seven, six and five. How dangerous could one little forbidden river be?

TIA TURNED BACK to her flight log, resisting the temptation to watch Cody right up to the moment he pushed through the trees and disappeared. Yep, it'd be a damn shame for the world to lose a specimen like that—and it'd break her heart to locate that body. He was muscular but easy with it, like he spent as much time doing yoga as lifting weights, like his power wasn't for show but function. A kayaker's shoulders, a soldier's athleticism, with the lived-in look of a guy who spent a lot of time outdoors.

She rapped her stubby fingernails on the clipboard. She'd give him until Wednesday night to call before hitting the phone. She didn't need another death on her conscience.

A gust swept through the tussock. The nor'wester, picking up ahead of the front. She'd take the downriver route home in case any bodies had been spat out. Or, hope above hope, she found four live ones waving up from the swing bridge above Auripo Falls. She rubbed the back of her neck, staring blankly into the scrub. The disappearances had been gnawing at her since the day it became obvious the Danes weren't going to arrive at

Wairoimata. One missing person wasn't unusual, even two. But four? She'd flown the river from glacier to sea, back and forth a dozen times, in case she'd missed some hazard that might explain things—a fallen tree, a crumbling cliff, a fresh rockfall.

She straightened, the tiny leaves on the trees coming into sharp focus. Something was out of place. She scanned the clearing. There, on a cluster of stones at the tree line, a twisted gray-brown clump. Damn. She crossed to it.

Yep, a kiwi. Mauled, bloody, decomposing. A big adult with a transmitter on its leg. Breeding stock. Would've been raised in captivity until it was big enough to defend itself. She crossed the clearing to the hut's stoat trap—one of hundreds she'd dropped into the forest this spring, for Koro's trapper mates. Another reason she wouldn't turn a profit this year.

The wooden box was on its side, bait untouched. Whatever knocked it over hadn't got in through the small wire tunnel, so not a rat or stoat. Possums didn't tear kiwi apart like that. It must have struck since the trappers had swept through on their fortnightly checks. She searched the ground.

There—animal shit. Dog? She swore. How the hell had a dog got up here? One feral dog could wipe out a hundred kiwi—the forest's entire population. She walked back to the bird, pulled out her phone and snapped photos for the rangers. They'd want to get here quick. If she left soon, she could bring them up before sunset.

Something rustled in the trees behind the chopper. Not a bird, something solid. She straightened. Nothing but tui warbling and trilling, and the rush of the river.

Cody, probably. Sheesh, she was jumpy. The only person he was a danger to was himself. There was no stopping adrenaline junkies with an obsession. She'd played dumb earlier, but of course she'd Googled him when he'd emailed her to book, seeing as it was so reckless to kayak the Awatapu solo. He'd competed in the extreme kayaking world champs with his brother—and if he was also a soldier, that was good enough for her. The profile of him she'd found was a decade old and hadn't mentioned the legion, but there were other hits she hadn't clicked on. They'd mostly been about some San Antonio software empire his family owned, and she couldn't care less about that.

The branches of a tall rata swayed. A kereru pigeon had swooped in, the sun catching the emerald of its breast, its weight bowing the branch as it twisted to eat berries.

A legionnaire, eh? What better way to stick it to your wealthy parents than run away to the legion? And she knew all about sticking it to your parents.

She was no sucker for a guy in uniform, but he'd look hot in khakis, with those broad shoulders tapering down to that tight arse, his sleeves rolled up over corded muscle, a serious slant to his jaw. Camo paint. Dirt. Sweat. Oh yeah.

She inhaled—and gagged on a filthy scent. Hell. That wasn't the kiwi. She'd transported enough bodies to know that smell. Something big and fleshy, and very dead. A pig? She swiveled, checking the leaves on the taller trees. The breeze had turned west. *Please, please, please let it be a pig.* She unzipped her jacket and pulled her T-shirt over her nose and mouth, her legs working robotically, nerves bringing her focus and hearing into high relief.

She shoved through the scrub, branches scratching her hands and slapping her face. The low drone of blow-flies, a lot of them. Her cheeks prickled. After a few minutes, she saw it, a flash of orange on the ground. Not a pig. Fuck, fuck, fuck. She pushed into a small clearing beside a boulder, her heart thumping.

Yep, a body. Curled up, sheltered under the overhang of the rock like it was hiding—that's why she hadn't spotted it from the air. The jacket. She remembered that jacket. Orange, with blue stripes. The Danish guy. Fuck it to hell.

CHAPTER THREE

TIA EXHALED IN a rush. *Don't breathe through your nose and you won't throw up.*

The guy had died this close to where she'd dropped him off? Maybe he and his girlfriend got into trouble downriver and he hiked back up to find help. But why not use their emergency beacons? Tia had insisted they each carry one. She crouched and nudged his jacket pockets. In one, a boxy shape. She carefully unzipped it. The beacon, still sealed.

"What the hell happened, mate?" The silence sucked up her whisper.

He had to have died of exposure, hypothermia, at least a week ago. She'd better radio in, get him in a body bag, load him. Cody could help—he'd be used to dealing with death. Once the body's smell was contained she'd have a better chance of figuring out if another one lay around here.

"Let's get you started on the journey home, eh?"

She blinked her eyes clear. A few meters away, a broken branch hung from a leatherwood bush. She stood, brushing her knees. A mobile phone lay in the grass. He'd crashed through, desperate? And then what—collapsed? She did a slow three-sixty, pulling back her hair. The roof of the hut was visible. He couldn't have been lost.

But then, people with hypothermia didn't always think straight.

A tragedy and a mystery. His phone was dead—no surprise there. She followed his trail through the scrub back as far as it was obvious. A lot of broken branches. Her nape prickled. Something else was wrong. She stopped, biting her lip. What wasn't she seeing? A kereru swooshed overhead—the fat one from the hut. She laid her hand over her heart, willing it to slow, and forced herself to focus on her environment. Her brother, Tane, teased her about her "premonitions," but he'd long ago learned to pay attention. The number of times they'd saved his arse... It wasn't anything spooky, as he liked to claim, just her brain taking a while to catch up with her senses, her subconscious registering alerts before her conscious did—hearing or seeing or smelling something out of place a few seconds before it became obvious.

Yes, there—a rusty smear on a brushy branch at chest height. Blood. More than you'd expect from the usual forest cuts and scratches. She walked faster. More blood. Now she knew what to look for, it was everywhere— on leaves, branches, the ground. She bit the side of her cheek as she returned to the body. Nothing visible on his back.

She crouched, taking a closer look. Chunks of flesh had been ripped from his thighs and calves. The dog? A hawk? Pressing her lips together, she grabbed the guy's shoulder and gently rolled him. A swarm of trapped flies flew up, their fat, furry bodies pelting her mouth. She swiped at them, her stomach lurching. *Hold it together, for his sake.*

Yep, a big, dark bloodstain on the chest of his torn

jacket. Through the tear, a gaping wound. On the leaf litter and grass underneath him a bloodstain had spread into an oval, the liquid long since seeped away. Dogs and hawks didn't puncture a man's chest. They might have come by after death. Was he knocked down and gored by a boar? Attacked by a stag? She lowered him and stroked his shoulder. Death would have come quickly, if not quietly.

Forget the body bag. This was beyond her job description. She'd radio it in, leave Cody with the body and go for the cops. It was probably an accident or animal attack but that wasn't her call.

She dragged her feet to the chopper. No sign of Cody but at least he was near. Suddenly the isolation wasn't so friendly. She reached the pilot's door and froze, her instinct pricking again. Oh God, what now? A pair of fantails flashed and dived beside the hut. The tea towel snapped in the breeze, making her flinch. Nothing amiss, so why did she have the urge to run? Maybe she was just strung out. A dead body could do that.

Her ab muscles tightened. Fuck it. Better to be paranoid than dead. She sucked in a breath and took off for the hut, her sneakers flicking up stones.

Crack. An echoing gunshot, from behind her. Shit. She upped her speed. A hunter, thinking she was wildlife?

"Stop shooting!" she yelled. "Identify your target!"

Another pop, the clank of a bullet hitting metal, the shot reverberating. The chopper. Potshots from a rifle. A hollow smack, a thump, and something flicked her hair.

Jesus. She clutched her head, the hut bouncing around in her vision. Her hair was hot but no wound. A third crack, another thump, and the hut's front win-

dow shattered. The shooter couldn't have her confused
with wildlife—he'd have stopped by now. He was hunting *her*. She veered off course and plunged thigh-high
into tussock beside the hut as a bullet punctured its front
wall, a meter away. She rounded the back of the building and pushed her spine against the cold wall, chest
heaving. A half-second gap between the sonic boom
and the thump, so he was maybe four hundred meters
away, elevated—any closer, she'd be dead. Holy shit.
What now?

A burst of fire this time, spraying the other side of
the hut, shattering glass, pinging into tin. Automatic
fire. Not your standard hunting rifle. Hosing the place
because he'd lost line of sight?

She couldn't stay here. Too obvious. And a matter of
time before a bullet went right through the hut.

Cody. Where was Cody?

Wait—a military loner with a death wish? Had she
got him all wrong? Exactly what had he stashed in that
kayak?

No. The tourist—the hole in his chest. That was no
goring. What about his girlfriend and the other couple?
The search had concentrated on the river but maybe the
river wasn't the culprit.

Whatever the situation, she had to retreat, one good,
quick decision at a time. Get Cody; get out of here.
Maybe lure the shooter away from the chopper and
double back to it. Raise the alarm over the radio, alert
the police Armed Offenders Squad. Alert the fucking
army. Fly over the glacier, find the climbers.

The shooter had stopped. Gone stealth to stalk
her? The forest had silenced, the birds flown off. She
couldn't even hear the river with her eardrums blown

by the gunshots, just her own fast breath. She leaped across the tussock, to leave less of a trail than striding through, and ducked into the trees. Her jacket was black, at least—unlike Cody's bright blue one.

She inched into the scrub, watching over her shoulder. Even tiptoeing, her sneakers crunched. When she could no longer see the hut, she exhaled. First task: find Cody.

Movement, to her right. Her breath caught. A weka charged from the undergrowth, its panicked little legs whirring like a squat brown Road Runner.

A noise, ahead. She swiveled and her nose smacked into a big navy-clad shoulder. She lifted a knee to the guy's nuts but he spun her and caught her tight around the waist, pinning her arms. She stomped but missed his foot.

"Tia! Jesus!" he hissed.

He released her and she wheeled around. Oh God, it was Cody, his eyes wide, checking their surroundings. He'd taken off the blue jacket, leaving a skintight long-sleeved thermal. Damn, how much noise had they made?

"What the fuck is going on?" he whispered.

"Some nutter with a rifle—I didn't get a look."

He nodded sharply. "Let's find cover."

She followed him toward the river and down a rock bank, ignoring the hand he held out. Ahead, through the trees, the water rushed over stones, lit bright by the sun. A dog barked. The shooting started up again. More automatic fire. She pressed her back against the clammy stone. Next to her, Cody did the same. Ricocheting shots, smashing glass, clanging metal. Another dog joined in. "They must be in the clearing," she whispered.

Cody's eyes met hers, his jaw squared. "He ain't conserving ammo."

"Did you see him?"

"No."

"How do you know it's not a woman?"

His mouth twitched. "I'm kinda more concerned about the firepower. Gotta be an assault rifle—pretty much the same weapon we use to hunt humans."

"Did you just make a joke about hunting humans?"

"Wasn't meant to be a joke. Sometimes when you're looking through the scope, it feels like that… You okay? You've gone a little gray. I didn't mean to—"

"It's not that." She told him about the body. His expression grew grimmer by the word. Jolted out of holiday mode and into work mode. Lucky for her he wasn't a lawyer or a…pianist. "He really is hunting humans."

"Okay," Cody said, as if that wasn't at all problematic. "I'll lure him away while you get to the chopper."

"Yes. Then you can double back and join me."

"No. You go without me."

"I'm not leaving you here."

"It makes sense. I'll have to lead him far enough away that he's out of range as you're lifting. Going by that firepower, I'm thinking maybe a mile. No point in me then giving him time to return."

"You don't know this bush. I'm guessing he does— and so do his dogs. You might get lucky for half an hour, but…"

"He?"

"For convenience's sake."

A flicker of a smile at his tiny victory. "You said it yourself—I'm a risk taker with a death wish."

"Cody, I'm not leaving anyone else here."

"You're leaving me." His hand went to his hip, then froze. Checking for a nonexistent weapon. He fisted his fingers, and released. "Look, I'm not some hippie backpacker. I'm good at getting shot at. I'll lead them away, then swim the river so the dogs can't get me—assuming they can't swim."

"If they're hunting dogs—and they sound like it—they're all muscle and mouth and no fat. No buoyancy, especially in fresh water. They'll sink like rocks."

"Good. Then I'll hide until help comes. Easy."

"That river is basically just melted snow and ice. You swim it without a change of clothes, you'll be hypothermic by midnight."

"My clothes are pretty much made of plastic. They'll dry quick."

She shook her head.

"Tia, none of the options here are good. There's no easy decision in a situation like this, no risk-free choice. You know that. You'll be taking a risk in lifting off. I'll be taking a risk in running and hiding. But if you don't get away safely, we're both screwed, and so are those climbers and the other tourists, if they're still alive, and so are the next people who come wandering up here."

Dammit. "Help probably won't come until first light."

"I can handle a night in the open."

"A lot of tough guys say that, going in."

A dog barked nearby. She shrank against the rock. Cody slung his arm across her belly, pinning her with his elbow. Like she was going anywhere. The gunshots had stopped.

She tiptoed to reach his ear. He was a couple of inches taller. In another situation she'd consider that the perfect height. "We're downwind," she whispered. "The dogs won't be able to smell us yet. I'll go back the way I came. You—"

She froze. A second later he held up a palm, frowning. Through the trees ahead skulked the silhouette of the shooter, rifle held low across his hip, machete slung across his back like a ninja sword, two dogs running alongside. One was a short dirty-brown mutt, wide across the forelegs, thick neck, big jaw. Bred for fighting. The other was a greyhound cross, its nose skimming the river stones. Pig dogs—an attacker and a tracker? With the sun in his eyes, the guy wouldn't spot her and Cody, but she stilled her breathing anyway.

"A man," Cody murmured, his lips grazing her lobe.

Her best *no shit* look was wasted.

The shooter turned back, briefly swinging his head their way. He was skinny, with a dirty-blond buzz cut and scraggly beard, wearing head-to-toe khaki camo. Snake tattoos circled his neck, as if they were trying to strangle him.

"Oh shit, him?" she said under her breath as he disappeared.

"You acquainted?" Cody removed his arm.

"A hunter. He came up to me on the tarmac a few months back, asking for a ride up here, but I turned him down because he wanted to take dogs—they're not allowed in this forest. He was pissed off but I guess someone took his cash."

"Ex-military?"

"In his dreams. More of a survivalist, I reckon. I figured at least he was taking out his fantasy on the deer and pigs. I got his name and Googled him 'cause it was bugging me. Shane something. Did time for armed robbery and assault."

"Good call not to take him."

"Yeah. Mostly I'm good with being up here alone, but being up here alone with him…" She twitched as an image of the tourist's body flashed in her mind. "Shit, so where's the dead guy's girlfriend? And the other couple who disappeared? If he's… Oh God, I delivered them to him. He could be living in the hut, lying in wait."

"Best thing we can do for all of them is get help. Let's do this."

She nodded. "True. Be careful, Cowboy."

Another grin, like this was a game. "Always. And you know, I'm a city boy. I earned a business degree and worked in a tech company, so this 'Cowboy' thing you got going…"

"*So* disappointing. See you tomorrow, Cowboy."

"Look forward to it." He winked, still grinning as he walked off.

Was that…? Was he…*flirting*? Now?

Hell. She'd better bloody see him tomorrow.

CHAPTER FOUR

TIA CLAMBERED UP the bank and retraced her steps as Cody melted into the bush behind her. She really didn't want to leave him but, like he said, it was the best plan they had. As the hut came back into view, the shooting resumed, bullets hammering metal like a thousand nail guns firing at once.

She crept to a point that gave her a limited view of the clearing—the closest she dared to get. The hunter—Shane—was standing on a half-buried boulder, his body jolting with the recoil. Shit. He was disabling her chopper—with an AR-15 with a telescopic sight. He paused, slammed in a new magazine, angled the rifle through the open pilot's door and sprayed the controls, left to right to left to right… She winced. Cartridges pinged against the hull. The dogs whined and yelped. The straining head of the attack dog was just visible around the side of the hut, an orange lead attached to its collar. He'd tied them up.

Movement behind her. She swung, tensing. Cody, a meter away. She thumped a fist onto her chest. "Oh my God, stop doing that."

He dropped behind a rotting tree trunk, gesturing for her to join him. "I'm thinking our plan's just been shot to hell."

"Yep. And he's taken out the radio."

"Could we set off my distress beacon?"

She pressed her lips together. Tempting, but... "Too dangerous for Search and Rescue. Out here it can take hours for the satellite to fly over and catch the signal. By the time they get here they'll be flying in darkness, with no clear place to land."

"And a madman going nuclear on them."

"They'd be prepared for a broken leg, not combat. Someone will come looking when I fail to return, but that could be days. They'll have me recorded as safely on the ground up here."

"What's the quickest way out if not by air?"

"We're not dressed to go over the peaks and down the glacier," she whispered, thinking aloud.

"Any other walking tracks? Roads?"

"Not this high up. And bashing through the bush could take weeks."

"Which leaves the river."

"We'd be sitting ducks."

"Except ducks can fly."

She rolled her eyes, but his focus was on the clearing— now quiet again.

"We gotta do it," he whispered. "River's near peak flow so it'll be fast. How's your kayaking?"

"Rusty. We did some white water in training. Team-building stuff." But she needn't go all the way to Wairoimata. If she could get a few hours downstream, she could go bush while Cody paddled out. "You can talk me through the tough bits."

"You can roll?"

"Yep."

"You done grade five rapids?"

She winced. "No."

"You'll be good," he said unconvincingly. "Now, how do we get to the kayaks and launch them under his nose?"

The shooting started up again. "Fuck. My chopper." *My life.* Just when she was getting something good going.

"Might be fixable."

More gunfire. Potshots. He was being selective. "You think?"

"You insured?"

"Enough to repay my loans, but I'll be left with nothing." She rubbed her face. "I'll look forward to worrying about that when we're out of here."

"So we tweak the plan. I'll lead him away while you get the kayaks to the river. I double back. Then we're gone."

"We'd be crazy to launch here. The river meanders for the first kilometer—he'd be faster on foot and have plenty of opportunity for potshots. And if he gets back and finds the kayaks gone, he'll assume we've launched from the hut and come looking."

"Got a plan B?"

"There's another entry point downstream, a Y-junction, where a big tributary joins the Awatapu. He can't cross either river without a boat, not with the dogs, and swimming that vortex would be suicide. He'd be trapped on an arrowhead of land with rapids on two sides. He'd have to backtrack up the tributary for a couple of hours to reach a wading point. If we launch at the junction, we'll be out of his scope in minutes—and we'll get a head start."

"How far away is it—this arrowhead?"

"There's a shortcut over a saddle." She pointed west, not that it was any help in the thick foliage. "He can't be two places at once, and he'd be more likely to watch for us up here."

The firing stopped. She swallowed, resetting her hearing. Shane paced along one side of the chopper, nodding in satisfaction as he swapped magazines again.

She shuffled closer to Cody. "Okay, so you get the kayaks while I lead him into the bush. I'll lose him, circle 'round and meet you at the arrowhead."

"Too dangerous for you. I'm playing decoy."

"It's my territory. I know it better. And...you'd handle carrying two loaded kayaks better than me." She pointed to his watch. "If I don't arrive by 1800, go without me. That'll give you a little over two hours of safe paddling. You need to be far downstream by nightfall."

No answer.

"Cody?"

His jaw tightened. "I'm not leaving you."

And here we go with the macho bullshit. "Like you said, the priority is to raise the alarm."

More silence.

"A few minutes ago you were happy for me to lift off without you," she whispered. "What's different about this scenario?"

"What do you mean?"

"You'd be happy leaving me if I was a guy, right?"

He blinked, jerking his head back. "Actually, no." His voice clanged with genuine offense.

"O-kay," she said. That intense look on his face... Something bigger than chauvinism was preying on that cool demeanor. A touch of PTSD? Guilt? "But we don't have a choice. If we stick together, he'll take out both of us."

"No."

"You have ten seconds to come up with a better plan." She checked her watch. "Nine, eight—"

"I lead him away. You kayak for help."

"I can't take on that river alone. We'll both end up dead, as will the climbers. And like I say, this is my *turangawaewae*, my home ground."

He swore under his breath. *Game to Kupa.*

"Wait here until I've lured him upriver, then get the kayaks." She gave him directions to the saddle. "If I don't show, you're paddling out solo. For everyone's sake."

She crept away before he could argue, her throat drying. He'd better bloody leave without her.

She circled the clearing, staying hidden. Shane had found her backpack and was shaking its contents onto the tussock. With the knife, he speared a pair of lacy knickers, lifted them to his nose and sniffed. Oh God, really? Looking for something for the dogs to track, or…? He pulled a hunting knife from his pocket and flicked it open. The spare clothes she always carried would be too clean for tracking but he pocketed the underwear anyway. Ugh. He swaggered back to the pilot's door. A tearing noise. Judging from the way he was bent over, by his jerky movements, he had to be slicing up the pilot's seat. That *would* have her scent on it.

She ducked farther into the bush, skirting to the upriver side of the clearing. How well could a pig dog adapt to tracking humans? If it was anything like a search and rescue dog, it'd go off both the scent of her in the air and the dead skin and debris that fell from her body. If he got the dog started at the hut, it should first lead him in a circle, via the bank where she and

Cody had sheltered. Best she could do was stay ahead of them and hope.

When she was a safe distance from the clearing, she yelped like she'd been hurt. The sound echoed through the valley, followed by a man's shout—Shane. The dogs barked and whined. She blew out a breath, imagining them straining at their leashes.

"Shut up," he shouted. The dogs silenced.

She trod quietly but deliberately left a trail—stepping in mud, snapping branches, striding through tussock. Once she'd laid a path far enough upriver, she would find a stream to wade along to interrupt the scent trail before heading back down through the bush. The birds had started up again. The river seemed to be rushing louder, like it'd frozen at the gunshots and was relaxing again.

She made steady progress, keeping the river noise within range on her right for orientation, keeping the breeze on her face to leave a scent trail, keeping her breathing and steps quiet so she could tap into her surroundings. The forest stretched up and darkened—thinner scrub and more towering rata. Less cover.

The going got steeper, the river noise deepening into the rolling roar of a white-water gully. Overtop, a trickle—a stream, ahead. She checked behind, her stomach flipping like a landed trout. Nothing moved among the twisted tree trunks. Shane had better be on her tail and not Cody's. She hadn't heard a gunshot since the hut. That must mean he hadn't found Cody. No scrawny guy with a gun would risk hand-to-hand combat with a man of that build.

The stream was narrow but it'd do. Clear water, a stony bed. Churn-proof, though she'd have to avoid the rocks that were furry with green moss. She slipped off her socks and shoes and stepped into the water, swallowing a gasp as the cold jolted her nerves. As the shock abated she waded upstream, the scalding sting giving way to numbness. She left the waterway at an impassable tumble of rocks, dried her feet as best she could and gratefully pulled on her socks and sneakers, her toes burning all over again when sensation returned.

As she tightened her laces, a shiver rolled up her spine. She turned, sucking in her lips. She heard panting, leaves crunching. Oh God, a dog. She couldn't turn back just yet—they were too close. She'd find another stream to follow, higher up. She leaped to the far bank and set off, faster. Behind her, footsteps thudded. Or was that her pulse? After a few minutes, light filtered through the trees ahead—a clearing. A trickle—another stream. She stumbled toward it, surged out of the scrub and stopped dead, gasping.

Not a clearing, not a stream. A cliff. She grabbed a thin black tree trunk. Way down below, the river churned and frothed around jagged rocks. How had she ended up back at the river? The trickle she'd heard was a waterfall sprinkling from a fissure in the cliff. A clod of earth gave way under her right foot. She tap-danced to reclaim firm ground. Below, the clod smacked into the white water.

She was farther upriver than she'd thought, at a sharp bend. A sheer drop blocked her exit on two sides, the shooter and his dogs on another. She'd backed herself into a corner.

She looked down, swaying. Tane would tell her to jump for it, taking a positive leap to clear the rocks, torpedoing with her toes pointed, lifting her chin so the water didn't flood her nose, bracing for the shock of the water. *You'll be sweet.* She tried to force herself to leap but her hands clutched the tree. She still had one escape route that didn't require plummeting to likely death—back the way she'd come.

A bark. A shout. Close—in the trees behind her. Another bark. She had to get out of the light. She talked her hands into releasing the trunk, crept along the cliff, clutching at branches, and gratefully ducked back into the forest. She could hear it, like a ghost dog—panting, scrabbling through dirt and sticks. Hopefully they'd lost the scent at the stream and were operating on guesswork.

She crept inland, following a ridge above a dry, rocky streambed. The roar of the river eased.

Behind her, something rustled. She swiveled. A dog leaped on top of a rotting tree trunk, its focus latching on to her. The brown one with the big jaws. Shit.

CHAPTER FIVE

THE DOG CROUCHED, growling like an idling motorbike. It threw up its head and barked, once, twice, three times, idled again. How the hell had it circled her so quickly? Tia dropped her gaze to the ground in a show of submission, and scanned for a stick. Nothing but twigs and leaves. She was in the middle of a fucking forest and she couldn't find a stick?

"Jaws! Attack!"

She jumped. The voice was right behind her. The dog launched off the trunk, teeth bared. She reared, and her right foot punched into air, throwing her off balance, dropping her feetfirst off the ridge. She grabbed a tree root but it tore away, spitting dirt into her eyes. She slid down a bank of sheer rock, scrambling for a handhold, her stomach in full panic.

She thumped onto the dry riverbed, arse-first. The dog stood on the ridge several meters above, barking, turning itself nearly inside out in indecision. From out of sight, Shane yelled the attack order again. She pushed to her feet. Uninjured and, for now, out of reach.

A noise, behind her. Something grabbed her calf and tugged. Pressure flamed into bright pain. She twisted. Another terrier, a white one, was clamped on the back of her leg. Its teeth pushed through the denim of her jeans, popped her skin, sunk in. The pain exploded. She punched blindly, yelling, her fists bouncing off solid muscle, her vision spotting. Oh God, Shane had three dogs, not two—and this one was about to rip her leg off. It yanked, and she slipped sideways, her shoulder clonking on dirt. No sound. Why was there no sound? She couldn't feel the rest of herself—nothing but the tearing burn in her leg. She flailed her fists but the angle was too awkward. The dog dragged her, stopping when its back hit the rock wall.

The sour stench of body odor smacked into her. Shane appeared, gripping the brown dog's collar. It lunged for her, gagging as he yanked it back, its eyes rolling. Behind, the greyhound tracker bounced side to side.

"She got a good strong bite on her, eh?" Shane said, his shoulder looking ready to jump from its socket. "Jaws! Release!"

It didn't.

"Yeah, nah, bit of a mongrel that one. Well, they all are, but must've been some monster jumped her bitch mother. Trick is, getting her to let go. Still working on that."

"Get it off me!"

"Yeah, hurts like fuck, eh? Hang on, just let me tie this bugger up. He's going apeshit. He can smell the blood, eh?"

What was this guy on? Tia tried to pant through the pain but it sharpened with every inhalation. Man, if she ever gave birth she was taking the drugs. Panting didn't do shit. The dog—Jaws—gave a rolling growl. She forced her leg to relax. Maybe if she stopped resisting it'd stop the goddamn tugging. Its hold slackened— just long enough for it to adjust its bite and bust through fresh skin. She yelled.

She vaguely registered Shane leashing the brown

dog to a tree and taking off a camo backpack. Something thudded down in front of the greyhound. A slab of meat. As it sniffed, Shane crouched and ruffled its ears. "G'boy. G'boy. What a good boy. Yeah, yeah, yeah." The bound brown dog yelped. Shane tossed another slab and it jumped and caught it, choking as it yanked the leash.

Shane grabbed a stubby stick from the bag and advanced on Jaws. "Yeah, bitch got me good, too, when I's training her." He thrust his left elbow at Tia and, with the stick—an artificial thing with rope at either end—pointed out a ragged red scar on his forearm, below his rolled shirt. "Right through the bite sleeve. Shouldn't a got the cheap one. Fucking li'l shit."

He turned to Jaws. "Release!" he barked. "Release! Nah, fuck, see? She's useless."

The dog stilled, giving Tia a split second of relief. Its nostrils flared, the whites of its eyes glowing in the dim light, ears pinned.

"Yeah, girl, you done good but you gotta know when it's time to concede, mate." He forced the stick between her jaws, the extra force threatening to snap Tia's shin. "Release! Release!"

The pressure lifted. Tia inhaled. Shane kicked the dog's stomach and it yelped and skittered sideways, tail down. He pulled another slab of meat from his bag. The dog slunk to it, eyeing Shane's boot.

Tia's leg throbbed, blood soaking her jeans, filling the puncture wounds. She closed her hands around her calf, which only cranked the pain from red hot to white hot. Whoa, so not the kind of wound that liked pressure. She eased off, blood dribbling over her hands.

"Jeez, she got you good. Gotta work on her people

skills, eh? I keep 'em right on the edge of hungry so they don't lose their fight. Keep 'em remembering they're working dogs."

Just what brand of psychopath was he? As Jaws chewed, Shane hooked a leash onto its collar.

"Who you dropping off kayaks for? You got hikers coming through? Three of 'em?"

Three? Shit. He hadn't seen Cody? She'd been alone when he'd opened fire.

The longer she stalled him, the more of a head start Cody would get. She surreptitiously checked her watch, pretending she was inspecting the wound. Eleven minutes until 1800.

"I'm flying a big group of kayakers up in a few days. Had to spread out the load."

"Yeah, you're not gunna be now, are ya?" He laughed, as if it was a shared joke. "You found that guy, eh? That weirdo German, or whatever the fuck. I went easy on him. He went quick. Shoulda seen what I done to his missus." His head bobbed in a self-congratulatory nod.

Oh God. She had to know if the woman was alive. "What *did* you do?"

"Oh, we just had a bit of fun, eh?"

Her forehead prickled. His voice held no malice. He wasn't taunting her—it was the conversational tone of a passerby who'd stopped to change a stranger's tire.

"What do you mean?" She couldn't keep the fear from her tone.

"Bit of a game. Cat and mouse. Well, dog and mouse. It's what I do—get rid of the guy and have a bit of fun with his missus. Hunt her like with the pigs—send the dog to find her, weaken her, then go in and finish off. You'll see, later. Not that I've done it heaps, not yet.

Only, like, four so far." He sounded apologetic, as if he was humbly underplaying his achievements. "Five, soon."

Not if I can help it. The pain had eased to a throb, giving her a beat of respite between pulses. Would she even be able to walk?

She'd be able to kayak.

Four so far. "Where are the others? The other three?"

"Ah, they're all up bush. Possum food. Wait, do possums eat meat? Hey, might be good to give 'em a taste for it, eh? We could stop 'em stripping the trees, get 'em going after the pigs and goats. You should see the damage they do, up the valley. We gotta do something about that shit."

"Totally agree. Tell me where and I'll report it to the rangers. Maybe you could help us cull them? I bet you'd be good at that."

He tilted his head, considering. "Nah, it's okay," he said finally, as if turning down a favor.

She chewed her lip. He seemed eager to talk. Too much time alone? The rock bank curved behind her like a sheer amphitheater. She couldn't climb or run or fight, but she could stall until Cody got away. "Your name's Shane, right? I'm Tia."

"Yeah, yeah, I remember you, course." He looped Jaws's slack leash around a tree, secured it and sat with his back against the trunk. "Pigs are pretty good hunting— they really fight ya," he said, like she'd just asked a question on the topic. "Especially if you use the knife and the dogs, not the AR. They're a bit of fun. Stags, nah, too big a target, too easy. Just, *boom*, and it's all over. Most animals 'round here are no fun with guns, unless you wanna go after birds, but they're mostly natives so I leave 'em alone. Just the hawks coz they're Australian—and they're fun when they fall." He made a spinning movement with a finger, emitting a low whistle. "I'm basically one of them, like, greenies."

"A greenie?"

"Yeah, you know. Saving the environment and shit."

O-kay. "You know your dogs are killing kiwi?"

"Yeah, yeah, that one by the hut? Knew you'd go off at me about that. Believe me, it's not how I trained them, the buggers. It's this one what's the problem." He swiped at Jaws and laughed when it flinched. "Nah, see, she's not that bad. Knows who's boss. We'll see, we'll see."

"We could really use a guy like you as a trapper," Tia ventured. "We always need people who know the bush, understand the problems. I could get you on the payroll when I return."

"Nah, I'm not into traps. They're cowardly, you know—well, except when you use them on humans. That's pretty fun. Nah, you wanna hunt with guns, and humans make the best hunting. Animals are too predictable, see? They do exactly what you expect, every time. I been hunting them all me life." He sniffed and wiped his nose along his knuckles. "Used to go hunting with the old man before he fucked off. And don't you go judging him for walking out because you never met my mother. Right bitch, that one. Nah, humans are all different, eh? They try and outguess you, you know? It's a fair fight."

"Not when you're armed and they're not."

"Ah, I give 'em a chance. Well, not the blokes. You never know when they're gunna try and be a hero and go after you. Nah, you get rid of them and go after the women." He licked his thin, dry lips. "See, the women, they're smart. They know they gotta use their brains, not try and fight. They gotta run, try and trick you, talk, beg, fuck with you, keep you guessing. Cat and mouse, see? The men, that's like cat and cat and that's never gunna be fun, right? Not enough of a game. Nah, with them you just—" He mimed lifting a rifle and firing, blowing his cheeks out with a poof.

Where did she even start with that? "You know it's wrong to hunt humans."

"Yeah, I don't reckon it should be. Humans are the fucking problem with this world. They could use a bit of a cull, eh?"

"You know it's against the law?"

"Won't be soon, when the end times come. No more laws. I read about it. I follow this dude's blog and he knows all this shit. Preppers, that's what we're called. Survival of the fittest and all that." His lips angled down in an exaggerated frown. "You seen all the shit that's happening in the world. End times are coming sooner than you think. It'll be dog-eat-dog. Except, you know, with humans. Except, well, I'm not *eating* anyone. Some people might, I guess, when it gets that bad. But not me. Not my thing."

She stole a glance at her watch. Past 1800. Cody might give her some extra time, but he'd know not to wait too long.

"How would you feel if someone was hunting you, if they hurt someone you love?" She was saying whatever bollocks came to mind, but the longer they sat here, the more time Cody had.

"I'd fucking slaughter them. But I don't give a fuck about anyone and no one gives a fuck about me, so all good there. I'm not the sort of guy people warm to." He said it like he was letting her in on a secret.

"Okay, well, just so you know, my brother and grandfather would be gutted if something happened to me."

"Huh," he said, unmoved. She'd met people like him before, desperate people with that dead look in their eyes, who'd shrugged off their humanity for the sake of survival.

She tried again. "Can I ask you a personal question?"

He shrugged. "Okay."

"Do you…feel emotions?"

"Nah, that'd be weak, eh? Sometimes I get angry, you know, but not so much up here, where no one pisses me off. It's peaceful, eh?" He smoothed his hands along the rifle resting across his knees. "I mean, I'm not thick. Lotta people think I am but I'm not. I know you're not *supposed* to hunt humans but I'm doing us all a favor. When the end times come we're gunna need the strong ones. *You* might survive, you know. We're gunna need some women but they gotta be tough. No fucking princesses, eh? Even a woman's gotta be useful for something. Well, something more than the obvious, right?" He laughed. "It's all about getting ready. Yeah, nah, those last ones, they were disappointing, eh? Especially those Germans. I thought they might of worked out better. You're gunna be good, though, you're gunna be good. I can tell." He looked at her bloody hands. "Your leg's pretty fucked up, eh? I'd give you something for it but it'd be cheating for you. Gotta do this organically and shit. I might have to shoot it. Really put it out of action."

Shit. "Wouldn't I be more of a challenge if I could run?"

He jabbed a pointer finger at her. "See, that's what

I'm saying about women. They try and get in your head and shit."

A distant artificial whistle pierced the air, above the birds, the river, the wind in the trees. Then the echoing yell of a man, far down the valley. Shit. Cody. He should have been way downriver.

Shane leaped to his feet and bounced around, rifle at his shoulder, peering into the trees like he had X-ray vision. Jaws shrank back at the sudden movement, tail tucked.

"Who's that?" he asked.

She shrugged. "Trapper?"

"Nah, they came through already. I watched them, tracked them, for practice. That your kayaker mates?" He narrowed his slit eyes even more. "You been lying."

More shouting. Another burst of the whistle. *Damn you, Cody.*

Half of Shane's face twisted into a smile. "Is it your boyfriend?"

"No."

He started pacing. "You been fucking sitting here lying to me this whole time."

Breathing became a conscious effort. Should she double down on denying she knew about Cody, or admit it?

"Nah, I like that. That's good." Shane stopped pacing and turned to her. "Coz I was starting to think you were okay, and that might make it hard, you know? But nah, we're good. If you're trying to fuck with me, I get to fuck with you. I'll go after him and come back for you. But first I gotta do this…"

He pointed the rifle at her knee and flicked the safety off.

CHAPTER SIX

TIA SHUFFLED BACKWARD but hit rock. Another whistle. Cody shouted her name, clear on the breeze. How was this going to go?

"It fucking is your boyfriend." Shane lowered the rifle. "Nah, I don't wanna give away my position, eh? I'll surprise him, take him out first. Heaps of time. You're right. It'll be more fun if I give you a chance. Dogs'll catch up with you in a minute anyway, with all that blood." He threw his backpack on and tightened the straps, then bounced on the spot three times as if warming up. "See ya soon, Tia. This is fucking *on*."

He strode off with an exaggerated swagger, pulling his machete from its sheath and swinging it, the greyhound bounding and leaping beside him like it was high on his adrenaline. The attack dogs whined after him, straining their leashes—leaving her path clear. She felt for the wall behind her, used it to climb to her feet. Inhaling, she put weight on her leg. Pain shot up to her thigh but it held. She took a step. Shane spun. She froze.

"Attack, Jaws!" he shouted, gesturing at her. "Attack, Rocky!"

She flattened against the rock as the attack dogs turned, their leashes slackening, then snapping taught—their jaws inches from her legs. They barked, teeth bared, whining, clawing. Shit. Shane hadn't tied them randomly. He'd tied them in overlapping arcs, trapping her. He laughed, and disappeared into the trees.

The bank behind her back was steep and smooth, a canyon carved by some ancient waterway. No chance of climbing. But if she slunk out along one side of the wall, she'd have to deal with only one dog. With what defenses? No sticks, no rocks, no handy slab of poisoned meat, just small stones and twigs—shrapnel.

Another shout arced over the valley. "Tiaaaaa! Help!"

Cody had to be bluffing, luring Shane away. Disrespecting the plan. Didn't trust her to save her own arse—not that she was doing a particularly good job of that. And, okay, she might have a bullet in her knee right now if he hadn't shouted, but that wasn't the point.

Blood dribbled into her shoe, pooling under her arch. She stripped off her jacket and T-shirt, ripped the shirt along the seams and bent over her leg. Between pulses of blood, a flash of white was visible. Her shin bone. Ugh. She tied the T-shirt around her leg. Blood everywhere, but just having the wound contained made her feel stronger. She zipped her jacket over her bra—then stopped.

Shrapnel. Shrapnel had its uses. She chewed the inside of her cheek. What the hell. She was short on options—and she didn't want to be here when Shane returned.

Checking that he was still out of sight, she took off her jacket and bra, and zipped the jacket back on. She filled one of the cups with stones and experimented with spinning it, holding it by a back strap, G-force keeping the stones contained. Big ups to industrial-strength bras. The dogs whined, eyes following the bra, jumping at it. She'd take on Jaws. If it was less well trained, it might be easier to scare and distract.

She settled her nerves, picking her route, weighing up angles. If this didn't work, she'd have a bitch of a time detaching the mutt. And what if it clamped onto her good leg?

After a few practices that had the dogs nearly tying themselves in knots, she paused and took a cool breath. *Here goes.* She did a wind-up, the cups humming as they sliced the air. She swung the bra and released a load of stones into Jaws's face. The dog jumped back, stunned. *Now.* She sprinted, her blood-slicked soles sliding on dead leaves. In wobbly vision, she registered the dog shaking its head, standing to attention, launching. Reacting quicker than she'd counted on. Shit, it had too much space. She'd misjudged the distances, misjudged the leash length. She spun to face it as it leaped for her arm. At the last second, she jerked away, grabbed an end of the bra in each hand, snapped it taut and shoved it into the dog's jaw.

The dog somersaulted backward and thumped onto its spine. She ran. It scrabbled, coughing, sprang up and lunged, but the leash jerked it back. It yelped, a bra strap trailing from its teeth, and shook its head, flicking the catch into its eye.

Her leg burned. Red splotches expanded across the T-shirt like dye. The dogs were barking like crazy. Shane had to be hearing that. Her only chance was to get to a kayak, and fast.

But what the hell was Cody up to?

TIA HADN'T BEEN kidding about the fucking sandflies. Rather than risk a slapping noise in the echo chamber of a valley, Cody slid his hands over his goose pimpled skin like he had a tic. Didn't help that he was standing on the riverbank dressed only in board shorts. But he was planning on doing some swimming and it'd be insane to get any more clothing wet. This plan had to work, plain and simple.

When Tia hadn't showed at the rendezvous, he'd returned to the hut, grabbed the third kayak, paddled it across the river and left its stern sticking out of a shrub, to make it look like he'd gone into the forest on foot. With luck, the shooter would assume he'd taken all the kayaks to the same spot. A little more noise to draw the shooter here, and then he'd swim for the kayaks waiting at the confluence downriver.

Since he'd started up with the whistling and yelling, no more screams had come from upriver. Just frenzied barking. If that psycho had done something to Tia, he was doubly dead. Cody blasted the whistle, yelled her name.

If I don't show, you're paddling out solo. You need to be far downstream by nightfall. And he would be—but not without her. Meanwhile he'd lure the shooter away, distract him, confuse him, buy her a chance to reach the rendezvous—if she still could. That yell she'd let out… He knew pain when he heard it.

A bark, closer. On the far bank, a breeze curled through the tussock. *Come on.* A minute later, a scattering of birds rose from beside the hut's red roof, just visible above the scrub. He stilled his hands—let the little fuckers feast.

One last time. "Tia!"

He crept downriver and slipped into the water. Holy fuck, he'd expected cold, but *that*. He forced himself down to his neck, his throat closing in protest, his skin shocking like an electrocution. Still the damn sandflies followed, dive-bombing his eyes.

A clanking, a knock. Boots on wood, on…metal? Movement, on the roof. Shit, the guy had climbed it for a vantage point, his beady eyes drawn to the bright green kayak. Cody filled his stinging lungs and submerged, a headache striking like lightning. His eyeballs threatened to snap-freeze. But—distraction accomplished. Now to get around the bend in the river, out of sight, and then swim fast for the kayaks. He pulled underwater in long, strong strokes, kicking hard. It was a relief to move—and to be away from those damn flies. How much cold could your body take before your blood iced up, your heart stopped?

He swam till his lungs caved, and silently surfaced, smothering the urge to gasp. No need for silence— gunshots boomed. A tree screened the shooter as he sprayed the green kayak. The bushes flinched with bullets, the water flicked. Perfect. Cody inhaled and sank again, following the current, his scalp shrink-wrapping his skull.

When he rose again, the shooting had stopped and the river noise ahead had changed—the tributary joining, and not real happy about it. With the crosscurrent and the cold against him, his swim back across to the kayaks would be twice as challenging as he'd thought. He was using too much energy keeping afloat, keeping on track, keeping from freezing solid. But he was committed now.

All muscle and no fat. They'll sink like rocks. The dogs weren't the only ones. Wasn't often you regretted those last twenty push-ups, that last ten miles on the trail, but…shit. If he got swept downriver he was *dans la merde*.

The tip of the beach came into view, then the orange and yellow kayaks. He upped his stroke and kick rate, pushing until his chest stung. The frothing current shoved back. A bark shot above the churn. Behind the kayaks, branches moved. Cody took a breath, ready to go under, as a figure stumbled through.

Tia! Thank *fuck.*

He tried to signal but a wave slapped him under. He pulled back up, the current sweeping him level with the kayaks but too far from the bank. Tia looked over her shoulder and pushed the tourists' yellow kayak until the water nudged it. He flailed like a maniac. Her head snapped up, confusion on her face as he struggled past. She yanked the paddle from where it was wedged, strode into the water and held it out. It was a good seven feet short. Under her other hand, the kayak bucked like rodeo roughstock.

"No chance," he called. "Kayak out. There's a towline behind my seat. Tow mine out."

A gunshot. Crouching low, she found the line and hooked the kayaks up, stern to nose. A dog shot out of the trees, the big one, bowling right for her.

"Tia!"

"I know! I fucking know." She squeezed into the seat of the yellow kayak. Using the paddle as a gondola pole, she pushed into the water, the boat swaying wildly.

The dog went for the orange kayak, but the stern swung out as Tia pulled, forcing it to spring sideways. More gunshots. No sign of the shooter—he had to be firing into the trees in hope. She met Cody's gaze as the water drove him past. Her jaw was tight, eyes narrowed. Her kayak caught the current and shot forward. Cody's biceps burned as he hauled through the water, fighting into a trajectory that would meet hers. In a minute they'd plunge into rapids, studded with rocks. *Swimming that vortex would be suicide.*

He ducked away as her kayak skimmed past, the hull grazing his forehead. Whoa. The orange one bobbed toward him.

"Unhook the towline," he yelled.

As she scrambled for it, he caught his boat, got ahold and launched over the cockpit, steadying himself so his weight was balanced, head sticking out over one side of the boat, legs the other, water surging by in a choppy blur. The kayak rocked but settled. Not his best mount but it'd do. He yanked out the paddle and held it flush with the boat. Inhaling, he channeled his weight evenly into his arms, flipped and twisted, and slid his legs inside, his butt bumping into the seat. The cool air blasted his wet skin.

Ahead, Tia was about to hit a grade five boulder garden—no helmet, no life jacket, no spraydeck. Gunshots surged—or maybe they'd been firing all along. Back on auto but still out of sight.

"Left!" he shouted at Tia. "Go left!"

As they shot 'round the corner he caught a glimpse of camo gear tumbling onto the beach. The shooter registered the kayaks, raised his rifle—and drifted out of sight.

Gunfire sprayed, hitting rocks and trees behind them. Wasted, frustrated, desperate shots. Fuck, that was close. One problem down, for now, but Tia was still angling too far right, the river funneling her toward an overhanging rock shelf.

"Tia, go left, quick!"

Too late. The current shunted her kayak under the shelf, giving her just enough time to panic before it flipped, taking her with it, face-first, mouth open. Her upturned kayak scraped the lip of the rock. Cody pulled toward her, his shoulders straining. He needed enough momentum to slip past without getting stuck, but if he misread the angles he'd plow straight into her. Black hair swirled under the water as her jammed kayak lurched downward.

Then she disappeared.

CHAPTER SEVEN

As HE SHOT PAST, Cody leaned back, swept a hand under Tia's boat and grabbed the first thing he touched. He compensated with his hips as she bobbed up next to him, spitting and gasping, still holding the paddle. He had her by the shoulder. He jammed his paddle into his webbing and hauled her astride his bow.

"Hold on to me," he yelled, retrieving the paddle. His nose was too low in the water. "Scoot up, quick!" Her hands flailed. She found the side of the cockpit and hoisted herself forward, jamming the crown of her head into his bare stomach, her face into his lap. Her ass stuck up over the lip of the cockpit. Her legs straddled the bow. Her paddle dug into his side. It was all he could do to hold the kayak straight, his arms and abs and quads sharing the strain, his hips and shoulders navigating them left and right as they flew around boulders, the bottom of the kayak scraping rock, her head bouncing in his lap.

After an age, a shoal island appeared midriver. They were far enough below the confluence that they could afford to stop and regroup. "Get ready to jump out," he said. He paddled fast and beached the kayak front-on. She pretty much somersaulted over the bow and onto the stones, freeing him to leap out and pull the craft clear. Her kayak was coming up fast, bottom up, low in the water.

He dived, grabbed it and dragged it onto the island. He flopped onto his back, heart pounding out of his chest, headache crushing his skull. As the adrenaline passed, the cold closed in. He raised his head high enough to check their surroundings. Deep, swift channels on either side. Thick bush along the banks.

"Cody?" Tia's voice creaked.

He crawled to her commando-style and slumped as she rolled onto her back.

"Not as stealthy as we'd planned," he said.

"Or as elegant."

A mental picture flashed up. Her denim-clad ass bucking in front of him, her face hammering his lap. Shame he didn't get to appreciate that at the time.

"You're grinning," she said.

His chest convulsed into a laugh, which he covered with a cough as he flipped, resting his back on sun-warmed stones. She propped up on her elbows, dropping a wet-lashed gaze to his chest. Her eyes widened.

"Yeah, the little fuckers got me good." Any second the itching would set in. Being numb had its advantages.

"The what?" she wheezed, her focus snapping back to his eyes.

"Those bugs you warned me about."

Her gaze dropped again and narrowed. "Oh. Yeah." She collapsed again. "Holy fuck, I'm cold."

He forced himself up to sitting. Her jacket, jeans and sneakers were drenched. "We better get changed, fast."

Something red was tied around her lower leg, dripping pink water onto the stones. He frowned, looking closer. "You're bleeding. You hit rocks?"

"I hit dog." Her voice vibrated. "Can't feel my legs, so all good."

"Must have been quite a hit. Damn, you're shivering."

"S-so are you. Your lips...blue..."

He crawled to the closest kayak—the yellow one—and pulled out the climbers' dry bag. "I grabbed the stuff from the green kayak, too. There are thermals, a microfiber towel." He dug through and found shorts, a pink thermal top and the towel and threw them to her.

Now for his clothing. You knew you were staring down trouble when getting dressed felt like an Everest expedition. He staggered to his feet, wove to his kayak like a drunk and keeled over, a meter short. He couldn't feel his feet, let alone get them in the right places. He crawled the remaining distance, yanked out a dry bag and grabbed his own thermals and shorts. A T-shirt would do as a towel. He faced away from her—she'd be stripping down, too. Once dry and dressed, he found his neoprene socks and slipped them on. His defrosting feet throbbed like they were being stabbed. He threw himself into his spray jacket and zipped it to the collar. Better.

Hold up—there was no noise behind him. "Tia? You good?" No answer. "Tia?"

Nothing. He turned. She was sitting shivering like a wet Chihuahua, tugging at her jacket zipper. Still in jeans and sneakers. In another minute she'd be snap-frozen. He clambered to her and took the zipper. "I got it, Cowgirl."

Her face was gray, her lips purple. She tried weakly to fight him. Under her legs, the pink water was turning red and thick. He yanked the zipper and shoved the jacket off her shoulders. Bare skin. Breasts. Nipples.

"Putain!" He stumbled backward, raising a palm to his eyes, and spun. "Fuck! I'm sorry, I didn't…"

"'S okay," she said. "Towel. Pass me…"

He patted the stones behind him and chucked it blindly in her direction.

"You were naked under that."

"Yeah," she said, her voice shuddering. "I didn't start the day like this."

"Oh fuck. Did he…?"

"No. My leg," she said. "I used my T-shirt…"

"…as a bandage." He slumped to his knees, still facing downriver. Of course.

"The look on your face was pretty funny."

He choked out a laugh. "They did kinda…jump out at me." Another thing to appreciate in hindsight.

She snorted and began giggling. Laughter exploded in his chest. He let it come, let it out until his abs ached.

"I don't know why I'm laughing," she said. "I'm freezing my…*tits off*." She cackled. Shit, she was probably delirious. "It's safe now, Cowboy. Nothing jumping out."

She was squeezing her hair with the tiny towel. The pink top finished halfway down her forearms and several inches above her waist, stretched so thinly over her chest he didn't need to rely on memory to picture what lay underneath. Not that he was looking, but man, it was hard not to.

"I think this top was intended for a normal woman." She pulled her knees up, as if trying to hide those *magnifique* curves.

"No kidding," he said, staring so intently at her face

that his eyes stung. "I mean… I didn't mean… It's not that you're not… It's more that you're…"

"Shut. Up."

Man, he was head-to-toe idiot and she was head-to-toe goddess. And he should not be thinking about that stunning body. Still, she was warming him up right when he needed it. As much as he wanted to be a gentleman, nothing could wipe the sexy image burned on his brain.

"Let me find you a spray jacket," he said, walking to the kayaks.

"Maybe the guy's jacket, if there is one."

"There is. I'll get his shorts, too. Sorry, I just saw the pink and…"

"It really is time to shut up."

Yep. He pulled out a fluoro lime jacket, strolled over and laid it across her shoulders.

"And don't worry about offending me," she said, pushing an arm into it. "I used to hate the way I look, but there are advantages to being man-sized. And hey, a guy who wants a petite princess to protect isn't a guy I'm going to get along with."

So what kind of guy *did* she want? And did that mean she was single? He cleared his throat. "What happened with the dog?"

She zipped the jacket, bent forward, wincing, and began untying her shoelaces. "Let me catch you up. It's pretty crazy."

By the time she reached the part where she limped to the kayaks, chased by the dog, Cody was a goner. The image of her swinging that bra… He knew some kickass women—most notably his legion buddies' girlfriends, unfortunately for him—but Tia was…was…

"Cody?"

She'd stopped talking. Damn. *Focus, Caporal.*
"Sorry. Did you say something?"

"Do you have a knife?" She smoothed long fingers
down long thighs. "I might cut off my jeans at the knee
and leave the bit around my calf—it's probably holding
the whole lot together. I don't know which bits are me
and which are denim."

"Knife. Sure." He wandered to his kayak and dug
around. "Want me to check it out? I could clean and
dress it, tape up the worst cuts."

"It can wait. We should get some distance behind us
before dark. He'll be backtracking awhile, and bush-
bashing, but—"

"You're sure he's on foot? No boat, no vehicle?"

"When he asked me for a ride, it was only him and
the dogs. Even a trail bike wouldn't get through this terrain. The river's only navigable by kayak and you can't
kayak with three do—" She frowned suddenly. "I told
you not to wait for me."

"I told you I wasn't leaving you." He walked over
and handed her his beast of a pocketknife. "I note you
weren't looking around for me when you pushed off in
that kayak."

"Because I was trusting you to look after yourself,
like you should have been trusting me." She grabbed
a handful of denim and attacked it. "You should go on
ahead. You'll be faster without me. Get through the Auripo Falls tonight and you'll be safely out of his scope.
Below them the forest is so thick and steep it'll take
him an hour to cover two hundred meters."

"Still not leaving you. *Tu n'abandonnes jamais ni
tes blessés.*"

"Meaning?"

"You never abandon your wounded. The legionnaire code of honor."

"I'm only marginally wounded, and I'm not yours." She studied him like she was trying to work him out. "So, how did you end up swimming?" she said, returning to her leg. Sensibly concluding that arguing was futile? While she worked on the jeans, he ran through his version of events.

"I'm surprised the kayaks didn't get shot when he was spraying the clearing," she said after he'd finished.

"A couple did. Mine caught a ricochet, I guess. I duct-taped it. The one I left upriver was worse hit. Wouldn't have lasted."

She rocked up to a crouch, then stood cautiously and unzipped her fly. A good time to study his topo map. He retrieved it from his kayak and crunched across to the tail of the island. He'd scrawled notes on it from kayaking blogs and websites. The next few hours would be much the same as the chaos they'd emerged through— wide pools funneling into narrow canyons where the water dropped fast and quick, twisting and thrashing around car-sized boulders. He rubbed his belly. The nerves were flipping.

She swore quietly.

"What's up?" He killed the urge to turn around.

"Nothing. Just…tight wet jeans aren't the easiest thing to take off."

Don't give me that mental image. "Tell me if you need help." He tried so hard not to sound sleazy that it came out stilted, like it was the last thing he wanted to do. Which was so far from the truth…

"I'm good."

After a minute she gave the all-clear. She smoothed her hands down her fluoro yellow life jacket. "We're glow-in-the-dark and he's top-to-toe camo."

Cody threw her a helmet. "We better go fast, then."

Once they pushed off, his gut settled. With the reprieve from danger he could appreciate the scenery, like a fog had burned off to reveal a pristine day. As they descended—through canyons so steep his stomach dropped, through pools so clear it looked like their kayaks were hovering over the stony riverbed—the terrain changed from subalpine scrub to primeval rainforest, with ferns crowding the riverbanks and marching up hillsides, studded by tufty Seuss-like trees and giant cedars. He'd be only slightly surprised if a velociraptor popped up, squawking. Or an orc.

Yep, with the vivid color of the water it did feel like a movie set, some fantasy epic in a parallel universe. How could he feel so goddamn calm with a murderer hunting them and his commando team half a world away?

But he had Tia. And like she said, she was no princess. She didn't talk much but she was easy company, and they settled into a partnership more through instinct than negotiation. At the rapids he'd check the lay of the obstacles, brief her and hope like hell to see her still with him when they got spat out. And every time, there she was, pulling alongside with a satisfied grin. They carried their kayaks over a few saddles and rocks to avoid treacherous stretches, though he shot longing glances at the surging white water. They powered through pools side by side, and at some point their sprints became an unspoken competition—one he didn't always win easily. The only gloating from either was a sly smile. The only concession was a slight shake of the head. Her stroke was uneconomical, but she compensated with strength and athleticism and a determination written in her jaw.

After one sprint, she glided slightly ahead and he shamelessly drank in the view. The sunset glow warmed her long, strong arms, glossed up the black hair curling out under the helmet, and picked out the freckled contours of her face and the glint of her eyes. Guilt churned in his chest. This was supposed to be a memorial to his brother, not a dating show. He powered up and overtook her.

True to her word, they smelled the tahr before they saw them, like wet, rotting wool. The tatty creatures would freeze and stare, or clatter away. Ducks bobbed in quieter patches, other birds weaved and dived, and dragonflies hovered and shot just above the water.

Even so, the forest was eerily quiet. On operations in South America it felt like everything was taking a number to kill you—malaria, caimans, garimpeiro gangs. But what did he know? He'd grown up in San Antonio and spent most of his legion career shaking African dirt or Middle Eastern sand from his boots, or hunting terrorists in locked-down French suburbs.

After the tenth, twentieth—who knew?—rapid ejected them, he balanced his paddle across the cockpit and retrieved a granola bar. As he bit in, the boat lurched, jump-starting his heart. Shit, he was tipping. Caught on a snag. He grabbed the paddle. The granola bar skidded down the fiberglass and plopped into the water. He backpaddled hard, the hull scraping as the snag released him. A submerged branch. The kayak bumped into the water and he veered away.

"I didn't see that." His vision had adjusted so gradually he hadn't noticed the river was in shadow. But yeah, his eyes were working hard. "We gotta get off the water. Where's this waterfall?"

"Got your map handy?"

He eased up alongside her and retrieved the map and his headlamp. He held her kayak steady while she fitted the lamp and origami-flipped the map so the rectangle she needed was facing up, the rest neatly tucked. Map-folding skills. Could she get any more perfect?

Her downlit face screwed up. "The falls are an hour paddle away, at least. Crap, I thought we were making better time."

"It'd be suicide to do it in the dark."

"Or in the light."

"Got a backup optio—?"

"We'll have to wait till first light," she said, her frown suggesting her brain had left his in dust. "Set up camp ASAP. We'll stay on the port side of the river, since he'll be coming down starboard. I mean, we stay left. Hell, you know what I mean." She trailed a finger along a thin blue line. "I've seen this from the air. A stream that leads to a small clearing—I had a good sweep over it when I was looking for the Danes—it's a place you might hole up in. Small but protected by a cliff and screened by thick bush."

"Sounds good."

"Only problem—it's a flash flood zone. If the rain starts up, with the melting snow in the tops, we're screwed. But we'll be safe enough tonight. We'll take on the waterfall in the morning." She switched off the light, but not before a flicker of doubt crossed her face.

"Waterfalls aren't as dangerous as you think, if you approach them right," he said. "The trick is to go with the current and not get stuck in the suckback. I can talk you through that."

"My brother says it's like being caught in an underwater washing machine. Of course he wouldn't go near that waterfall."

Something caught Cody's attention, on the dark far bank. "Shit, a light," he whispered, narrowing his eyes. Dozens of lights—a constellation of bluish pinpricks.

"Gotta watch those glowworms." He didn't have to look to know she was smiling. "One drop of their lure on your skin and the neurotoxins crawl into your veins. They reach your heart and boom, game over."

"Whoa, serious?"

"No."

He flicked his paddle, sprinkling her with water. "It's not polite to take advantage of the dumb tourist, you know."

"Oh, I'd take advantage of you any da—"

Her grin died. She looked down at the map and quickly refolded it. *Tried* to refold it. She didn't find the right creases. She swore, thrust it into his hands without meeting his eyes and ripped off the lamp. As he put the map to rights, she swept her paddle and pulled away, back straight, focus fixed ahead.

He blew out a long, slow breath. Did she clam up because she hadn't meant to infer she wanted to jump him, or because she regretted admitting it? And why so flustered? She didn't strike him as the easily embarrassed type.

Interesting. Was it possible this attraction wasn't one way?

CHAPTER EIGHT

By THE TIME they hauled their kayaks into the clearing, pulled on warmer layers and began unpacking supplies, thick darkness had fallen and Tia's belly was flip-flopping. And not because of the madman hunting them. Tonight that threat was distant. No, right now it was Cody who had her nerves strung tight. She'd spent far too much of the evening admiring the way the tightly packed muscle of his arms and shoulders and back shifted as he pulled the paddle through the water and flicked it out again. He had an easy command of the kayak, like he had an easy command of his body.

She'd be such a cliché if she had a fling with a tourist. Not that he was offering.

"Good spot," he said, unrolling a thin sleeping mat.

"Yeah." She stretched backward, her spine giving a satisfying crack. The overhanging cliff jutted into a starry sky. It'd be a chilly night.

"Even if he figures out where we are, which I doubt, he can't… Holy shit!"

She snapped straight, her pulse vaulting. "What is it?"

The slap of palms on skin. Ah. The locals had found Cody. She grabbed the spray from the pile of supplies and limped to him.

"Hold still," she said, spraying his legs. "You might want to rub it in." *Before I do it myself.*

He coughed, swatting the air. "What is that—mace?"

"Lethal, eh?" she said, spraying her own skin, avoiding the wounds. "I'm guessing citronella, peppermint, lemongrass, *mānuka*… My *koro*'s trapper mate makes it, especially for the sandflies around here. He makes a killing at the Wairoimata markets but won't tell anyone the secret recipe. We call him 'the Colonel.'"

"You're really limping now."

She zipped the little bottle into the pocket of her spray jacket, ready for the morning, and stretched her neck side to side. "Lucky we're not walking out."

"We better fix you up." He picked up a long nylon bag and untied it. "The tent's bright yellow so we'll just use it as a groundsheet." He laid it on the grass, its dark underside facing up, and slapped the mat on top. "We only have one sleeping bag."

"The climbers are carrying theirs."

"You can have it." He shook it out and tossed it onto the mat. "Come sit. I'll get the first aid kit."

Her leg throbbed as if it'd heard. She lowered herself onto the sleeping bag, digging her fingers into her aching right shoulder. The reflective white cross on the kit stood out against the dark, bobbing along beside him like it was floating.

"Where did you fly in from?" she said. "America, or…?"

"Started out in Corsica—a mighty long time ago."

"Is that your base?"

"Yep."

"Do you normally holiday alone?"

He settled in beside her leg, strapping on his headlamp. "No one is fool enough to join me. Like you say, it takes a special kind of death wish."

He switched on the lamp, flicked out his pocketknife and slid it under the hem of her jeans. She'd rather avoid light but she'd also prefer he didn't do this blind.

"What about your brother?" she asked.

He stilled. "How do you know about my brother?"

Shit. "You mentioned him."

"Pretty sure I didn't." A definite bitter note. He stabbed the fabric from underneath and sawed. "Did you Google me?"

Honesty is the best policy, as her mother used to say before she got convicted. "Had to check I wasn't delivering a novice kayaker to his…"

"…death?"

"So…your brother?"

The pressure around her leg released as he cut. "What about him?"

"He's into suicidal kayaking, too, right?"

Cody pocketed the knife and began to unpeel the denim, stopping where he met resistance. She held her breath.

"Was," he said.

"He gave it up? Smart guy."

"He died. Kayaking."

Oh my God. "I'm sorry. That was…"

"Don't worry."

"No, seriously, I am sorry." She'd intended to tease him, not upset him. "How long ago?"

"Seven years."

"That's why you joined the legion?"

He grabbed nail scissors from the kit and started snipping around the wounds. "I enlisted a year later."

That tightness in his tone—he wasn't just grieving, he was angry. There was something unresolved, something he wasn't going to volunteer.

"Were you with him when he died?"

Snip. "Yep."

Yikes. "So is it him you blame, or yourself?"

He jerked his head up, his brow stern, the light drilling into her. "What?"

She shut her eyes and pressed the heels of her palms to them. "You're pissed off about it."

She sensed a return to darkness. When she opened her eyes, the night was twice as black, apart from a cone of light around him and her leg.

"Shouldn't have happened," he said, drawing her lower leg across his lap, sending tingles over her skin. *God, Tia, he's talking about his brother's death.*

"Accidents never should," she said. "That's why they're so hard to accept. Though, to be fair, any death that isn't from extreme old age is hard to accept."

"I guess." As he cut away the fabric, the points of impact became clearer. The dog had attacked from the rear, but its top teeth had embedded near the front of her shin and the bottom ones in the flesh underneath.

"Is that what happened to your family—an accident?" he asked.

She shook her head, not that he'd see.

"It's okay. You don't have to tell me."

Hell, the whole of New Zealand knew the story. Why not him, too? "My mum and dad got sent to jail."

He lifted his gaze, shielding the light. "Whoa. *That* I didn't see coming. The way you spoke about accidents— I thought..."

"No, that's more professional. I've mopped up after

a lot of tragedy. Guess I'm a little desensitized," she said, feeling the need to explain her tactless questioning.

"Happens." He pulled tweezers from his kit. "Is that partly why you left the air force?"

She frowned. Did she want to share details? She'd met the guy only a few hours ago.

"Talk to me, Tia. It'll take your mind off this."

Good point. And she felt an urge to connect with the part of him that was still living his hell. "I'd had enough of senseless death. I wanted to return to the land of the living where sudden, violent death is the exception, not the norm."

"I hear you."

"I know it's a cop-out to leave other people to do that job, but after a while you either go mad or you go numb. I could feel myself swinging between the two, sometimes empty, sometimes furious, as if my mind was trying to settle on which way to go. When you start laughing at the other guys' dark jokes, about the bodies, about death…"

He tilted his head. "Yeah."

"I didn't want to reach the point where it was me making the jokes. And you can't shovel that shit while you're swimming in it, no matter how many psychologists they dump you in front of."

"You're still doing good work, with the search and rescue ops."

"It's as much death as I can handle."

"These tourists—it's hit you hard, hasn't it?"

"Yeah." She swallowed. "Must be hard for you, too, after your experience."

"This next bit…" The corners of his eyes wrinkled.

"It'll hurt, I know. Just do it."

He gave a grim nod. She guessed that was him slamming the door on sharing his story. He bent closer, his warm breath coasting over her skin. She closed her eyes, concentrating on that, not on—

"Yeow," she breathed, her eyes flicking open.

The tweezers held a bloody tuft of denim. Mate, it felt like he'd stabbed her, not removed something. Blood rolled down her shin. She bit her lip and rode out the pain, switching focus to his face. His stubbled jaw was square and serious, his brown eyes sharp, lines etched between them. His brow hunkered as he tugged again. She braced, keeping her gaze on him as the pain struck. As he worked, she kept staring, kept breathing. If he looked up, she could avert her eyes. In the meantime, she'd run with the only pain relief on offer.

"My brother, Zack," he said quietly, still focused on her leg. "We were doing a river in Spain. He went down a waterfall and got impaled on a branch. Total freak accident. It was a mess." He examined a fragment of denim in the tweezers like it was a portal into the past. "Years later, a doctor buddy—the medic in my commando team—went over the medical report for me. The way the stick hit was crazy unlucky—the speed he was going, the trajectory, how it snuck in under his life jacket and jammed between his ribs. A quarter inch either way and it might have just cracked a rib."

Her chest tightened. "Was anyone else with you?"

"No. It was like this. Isolated. That's why we picked it. He begged me to stay with him, but I figured if I did he was definitely dead. So I paddled for help. By the time we got back…" He gulped, his Adam's apple bobbing. His eyes shone. "He'd only lasted half an hour. Half an hour."

She shuffled forward awkwardly and laid a hand on his shoulder.

"I don't usually talk about it," he said, pinching the bridge of his nose. "For exactly this reason."

"I get that. So you blame yourself."

"Should've known going for help was futile. Should've listened to him. He died alone, in so much pain… When we found him you could still see it on his face."

Her eyes stung. She knew that look. You didn't get that look out of your head, even with a stranger. With someone you knew, with your *brother*… "I would have gone for help, too. I'm so sorry that happened to you." Sheesh, you'd think that after all this time she'd have found something more helpful to say than *I'm sorry*.

"I think that's all the denim." He ran his fingers around her calf and grabbed a packet of antiseptic wipes. "This is gonna hurt."

She released his shoulder. "It's fine."

"Thank you for being the first person ever not to say, 'It wasn't your fault, there was nothing you could have done, you couldn't have known…'"

"I figure you already know all that."

He started wiping, his touch so gentle she could barely feel it, though she could feel the sting, all right. "My parents made such a point of not blaming me that I knew they were struggling not to themselves. They were so determined that it shouldn't destroy us as a family, but something like that—it can't help but screw everything up. So I did the adult thing and ran away."

"Oh, believe me, I get that."

"Thing is, because I've upended my daily life, it seems possible that Zack's back in San Antonio, doing his thing. It's not like I'm walking past his old office every morning, or sitting at the bar where we used to hang, or driving past his apartment. It's mostly when I go home that…" He shook his head. "And I don't go home, so…"

Her chest twisted. If she lost Tane…

"So, yeah, you asked before if I was pissed? I don't know if it's that anymore, but the regret sure follows you around." He grabbed another wipe. "Are you angry, about your parents?"

"Hell, yeah. Whenever I think of it—which is a lot—I get this knot of rage right here." She thumped her chest.

They fell silent. The pain dulled to a stinging throb, which had to be progress. She pulled her right arm across her chest and then her left, but the ache remained.

"To risk stating the obvious and saying what everybody says," she ventured, "you know you shouldn't be angry at yourself for your decision, right?"

"In theory, sure. But it's not something I can rationalize. Not an hour of a day goes by that I don't wish I'd stayed. Of course, I wish that fucking branch had never happened, but that wasn't the direct result of a choice I made." He tossed a wipe in a growing pile. "What did they go to prison for—your folks?"

Tia bit her cheek. How could she clam up after his admission? "They used to own a big retail chain. High profile, you know? Always sponsoring this and mentoring that and sitting on boards and getting awards and going to black tie functions. All over the social pages. Media darlings."

He opened a tube of antiseptic cream and started

dabbing her wounds. "I'm guessing you didn't live around here."

"No, I grew up in the city, in Auckland." She massaged the muscles at the top of her back. "My dad didn't want anything to do with my *koro*, with his working-class roots. He got out of Wairoimata as soon as he was old enough and only grudgingly came back to argue with Koro every Christmas. He sent my brother and me to private schools, hired tutors, sent us for music lessons and golf lessons. They were grooming us to take over the business."

"You, too, huh? But you enlisted?"

He fixed a dressing to her shin and grabbed another. "My great rebellion. I always had this uncomfortable feeling about their business. I guess I picked up on the undercurrents in their conversations, their body language, but I was too naive to know what it meant."

"Which was?"

"They were committing massive fraud and tax evasion. Usual story—the company was failing but they kept lying to shareholders to prop it up, lying to the tax department, hoping they could work their way out of it. But it just got worse until… Two years ago I was on transport duty in Iraq when Tane sent word. They'd been arrested—him, too. It was one of the biggest fraud cases in New Zealand."

"Tane?" he said, carefully matching her pronunciation. *Tah-nay.*

"My brother. He very narrowly avoided jail. He'd been working with them a few years, but they'd kept him in the dark and he managed to prove it. The whole thing broke him, though."

"Ah, man, that's tough."

"Sucks to be us, eh?"

He met her gaze, shielding the light, and grinned. "Sure does."

She chewed her bottom lip and his gaze dropped to it, making her décolletage warm. If she leaned in a little and he leaned in a little... Her breath shallowed out. His jaw twitched and he looked away. As he grabbed another dressing, she allowed herself a full inhalation. Turned out she was a sucker for a sexy man listening to her pity party.

She eased back onto her elbows, buying some distance. "So this solo kayaking thing. Is it a tribute to your brother?"

"Exactly that," he said, resuming his task. "Once a year, every year since—except when I enlisted and hadn't earned the leave. Before he died, we narrowed down a list of the wildest runs in the world and made a pact to kayak them. We'd only just started when..."

"So you're finishing it for him."

"And for me. When I'm alone in a place like this, I can imagine he's here with me. This is gonna make me sound crazy but..." He shook his head.

"Hey, I already think you're crazy."

He smiled, a meltingly sad smile. "After a day or so I hear his voice. It keeps him alive for me, kind of fills up the hollow." He tapped his chest. So he had a hole there and she had a knot. "And when I'm kayaking, when it gets gnarly and I have to focus, the world vanishes. I feel like me again—the me I used to be."

"Some people meditate to get that feeling."

"If only that worked. But then, if it did, I wouldn't be here right now with..." He glanced up, then quickly back down, like he had a guilty conscience.

Here with…*her*?

No. He couldn't mean that, not in the way it sounded.

"But every year it's harder to bring him back," he continued. "He's fading."

"A psychologist would probably say that's natural, healthy."

"Would that psychologist also say you're hiding down here from what happened with your folks?"

"Mate, I don't need a psychologist to tell me that's what I'm doing. But I'm happy enough. Down here I'm less my criminal parents' daughter and more my *koro*'s *mokopuna*—his grandchild. And most of my clients are tourists who have no idea of my history and couldn't care less." Hang on—when did the attention land back on her? "So…your parents are still in Texas?"

"Yep."

"Let me guess—they're not so keen on their surviving son running off to fight someone else's wars?"

"See now, you're the psychic one." He stroked her calf—checking for more damage. She resisted the urge to shiver. Now that the pain had subsided, she was buzzing with far more interesting sensations. "That's as good as we're gonna get it. I'll tape it all up." He rummaged in the kit. "Yep, I lived the cliché and ran away to the legion."

"And when you take leave you run even further."

He raised his eyebrows as he tore the wrapping off a roll of tape. At some point he'd dropped the devil-may-care act. This was a guy who thought deeply, felt deeply and was man enough to share. "And the farther and longer I run, the less I want to go back. I guess one day I'll find the point of no return and the decision will be made for me."

"Oh God, you do have a death wish. And I'm stuck with you."

He laughed. "Don't worry. I have excellent luck. But I leave my fate up to fate. If I die, I die."

"That's supposed to make me feel better?"

"Hey, I take every precaution. I make it hard for Death, but I'm not scared of it." He fixed an end of tape on her shin and began winding it. "Ah man, I don't usually dump this shit on people I've just met—or even people I've known for years."

"It's being out here. Like you say, the real world doesn't exist."

He nodded, making the light nod, too. As he smoothed on the tape, he followed its path with a warm, rough hand, which sent a whole lot of inappropriate tingling up her legs. It was sexy, the way he concentrated— the way he concentrated on *her*.

"So you live with your *koro*?" he asked, his pronunciation perfect—the long vowels, the rolled *R*.

"Yeah."

"Will he worry when you don't come home tonight?"

"Nah, I stay out a lot."

"Do you, now?" He grinned.

"Not like that! Sometimes I fly up to remote huts when no one is booked in and stay a night or two. Tane and Koro will assume I'm overnighting somewhere. Everyone around here knows not to worry if I don't radio in for a while—the coverage can be patchy."

"You do that—disappear?"

"I like the peace. That's what I didn't like about the military—you don't get much time alone."

"I don't mind that. My own head is not always the nicest place to hang out. So," he added quickly, like he'd slipped into dangerous waters, "I'm good at running and you're good at hiding. That could come in useful." He tossed the tape into the kit. "Done," he said, though he kept her leg on his lap, a hand on her knee. "When will you be missed?"

"Not for a couple of days, when I don't show for my next job."

For her sanity, she pushed up to sitting and retrieved her leg, pretending she was inspecting it. What would it be like to have someone looking out for her, missing her? Not Tane or Koro, who had better social lives in Wairoimata than she'd had in the city, but someone all hers, whose evening would be too quiet without her. She'd had casual boyfriends who treated her like one of the guys, who hadn't felt the need to buy her flowers or dinner. But she'd never had someone waiting for her. She rubbed her right shoulder, rolling it back.

"You been doing that for an hour. Here, let me." Cody shuffled behind her, kneeling, and clicked off the light. Before she could react he'd pulled her hair to the side and his fingers were digging into the muscle, into just the right spot. Wow. And her reaction was not limited to her shoulder. She wanted those hands everywhere, all at once. She wanted *him*.

She forced herself to pull away. "It's okay. You don't have to—"

"I don't want you seizing up tomorrow."

By the time he reached "tomorrow" her objections had melted into a warm bath of bliss. He sure knew what he was doing. But what was *she* doing? This wasn't real intimacy. Just… TacMed. Silence fell—awkward, on her part, like when the hairdresser launched into a head massage and she nose-dived from small talk to swooning, aware she must look like an idiot, lying back with her tongue lolling while everyone around her was bustling on, but unable to pull herself together.

Except here no one was watching. There were just his warm hands and strong fingers rubbing and sweeping and digging. And there came the belly flips again... Her breathing should have been easing but it grew ragged. At least by making a conscious effort to still it, she was diverting attention from other parts of her body that were demanding it. She inhaled. Earth, decay, the metallic scent of stone, *him*. Okay, that didn't help.

His hands stilled, one on each shoulder. Then he swept them up into her hair, lifting it. He coaxed her head to one side and something warm and soft touched her neck.

His lips.

CHAPTER NINE

TIA FROZE. SO DID CODY, as if it were just as much of a shock to him. His fast, warm breath caressed her skin, the heat fanning out in concentric circles, like the spread of aftershocks following an earthquake.

He released her and cleared his throat. She quickly steadied her head before it lolled.

"I don't know why I did that," he said, his voice clipped and gravelly.

Her stomach went into free fall. He'd got carried away and he was regretting it.

No, Tia. She wasn't that girl anymore, the insecure teenager who didn't think she was worth the popular boy's attention. Cody was an attractive man and she was a strong woman who knew her own mind, knew that right now there was nothing she'd rather do than strip him naked and screw him, and why the hell not? He couldn't be hers forever, but he could be hers tonight.

"I don't know why you stopped," she said, the words shakier than they'd sounded in her head.

Silence. Stillness. While he figured out how to let her down gently? Her breath was so shallow she could well flake out. *Ball's in your court, Cowboy.* Her scalp prickled—in a good way—and then his fingertips touched her temple and combed through her hair, gently twisting it aside. She let her neck fall sideways. This had better not be him letting her down gently.

A shifting noise and he leaned over and touched the tip of his tongue to her collarbone. She gasped, and he slowly circled up her neck until he grazed her earlobe.

"I can feel your pulse," he murmured. "Hot and fast."

"Oh."

This was really happening. She'd wanted this to happen and now it was, way out here where the real world didn't exist. She spun, her hair tumbling onto her shoulders, and there he was, kneeling above her, his eyes veiled by shadow, one cheekbone cut by a shaft of moonlight. She propped her knees up on either side of him, her shin tight, and he leaned in and cupped her jaw with one hand. His breath coasted over her lips. Magic.

"This is crazy," she whispered.

He pulled back slightly. "Depends what you compare it with."

"True. My definition of crazy got a whole lot crazier today."

"Definitely not where I thought my day would end."

"I was going to do my taxes tonight. They're overdue."

His hand slipped from her face, making her skin tingle with cold, and he jumped into a crouch. His skull smacked on a jutting rock. He swore, rubbing it. *Taxes? Really, Tia?* So much for leaving the real world behind.

"It's the stress," she said, giving him an out, though her belly hollowed. It would be an awkward night. And no way would she be able to shake the feeling of his tongue and lips on her neck.

He sat heavily beside her, fingers smoothing his eyebrows as if he had a headache. "You're right. The stress."

He'd taken the out. "We should eat," she said robotically, though food was the last thing her body wanted.

"Yeah."

He dragged a bag over and they ate in silence—joyless

freeze-dried food. Afterward he gathered the rubbish and strolled to the kayak to stash it. She cleared her throat and he looked up, as if expecting her to speak. She coughed unconvincingly. The air thickened. High in a tree, a ruru gave a breathy hoot.

"You know," he said, "kissing you…your neck…"

She broke out in full-body goose bumps.

"It ain't about stress, not for me," he continued, his voice deep.

"What…what is it about?"

"Some pretty whacked circumstances planted you and me here, but I reckon if I'd met you somewhere else, some other day, we would still have ended up in this situation, where something might happen. And I'm not saying that just because you're hot."

Holy cow. *Something might happen*? And *you're hot*?

"I can honestly say I've never met a woman like you."

She snorted involuntarily.

"I'm serious, Tia."

"Yeah, I get that comment a lot." Usually from guys who wanted to play friends with benefits. *You're basically a guy with tits,* one hopeful had said, in a tone of awe like it was a compliment. *You know you're not girlfriend material, right?* said another as if stating the obvious— after a weekend of behaving as if she were exactly that.

"I'm not surprised," Cody said. "You're incredible. Smart, funny, tough—"

"—just one of the boys."

"Uh, no, that wasn't where I was going with that. You're seriously the sexiest woman I ever met and I'm insanely turned on by everything about you."

She blinked. Behind him, the stream bubbled, the river rushed.

"But if you get that a lot…" he said.

"Yeah, no, not so much." She felt like she was suddenly breathing at altitude.

"So…if you feel you wanna…see where this ends up tonight, I'm good with that. Very good with that. But no pressure."

Tonight. One night, which was all it could be. What was with the fear shrinking her chest? Even if he wasn't being genuine—and she could swear he was—she couldn't get her heart broken. He was a hot tourist she'd never see again, but he was also a real guy with raw scars, who wasn't trying to be anyone else.

"Okay," she squeaked.

He didn't move. "Honestly? I was looking for a little more enthusiasm."

She laughed nervously. The cold seeping from the ground was no match for the heat going the other way. She shifted, the fly of her shorts putting more pressure on the area that wanted the pressure. What the hell? Why not be that woman who took what she wanted? And damn, she wanted him. He was all hers, just for tonight, in this sanctuary.

He was motionless, his face in shadow. Waiting—for her. At this rate she'd catch alight, and he'd hardly touched her.

Do this, Tia. Be this woman. She pushed to her feet and stepped toward him. Her bad leg buckled and she hopped for balance, her skin tightening in panic. Suddenly he was there, his hands circling her waist. She grabbed his upper arms and righted herself. Not the sexy saunter she'd intended—but it'd landed her right where she wanted, staring up into his dark eyes.

"I'm good with it, too—us, this, tonight," she said. Damn her wavering voice. "Very good."

"Estupendo."

"Indeed."

She slowly unzipped his jacket and smoothed her palms up the hard contours of his chest, bunching his silky merino thermal. His lungs were working hard, just like hers. He wasn't as cool as he'd been a minute ago, like this meant something to him. Temporary could still be real.

She linked her fingers behind his neck, as he slid his hands to her hips and coaxed her closer. He dropped his forehead to rest on hers, unhurried, like he was savoring the moment as much as she was. He bent lower, his stubble grazing her cheek. She closed her eyes, letting her head fall back a little. Those soft lips touched hers, released, touched again, slowly evolving from gentle probing to one long, searching kiss. Her body prickled head to toe with warmth and desire.

Like it was mutually agreed upon, he deepened the kiss the same moment she pressed into him. They explored each other until she felt like she was entering a new reality, until the give and take came as naturally as if they'd been doing this together all their adult lives. Her body cried with need but this part was delicious, too. The calm before the storm.

And boy, did she love storms.

MAN, TIA FELT like even more of a goddess than she looked. Cody shrugged off his jacket, unzipped hers and slid his palms under her sweater and thermal. He caught a breast in each hand, round and supple and heavy. She groaned into his mouth. Oh yeah, that satiny skin he'd glimpsed earlier, those big, dark nipples, tight now with desire instead of cold. She shuddered against him, wobbling on her injured leg. Time to take this horizontal.

He dropped his hands to her waist and walked her

backward, releasing her lips long enough to guide her onto the thin bed. She let her knees fall apart and he eased his weight onto her, pushing his fingers into her hair and again seeking the silky paradise of her mouth. Damn, he couldn't get enough of her—but he sure as hell was going to try.

She tugged the hem of his thermal, and he lifted away and let her pull it over his head. He hungered to feel her warm, soft skin against him. As if reading his mind, she dived for her sweater. He got there first. As he discarded her layers, her hair fell in heavy curls on her shoulders, the curves of her breasts catching the moonlight. *Increíble. Magnifique.* A goddess in any language.

She circled a fingertip on his chest, over his tattoo.

"I saw this earlier," she said huskily. "Some French words, right?"

"Yeah."

"What's it say?"

"Je ne t'abandonnerai jamais."

"Meaning?"

"I will never abandon you."

"Your brother."

"Yeah."

"It's over your heart."

"A few of us got tattoos at the same time. We'd had a little too much cognac. Got all sentimental."

And sentimentality was not what he was after tonight. He lowered his head and caught one of her nipples in his mouth. She gripped either side of his head, moaning and sinking onto the earth like she'd lost the strength to hold herself up. Which was cool because he'd found a ton more energy.

"Cody, do you have protection?"

He released her, his cock straining against his shorts like it had ears. "Somewhere. Let me find it."

Her freckles stood out against her cheeks. Maybe later he'd lie beside her counting them, memorize every detail of her, of this. Get enough of a fix that he could return here whenever he needed to remember happiness and normality. He caught a lock of hair and rubbed it between his fingers. So soft.

"In a minute," he said, catching her lips and easing onto her. Yep, she felt amazing against him. Soft and strong and pliant, her fingertips pressing into his back. Not a fragile bird who might break but a real woman who smelled of shampoo and desire. He slipped his fingers into her shorts, under her panties, and slid into her slippery curls. He circled and played, as she groaned and thrust against his fingers. So sexy. He dived into her neck, kissing her silky saltiness as she got wetter and wetter under his hand, her moans ever more desperate. Her nails clawed his shoulders and she arched those beautiful breasts into him. Holy shit. This could well be heaven.

Suddenly her hand was on his cock, squeezing and stroking through his shorts.

"I want you inside me," she said, panting. "Shall we...?"

"...move this along?"

"No, wait." She closed her eyes. "Keep. Going." Her mouth fell open.

"Yes, ma'am." *We have all night.*

She gave a muffled cry and bucked against his fingers, clamping his cock like she was taking the impact out on him. As she crested, he slipped two fingers into her, his groans matching hers as her muscles pulsed around him. Hell.

She slumped, her hand—blessedly—releasing.

"Wow." She exhaled, her breath cool on his shoulder. "That's been building longer than you might think," she added, as if she felt the need to explain.

"You'd be surprised how much I identify with that. Or maybe you wouldn't."

"We were...talking about condoms." That desperation in her tone—oh man.

"I'm on it," he said, crawling to his gear, because crawling was about all he could manage. He found two in his wallet.

"So you *are* that kind of tourist," she teased as he returned.

"Are you slut-shaming me because I carry protection? After you asked if I had any?"

"I thought you could only slut-shame a woman."

"So sexist. I can totally show my respect for you by stopping right now."

"*Do* you respect me?"

"Let's see," he said, dropping to his knees and kissing her soft belly. "You fly a chopper, you're kickass, you're smart... So yeah, I respect you. And did I mention you're goddamn gorgeous?"

"Okay, that's good enough."

"So you don't want me to stop?"

"Uh. No. Just stop talking shit."

"It's not shit. And for the record, the last time I slept with a woman was a year ago. The condoms are wishful thinking."

She laughed, her belly shuddering. He licked her navel, earning another shaky giggle.

"Let me guess," she said. "That was the last time you went on a kayak trip? A hookup with a local?"

"Ah, actually, yeah. But it's not a habit, believe me."

"Don't sweat it. I'm okay with you not being a virgin."

"So we're doing this, right?" he asked. He couldn't help sounding a little anxious.

"Hell, yes. Just…let's not get too carried away."

"It doesn't really work unless we get somewhat carried away."

"True. Well, let's get carried away in a silent, slow kind of way."

Yes, ma'am.

It wasn't the impersonal shag Tia had expected. With her limited mobility and the need for quiet they took it lazily, cocooned in warmth and safety and trust, hiding from sandflies under his unzipped sleeping bag. Hiding from everything. When they weren't kissing, she was staring into his dark eyes, her climb into bliss reflected in his gaze like it was a meeting of souls, not just bodies. Intimate. Loving. Like a couple who had known and loved a long time. His back muscles tensed and released under her fingers as he moved inside her, the occasional haunting call of the ruru marking the passing of time. She had an urge to close her eyes and concentrate only on how good it felt, the steady build of agonizingly sweet pleasure, the solid weight of him, his chest flattening her breasts. But she didn't want to break the connection in their gaze, the comms link between their thoughts.

When her release came again, it was more of an implosion than an explosion, her body splintering in on itself. At that point, she did close her eyes—and held her breath to stop from crying out with the exquisite force. He moaned, crested and collapsed on top of her. She wrapped her arms tight around his wide, slick back and he slid to one side, easing his weight off her. She slung her bad knee over his hip, ignoring its half-hearted protest, and he sought her gaze again. Swallowing, he pushed a lock of her hair behind her ear and trailed his hand down to her waist. She adjusted the sleeping bag to cover them again—not that she needed the warmth—and they lay still and silent as the night reformed around them, a frown caught on his forehead like he was trying to figure it all out.

Good luck with that, Cowboy. A breeze caught the ferns bordering the clearing, the brush of the fronds echoing the rush of the water beyond. Somewhere far away a female kiwi trilled. Tia listened for the mate's reply but it didn't come.

She was grateful Cody didn't talk. Let their bodies have the last word, let their connection remain unspoken, let the beauty of it breathe. What good would come from words—a joke to break the spell, a briefing of tactics for tomorrow, the inevitable panicked disclaimer? *You know I'm not in a good place for a relationship, right? But this was fun. Let's do it again sometime.*

She realized her eyes had drifted shut when he shifted onto his back and she jolted out of the delirious dawn of a dream. He shushed her, slipping his arm around her shoulders and pulling her in so her body pressed into his side, her cheek on his chest. He kissed her crown for a long moment.

"Mmm-hmm," she murmured, snaking her arm across his waist, giving in to the weight of sleep, to a sweet bliss that wasn't hers to keep.

CHAPTER TEN

CODY CROUCHED AT the junction of stream and river, watching colors seep into the landscape after the gray dawn, long enough to be satisfied their stalker wasn't lying in wait. If Cody was doing the sniping, he'd set up in that dip between the boulders on the far bank, in that clump of ferns upriver, on that rocky bluff.

The concrete sky sagged. The forest drooped with dew, as if salivating at the promise of rain. Far away one of Shane's dogs barked, the echo bouncing around the valley. Cody turned his head to one side, listening. More barking. They were still a fair distance upriver but it was time to push on. He stood, rolling his shoulders. Time to wake Tia. He'd packed everything in the kayaks except the bedding.

He followed the stream back up, rubbing his nape. He'd hardly slept, but when did he ever? Having Tia naked in his arms was enough of a recharge. He'd lain there thinking too much, listening to the piercing calls of night birds, the hoot of a tiny owl that swooped in and out of a tree, the trickle and rush of water, the odd scraping and shuffling that had him on alert.

At the clearing, Tia sat studying the map, crunching into the apple he'd left for her, along with a nut bar and water. The sleeping bag, mat and tent were neatly stowed. She'd pulled back her hair, and her face was fierce with concentration. It was true what he'd said—she wasn't like any woman he'd met. Tough and passionate. It'd take one hell of a man to count as her equal—and not a guy who'd spent six years on the run. *You can't shovel that shit while you're swimming in it.* Was that his problem? He was counting on time and distance to heal him, but the farther he ran from his guilt and grief, the heavier it got.

Tia looked up, rubbing her lips together as she spotted him. How would this go? It wasn't your usual morning after. They'd crossed a line last night, and not just a physical one. The last couple of years he'd watched his best buddies hook up with the right woman at the wrong time. Never thought it'd happen to him.

And it wouldn't happen. It wasn't happening. Like she'd said, this was a fling between a local and a tourist, the kind of thing that happened every day—had probably happened that very day to a thousand people, from Kenya to Manhattan. Two people pairing up, having a good time, moving on. Happy blips. The what-if moment was inevitable but you pushed on through.

"We'll need to bust a gut to get to the falls," she said, snapping her gaze back to the map. "There's a river crossing right before it—a swing bridge. I'll feel better when we're past that."

He crossed the clearing. So that's how it'd be—they'd forget it ever happened. Well, he'd never forget, but he could pretend, if that's what she wanted. He'd also be good with stripping naked and resuming where they'd finished up last night, but maybe it was lucky they couldn't.

"A bridge," he said, catching up with her words. "Does that mean there's a track?" Another escape route?

"Yeah, but it's rough. An old hunting track that goes nowhere to nowhere, slowly." She stretched her legs out. The dressing was soaked with blood. "The river's still our best bet."

"Want me to change that?" He nodded at her leg.

"Nah. It's holding. We should go." She went to push to her feet and stopped, wincing. He held out a hand. "I'm fine." She tried again, smacked onto her ass, swore.

"It'll take a while to loosen up again, after a night's… rest," he said.

Sighing, she clapped her hand into his and he pulled her up. He liked the weight of her. He liked that they were nearly eye to eye when standing. And he liked it even more when she gave in to a shy smile, pulled him closer and kissed him, as tender and intimate as sex had been last night. Is that what a relationship with her would be like—hot and fun but calming and fortifying, too?

Way too soon, she pulled away. Her smile faded, her eyes turning down in the creases. Laid bare and uncomfortable with it. "Thanks," she whispered. "Last night was… Thanks." There was a finality in her tone. Officially sealing the experience into the box marked One-Night Stand.

He should say something profound that would convey how much more it'd meant, without suggesting they had a future. He said the first words that came: "My pleasure."

He felt like a jerk, but what could he say? *I'll call you. Let's do this again sometime. Run away with me because you're the hottest—and coolest—woman I've ever met.* And then what? A woman couldn't join the legion. And what would he do in Nowheresville, with too much time and space for dark thoughts? A few days in a year of days was cool, but any longer and he'd drown in the silence. Even if they went somewhere new, somewhere busy, his regret and heartache would come, too. She deserved better.

She stepped back and turned with a clumsy hop. "Right. Let's get on the water."

And there it was. The End.

Their awkwardness lifted after they pushed off, with rapids to force their concentration, and hard paddling in calmer waters. Her leg impeded her more than the day before, not that she complained. Hard to use the force in your arms without a solid anchor in your legs. After half an hour a light drizzle settled, more mist than rain. Icy drops trickled down his nape. Below Tia's helmet, her hair glistened like a spiderweb beaded with dew.

The forest was noisy with birds—bells and whistles and coos and clicks and warbles and screeches and rustling that had him itchy with nerves. The hunter whistling? The clunk of a bolt sliding home? The rustle of dogs?

As he rounded a sharp corner approaching rapids, a parrot with a rust-red belly swooped across the river, screeching. He flinched. It barreled into foliage and disappeared.

"Kaka," Tia said behind him. "I've never seen one up here. There used to be thousands."

"Let me guess. Before humans?"

"Yep. We suck. Seriously, the world would be a better—"

He glanced over his shoulder. She was frowning at something ahead, on the right bank. He followed her gaze. A wire trailed downriver, attached to a tree root.

He paddled into an eddy, skimmed his hand through the water and picked it up. It was no random piece of rubbish—someone had knotted it tight.

"Any good reason for this to be here?"

She eddied out behind him. "Look," she said, nodding at the far bank. "Straight across. Another wire."

It was tangled in scrub on the water's edge. "The other end of this one? Why would you string a wire across a…" He blinked. "Shit. He clotheslined a kayaker?"

Cody yanked and the wire pinged free, the root splashing into the river. He coiled it and stashed it in his kayak.

"Cody." Tia's voice was flat and urgent. She pointed downstream. Something red was caught in a sieve, under a tree canopy. A paddle. "He boasted about setting traps for humans, about hunting women. Maybe this was him trying to get a woman off the river, force her into the bush where his dogs could catch up." Tia scanned the ferns along the banks, backpaddling. "So where is she now?"

"Maybe the kayak overturned. Maybe she bailed. If we find her kay—"

A bark, low-pitched and husky. A shout: "Shut up!" Close behind. Shit, Shane had caught up fast. Cody kicked into gear, pulling hard into the current.

"Tia, I want to find her, too. But right now we gotta stick to the plan, stay ahead of him."

She nodded curtly, her lips thin.

"We get past the waterfall, we're home free."

Another nod.

The next rapid was short and brutal. No more sign of kayakers. Then the goddamn river began to meander, just when they could have used a solid patch of straight water to pull ahead. Every bend, every cliff, every bay, Cody expected to see camo gear, hear the zing of a potshot. The dogs had silenced—under control, on the hunt? The rush of the rapids turned into a roar, the roar into thunder. Mist billowed around an upcoming blind bend. The waterfall. A sudden scream cut overtop.

Tia charged up alongside him. "Hear that?"

"Yep."

"It was close—just through there." She nodded at a strip of stony beach on the right bank.

"Tia, we gotta get to the waterfall before he does."

"It could be her." Another scream, indistinct. "I can't not…"

His gut churned. Fuck.

"You go ahead," she said, paddling for the beach. "I'll check it out."

Dammit. He followed, ripping off his spraydeck as his kayak skimmed to a halt behind hers. He jumped out with a crunch and pulled the boat under a clump of ferns as she did the same.

"You have to keep going," she said, stepping out of her spraydeck. "Stick to the plan."

"I'm not leaving you."

She unclipped her life jacket and tossed it on the kayak. "This is about your brother, isn't it?"

"Don't bring him into this. It's about you." He nodded into the forest, trying not to shout above the crashing water. "It's about her."

"I can look after her—and me. Best thing you can do is raise the alarm. You're not thinking straight because of what happened before."

"Don't tell me what I'm thinking."

"We don't have time to argue. Staying is a bad decision. Go."

Another scream, almost inhuman. He frowned. There was something odd about it. His ears couldn't get a fix on it over the roar of the falls.

"Cody, go." She scrambled up a mud bank.

Leaving made sense. Of course it did. He dragged his palms down his face, slick with mist and sweat. But, fuck it. Maybe staying *was* a bad decision, but it was the only one he could live with.

He caught up with her in a dark gully where the forest muffled the waterfall to a bass boom. She shot him a disapproving look, then started.

"Hear that?" she asked.

A snorting, ahead. Not dog, but he'd swear it wasn't human. He overtook her—and froze. Farther down the narrow gully, a monster of a black boar tottered and swayed to its feet, curved tusks glowing white in the gloom. Holy shit. Grunting, it lowered its huge matted head—and charged. Cody reared and smacked into Tia. She yelped. An instant of weightless panic and then he landed on dirt, taking her out on the way down. The boar barreled toward them, getting bigger by the second. It threw up its head and squealed. Then its legs buckled and it thudded to the ground, the impact shuddering like a quake. It slid to a stop so close that Cody could feel its hot breath.

"He's bleeding," Tia whispered, pointing past Cody to a deep, dirty gash in its flank, oozing with fresh and dried blood and yellowy gunk. Behind it, on the leaf litter, was a long red smear. "The dogs must have had a go at him—a while back. He's dying."

"Jesus, a lucky break for us. Let's go." He shuffled off her legs and pushed to his feet. "You okay?"

"We can't leave him like that," she said, hopping to her feet. "That knife still in your pocket?" She held out a hand.

"Ah man." They were sniper fodder and she was stopping to be humane? "I'll do it."

"I can do it."

"Tia, I would totally be cool with watching you take on a wild boar. Hell, I'd buy tickets. But you're injured."

She pressed her lips together. Her skin had paled, her freckles standing out. He'd landed right on her leg. Fresh blood stained her bandage. The pig squealed, the sound digging into his brain. A dog barked, the echo masking its location.

"Make it quick," she said.

The exhausted beast didn't give much of a struggle. It'd had enough of fighting. Still, it stung Cody in the chest to watch its life end, with a twitch and a slump. *I've had enough of death,* Tia had said. Cody'd had enough of death seven years ago. *You go mad or you go numb.* Which way was he headed? He felt warm pressure on his lower back, under his life jacket. Tia. She jerked her head the way they'd come, her face grim but back to normal coloring. He nodded.

A few steps from the beach, Tia stopped, grabbing his arm. Something was churning through the undergrowth, still out of sight but coming their way. The ferns carpeting the gully remained still.

"Run," she whispered.

He pushed her ahead but she stopped short, forcing him to sidestep to avoid taking her out. A dog flew off a bank and landed in front of her. Squat and white with pink-rimmed eyes. It advanced with a rumbling growl, saliva dripping from bared teeth like some demon hound. The growl grew into a bark, then another. A whistle answered—from downriver. Shit, the shooter had gotten ahead of them. Cody drew out his knife and flicked it open.

Tia cursed. "Shane must be on the swing bridge, above the falls. Waiting for us to round the corner in the kayaks."

"We almost did."

"We need to lure him away." She straightened. "I have an idea. Sit, Jaws, sit," she commanded.

"Was *that* your idea? It ain't working."

"No, that's me giving it a chance to cooperate. Take off your life jacket. Wrap it around your arm."

Cody blinked. "Holy shit, for real? I liked your first plan better."

"When Shane told me about training the dogs to go after humans he held out his left arm, like this." The dog snapped as she raised her arm, elbow wide. She pulled it in. "That's what he trained the dog to go after. If we get it to latch on, we can contain it long enough to leash it. And shut it up in the meantime."

"You make it sound so simple." He unclipped the life jacket and slid it off. "Is this the dog that attacked you?"

"Yep."

"It went for your leg, not your arm."

"You have five seconds to come up with another plan. Four, three—"

"Ah, fuck it. You take the knife, just in case."

He placed it in her nearest hand, wound the jacket around his arm and jumped in front of her, offering his forearm.

"Jaws!" she said, her voice low. "Attack!"

"Whose side are you on?"

The dog pulled back slightly, scrabbled on dead leaves and jumped. Cody winced. Its teeth locked around the jacket. Holy shit, the pressure... He clenched his teeth so hard his jaw clunked.

"Hold on," Tia said, limping toward the beach.

"You talking to me or the mutt?" Its canines pierced the jacket, scratching Cody's skin, but the pressure was the bigger problem. Any second he'd pop like a balloon. "This thing must weigh sixty pounds."

"I'm more of a kilograms girl."

She returned with the towline and clipped it to the dog's collar. It rolled its eyes back, trying to figure out what she was up to. *Me, too, mutt.* Another whistle from downriver. The dog whined.

"It has an attachment problem," Tia said. "Well, a *detachment* problem. Doesn't know how to let go."

"You tell me this now?"

She hoisted its hind legs, easing the strain. It twisted, eyes rolling back, paws scrabbling in air, like it wanted to turn and take out her instead but didn't know how. "Walk inland. To the pig."

"You're not tying it up?"

"Got a better idea."

"I'm not really warming to your last idea."

His body was chilling with panic, his nerves screaming at him to do something. His medic's Scottish brogue landed clear in his head: *"Suck it up, Princess."* Tia had done this without the armor.

After forever, they reached the dead pig.

"Now what?" he asked.

"Sorry, that's as far as my plan went."

"What?" Another whistle. Closer. The shooter was on the move.

"I'm kidding. Let's lower the dog."

Bad idea. As soon as its paws hit dirt it yanked, trying to drag its prey down. Tia leaped to a tree and tied the towline around it.

"Jaws, release," she hissed.

It didn't.

She scanned the ground, grabbed a stick and caught the dog around its middle, which triggered more head thrashing. She angled the stick up and tried to wedge it into the corner of the mutt's mouth. With the jacket and Cody's arm stuffed in, there wasn't room.

"Hold tight," she said.

"Again, me or the dog?"

Cody braced as she shoved the stick. The dog released and dropped onto its spine with something between a cough and a bark. Tia grabbed Cody's good arm and they stumbled away. With another cough-bark, the dog lunged. The towline snapped tight and yanked the mutt back. It whined and shook its head, then found its voice, barking to burst an eardrum.

Ah, now he got it. Not only were *they* just out of reach—so was the pig. Dog goes bat-shit crazy at pig, shooter thinks it's guarding Cody and Tia and leaves the bridge to come find it, they get over the falls. Genius.

Tia shoved Cody. "Get the kayaks ready. If I'm not back in two minutes, go without me."

"What the fuck? He's coming!"

"Go!"

"I'm not leaving you behind, if that's your pl—"

"It's not. Trust me. I can't waste time explaining. I'm a soldier, too, Cody—show me some respect and go."

She was right. He wasn't her bodyguard—they were a team. He'd give her two minutes but no way was he pushing off without her.

He'd just gotten the kayaks to the water when she leaped down the bank. Blood everywhere—her shorts, her jacket, a smear across her forehead.

"Shit, Tia, what happened?"

She held up a couple of dripping slabs of meat, hairy black skin still attached. "Ham steaks happened. He keeps them hungry. If we have another encounter..."

She zipped them into her jacket pocket. Shee-it, this could well be love. As they pushed off, stretching their spraydecks on, he ran through instructions for clearing the waterfall. "Only thing you gotta remember—you *have* to hit it from the left. You go down in the middle, you'll get caught in the suckback. Too far right, you'll hit a nasty undercut ledge."

"The left. Okay."

"Coming up to it, the current will push you right, so be ready. You gotta shoot out of that left-hand corner with nose straight and as much momentum as you got."

She nodded, her face locked in calm focus. *Show me some respect.* Man, that'd stung. He had total respect, total faith in her, like he had in his commando team, like he'd had in Zack. Like Zack once had in him...

Cody rounded the bend in the river, his hull scraping a submerged rock. The current was already forcing him right. A stream of sunshine lit a rainbow in the curling mist. Fifty feet ahead, an old rope-and-wood bridge swooped low from bank to bank. Beyond it the water vanished over a crisp, smooth line, like his folks' infinity pool, and reappeared much smaller far down the valley. *Merde.* Was this a waterfall or the fucking

Hoover Dam? He pushed away from the rock and corrected to avoid the wake of a fallen tree splitting the current. One hell of a sieve trap. He glanced back to warn Tia—and caught movement on the stony beach they'd just left. The beach drifted out of sight but he knew what he'd seen. Camo gear.

A gunshot. Tia cried out, her boat rocking. *Crack.* Her paddle splintered, leaving a stump in her hand. Her gaze met his, eyes wild. A bullet had ripped the side of her kayak open. The current pulled her into a spin, going downstream fast. Another gunshot. The bullet smacked into the water behind her. She was using her half paddle as an oar, desperately pulling herself right— to the sieve. He veered violently and caught a branch of the fallen tree with one hand, his biceps straining to steady the kayak against the charge of water.

She was out of the hunter's sights, but her nose was dipping, threatening to flip the kayak end over end and send her down the falls belly-up. Not a fucking thing he could do but watch her fight. And man, was she fighting, her cheeks blown up with the effort of feeding oxygen to her overworking muscles. She leaned hard to the right and the kayak swung—and wedged neatly between the tree's upended roots. Good plan but it wouldn't hold her long. His kayak lurched. The branch slipped from his grip. She thrust out her paddle, and he caught it with one hand while backpaddling with his other hand and wrangling the current with his hips and abs. Not sustainable.

"Go!" she shouted. "Get help." He could hardly hear her over the thunder of two hundred smashing cumecs.

"Not leaving you."

She glanced at the bank, her eyes huge. "He won't

kill me straightaway. He's doing this for sport. He'll draw it out, hunt me."

Cody's boat shot forward, his glove slipping down the paddle. "Tia, pull me in!"

"You're good at running and I'm good at hiding, remember? We play to our strengths. I'm letting this go. You'd better be ready because I sure as hell don't want to search for your body."

"No!"

"If something happens to me, don't blame yourself or I swear I'm coming back to haunt you."

"Tia…"

"Three. Two."

"Tia!"

"One." She let go and the current took its chance, sweeping him downriver. "Don't come back without the army, Cowboy."

Fuck. He swiveled, tossing her broken paddle and gripping his. He was too far right. He paddled hard. The current swung him sideways, accelerating on approach of the drop, shooting him under the bridge. His abs burned. The watery horizon was coming up fast. He was going down sideways, smack in the middle.

Not a great time to find out he was scared of death, after all. No way was this gonna beat him. No way was that freak gonna win. No way would he abandon Tia like he had Zack.

His kayak fell away under him, yanking him down. Weightless. White water, rocks coming up fast. Screw the death wish. Turned out he did have something to live for.

Someone to live for.

CHAPTER ELEVEN

TIA WAITED TO hear something—the crack of Cody's kayak hitting a rock, a shout. The roaring falls smothered everything. The current shunted her kayak, lurching the stern up. Water gushed into the nose, submerging her feet.

Cody was a pro. He was wearing a helmet, a life jacket. He'd gone down on the current's terms but he'd recover it. That was *not* how they'd say goodbye.

She yanked the spraydeck off the cockpit and clambered onto the tree. It rolled a little, sending her heart into palpitations. Time to swim. She'd be safer on the far bank, away from Shane, but that meant crossing the main mass of water—and the current was charging like a burst dam. But maybe she could lay a false trail. She unclipped her helmet and, with a grunt, hurled it across the river. It bounced onto a stony shoal. She shimmied out of the spraydeck, tightened her life jacket and leaped.

The current slammed her like a train. She stroked and kicked hard, icy spray pelting her eyes. Her arm hit a rock, spinning her. Something scratched her leg. A branch? She grasped for it, got a hold, stopped dead, the water tugging her. A tree root. She clamped her other hand around it. She was just short of the swing bridge. The root led to a gnarled tree clinging to the bank. *Keep clinging, tree.* She pulled hand over hand over hand, her belly clenching so hard she fought the urge to vomit. Her feet hit stones and she pulled into the rocky shallows, shaking all over.

Her instinct pricked. Goddamn, she was sick of that feeling. Shane? The dogs? She looked around. There, under the bridge, caught in debris corralled behind a pile of rocks—a square of yellow fabric, billowing and sucking like a jellyfish. A jacket? Clamping her jaw to kill the shivering, she waded up and grabbed it. It was heavy. Not just a jacket. Oh God. Something brushed her knee and bobbed to the surface. She stumbled back. A pair of legs, swollen, pasty, skin peeling off the feet, ankles tied with an orange strap—a dog lead.

She smacked a hand over her mouth and squeezed her eyes shut, riding out the hit of shock. That fucking monster.

A squeak. Her eyes flicked open. *Squeak.* Above her the bridge lurched and started jumping around. *Squeak. Squeak.* The sole of a boot appeared between the planks. Paws scrabbled. She held her breath, heart pummeling her ribs. The boots passed and a dog followed, nose down. The greyhound. It clawed the wood and whined. Tia slunk down, her skin stinging as the water reclaimed her. The whine rose to a bark, and another.

"Shut up," Shane shouted.

The dog kept barking. Shane stopped in the middle of the bridge. *Keep walking, keep walking.* The dog flew back into the bush, still yapping. Damn. She sank until only her face was above water, the cold piercing her skull, her hair swirling.

From the corner of her eye, she spotted frantic movement by the bank, under the bridge. The greyhound.

More barking. A crack. She lurched up. A gunshot? The brown dog bolted out of the undergrowth to join its friend, both baying like their lungs would burst. Shane was still on the bridge. He wasn't aiming at her. He was aiming...downriver. *Crack*.

"Got him!" Shane yelled. "Fucking got the motherfucker!"

Tia stilled. No. No.

"Woo-hoo! Rocky, come here, boy."

The dogs stayed put, barking, whining, pawing the lapping water. The bridge groaned and starting swaying. Shane was coming for his dogs.

"Yeah, yeah, I know she's down there."

Holy shit. He knew? He trod slowly, heavily. Taunting her. Cat and mouse. Oh God, what now—take her chances with the waterfall? She scanned the river ahead. There was one more spot where she could pull out—a tower of boulders right before the drop. She could scramble up and over and head into the bush. If she missed it, she'd hit the waterfall on the right and smack onto the rock ledge Cody had warned her about.

Oh God, Cody.

Maybe he wasn't dead. Maybe Shane had missed or just holed the kayak and Cody was right now swimming to the bank.

"Shall we pull her out and let you play with her while we figure out where the other bitch went?"

Wait—what?

Shane thought the dogs had found the body, not Tia. The boots passed overhead. He was seconds from discovering the truth. She'd wait until he reached the end of the bridge, anchored back in the trees, where his view would be obscured for a few seconds.

When his footfalls faded, she silently pushed off, skirted the body, drifted, stroked in and got ahold of the lowest boulder. Her numb fingers slipped right off. She flung her arm over it, the shock of the hit reverberating to her shoulder. She forced her fingers to grip, and hoisted up. The dogs hit desperation pitch. She threw herself onto the rock like a seal, climbed the next one, and the next. She hurtled, swaying, to a tree and pressed her back into its far side, panting. Her scalp tightened with cold.

Downriver, through the trees, through the haze, she made out a stony beach—with an orange kayak on it. She stumbled forward. Cody was slumped over the bow, still in the spraydeck, the back of his life jacket torn up. By bullets? As she watched, the river tugged the boat back in, spinning it. Cody sagged sideways and the boat flipped.

Come on, Cody. Roll. Pull out.

The overturned kayak drifted downriver, bouncing off rocks. She stifled a sob. He'd died alone on a river, like his brother. She'd told him to go. *She'd let the paddle go.* This was it—the stupid split-second decision that would haunt her, like Zack's death haunted Cody.

Barking. She straightened and wiped her eyes with clammy hands. Time to get this bastard. Her chest tightened. *Yes, use the anger. The grief can come later.* If she could catch up with the kayak, with Cody's—oh God, his body—she could...what? Tip him out and take the kayak? Trigger the beacon?

First she had to get there. At a sickening distance below, the waterfall boiled and hissed as it hit the river, its spray hazing towers of boulders. Directly under her, the rock ledge jutted out like a giant's diving board.

She could climb to it, boulder by boulder, and go bush. A head start.

A growl, right behind her. She spun, catching her breath. The greyhound, alone, advancing. It barked harshly, like it was losing its voice. It tipped up its head, sniffed, whined. Getting her scent. Or maybe…? She patted the bulge in her jacket pocket.

Slowly she unzipped it. She pulled out a bloody chunk of meat and waved it. The sandfly spray bottle flew out and landed on rock. The dog followed the path of the meat like a hypnotist's watch, barking. She shuffled closer, letting it catch the scent. It whined and jumped but she snatched the meat away. *Atta boy.* It crouched, clawing the earth, whining, *begging*.

She tossed the slab high into the air behind the dog. The creature skidded around and bounded off. She retrieved the repellant, ran to the cliff, sat on the edge and pushed off to the first boulder. She landed awkwardly, sheering to the side and smacking her thigh on rock. A bolt of pain, but no damage done.

She slid to the next boulder, and the next, and the next. The final drop to the ledge was a leap of faith but she made it, knees bent, the impact jolting her frozen feet. To her left, two meters down the cliff, was a rocky alcove—but there was no way off it. She'd be trapped. The bush was still her best chance.

She limped for the trees. As she neared them, something barreled out. The brown dog. She pulled up, forced her shaking fingers to unzip her pocket, and grabbed the other slab of meat. The dog didn't even look, just fixed beady eyes on her, barking. She held up the meat, shook it. Nothing. Waved it. Nope. Threw it into the bush. Not a flinch. A whistle, nearby. If she could skirt the dog, get to the trees… She took a step and it lunged, driving its teeth into her ankle. She bit her cheeks to keep from screaming. It released and stood its ground, barking. Blood dribbled from several new holes. The pain felt distant, numbed by the cold. Jesus, if that was just a warning nip…

She backed up, hopping. The dog followed her, barking, to the edge of the precipice. Spray washed over her, pinpricks of ice on her skin. Far downriver, Cody's kayak was a tiny orange oval floating through a turquoise pool. Another whistle. Shane had to be following the dogs through the bush.

She wasn't going to stand here waiting. One last trick up her sleeve. She held up her left arm, elbow out. Her hand shook like it knew what was coming.

"Attack," she hissed, jabbing her arm at the dog.

It whined, tilted its head, pawed the rock.

"Attack. Attack." What was the dog's name? Some eighties movie, like *Jaws*. Sylvester Stallone's face popped into her mind. "Rocky! Attack!"

The dog lunged. She twisted away, shot her other hand forward and released the trigger on the repellant. Spray blasted the dog's eyes. It yelped, smacked onto its side and slid off the cliff sideways, scrabbling air like a cockroach. Its thick body thudded onto the alcove. It leaped up and shook itself.

A whistle. Now to get to Cody's kayak. She hobbled to the trees, her foot slippery with blood, blinking as she passed into the dark shade of the canopy. A breeze prickled her face.

No. This didn't feel right. Well, God, none of it felt right, but this… She backed out into the sunlight. Her lungs felt like they'd shrunk to the size of grapes.

Maybe there was another way off the ledge, to the river. Running through the bush, dripping blood, with the greyhound out there was suicide. And no way was she jumping.

"Knew I'd find ya."

She froze. Shane stepped from the trees, rifle raised, the two dogs at heel.

Her throat dried. "Are you going to track me now?" She hated the hope in her voice. The pleading.

"Nah. I've had enough fun with you." He flicked off the safety.

Her breath skittered. But the thing with a rifle like that, it made the person behind it feel bulletproof. And the thing with a guy like Shane? He underestimated women. He thought the weapon and the dick put him at an unassailable advantage.

"You think I'm too much of a challenge," she said, walking backward. "I know this forest better than the other women so you're taking the easy way out. What happened to cat and mouse? You giving up?" Her voice shook. Hell, her feet shook. No, that wasn't her feet—the ledge was vibrating from the force of the falls.

His Adam's apple bobbed, his need to be respected battling his fear of being played. "Yep, and now the mouse starts to squeal, right at the end of the game."

"Let's talk about this." She reached the end of the ledge and peered over, swallowing. In the alcove, Rocky jumped to attention and barked. Nowhere to go but the waterfall. Breathing through her nostrils, she stood rigid, hands fisted by her sides, making out she was frozen with fear. Which she kind of was. "Maybe we could come to some—" she made a show of gulping "—arrangement."

"Ah fuck. Yeah, they all do that at the end." He jabbed the air with the muzzle, in emphasis, strutting ever closer. "Think that'll put me off my game but nah, that's not the game. I got plenty of bitches wanting to suck my cock. I don't need to rape anyone."

"Let me go. Please. I won't tell anyone."

He shook his head slowly, the tattooed snakes twisting on his neck. "You're just saying any-fucking-thing now. I really thought you'd be more of a challenge."

And you've just got too close. She filled her lungs. "Let me go and I'll show you what a challenge I can be."

"Nah, this is just you trying to mess with—"

She sprang to one side of him, gripped the muzzle with one hand and shoved it sideways, away from her. Before he could recover, she slammed her other hand down on the buttstock, flicked the muzzle up and cracked the sights into his nose. The dogs went ballistic. Shane's grip loosened, just enough. She flipped the rifle, snatched it from his hands, spun it and crunched the butt into his face.

As she twisted the weapon into firing position, he launched at her and grabbed it. His boot smacked her wounded shin, and her leg gave in a blast of pain. She stumbled back, stones falling away under her feet. Her ankle skidded, her stomach dropped. She was going over.

CHAPTER TWELVE

TIA CLUNG TO the rifle. So did Shane. For a microsecond he held them, the veins bulging in his neck. Then he buckled and they were skidding down the cliff.

She bounced out into thin air. Rock, blue sky, clouds, Shane, water, the rifle flying end over end. *Fall like a seal, not a giraffe,* Tane had said. Toes first, arms by your sides. Aerodynamic. She thrust out her legs. *Smack.* She gasped. Too late. Pain shuddered through her legs, her back. She'd hit rock. This was it. She was dead. She kept falling, through the earth. The roar muted. Not falling—plunging. She'd hit water, not rock. Cold shocked her heart, her skull, her eyes, her ears. Her descent slowed, like she was in a cushion, but she was still going down. Her elbow hit a rock. She tipped forward and kept tumbling, bubbling water filling her nose, her mouth. Everything was white, like a blizzard. Caught in the washing machine.

Swim down. Find the calm water under the whirlpool. But which way was down? She stroked, her lungs stinging. The water tossed her back into the spin. She tried again but she was helpless. The water was in charge. She was too…

Too buoyant. The life jacket. What if…? She lunged for the quick release, her hair swirling into her mouth. Found it. Tore the thing over her head, her legs pedaling. Her chest threatened to cave. She plunged down, channeling her energy into kicking and pulling. The water pushed her up—the cyclone, sucking her back in. Oh God. Her vision darkened. *Fight, Tia.* She felt herself slipping, out of the churn, into…smoother water.

She was being pushed forward. She stroked up—and her hand hit air. She kicked fast, popped out like a cork, scraped in a breath. The water pushed and tugged, and slapped her face. The beach—she could see the stony beach Cody had pulled up onto. The water relented and her hand hit stones. She crawled up, coughing. The ground seesawed, left and right, left and right.

She heaved into a sitting position, hunched over, her breath wheezing. Water swirled around her legs, blurry veins of pink entwining with the bubbling white. Her blood. No pain, just cold clawing deep into her bones. She raised her head in a zombie lurch. No sign of Shane in the churning river. But she should hide. Just as soon as she could stand.

Crunching, behind her. Heavy footfalls. Cody? She started to turn. A green-swathed figure grabbed her from behind, pinned her arms, trapped her in a headlock. Shane. Not Cody. Cody was dead. Something cold jammed against her neck.

"It's over," he snarled. She tried to twist away but she had no fight. Above her, his face was slick with blood, one cheek a pulpy mess. He had a knife to her throat.

"I win, bitch."

She bucked but her body felt weighted. She saw it from the air, as the search pilot would—her body sprawled on the stones, Cody's overturned kayak. They'd fought and lost. Loved and lost. Her eyes burned.

Shane pushed the blade. A second of pressure and the skin gave.

Crack. His hold released and he fell back, taking her with him. Her skull bounced on his shoulder. The noise emptied from her head, like she was back underwater. He twitched and was still. She lurched up and rolled away, the effort like swimming against the current. He lay motionless, legs splayed. Beneath his head, thick blood hobbled through the stones. She pushed onto hands and knees, swaying. He stared at the sky, one eye bloody, the other clear. A deep red puncture hole between his eyes.

Her name. She could hear her name. She could hear the waterfall crashing, hear a dog barking, feel the spray peppering her, but it was all so distant.

Her name. Again. She spun, her butt plonking down on the stones. The world kept turning for a second. Her gaze locked on something on the opposite bank. Someone.

"Cody?" she croaked.

He threw something to the ground—the rifle—strode into the river and dived. He churned across with strong strokes, his head flicking side to side. She pinched her cheeks. Wasn't that how you checked if you were dreaming? Her skin was so cold it felt like someone else's fingers on someone else's cheeks. Maybe she was delirious. Hypothermia could do that. Maybe she was dead. The fall, the washing machine, the knife…maybe she was dead three times over.

The Cody hallucination reached the bank downstream of her and staggered up the stones. He was shirtless, his chest slick, shorts clinging to his thighs. Totally how she'd picture him if she were dreaming, right down to the tattoo. A strap was slung diagonally across his torso, a dry bag on his back.

He bent over Shane and shoved two fingers against his throat, then turned to her. Eyes deep and brown, just as they should be. If this was heaven, she was all for it—but would she have to spend eternity this cold? He stepped over the body, dropped to his knees before her and took her cheeks in his hands, searching her eyes. His palms were so warm. She began to shiver.

"Tia. Oh God, Tia." Husky, but yep, that was his voice. He pulled her into his arms, pressing her cheek against his chest, their legs in an awkward tangle, his lips on her hair. Her shin throbbed but that was the least of her concerns. How was he so warm after swimming through that ice bucket? There it was—the flaw in this vision.

He drew back, holding her upper arms, and swept a worried gaze down and up. He touched the side of her neck. His fingers came away bloody. She shot her hand to the spot.

"Just a scratch," he said. He shook his head and swore. She knew what he was thinking. A few more seconds...

"Are you...?" she started.

"I'm okay."

"But are you...real? Alive? Am *I* alive?"

His eyes creased in the corners.

"He shot you. I saw."

"He didn't shoot me."

"But... I..." Her bottom teeth hammered her top teeth.

He unrolled the bag. "We gotta get you into dry clothes."

"You just wanna see my…tits."

"Damn straight, Cowgirl," he said, but his smile was forced.

She was in trouble, wasn't she? She sat like a baby while he stripped her, barely able to lift her arms or hips to help. He rolled on layers of clothes—leggings, socks, his navy top, still smelling deliciously of him, a fleece… As he dressed her, the shivering released its hold and she could almost feel her blood begin to flow again, hot and thick. He shrugged into his own clothes and helped her to a flat rock in the sunshine, out of the breeze, away from Shane. She lay on her side, the stone warming her, her body tingling and buzzing. Life, returning. A second chance. And Cody…

He pulled something from a pocket. The rescue beacon. "Permission to set this off?"

"Mmm-hmm."

He rolled the bag and stashed it under her head, settled in behind and drew her close. Spooning. The sun on her face, his chest against her back, his thighs under hers, his arm slung over her.

"Je ne t'abandonnerai jamais," he whispered.

"Mmm-hmm."

As she relaxed, her body ached and stung. But she was alive. He was alive. They were together and it felt so right.

"How did you…?" Her throat closed.

In a low murmur, Cody caught her up. He'd managed to swing the kayak on descent and survive the waterfall. He'd paddled to the beach and built a target for Shane—stuffing the sleeping bag and mat into his spray jacket, helmet and gloves, and fixing it all in place with duct tape and the spraydeck, with the paddle taped across the top. He'd attached the wire to the front of the boat, hid behind a rock and yanked it through the water when Shane arrived on the bridge, to make it look like it was moving on its own momentum.

"With the haze from the waterfall, I figured even the scope wouldn't give away that it was a dummy. I was climbing up to find you when I heard you on that shelf. And then you fell." His voice cracked. "I saw the rifle land in the trees and went after it. When I got back you were on the stones, and he was…" He swore.

"You're alive," she said.

He laughed, his chest rumbling under her back. "Yep."

"You're here."

"Yep."

"What happened to 'Yes, ma'am'?"

"Happy to 'Yes, ma'am' you whenever you like."

"Maybe just sometimes." His forearm tensed under her hand. Yeah. That sounded like this thing would continue beyond the river. They both knew it wouldn't.

"Come traveling with me," he said, so quickly she might have imagined it.

"What?"

"I have three weeks until I fly out. You're grounded anyway, so…"

Her turn to tense up. With mammoth effort, she pushed up and rolled over. This was a conversation that should happen face-to-face. He smiled but there was a seriousness in his eyes. A vulnerability. Like he was afraid she'd say no. She lay down facing him, her knees grazing his.

"I don't even know you," she said, pulling the dry bag back under her head.

"You could get to know me."

"You don't know me."

"I'd like to get to know you."

"What would we do for three weeks?" She could barely hear her own words over the pulse pounding in her ears.

His lips curled up. "Something slow. Something quiet." He slid a hand onto her cheek, into her hair. It jammed in a knot. "What do you say?"

Her stomach plummeted—with nerves this time. Good nerves. In the last hour she'd almost died three times. And now…this? Just a fling but she'd take it. Oh hell, would she take it. "Okay," she whispered.

"To be honest, I was looking for a little more enthusiasm."

Laughing, she shuffled forward, cradled his jaw in both hands and touched her lips to his. He groaned and pulled her on top as they deepened the kiss. He tasted curiously salty. His hands pressed into her lower back. Bliss. Three weeks of bliss. Three weeks of *him*. That was enough to last a lifetime, right?

CODY CLUNG TO a safety railing as the bungee jump guide did final checks of the harness and the giant woven elastic wrapped around his legs. A hundred and fifty feet below, a thick turquoise river carved through a steep, silvery canyon.

"Last chance to join me," he shouted behind him.

"Yeah, not feeling the urge right now," Tia called, leaning on the handrail of the old bridge. "But you go ahead. Enjoy."

With glossy curls blowing into her face, skin warmed by the sunset and a broad smile, she looked like the cover of a healthy living magazine. Right down to the fifty-three freckles across her cheeks. Yep, he'd counted. For three beautiful weeks he'd worshipped her.

Not that it'd been all sightseeing and sex. After getting Tia's wounds stitched up, they'd given police statements, dodged the media, arranged the salvage of her chopper, filed her insurance claim, sent her *koro*'s buddies in after the dogs. "Not their fault," the Colonel had muttered. "I'll give 'em a home on the farm. Put 'em right."

They'd stood hand in hand in the old Wairoimata Hall at a memorial for the four tourists. They'd returned to the Awatapu with Koro and Tane for a spine-tingling Māori blessing. And tomorrow Cody would fly out. Three weeks had dissolved into hours. One more night of heaven, and then it was Queenstown to Christchurch and back to a life that suddenly felt hollow.

"She's scared of heights," he said to the bungee guy, loud enough for Tia to hear.

"I'm reluctant to plummet uncontrolled through thin air," Tia shouted. "Perfectly logical."

"You can't control everything. Sometimes you have to dive in and trust that the cord will stop you."

The man guided him to the edge of the platform, which wasn't much different from a plank on a pirate ship. He inhaled the crisp air, waiting for the adrenaline to hit. He breathed again. It didn't come. He felt... serene, happy.

Why the hell was he about to mess with that?

"I'm not sure I want to do this anymore," he muttered.

"Sometimes it helps not to look down," said the guy,

holding the back of Cody's harness. "Take as much time as you need to make up your mind."

Cody looked up at Tia. Her head was tipped, trying to decipher the conversation. "You know what?" he said to the guide. "I've already made up my mind."

"You serious?" the guy asked.

Cody kept his gaze on Tia. In the last few weeks she'd been every bit the woman he'd admired on the river—strong, passionate, sharp—and so much more. They'd talked late into the night, laughed a lot, even cried… "Very serious."

"You're not gunna jump?"

"I'm not gonna jump."

As he stepped back onto the bridge, unbound, Tia hurried up. "What happened?"

"Suddenly I just didn't see the point."

She smiled, her lip gloss catching the sun, making her even more kissable, if that were possible. "Was there ever a point?"

"I once thought so. But I just realized…there's no reward anymore, in any of this." He waved at the plank. "I've been taking all these risks and if I fail, the consequences are dire. But if I succeed I just end up back at the beginning, looking for the next quick thrill. So no, there's really no point."

She slipped her hand into his and squeezed. "Congratulations. I think you just grew up."

He pulled a strand of hair from her lip gloss and planted a kiss. She tasted like candy, and smelled like clean air and distant snow. "I thought all this *was* my way of dealing with it, of living with it. But it's just another way of running."

"I did wonder if it was about that."

"I think you said as much but I needed to figure it out for myself." He took her other hand. "Right now, there's only one risk I want to take and it scares the life out of me, more than jumping off a damn platform or hurtling down a river." He looked at their hands. So *now* the adrenaline charged in his veins. What was with that? "Except with this risk, if I succeed I might actually get somewhere in life, something might change for the better—which makes a hell of a lot more sense."

He lifted his gaze. The breeze had blown her hair back onto her lips.

"I'm really not following," she said. "What risk are you talking about?"

"It involves you and a plane."

"You want me to take you stunt flying?"

"No, ma'am."

"Gliding?"

"No, ma'am."

"I am *not* skydiving."

He cleared his throat. "My big risk is…asking you to come with me tomorrow."

Her smile melted.

"This is gonna sound silly, but I'm thinking maybe Zack brought me here to meet you so I could move on, live again. Maybe he was sick of me and my stupid death wish."

"Oh God, don't make me cry."

He brought their hands up to bridge the gap between them. Her eyes glistened, which kicked him in the chest. "I don't want you to cry. I want you to say yes."

"Cody, I…"

"See, the risk is that you'll say no, which would suck, and I would honest to God be heartbroken. But the reward…the reward is us getting to see where this thing between us goes. And I reckon it'll go somewhere good. And I reckon maybe you need the chance to move on, too."

"You mean I come to France?"

"Yep."

"For a holiday?"

"At first, yeah, I guess. You're gonna be grounded awhile, and I should be on base awhile, so come to Corsica, see if you like it. See if you like me."

"Oh, I'm pretty sure I'll like you. And Corsica. But—"

"Plenty of call for good pilots in the Mediterranean. Or we could end up back here—or any damn place we choose. Who knows? Let's just take off and see where the plane goes."

"I don't know if I can—"

"Fly away with me, Cowgirl. Take a risk."

Panic darted across her eyes.

Don't say no. Please don't say no.

"Cody, I'm not good at taking risks."

"And I'm too good. Which makes us perfect. You'll keep me grounded and maybe I'll scare you, just a little, in a healthy way. But we might have to make a stop on the way to Corsica."

She frowned. "Texas?"

"Time to front up. Stop running. Stop pretending that all this extreme stuff is helping me, is bringing my brother back."

She smoothed her thumbs over his. "It'll be good for you."

"Be a damn sight easier with you there. Wait—is Texas even on the way to France?"

"When you're going from one end of the Earth to another, pretty much anywhere is on the way."

"So? How about it?"

Her face fell. "I can't. For starters, right now I'm financially in the sh—"

"I'll pay for everything. Not because I'm a misogynist, you understand. Just because it makes sense."

"I can't take your money."

"Tia, your helicopter wouldn't have gotten shot if you hadn't taken me up there."

"I would have gone up anyway to drop off the climbers' kayaks. I would have died."

"I'm not so sure about that." He kissed her knuckles. "Just promise me you won't let this decision be about money—I'd hate to lose you over something that doesn't have to be a problem."

"I could pay you back when I'm on my feet again." She was just thinking aloud, thinking hypothetically, but it filled his lungs with hope. "That could take years."

Years. Years was good. He cleared his throat. "Was that a yes?"

"No!"

He flinched. Crap.

"I mean," she said softly, "I can't make a decision that big so quickly."

"I think you already made it. You know it right there, don't you?" He pressed their hands to her heart. "Just like I do. You just need to go with it. Maybe we both need to stop shutting ourselves away."

"I can't…" She shook her head, her brow scrunched.

"While you're thinking about it…" He leaned in and kissed those shiny, hair-streaked lips. She kissed him back. They'd been doing this for weeks, but every time, he got a buzz like it was the first. He would never get enough of her.

Please, Tia. Say yes.

TIA GENTLY BROKE the kiss and rested her head on Cody's shoulder, looking out over the river. This time tomorrow she'd be back in Wairoimata, alone.

Or maybe not…

There's only one risk I want to take and it scares the life out of me.

It scared *him*? She was the one who liked playing it safe. And so far that'd got her nowhere but alone. Was she brave enough to do this? It was pretty bloody obvious she was falling in love. She got breathless whenever she looked at him. She felt like she was permanently high on happy pills.

She breathed in the fresh cologne that had become achingly familiar. He was right. Time to take a risk, challenge her instincts. She stepped back, smiled at him and walked to the bungee guide, who was sorting harnesses.

"Can I use his jump?" she asked. "He's too chicken."

The guy shrugged. "Yeah, sweet. You'll have to do the safety briefing, but we can fit you in." He raised his voice. "That okay with you, mate?"

"Sure," said Cody, crossing his arms, looking baffled.

Hell, she was a little baffled.

Half an hour later, she stood on the platform, trying not to look at anything. Definitely not down. But straight ahead at the plunging cliffs wasn't much better. Or the packed viewing platform to her left. Who were those people? What the hell was she doing?

"Ready to fly?" asked the guide.

"I don't know," she said, looking at Cody, who was standing in the spot where she should have been. The safe spot. The sensible spot. Now, *he* was a view she could look at all day. "Am I?"

"Only you can make that choice." Cody gave a half smile. "But you can do anything. You're *increíble*."

Oh yeah, he was good for her.

"Time to leave the safe harbor," she called. "See if that bungee cord stops me."

His smile dropped. "Does that mean you're coming?"

Wind buffeted her jacket. Her throat felt like it was closing. Her stomach ping-ponged. Nervous about the jump, or what lay beyond? The guy counted down, Cody joining in.

Screw it. She jumped, her body clenching in cold panic. She shouted, channeling all the stress and elation of the last three weeks into one word: "Yeeeeeesssss!"

Over the rush of air, over the spectators' cheers, she heard the voice she was in love with, along with everything else about *Caparol* Cody Castillo.

"Estupendo!"

Indeed.

* * * * *

ACKNOWLEDGMENTS

AFTER SETTING BOOKS in Asia, Africa, Europe and the UK, with American, European, Scottish, Australian and Ethiopian heroes and heroines, I've loved coming home with a New Zealand setting and a Māori heroine.

Thank you to my insightful editor, Allison Carroll, who always *gets* my stories and knows just what tweaks they need, and the talented team at HQN Books. And to my agent, Nalini Akolekar, for your calm and steady presence.

And a huge thank-you to all the generous and enthusiastic critique partners, beta readers, technical advisors and cheerleaders who helped bring this novella to life, including Brad McEvoy, Mia Kay, C. A. Speakman, Rosalind Martin, Christine Sheehy, Priscilla Oliveras, Griffin Jenkins and Leah Fitzpatrick.

Me te aroha nui ki a koutou katoa.

Fast-paced, sexy and full of heart-pounding suspense, don't miss the gripping *Killer Instinct* novels by *New York Times* bestselling author

CYNTHIA EDEN

Prequel Novella